NIGHT SCHOOL
Fracture

BY C. J. DAUGHERTY

Night School
Night School: Legacy
Night School: Fracture

NIGHT SCHOOL
Fracture

C.J. DAUGHERTY

www.atombooks.net

ATOM

First published in Great Britain in 2013 by Atom

Copyright © 2013 by Christi Daugherty

A CIP catalogue record for this book
is available from the British Library.

ISBN 978-0-349-00171-5

Typeset in Bodoni by M Rules
Printed and bound in Great Britain by
Clays Ltd, St Ives plc

Papers used by Atom are from well-managed forests
and other responsible sources.

MIX
Paper from
responsible sources
FSC® C104740

Atom
An imprint of
Little, Brown Book Group
100 Victoria Embankment
London EC4Y 0DY

An Hachette UK Company
www.hachette.co.uk

www.atombooks.net

For Jack

We have to be continually jumping off cliffs
and developing our wings on the way down.

Kurt Vonnegut

ONE

Shoving the phone back into her pocket, Allie shivered as the bitter February wind cut through her and moved closer to the tall pine tree that sheltered her.

She'd been waiting nearly twenty minutes. If it took much longer ...

Her throat worked as she swallowed hard.

The gate in front of her was tall and imposing, topped with sharp spikes of black metal. As far as she knew, this was the only way in and out of Cimmeria Academy's grounds. Nearly a mile from the school building at the end of a long drive, it was opened and closed by remote control. Only the headmistress and a cadre of carefully chosen security guards were allowed to operate it.

Cars were relatively rare at Cimmeria Academy. Most teachers and staff lived on site. Still, delivery trucks and post vans came and went each day, as did the security guards who worked for Raj Patel. She'd been observing the rare traffic for a few weeks and she knew a delivery van arrived just before four o'clock most days. It was nearly four now. If she was lucky, the van would enter through those gates before she was discovered.

Her hiding place was very close to where she'd been when Jo was killed. The memory of that night, eight weeks ago, tortured her. If she closed her eyes, she could see it all – the blanket of white snow, the blue moonlight, the fragile body thrown like a rag doll on to the road ... The cloud of blood blooming around her like the petals of a deadly flower.

She opened her eyes.

Tonight there was only an empty dirt road.

She took a shaky breath.

Am I really going to do this?

She'd been asking herself that question ever since she'd reached the gate. Part of her wanted to cry. Part of her wanted to run back to her room. But she did neither. Instead, she steeled herself.

She had to get out of here. If she wanted answers about what was really going on, she needed to get away from this school and find them.

An icy breeze shook the trees, showering freezing raindrops down on her. Shivering, she wrapped her scarf tighter around her neck. The roar of branches swaying above her disguised the noise of the car engine for a long moment. By the time she'd clocked it, headlights were visible in the distance.

Dropping into a crouch well out of the path of the high beams, she waited, poised like the athlete she'd been before the attack. The stance hurt every part of her damaged body – her knee most of all – but she ignored the pain. Now wasn't the time to listen to her body. Now was the time to run.

Breathless, she watched through the bars of the fence, invisible in the shadows in her dark coat and jeans. She expected a white van, but saw instead a dark, low-slung car.

Allie's breath caught in her throat. Several of the security guards drove cars like that. It had to be one of them.

The sleek car approached the gate slowly and rolled to a stop.

In an instant Allie decided: she would do it anyway. Whoever was in that car, it didn't matter. She was going to run.

She readied herself. This was her chance. Maybe her only chance.

But nothing happened. The throbbing in her injured knee became more acute. Staying still was excruciating. She couldn't do it for long.

Closing her eyes, she willed the gate to open but it didn't move. Something must be wrong.

Maybe they know. Maybe it's a trap and Raj has already sent the guards to grab me. Maybe they're coming for me right now.

Her mouth went dry. It was hard to breathe.

Then the big metal gate shuddered and, with a metallic creak, began to roll open.

Her lips moving silently, Allie counted eight breaths in and out before it clanged to a stop, fully open. The road beyond curved into the dark woods. In the deepening twilight it seemed to disappear just beyond the gates – as if there was no world out there any more.

3

Pulling the phone from her pocket, she dropped it on to the ground. She hated to do it, but its signal could be traced – it was no use to her now. She had to trust that Mark would do as they'd agreed.

All she needed was for the car to drive far enough into the school grounds to allow her to get out without being noticed by the driver.

But an achingly long moment passed and the car didn't move. Its engine idled like a cat purring as it toyed with its prey. From where Allie crouched, she couldn't see the driver.

What the hell is the problem? Frustration made her want to scream. *Will you just drive?*

Just as she was beginning to fear she'd been spotted, the black Audi's tyres crunched on the gravel drive. Slowly, it began to move towards the school building.

Almost immediately the gates began to close again but she didn't dare move. The car was still too close – the driver might see her in his mirror.

With all her muscles tense and burning she waited, eyes fixed on the gates as she willed the car to pass out of view. But it moved with slow deliberation. Almost as if the driver was looking for someone.

The thought made her queasy; she took a deep calming breath to steady her nerves.

Don't lose it now, Allie, she told herself. *Focus. If he knew I was here he'd get out of the car.*

Watching the gate's slow progress, she counted three breaths. Four.

Five.

It was nearly shut now. The car was still within view but she had no choice – if she didn't go now she might never get out.

And that was not an option.

Springing from her hiding place she tore through the trees, legs pumping, knee aching, breath burning her lungs. The gap between the gate and the fence looked tiny. Too tiny. Had she miscalculated? Was it too late?

Then she was there, hands clutching the cold bars as if she could somehow slow their progress. But the gate was automatic – unstoppable. Its movement was steady. Uncaring.

Allie didn't hesitate – shooting through the tight gap as the bars yanked at her jacket like bony fingers, shoving her shoulder so hard her breath hissed between her teeth at the pain.

With a strangled cry, she ripped herself loose, tumbling to the ground on the other side just as the gates clanged shut.

She was free.

TWO

Allie hadn't started out that day planning to run away. She'd started out intending not to go to class.

She'd been doing that a lot lately.

Studying just didn't seem pertinent to her life any more. So why bother?

After being dragged, sullen and unrepentant, to class on several occasions, she'd begun using hiding places to avoid that unpleasant possibility. The rambling Victorian school building provided numerous nooks and crannies for this purpose – she was especially fond of unused rooms and servants' stairwells where no one ever thought to look. The crypt, the chapel . . . really, her hiding options were limitless.

Today, after enduring a few morning classes, she'd climbed out of her bedroom window, tiptoed along the narrow stone ledge to a spot where the roof dipped low and made her way up to the rooftop where Jo had once danced madly with a

eager for this insider information. 'He said blame is a kind of crutch; it allows the anger phase of grief to extend indefinitely. Until she gets through it she will never accept what happened and learn to deal with it.'

Whatever, Allie thought with hot impatience. *I'm angry for a reason. Because of you.*

Still, underneath her anger she knew there was some truth in what Isabelle said and it nagged at her.

Below her, Isabelle was still talking. 'But then Allie decided she didn't like him. He's meant to meet with her this afternoon and' – Allie could almost visualise Isabelle's weary shrug – 'right on schedule she's AWOL.'

Raj's voice grew louder – even from the rooftop Allie could hear his anger. 'This can't go on, Izzy. You have to take action. My entire team is out looking for her right now when they should be working to keep the school safe. We still don't know what Nathaniel is planning. He could hit us at any moment. She is *wasting our time*. We can't keep doing this. Allie is behaving like a—'

'Like she used to behave,' Isabelle said, interrupting him. 'This is exactly how she was after her brother disappeared. She's just angry and I can't really blame her. I'm angry, too. But I'm not sixteen so I have ways to channel it. She doesn't.'

The sound of someone knocking interrupted them.

Who could that be?

Straining to hear, Allie leaned over further, until her head and shoulders were hanging right over the edge of the roof. But Raj and Isabelle had clearly gone to answer the door. She could hear the murmur of voices but they were too far away for her to make out their words.

After a moment, the door closed with a decisive bang. Then ... silence.

They were gone.

Disappointed, Allie pulled herself back into a safer position on the roof; as she did, her eyes swept downward.

Two of Raj's security guards stood on the ground below. They were staring right at her.

Allie's heart leapt to her throat.

Oh bollocks.

Panicked, she scrambled out of view, her shoes skidding on the wet roof tiles. When she thought she was hidden, she leaned forward just far enough to peek down. Below her, the guards gestured for someone she couldn't see to join them. After a second, Raj walked out to stand beside them. They pointed to Allie's spot on the roof. Crossing his arms, he locked his unforgiving gaze on hers.

Allie swallowed hard.

Time to find a new hiding place, she thought.

Leaping to her feet, she ran across the rooftop to the place where the roof dipped down, sliding down the slope on her behind. Her short pleated skirt, not made for such activity, bunched up beneath her and water from the wet rooftop soaked through her dark tights. Holding on to the gutter with her fingertips, she slid along the stone ledge to her open window and vaulted through it on to her desk.

Once safely inside, she straightened triumphantly, only to find Isabelle standing in front of her with her arms crossed.

The headmistress didn't wait for her to make excuses.

'This is too much.' Her tone was angry but Allie could hear the sadness in it. 'You can't keep doing this, Allie.'

Some part of Allie felt guilty for hurting her. But she easily suppressed that voice. Instead, she gave a disdainful shrug. 'Fine. Whatever. Totes reformed. Never do it again, etc.'

Isabelle drew in a sharp breath. Her wounded expression threatened to make Allie feel something so she didn't linger, heading straight for the door.

Isabelle seemed to gather herself. 'I am not your enemy, Allie.'

'Aren't you?' Standing by the door, Allie studied her as if she was a specimen on a tray.

'Allie ...' Isabelle reached for her arm then, rethinking it, let her hand drop to her side. 'I'm worried about you. And I want to help. But I can't help you if you won't let me.'

There was a time when Allie would have gone to Isabelle for help and advice – when they were close. When she trusted her.

Those days were over.

She fixed the headmistress with an uncaring look. 'The thing is, Isabelle, your help gets people killed. So ... no thanks.'

A direct hit. As Isabelle's face crumpled, Allie ran out of the door.

Fighting the urge to cry, she limped down the grand staircase. Her knee ached, and the sound of her uneven footsteps (*thump-THUMP thump-THUMP*) echoed in the quiet like a cruel laugh.

With her head down, she took no notice of the polished oak panelling covering Cimmeria Academy's walls. Or the grand oil paintings – some of which stood twice her height and held the images of long-dead men and women draped in gleaming silk and jewels. She was oblivious to the chandeliers made of hundreds of pieces of faceted crystal sparkling in the faint afternoon light, the heavy candle-holders that stood five feet tall, and the tapestries of wan medieval ladies and horses pursuing unworried foxes.

She saw none of it as, ducking into the great hall, she shoved the door to behind her. The vast ballroom was empty, illuminated only by weak afternoon light filtered through enormous windows at one end of the long room. Allie's footsteps echoed hollowly as she paced the floor, her mind teeming with angry thoughts that pestered her like demons.

Thirty-three steps one way and pivot. Thirty-three steps back. And again.

Why should I be sorry? she fumed. *Isabelle's responsible for everything that's happened. Jo trusted her. And now Jo's dead.*

Spinning on her heel she paced the other way.

As it always did, her mind flashed back to snow-covered woods, the flutter of a magpie's wings, a small figure hurtling through the snow . . .

It was like a scab she couldn't leave alone although it hurt to touch. She kept worrying at the edges of it so the pain never lessened.

Maybe she didn't want the pain to lessen.

Jo is gone. Everyone failed her. And now Isabelle wants me to get back to 'normal'? Screw her.

Allie pivoted and paced.

She'd never trust Isabelle again. It had all happened

because of her and the fight she had with her brother that Allie didn't even understand. They'd all been caught up in it, and Jo paid the price.

She didn't trust Raj either. He was in charge of security for the school. He was supposed to be such an expert. But he'd gone off and left them alone, even after Allie begged him not to go. *Begged him.* So he wasn't around when someone inside the school – someone Allie knew and trusted – opened the gate so Gabe could kill Jo.

She pivoted again in a tight, painful spin, rage giving her strength.

In the eight weeks that had passed since the murder, Raj and Isabelle hadn't been able to find out who opened the gates that night. Who had been helping Nathaniel all along. A teacher, a Night School instructor, a student – somebody she passed in the hallway every day wanted her to *die*.

And they'd done nothing about it.

They all let me down. They all betrayed us. And I'll be damned if I'm going to let that happen again.

Suddenly, she stopped pacing. She knew what she had to do.

Yanking the heavy door open, she headed straight for Isabelle's office, running to get there before she lost her nerve. She was going to tell the headmistress she didn't want to go to school here any more. She couldn't go on like this. She'd go anywhere in the world as long as it was far away from here. Out in the real world she could find out what was really going on. She'd talk to her grandmother and together they'd find Jo's killers. And they'd punish them.

Tucked away under the main staircase, which soared upward

from the central hall in a theatrical swoop of ornate polished oak, Isabelle's door was hidden so cleverly in the intricately carved panelling that when Allie first came to Cimmeria she'd had trouble seeing it. She didn't have that problem any more.

Her jaw clenched, she shoved the door open without knocking. 'Isabelle, you have to—'

The office was empty.

The headmistress had obviously left in a hurry – the black cashmere cardigan she'd been wearing earlier was draped carelessly across the back of a chair. Steam still rose from a cup of Earl Grey tea, which sat in the middle of the leather blotter on top of her desk next to her glasses . . .

And her mobile phone.

Her mouth slightly open, Allie stared at it. Her brain couldn't register what she was seeing.

All electronic devices were banned at Cimmeria. Of all The Rules, this was the most strictly enforced. No computers, no televisions, and absolutely no phones.

If students wanted to phone someone they needed permission from the headmistress. They were only allowed to call their parents, and even then only if they had a good reason. But here was a phone, right within her reach.

As she'd stared at it, Allie's mind had whirred through a checklist of things that would happen. Isabelle would never forgive her. She'd be expelled. She'd lose her friends. But she might also find out what was really going on. And that could force Isabelle and Raj to finally *do something*.

So she picked up the phone, stuck it in her pocket and walked out of the door.

THREE

Outside Cimmeria's gates, the forest was wilder, blocking the weak rays of late afternoon light. Here, it was already night and Allie looked uneasily over her shoulder as she hurried through the gloom.

With every step she assured herself she was doing the right thing. Nathaniel was out there somewhere and he was looking for her but Allie didn't care any more. She was so exhausted, so angry, so *broken* ... staying wasn't an option. She had to go.

But she'd never felt more exposed. She was completely alone now. And Jo's killers could be anywhere.

It was unnervingly quiet, the only sound the crunching of dried twigs under her feet. The sun was setting and the cold was growing intense – the wind cut through the fabric of her coat, chilling the sweat on her skin. In her pockets her hands balled into icy fists.

At least I know where I'm going, she thought.

She'd made so many trips to hospitals recently she'd come to know the local roads pretty well, and as she walked she calmed herself by thinking through the route in her head – visualising a map. By her own calculation she wasn't far from the main road. Once there, all she had to do was turn right and then follow the signs. There were fewer trees around the main road, and more light. It wouldn't be as spooky.

All she had to do was get through these woods and she'd be safe. It was simple.

And it all went perfectly. In fact, she'd almost reached the crossroads when a sound, as faint as an intake of breath, made the hairs on the back of her neck stand on end.

Stifling a gasp, she darted right, ducking behind the thick trunk of a tall pine. Crouching low, her hands pressed against the rough bark, she peered into the gloom.

Whatever that was, she didn't think it had been made by the trees.

From her hiding spot, she could see no one. But the woods were dark and filled with shadows that shivered and danced with the breeze. Each one could be a person. Each one could be a killer.

She was beginning to find it hard to breathe.

Someone could be standing right behind me and I'd never see him. Gabe could be standing a few feet away watching me right now. The thought made her queasy with fear and she pounded a fist against her forehead. *Why did I do this? I'm such an idiot. I've walked right up to him . . .*

Clinging to the tree trunk, she fought for calm. If someone really was out there, she needed to *think*.

For a long moment she froze, listening; poised to run at the slightest sound. But there was only silence and wind and trees swaying above her.

After a while, Allie reasoned with herself. She could see nothing and hear nothing. The only hint she had that anyone was really out there came from her battered instincts. She tried to force herself to remember her training. What would Raj say if he were here?

Trust your instincts but don't be a slave to them, she thought. *He'd say don't react to fear – react to evidence.*

She could almost hear her instructor's calming voice in her head. 'And what does the evidence tell you now, Allie?'

I can't see anyone, or hear anyone. I've followed procedure and found no true threat.

'The evidence tells me there's no one there,' she whispered, trying to believe it.

Either way – whether someone was hiding in the woods nearby or not – she had two options: wait and see if they appeared, or keep moving and hope they didn't.

She chose the second.

Grimacing from the pain, she limped as she ran through the forest towards the road. Her woollen hat slid to one side and she yanked it off, gripping it tightly until she'd made it into the middle of the crossroads. Only then did she stop and look back.

She saw nothing but empty woods.

Panting hard, she bent double, resting her hands on her knees. Her lungs ached from the exertion and the cold.

And there was still a long way to go. They could come after her at any moment – she had to keep moving.

She turned in the direction the map in her head pointed her. The one-lane road was bordered by tall hedgerows, bare and bristling at this time of year. Beyond them, muddy pastures and fields were quickly disappearing in the fading light.

But the road was smooth and, if she was right, the town was a couple of miles down this road. She pulled her hat back on.

All I have to do is keep moving and not have a nervous break-down on the way.

To pass the time, she went over her escape in her mind.

It had been so easy, in the end. Almost as if they'd wanted her to go.

After grabbing Isabelle's phone from her desk, she'd hurtled up the stairs. In her pocket, the small device had seemed as heavy as a block of concrete; as hot as fire. She was certain people would somehow see it through the thick blue fabric of her skirt.

On the landing, she'd shoved through the crowds of students chatting and laughing to reach a narrower staircase to the girls' dorm. She'd kept her eyes on the floor in case her guilty expression should betray her.

'Psycho,' somebody said behind her, low and mocking. The cut-glass accent was unpleasantly familiar.

Allie didn't look up. She didn't need to – she'd know Katie Gilmore's voice anywhere.

'Get out of her way or you die next,' somebody else said and they all laughed.

Fighting the urge to punch Katie in the face, Allie kept her eyes on the floor, counting each step under her breath. The numbers soothed her as they grew.

... fifty-five, fifty-six, fifty-seven, fifty-eight, fifty-n ...

'Allie.'

She jerked to a halt, eyes fixed on the pair of soft, cream-coloured sheepskin boots in her path.

Slowly, she raised her gaze.

Jules, the girls' prefect, stood in front of her, razor-straight white-blonde hair just brushing the tops of her shoulders, arms crossed disapprovingly. 'Isabelle sent me to look for you.'

Allie's heart skipped a beat. Unconsciously her hand drifted to her skirt pocket, where it clutched the stolen phone.

How had she already found out?

Somehow though, despite the adrenaline racing through her veins, her voice was steady. 'What does she want?'

Jules gave her a strange look, as if she hadn't expected that question. 'I don't know. She just said she was looking for you, and if I saw you to send you to her office.'

Relief washed over Allie like cool water. *Isabelle doesn't know about the phone. Yet.*

The realisation made her bolder. 'Right. Well, you've delivered your message, Jules, so your job is done.' She took a step towards the prefect. 'Isn't your *boyfriend* waiting for you or something? Shouldn't you be with him?'

Jules didn't flinch but a red flush stained her neck, creeping to her face.

Ever since the winter ball, Jules and Allie's ex-boyfriend, Carter, had been an item – *the* Cimmeria power couple. Allie had got used to seeing them walking down the hall with Carter's arm draped loosely across her shoulders; his dark hair juxtaposed strikingly against her blonde head. Like chess pieces – the black king with the white queen.

It still made her stomach churn each time she saw them.

'I don't want to fight with you, Allie,' Jules said evenly.

'Oh good. Well, I'm going to my room for a second then I'll run right downstairs to talk to Isabelle, like a good little girl.' Allie knew it was petty to be bitchy to Jules but she couldn't seem to help herself. She wanted a rise out of her – she longed for a screaming match. Or a fist-fight.

But Jules refused to engage and, shoving past her, Allie hurried on to her room, closing the door with a bang. She didn't have much time. Isabelle was bound to notice her phone was missing and it wouldn't take long for her to figure out who'd taken it.

The room was in chaos. Dirty clothes lay strewn on the floor, along with papers, bedding and rubbish. When she'd got out of the infirmary Allie had told Isabelle she didn't want the cleaners in her room and the headmistress had reluctantly agreed. Now the place was a tip.

Just the way Allie wanted it.

Kicking off her skirt and sensible, school-issued shoes, she yanked on a pair of black skinny jeans. She'd lost weight after Jo's death and they hung a bit loose on her but they'd do. Hastily lacing her red Doc Martens up to her knees, she grabbed a dark coat from the wardrobe and rummaged through the clutter on the floor for her hat and scarf. She was still shrugging on her coat as she dialled a familiar number.

'What?' The voice that answered her call was aggressive. But to Allie the thick London accent sounded like home.

'Mark.' Her voice was urgent but low. 'It's me.'

'*Allie?*' His tone changed. 'Holy . . . How the hell are you?'

'I'm in trouble.'

The pleasure left his voice. 'Where are you? Are you at home? Is it your parents?'

'No,' she said. 'I'm at school. But something's happened. Something bad.'

He didn't hesitate. 'What do you need?'

She looked out of the window where the daylight had begun to fade. 'Want to run away with me?'

The road was quiet at this hour. Picking up a stick, Allie threw it hard into a darkening pasture, listening for the faint thud as it landed on the rich soil, out of her sight.

There were no streetlights, and the only houses were in the distance – she could just make out their lights twinkling across the fields. But she felt better out here, without trees blocking the ambient light. In fact, the further away from the school she got, the better she felt.

Her left knee was a bit numb but it was taking her weight. She thought it would hold out until she got into town.

Lost in thought, Allie tripped over a stone on the edge of the road and only just stopped herself from falling.

Focus, Allie, she chided herself. *Break your leg now and you'll end up back in that stupid infirmary.*

In the distance, the rumble of a car engine disturbed the quiet country lane. She scrambled for a place to hide but the hedgerow was a solid wall on either side of the road. The car's headlights brightened as it curved towards her.

Panicking, Allie dived into the hedge, ignoring the sharp branches digging into her sides. She pushed back until she could go no further and waited.

It could just be someone who lives around here, she told herself. *It might not be a guard from Cimmeria.*

But she still held her breath as the car growled past her, exhaling only when it sped on into the night.

They hadn't seen her.

The darkness seemed heavier after that as she resumed her walk, plucking bits of dried twig from her hair.

Her whole body ached and the chill had permeated to her bones. To distract herself, she tried to imagine what Rachel was doing back at school right now.

Rachel was her best friend and an utter bookworm, so Allie was fairly certain she knew precisely what she'd be doing: her advanced chemistry homework. She'd be sitting in the library in a deep leather chair, her books spread around her in the glow of the desk lamp. Her glasses would be sliding down her nose and she'd be happily lost in complex formulas and diagrams.

At the image, Allie smiled to herself. But the smile faded quickly.

Will she forgive me for running away without telling her?

She shook her head to clear the thought away. It didn't matter what anyone thought – even Rachel. This had to be done.

Jo's killers had to be punished. And since nobody else was doing it, Allie would do it on her own.

FOUR

In the end she was right about the directions but wrong about the distance – it was much more than two miles. She could hardly feel her feet by the time she arrived in the town two hours later.

After the long walk on the dark road, the town's bright street-lights were blinding and the traffic noise startling, but it wasn't a particularly big place and Allie knew if she walked towards the centre eventually she'd find what she was looking for.

Sure enough, a few minutes later an old-fashioned wrought-iron sign pointed her to the train station. It was nearly empty – the next train wasn't due for quite a while. The waiting room was locked tight, along with the ticket office, so she lowered herself on to a cold, metal bench on the platform and waited. The night air was freezing; her breath puffed out in little clouds and for a while she amused herself trying to make smoke rings of steam.

But that was only so much fun. And soon, shivering, she

gave up, burrowing further into her coat, yanking the collar up to her ears.

She must have dozed off because the train woke her with a start as it roared into the station. The long red carriages were packed with well-dressed commuters coming home from a day in the office. Allie watched blankly as they hustled down the platform without even a glance in her direction, hurrying to their waiting cars, their warm homes and happy families.

She was so absorbed in watching them, wondering what it would be like to *be* them, she didn't hear the boy sneaking up behind her.

'Do you have permission to be here, miss?'

Jumping to her feet, she launched herself at him with such force she nearly bowled him over. Her hat flew off her head, landing on the platform a foot away.

'Mark!' She hugged him tightly, breathing in the faint but not unpleasant scent of cigarette smoke that always clung to his clothes.

He'd dyed the ends of his dark hair blue and mussed it into a swirl of black and blue; a tiny gold hoop earring peeked out through the tangles, matching the one in his eyebrow. While she'd been away his pimples had cleared up – he looked more grown-up. But his clothes were the same – tonight he wore torn jeans and a faded black T-shirt with 'Revolution' on it in mirror writing.

Clearly surprised by the force of her greeting, he hesitated briefly before hugging her back. 'What the hell, Allie? What am I doing here in –' he paused to watch the last commuters in suits and high heels make their way out of the station – 'wherever the hell we are?'

At that moment she must have stepped into the glow of a security light, because she saw him notice the scar at her hairline – the doctors had shaved her temple to keep the wound clean. The hair was growing back but the jagged red line still stood out starkly.

He whistled admiringly. 'That's a nice scar. Who hit you?'

She grew serious. 'It's a long story, but it's why I called you. I need your help.'

'No kidding. You look like crap, Al.' She saw him noticing with growing concern the circles under her eyes, her thinness and pallor. 'What've they done to you?'

The station was empty now. Behind them, with a groan and a screech, the train began to depart. But Allie lowered her voice anyway.

'Some people tried to ... to kill me. And now I can't ...' She stopped. How could she explain this? Mark knew nothing at all about what had been happening in her life since she left London. Nothing about Cimmeria or Night School. Nothing about Nathaniel or murder. He was utterly outside that world.

'Look, let's just get on a train and get out of here, Mark,' she said, grabbing his arm with sudden urgency and dragging him towards the station timetable. 'I'll tell you on the way. The next train to London, when is it?'

Her mood change seemed to catch him off guard and he held up his hands. 'Whoa, hang on. Look at the board.' He pointed at the lighted schedule near the door. 'The next train's not for two hours. This is the back of beyond, remember?'

Allie's face must have fallen because he scrambled for an alternative. 'Let's go and get a drink and find somewhere to talk. We got plenty of time.'

Glancing longingly back at the quiet rails behind them, she gave in and let him lead the way out of the station. What other option did she have?

'OK,' she said. 'But let's just ... be on that train.'

'Where should we go?' Mark said as they emerged on to a dark street. Ahead of them, Allie could see the lights of the high street. 'What's in this town anyway?'

Mark had been her closest friend before she came to Cimmeria. They'd been arrested together several times, tagging bridges and schools. He'd shown her a side of London girls like her rarely saw – a world of rebellion and anarchy.

The main thing they'd had in common in those days was anger.

'I don't know,' she admitted. 'I've never really been anywhere but the hospital.'

When his eyebrows winged upward his piercing glittered. 'Well, come on.' He pulled her with him towards the lights. 'Let's find an offie and a place where you can tell me all your troubles. I want to know more about those battle scars.'

Allie nodded and followed him down the street. 'Right-o.'

'Right-o?' Mark imitated her accent with open incredulity. '*Right-o?*'

'Oh shut up,' Allie laughed, giving him a shove. She hadn't realised her accent had changed so much while she'd been at school.

After that she tried to sound less posh.

The high street was lined with expensive-looking boutiques. Mark shot the piles of silk and cashmere in the shop windows bilious glances and grumbled under his breath about 'snobs' until they found an off-licence in a side street.

'I'll go inside and see what's on offer.' His eyes swept over Allie's decidedly underage features. 'You better stay here. If we go in together they might get curious.'

She waited in the cold, stomping her feet to keep warm until he reappeared a few minutes later carrying a plastic bag. She could hear the cans rattling inside it.

'Right,' he said, looking around. 'We need a venue.'

For nearly ten minutes they trudged up and down the quiet streets looking for a drinking spot until Allie spotted a narrow cobblestone lane leading to a quiet churchyard.

The ancient church building was surrounded by spotlights illuminating its crenellated bell tower but the graveyard around it was ghostly and dark. They found a damp wooden bench sheltered beneath the sprawling branches of an oak tree and settled down.

Pulling out two cans of cheap cider, Mark handed her one. He popped his own can open and took a deep draught then sighed with pleasure. 'That's better.'

Allie followed his lead. The fizzy, apple-flavoured alcohol went down easily, warming her insides. After a while she stopped shivering. Maybe sitting outside wouldn't be so bad after all.

After they'd drunk a little, Mark turned to face her. 'Now. What happened to your head?'

There was no way for him to know how huge that question was. How long the answer could be.

She took a long, deep gulp and let the fire of the alcohol burn through her veins.

'There's this group,' she said, 'at my school. I'm in it. It's all secret. We train in lots of weird stuff . . . '

'What weird stuff?'

Crumpling an empty can, Mark tossed it into the grass. Instinctively, Allie winced. But she told herself to get over it. Mark was the way he was.

She needed time to think. So she up-ended her own can, finishing it off in a few swallows, then gave a loud belch.

'Nice one,' Mark commented as he opened a fresh can.

'Thank you,' she said primly. 'Weird stuff like self-defence. Martial arts. How to kill people with your hands.'

His can half open, he stopped and stared at her. 'What? Seriously?'

'Seriously.' Shoving the empty can back on the bench next to her she held out her hand for a new one. With a puzzled frown he handed one to her. 'All the kids in this group are from super-rich, powerful families. And there's this man who wants to take over that group and the school and . . . me.'

He was looking at her with new caution, as if she might bite. 'Is this some sort of a joke, Allie? Because if it is—'

'It's not a joke, Mark.' Her voice was sharper than she intended and she tried to calm down. 'It's all real. I promise you.'

But he didn't appear convinced. 'So this man, he wants you . . . why, exactly?'

Allie's mouth opened and closed again. He had her there. Because even today she wasn't entirely certain what Nathaniel wanted from her. 'It's something to do with my family and his family. Some sort of a fight and I'm just a small part of it . . . '

It sounded unconvincing and she knew it. She could see the puzzlement in his eyes. But he had to believe her. She needed him to understand. Without his help she was lost.

She held his gaze. 'I know it sounds crazy, Mark, but it's real. He's dangerous. Last Christmas he killed my best friend.'

He looked stunned. 'Wait. Are you telling me a girl got axed at your *school*?'

Allie tried not to remember how Jo had looked as her life ebbed away but she couldn't make that image fade.

'I found her. It was bad, Mark. So much blood . . . ' Her voice trailed off.

For a long moment he sat staring at her as if looking for assurance that he could believe her; he didn't seem convinced by what he found.

'But, Al, why didn't I read about it in the papers? Posh bird gets done at some boarding school – that'd make headlines.'

His tone was dubious and Allie's heart sank. He didn't believe her.

'They covered it up,' she explained, knowing even as she said the words how crazy they sounded. 'They always cover things up.'

He didn't appear convinced. Opening her new can, she took a long draught. If only she could drink enough to make every-thing better.

Mark was still trying to figure things out. 'Come on. How do they do that?' he asked. 'I mean, how do you cover up a murdered rich girl?'

'I don't know,' she admitted, helplessly. 'They just . . . do it. Lots of really powerful people went to my school. They can do things like that.'

'Is that how you got hurt?' He gestured at the scar on her hairline. 'Were you with her?'

'Gabe – the guy who killed my friend – he'd tried to grab me once before and my friends protected me.' Something about that bothered her – something important – but the cider was doing its job and almost as soon as the thought arrived it slipped from her drunken grasp. She frowned at the can in her hand.

'Then what happened?' Mark nudged her.

'Gabe came back,' Allie said quietly. 'He and another guy stabbed Jo and then kidnapped me. Put a bag over my head and threw me in a car and drove me away.'

Mark had gone still.

'But you see . . . I've had this training now in self-defence. So I knew how to hurt them. So I did.' She nodded to herself. 'I hurt them.'

Mark's Adam's apple bobbed as he swallowed nervously. 'What did you do?'

She spoke without emotion. 'I jumped over the seat and shoved my nails in the driver's eyes so he couldn't see, and he screamed but I didn't let go, and Gabe hit me, but I didn't let go, and then the car flipped over and I broke my arm and my knee and my head and stuff.' She took a drink. 'But I got away.'

'Bloody hell, Allie.' Mark looked stunned – maybe even a little afraid. 'I mean ... What the ... ?'

'But it didn't matter, don't you see?' She leaned towards him, her gaze intent. 'I got hurt trying to help Jo but it didn't matter because he killed her anyway. He *killed her* and I loved her and now she's dead and it's all my fault.' She stopped suddenly. 'My fault.' She repeated it again and decided it was true. 'My fault. All my fault.'

An icy tear rolled down her cheek and she swiped it away with an impatient gesture.

There was so much she wanted to tell him but couldn't. She wanted to tell him how Night School made her take chances. That it made her risk her own life and other people's lives. Being in Night School made her arrogant and stupid. It had created a wall between her life and Jo's life so Jo didn't tell her things. Like that Gabe was writing to her. That he wanted to see her. So Allie never had the chance to stop her from going to meet him that night. The night he killed her.

It was too hard to explain to an outsider. And besides, there was something else he needed to understand.

'I had to get out of that school because they haven't done anything about it – that's why I called you. One of them helped Gabe. Someone opened the gates for him, you see? Someone on the inside. But whenever I bring it up they just go on and on about how I need help "dealing" with what happened.' She made sarcastic air quotes around the word to show what she thought about that. 'They said I should leave it to them. So I did. And they have done *nothing*.'

She took a long drink of cider then fixed him with a

determined look. 'So I have to do this on my own. For Jo. I have to find Gabe and whoever helped him. And I have to punish them.'

They talked on the bench until they ran out of cider. She was in the middle of explaining how she'd escaped from the school when Mark glanced at his watch and swore.

'What?' Allie peered at him drunkenly.

'The bloody train.' He yanked his phone out from the pocket of his jacket. 'We've missed it.'

'Oh bugger.' Allie had drunk too much cider to be helpful but she tried to look focused as he typed things into his phone. 'When's the next one?'

For a long second he stared at the screen. Then he swore again with more vigour.

'Tomorrow.' He sounded disgusted. 'That was the last useful train tonight.'

Allie stared at him open-mouthed.

'*Tomorrow*? What are we going to do?' Her head had begun to throb and, without the shield of a constant stream of warming cider, the cold penetrated through her layers of clothing right down to her bones. 'Is there a bus?'

Mark typed more things into his phone then shook his head. 'No buses.' He shoved his phone back into his pocket hard, as if it had betrayed him. 'Stupid country town. We're stuck.'

'But' – Allie looked at the gravestones surrounding them, suddenly aware she was surrounded by dead people – 'we can't stay here all night.'

Mark stood up stiffly, the last can falling from his lap on to the ground with a dull clang. 'The first train goes at half six tomorrow. We'll be on it. Let's go and find a place to crash for a few hours.'

That was easier said than done. They had no money for a room. And after spending twenty minutes searching for an unsecured door or vacant building they returned to the church-yard, feeling increasingly hopeless.

Allie's headache had worsened; she shivered uncontrollably. It was only then they thought to check the church door. To their surprise, it swung open silently.

'Home sweet home,' Mark whispered as they stood in the doorway looking in at the dark nave.

It wasn't much warmer inside the old stone building than it was outside but at least there was no wind.

After fumbling for the switch, Mark turned on the lights just long enough to gather the covers off the altar tables and collect all the candles he could find as Allie stood by the door, her arms wrapped tightly around her torso. After that, he switched the lights off again and used the glow of his phone to light their way.

'Don't need a nosy vicar coming over to see who's praying so late at night,' he explained.

They stretched out together in one corner with the gold and purple satin cloths draped across them like oddly festive blankets. Placing the candles on the floor around them, Mark lit them with his cigarette lighter.

As she stared into the flickering shadows surrounding them, Allie's teeth chattered.

Mark wasn't much of a hugger ordinarily, but when she burrowed her way into the crook of his arm he didn't object.

'What happens tomorrow?' she asked.

'Tomorrow you'll come to London with me and we'll find some place for you to stay. I know some guys who have their own flat – I'm sure they'd let you kip on the sofa. Then ... we'll figure something out.'

His voice was gruff and Allie could hear the doubt in it. He wasn't certain about this at all.

She knew he hadn't entirely believed her story – he probably thought she was drunk and exaggerating. Or losing it completely. But at least he was still offering to help her.

As she watched the candle flames shudder, she tried to imagine living with his friends. Being alone in the world. Sleeping on dirty couches surrounded by strangers. Trying to figure things out on her own.

Had she made a terrible mistake?

FİVE

'**R**ight back here.'

The sound of strange voices and heavy footsteps on stone woke Allie with a start from an awful dream in which Jo cried out for her but she couldn't find her anywhere.

Her eyelids seemed stuck together and her head pounded with nauseating intensity. She rubbed her eyes and they fluttered open to an extraordinary vision – bright yellow, vivid blue, green, and red light flooded the room, blinding her.

It was like being in the middle of a rainbow.

'What the ... ?' Squinting, she shaded her eyes with her hand.

Mark grumbled in his sleep as her elbow dug into his ribs.

'Sorry.' She said the word reflexively just as she recognised the stained glass, the pulpit, the flickering candles melting into pools of wax, and the crowd of people standing around them.

'Oh bollocks. *Mark*.' She shook his shoulder hard. 'Wake up.'

Without opening his eyes, he swatted her hand away. 'Don't. Jus' fell asleep.'

In front of them, a police officer stood with his hands on his hips, disgust in his gaze. 'Both of you: Up. You're coming with me.'

The local police station was in a small, squat building near a slow-moving stream at the edge of town. After a short, nearly silent ride together in the back seat of a police car, Allie and Mark were led through the utilitarian entrance.

As the police led them from the church to the car, Allie had heard someone complaining to the officers in strident tones about 'hooligans' and 'vandals'.

There was a time when that would have made her proud.

Once they were in the station, the two were steered into different rooms. As she saw Mark's blue head disappearing down the corridor, a sudden surge of panic made Allie's heart leap into her throat. She turned to run after him but a police officer shut the door in her face.

The room where they held her was small and crowded with desks, filing cabinets and shelves. It smelled unpleasantly of mildew, but at least it was warm, and Allie's limbs slowly began to thaw. Windows set too high on the wall for her to see out let in bright daylight.

Two officers stayed with her. One was young, with a penetrating gaze. The other was older, and had a beard that needed trimming. Neither of them seemed openly unkind.

Allie sat in a battered metal chair, facing them. The younger one was at a computer, where he typed things in using only his index fingers. The older one made notes on a pad of paper. He asked her name and age, and she answered numbly as the young one entered the information into the computer with surprising speed.

When the older one asked for her parents' names and address, though, she pressed her fingertips hard against her aching temples.

This was so bad.

'Please. Could you just call Isabelle le Fanult at Cimmeria Academy?' she said after a long pause. 'She knows me. Can I have some water?' Her mouth was so dry it felt like her tongue was permanently attached to the roof of her mouth.

At the mention of the school, the two officers exchanged a look.

'Are you a student at the school?' the older officer asked. With a fatherly face and greying hair, he didn't look threatening.

Allie nodded.

'Now that is interesting.' He turned to the younger officer, who was typing busily. 'Have we ever had a Cimmeria student in here before?'

Without looking up from his monitor, the younger officer shook his head. 'I don't think we have.'

The fatherly cop turned back to Allie, studying her with open curiosity. Squirming a little, Allie had a good idea what he saw – a teenage girl with dirt on her face, tangled dark hair and a pounding hangover.

'What's a nice boarding-school girl doing burgling a church? Couldn't your parents just buy one for you if you really wanted one?'

The computer cop snorted a laugh.

Looking back and forth between them, blood rushed to Allie's face. She hated being laughed at.

Tilting up her chin, she met the officer's gaze coldly. 'You have no idea what my life is like.'

But the cop didn't seem intimidated by this in the slightest. In fact, he looked as if it was the reaction he'd hoped for.

'Oh really?' He leaned back in his chair so far the front legs came off the ground. 'Why don't you tell us?'

Sullen, Allie shook her head. 'I don't want to talk about it.'

'That is a shame,' he said, his smile disappearing. 'Because talking about it is the only thing that's going to get you out of here in a hurry.'

A tingling sense of suspicion made goosebumps rise on Allie's arms. This wasn't right. She'd been arrested several times before and the police had never acted like this. They never cared where she went to school. It was always straight-forward and no nonsense: 'What's your name? How old are you? Who's your parent or guardian?'

Keeping her voice steady, she held his gaze. 'I am sixteen years old. I can't talk to you without a responsible adult present. Call my headmistress, Isabelle le Fanult. She will tell you everything you need to know.'

'Oh, we'll do that,' the officer assured her. He didn't look so fatherly now. 'But first we want to ask you a few questions.'

For what seemed an interminable amount of time, they asked questions and she refused to answer them. How many students were at the school? How many teachers? What were their names? What went on at the school? Any strange classes? Any odd behaviour? Anything illegal? Drugs?

Allie just stared at the floor, angry and exhausted. All she would say was, 'Call Isabelle le Fanult. She will answer your questions.'

When she finally heard Raj's familiar voice from the front desk, the relief felt like fresh oxygen in her lungs. She took a steadying breath – she was going to get out of here.

The two officers left her alone then. The walls were thin, and she could hear Raj calmly presenting paperwork proving she was a student at the school, explaining – lying – that Mark was a student too, and that it was all just a childish prank. The school would, he said, pay for any damage.

He was nothing but polite although she could hear simmering anger beneath the surface of his voice. Whether that anger was directed at her or the police, she couldn't tell.

When the police asked him about the school's security system, he never raised his voice but his tone was chilling.

'I could answer your questions, of course,' he said. 'But first, why don't you tell me how long you held these children before you notified the school they were in your custody?'

A pause followed.

'We would have called you sooner,' the officer replied after a moment, 'but they refused to tell us who they were. We had a devil of a time identifying them. Seems you've got some problem kids up at that school.'

Hearing the flat lie, Allie stared at the door in disbelief.

But the unspoken threat in Raj's question seemed to have the intended effect. After that they asked no more questions.

When she walked into the room a few minutes later, Raj's eyes searched her face for signs of harm.

'You OK?' he asked.

'No thanks to them.' She shot a contemptuous look at the officers.

Raj's face darkened. 'Don't blame them. You got yourself into this trouble.'

With that, the sense of relief evaporated – Raj might be rescuing her from the local cops but he was also still angry.

As they walked from the police station Allie squinted tiredly into the sun. The sky was bright blue, the late winter air crystalline and cold. The beauty of the day struck her as ironic.

At that moment, Raj's black-clad security guards appeared at her side to escort her across the small car park. Her eyes were sandy with exhaustion and her head pounded as if someone was beating her skull from the inside. She was being ushered into a black SUV when she spotted Mark being placed in another car driven by one of Raj's guards.

'Mark!' she cried after him. He didn't look up.

Anger – always looking for an excuse to strike these days – uncoiled inside her.

'Where are you taking him?' From the back seat, she leaned forward to where Raj was climbing into the driver's seat.

When he didn't reply, she just kept asking, her voice shrill. 'Where? Where?'

'To Cimmeria,' Raj snapped as he started the engine and pulled out on to the road. 'The same place we're taking you. Now be quiet.'

'You can't do that!' She stared at the back of his head in disbelief. 'He's not a student. That's kidnapping. You have to let him go.'

'He's been released into our care legally,' he said evenly.

'Legally?' Her voice rose. 'You *lied* to the police. You said he went to Cimmeria and he doesn't. How is that legal?'

A wave of helpless rage left her trembling.

When he didn't respond, she reached for the door handle, glaring at the back of his head. The car was moving fast now but she was so angry she didn't care. 'Maybe I should just go back and tell them the truth—'

Without warning Raj slammed on the brakes. The car screeched to a halt, skidding from the force of it.

Allie was thrown forward against her seatbelt, and back again hard.

Raj spun round in his seat to face her – for the first time she noticed the dark circles under his bloodshot eyes. 'You have caused enough trouble for one day. Isabelle has been worried sick. I was up all night searching for you. My team hasn't had a break in fourteen hours because they've been out looking for your *body*.'

Flinching at the last word, Allie struggled to make herself hold his condemning gaze.

'Now, unless you want to be restrained for your own protection,' he said, each word sharp as a blade, 'you need to sit back. And be quiet.'

She knew he was right. Knew she was behaving like a child. But she couldn't back down – he wasn't the only one who was angry and tired. With an exaggerated gesture, she lifted her hand from the door handle and rested it in her lap, holding his gaze defiantly.

After a moment, he turned back to face the front and the car began moving again.

For the rest of the journey she stared out of the window.

I have no one left, she thought, fighting back tears. *Even Raj hates me.*

When they arrived at the school the grounds teemed with activity. At first Allie was puzzled to see so many people around, but then she realised it must be lunchtime. The rare February sunshine had drawn everyone outside.

Students gazed curiously at the line of cars as they rolled up the long gravel drive to stop at the front door. Raj stepped back and let his guards open her door. She climbed out of the car with a guard on each side of her, like a prisoner. She saw Mark being similarly escorted.

As the students gathered around them to watch and whisper, Allie shrank back behind the guards. Within half an hour, everyone in the school would know about this. Rumours would spread like wildfire.

The thought made her feel sick. All she wanted to do was curl up into a ball and hide from their prying eyes. But she couldn't let them see her humbled.

Raising her face, she swept the crowd with an imperious look – as if this was exactly what she wanted. As if the security guards worked for her.

Suddenly, though, her gaze encountered a pair of extraordinary eyes the precise colour of the clear winter sky above them.

Allie froze.

Standing at the top of the steps leading to the front door, Sylvain watched her incredulously. She could see his tension in the way he held his shoulders and the set of his sharply defined jaw.

For one bittersweet moment she let herself wish he would sweep her up and take her away from this moment. But no one could do that.

Holding her gaze, Sylvain held out his hands questioningly.

Colour rushed to Allie's cheeks and she dropped her eyes. Because what was there to say?

When she glanced up again he was gone.

Inside, she was met by a furious-looking Isabelle who didn't say a word to her. As she led the way to her office, Allie couldn't take her eyes off the stiff, angry line of her back. Her heart sank with every step.

Without saying where she was going, the headmistress left her there, in the care of one of Raj's guards, who stood silently in front of the door, his arms crossed.

She didn't see where they took Mark.

Her nerves on edge, Allie looked around the familiar room as she waited for Isabelle to return. Low wooden cabinets lined one wall, while Isabelle's large desk took up much of the remaining space – her eyes darted to the elegant leather blotter where she'd found the mobile phone yesterday. It was empty now.

Isabelle would never make that mistake again.

Before she could think about that further, though, Isabelle returned accompanied by Night School instructor Jerry Cole.

The two looked solemn and tense as they asked the guard to leave them alone.

Isabelle sat at her desk; Jerry perched on a filing cabinet. Isabelle was white with anger.

Jerry spoke first, his voice stern. 'Allie, you are in a tremendous amount of trouble. We need to know exactly what happened, and you will make things better for yourself if you answer our questions.'

Her stomach roiling, Allie nodded to show she understood. 'I just . . . could I have something to drink? I'm really thirsty.'

Silently Isabelle opened the small refrigerator she kept in one corner and handed her a bottle of water.

Allie didn't think anything had ever tasted as good as that water.

Their questions were straightforward. How had she got Isabelle's phone? How had she escaped? How had she got into town? Had anyone helped her?

She tried to answer as clearly as she could – hoping that would get her out of there quicker – but they just kept asking more questions.

When she told them what happened at the police station, Isabelle and Jerry exchanged a dark look.

'I'll take care of it, Isabelle,' Jerry said placatingly. But Isabelle didn't appear mollified.

'Find out who they are,' she said. 'I want to take care of it myself.'

Still the questions continued. The pain in Allie's head had worsened, and she was hungry and tired. Her temper grew short.

'I wish you'd worked this hard to find out who's helping Nathaniel,' she snapped.

Jerry glowered at her. 'How do you know Mark doesn't work for Nathaniel?'

'You must be joking.' Allie scoffed, the very idea making her laugh. That was a mistake.

'Do you think this is funny?' He nearly shouted the question.

Before Allie could reply, Isabelle held up her hand. 'That's enough. Both of you.'

Allie's shoulders slumped. She was so tired. The pounding in her temples was growing into a kind of banging. She couldn't think straight any more.

Isabelle turned back to face Allie. For the first time today, she didn't look angry. She looked sad. 'Just answer this one last question, Allie: what did you tell Mark about Cimmeria?'

Allie's mind unspooled hazy drunken memories of rambling about Night School and Carter. Nathaniel and Isabelle. Security and threats. Jo.

But she didn't blink. 'Nothing.'

'You expect us to believe you ran away from school and spent the night with that boy, but told him *nothing*?' Scepticism was clear in Jerry's voice.

Allie whirled to face him, her anger spilling over. 'I didn't run away with Mark to tell him all your amazing secrets. I ran away because I didn't want to be here any more. Because someone here helped Nathaniel kill Jo and you haven't done one thing to find him. I'm not safe here. No one is. And I just . . . ' She pressed her fingertips against her burning eyelids. 'I wanted to be with my friend.'

'You may yet get the chance to do that permanently,' Jerry muttered.

From beneath her hands she shot him an irritated look. 'If you want to throw me out so badly, why'd you bother bringing me back? You should bloody thank me—'

'Language.' Isabelle's tone was sharp. 'I will not have you swear at a teacher. All the rules of civilisation have not been cancelled simply because you are having a bad day, Allie.' Turning, she said, 'Jerry, if you don't mind I'd like a few minutes alone with Allie. Could you please leave us?'

When he'd gone, the headmistress leaned back against the door, her shoulders drooping, staring at the floor. She looked uncharacteristically vulnerable and an unwanted bitter rush of guilt stung Allie's heart.

'Look, Isabelle,' she said hesitantly. 'Maybe I should just go—'

Isabelle raised her head, fixing her with a steely, incriminating gaze. 'You do not get any say in what happens right now, Allie. You have broken every Rule Cimmeria has. You betrayed my trust. You *stole from me*.'

Her hurt and anger cut through Allie's battered defences – her lower lip trembled. There was truth in what the headmistress said. Isabelle had taken care of her, looked out for her – maybe even *loved* her. And she'd betrayed her.

My reasons were good, she told herself for the thousandth time.

But somehow that wasn't comforting any more.

As if she could read her thoughts, Isabelle spoke quietly. 'I don't know how we will ever trust each other again. Maybe

Jerry's right. Maybe things have gone so far you don't belong here any longer. Perhaps I should give you what you want.' Reaching into her pocket she pulled out her phone – *Somebody must have found it in the woods,* Allie thought – and scrolled through her contacts. Pressing the dial button she said, 'But that is not my decision to make.'

A voice answered.

'Would you like to speak with her now?' Isabelle asked. After a second, the headmistress crossed the small room and held out the phone. Suspicious, Allie made no move to reach for it but Isabelle didn't back down.

'Take it,' she said, her voice icy.

Swallowing hard, Allie took the device, still warm from Isabelle's hand.

'Hello . . . ?' she said hesitantly.

'Allie,' a brisk voice replied. 'This is your grandmother. I understand we need to talk.'

SIX

'I understand why you don't feel safe at Cimmeria any more, but you will most certainly not be safe if you leave the school.' Lucinda spoke in a curiously monotone manner, as if they were in a business meeting and she was listing the facts about a project. 'Yes, there is someone working against us at Cimmeria and, yes, that person is dangerous and, no, I don't know who it is. But while you are at school, you are at least surrounded by people who are trying to protect you.'

Allie made an impatient noise – she knew all this already. Lucinda paused. When she spoke again, her tone was more urgent.

'Allie, so far we've failed to keep you safe. We failed your friend Jo most of all. And I am truly sorry about that. But if I promised you nobody else will be hurt, I'd be lying. This is a dangerous situation.'

Her words rang true. Allie's heart speeded up and she squeezed the phone tight, as if afraid it might escape.

'I know exactly what Nathaniel's thugs did to her and to you. If I were you, I'd want to run as far and fast as I could to put all this behind me. But no matter how fast you run, Nathaniel will find you in the end.' Lucinda's tone intensified. 'So don't run, Allie. Stay. And fight back with me.'

Allie was stunned. Was her grandmother asking for her help?

'Fight back?' she asked. 'How?'

'Nathaniel is out of control, Allie, and I want to see him suffer. I want his plans crushed. I want his hired guns in prison. I want to find out which of our friends is helping him, and I want to deal with that person myself.' Lucinda's words were as cold and precise as an ice-pick. 'I want everything Nathaniel cares about destroyed. But to do that, I need your help. If you stay at Cimmeria, I promise you, Gabe will suffer for what he did. And so will the person who opened the gates that night and let him in.'

The venom in her tone left Allie with no doubts about whether Lucinda was serious.

Revenge. The idea grew in her mind until it blocked out everything else. She could avenge Jo's death. Pay her killers back for what they'd done.

But to do that she'd have to trust Lucinda. And could she do that? On what would she base this trust? A word. A feeling. The delicate, twisting strands of DNA that connected them.

It wasn't enough. She needed to be certain that Lucinda was trustworthy. She needed to know more.

'Why can't we just call the police?' she asked. 'If we tell them what's happened they'd arrest him. Wouldn't they?'

Lucinda's hesitation was slight, but Allie noticed it. 'I'm afraid that at the moment the government minister in charge of policing finds Nathaniel very convincing.'

Puzzled, Allie frowned at the phone. Why would a government minister listen to Nathaniel? He was utterly mad. But then she thought about the way the local police officers had acted this morning and her heart went cold.

Her voice was plaintive. 'But the police should arrest him. How is this even *possible*?'

'It's all about power,' Lucinda said. 'And control. I have it. Nathaniel wants it. It is that simple.'

'No, it's not simple,' Allie said sharply. 'Because I don't understand it at all.'

'Yes you do. Think it through, Allie.' Lucinda's response was low and dangerous. 'After all these months, don't you know what you're part of? In your heart, don't you already know?'

The phone felt hot in Allie's hands as her mind flipped through the last few months – the things she'd been told. Bits of information like puzzle pieces sliding into place.

Night School is part of a much larger organisation ... Cimmeria is more powerful than you know ... The Board of Night School is also the Board of the Organisation ... The board controls everything ... The prime minister ... Several ministers are coming to the ball ... Lucinda is in charge of the board ... The government ... Lucinda ...

How can you not know?

'Night School controls the government.' Allie's words came

out in a whisper, but as soon as she said them she was certain she was right.

'Not Night School,' Lucinda corrected her. 'But the organisation.'

For a long moment Allie sat still, trying to absorb all this information. It was too much to grasp. Too horrible to accept.

'I don't ...' she said. 'I mean ... how?'

Lucinda's reply was brisk. 'The important thing is that it does. And if Nathaniel defeats me, all that power will be his. He will be unstoppable.'

Imagining a world in which Nathaniel ran everything, Allie bit her lip so hard it bled – the coppery taste was bitter on her tongue.

'You can't let that happen.'

This was what Lucinda was waiting for. She pounced. 'I want to stop him. But I can't do it without you. So ... will you stay and fight with me?'

There was no doubt in Allie's mind any more. It was so much worse than she'd thought – so much more dangerous and frightening. She didn't have a choice ... did she?

'Yes,' she said tiredly. 'I'll stay.'

'Good.' Lucinda sounded grimly pleased. 'But now that you know what's at stake I expect you to be part of this. You're in danger no matter where you are – even at Cimmeria. We don't know who the spy is among us so you must be constantly alert.'

'I will be,' Allie said numbly.

Lucinda continued, 'Do everything Isabelle asks without question; I trust her completely and you should do the same.'

Allie's eyes were drawn to where the headmistress sat watching her, a pen forgotten in her hand. Perhaps she could hear Lucinda's voice through the phone; her gaze was sharp and knowing.

'OK.'

'It won't be easy,' Lucinda warned her. 'You have a great deal of atoning to do for last night's incident. Isabelle will punish you and it won't be pleasant – she is very angry with you. I expect you to do every piece of menial, exhausting, pointless labour she hands you without complaint. Also, there must be no more running away – I can't protect you if I don't know where you are. In fact, there can be no more breaking of The Rules whatsoever – those Rules will keep you alive. And finally, even with all this happening, you are still in school so you must catch up on your coursework and excel in your lessons. Are we agreed?'

Her mind reeling from this litany of demands, Allie nodded mutely before realising her grandmother couldn't see her.

'Yes,' she said finally. 'Agreed.'

But Lucinda wasn't finished. 'Good. Understand this, Allie: violate any part of our agreement and our deal is off. I don't want to but I *will* cut you loose if I have to. And you do not want to be out there on your own, I promise you.

'But give me everything I've asked for and, I swear to you, I will give you your revenge.'

By the time Allie left Isabelle's office, the light had begun to fade from the sky.

She felt exposed, walking through the halls in her street

clothes, surrounded by the students in their matching dark blue blazers with the white Cimmeria crest over their hearts. Even with her head down, she could sense curious eyes studying her, hear quiet voices whispering, giggling. But when she glanced up no one met her gaze. She was invisible.

Hurrying her pace, she sped up the stairs to the girls' dormitory wing and then down the quiet narrow hall to her bedroom. Once inside she leaned back against the door – relishing the privacy. But when she turned on the lights, she stopped in her tracks.

Her room was spotless.

The dirty clothes had disappeared. Papers had been filed. Books were lined up on well-dusted shelves. The wooden floors had been swept and mopped; the bed covered in a crisp white duvet, a blue blanket folded neatly over the footboard.

This was a message from Isabelle and Allie heard it, loud and clear: no more special favours.

In the mirror by the door, she caught a glimpse of her wild hair and smeared makeup. She already knew she reeked of cider and sweat.

She didn't belong in this room looking like that.

Stripping off her grubby jeans and jumper, Allie wrapped herself in a warm dressing gown, grabbed a fluffy white towel and headed for the door.

At the last second, though, she turned back and picked the clothes up from the floor, dropping them in the laundry basket in the corner.

A deal was a deal.

'Satisfied?' she asked the empty room.

As she made her way down the hall she tried to clear her head of the memory of Mark's expression as she told him she'd decided to stay at Cimmeria. Isabelle had given them a few minutes alone before he was put on a train back to London.

'You must be joking.' Disbelief had filled his eyes. 'I've just been held prisoner. For hours. You're covered in scars and your teachers are fascists, but suddenly everything's *fine*?'

Allie hadn't known what to say. How could she explain to an outsider everything she now knew?

'Look,' she said, 'there's a lot you don't know—'

He'd cut her off with an impatient gesture. 'Come on, Allie. I've seen your school – it's like a bleedin' castle. And I've heard how you talk – you were always a little posh but now you sound like the bloody Queen.'

Stung, Allie felt the blood rush to her face. 'That's not fair, Mark. I'm still the same person.'

'No you're not.' With his hands resting on his narrow hips, he studied her as if he was seeing her for the first time. 'Maybe you don't know it but it's obvious to me. You're not one of us any more. You're one of them.'

Remembering how he'd looked at her then, Allie shivered and pulled the robe more tightly around her.

With a sigh, she pushed open the door to the girls' bathroom. It was blessedly empty at this hour. In a pure white shower cubicle, she turned the hot water up until the temperature teetered on the brink of painful and let it flood over her, washing away the grime of the last twenty-four hours.

She ran the soap across her skin, noticing the changes the

car accident had made to her body – the scars were slick bumps beneath her fingertips.

Each one was a reminder of what she still had to do.

Something Dr Cartwright had said to her in one of their meetings nagged at her. 'It is OK,' he'd said, 'for you to be alive even if Jo isn't.'

She hadn't believed him at the time.

But maybe he was right, she thought now. *Because I have to be alive to kill Gabe.*

Back in her bedroom, she wrestled a comb through her tangled hair and dabbed on foundation. But even when she'd done it, dark shadows still underlined her grey eyes; her skin looked sallow.

Flinging open the wardrobe, she surveyed the row of dark blue options in front of her. The choice of what to wear at Cimmeria was rarely complicated. Dark tights and a short pleated skirt went on first. Then a crisp, white, button-down blouse topped by a blue blazer. A pair of sensible, school-issued shoes and she was fully disguised as a Cimmeria student.

She glanced at her watch – it was nearly dinner-time.

Now, she thought with grim determination, *let the atoning begin.*

As she hurried down the stairs, the low roar of conversation and laughter emanating from the crowded dining hall grew gradually louder. The happy buzz felt alien and for a long moment she stood outside, unable to make herself go in. She'd been skipping dinners for weeks.

But in her office today Isabelle had made it clear that was no longer an option. She had to be in the dining room on time for every meal from now on, as The Rules required.

That was just one of many things Allie had agreed to do. Because once she'd agreed to stay, Isabelle had read her the riot act.

Allie would attend all classes and make up for all the work she'd missed so far this term. She would maintain perfect grades.

And she'd rejoin Night School.

The last requirement was the one that frightened her – the one that twisted her stomach into knots.

She knew it would be irrational to refuse – she had to be in Night School to train, to learn, to find out the truth about what was happening. It was the heart of Cimmeria, and she had to be there. But the idea of doing that again – of slipping into that world – scared the hell out of her.

But what was the point of telling Isabelle that? She knew it already. And she didn't care.

When she hadn't agreed immediately, Isabelle had fixed her with a cold gaze.

'Participation in Night School is a requirement for your continued attendance at Cimmeria. So you need to make up your mind now, Allie. Do you want to stay at Cimmeria Academy? Or not?'

Defeated, Allie had nodded her acquiescence. She did want to stay. She wanted her revenge. She would do anything for it.

And if she could rejoin Night School, then she could walk through that door now, into the dining hall. And eat supper.

Setting her jaw, she marched resolutely through the door just as Zelazny began to shut it. Out of the corner of her eye she saw him shoot her a strange look but she didn't slow down until she reached an empty seat at her old table and slid into it.

At the table, all conversation stopped.

Cringing at the silence, Allie forced herself to look around the table; here were all the people she'd been avoiding or ignoring for weeks – all the people she loved.

Isabelle had raked her over the coals for how she'd treated them. Looking at them now, her words rang in Allie's ears.

'I know you've been through a lot over the last few months, but your reaction to Jo's death was to strike out at the people who love you most,' she'd said. 'You hurt those people very badly. You never seemed to realise this fact: *they were grieving, too*. You've been cold to Rachel for weeks, so she's gone through this painful time alone. And you've virtually ignored Zoe. She thinks of you as a big sister. She needed you but you were too self-absorbed to be there for her.'

Across the table from her, Carter sat next to Jules. Each time she saw them together, a tiny shard of ice seemed to lodge deeper in her chest, but Carter had always been her friend and she didn't want to lose him.

If that meant being nice to Jules then . . . fine.

Next to them, Zoe looked very small as she scanned the faces around her with quick, puzzled eyes. Rachel kept her gaze lowered, as if she couldn't bear to see what had become of Allie. Next to her, Lucas gripped her hand tightly.

She got the feeling they were all waiting for something to happen. Maybe they expected her to act crazy. Run away. Shout at them.

She cleared her throat. 'Look, everyone. I want to say something. I know I've been messed up and I want to tell you all I'm sorry. I think I needed time to go ... I don't know ... a little crazy for a while. And I know you all know I ran away yesterday but I want you to know that I wasn't running away from you ...' She paused. Was that the truth? She didn't know any more. 'But now I'm trying to get myself together. I wasn't really trying ...' Flitting around the table, her gaze rested for a moment on Carter's face. His dark eyes avoided hers. 'I know I've been selfish and scary and I just hope' – she looked at Rachel helplessly – 'that you can forgive me. And help me ... get better.'

A brief stunned pause was followed by a rush as everybody spoke at once.

'Of course we can ...'

'Don't even think ...'

'Anybody would have ...'

They were all kind but when the conversation veered away from the uncomfortable reality of Allie's breakdown and wandered to the safer territory of her escape, she was relieved.

'How did you do it?' Lucas asked, with real interest in his eyes. 'They say you climbed over the fence.'

'No way,' Allie scoffed. 'That's impossible. For me anyway. That thing is *huge*.'

'Did someone help you?' Jules asked, her voice cautious.

Thinking of Mark, Allie paused. 'Not exactly ...'

'What are they doing to you?' For Allie, Carter's voice made all other sound stop and her eyes flashed up to meet his. 'What kind of punishment?'

'Loads of homework. Garden detention for the rest of my life.' She faked an insouciant shrug. 'The usual.'

The look on his face told her he knew there was more to it than that. But she couldn't tell them everything. She couldn't say what Lucinda had promised her. Not now anyway.

At that moment, the kitchen doors opened and staff poured out in rows of two into the room, steam rising from the platters they carried. As Allie watched the waiters enter in their crisp black uniforms, her gaze fell upon Sylvain, watching her intently, knowingly. His eyes as bright and cold as chips of glacier ice.

SEVEN

The next day Allie went to all her classes for the first time in weeks.

Her teachers must have been warned to expect her because none of them commented on her sudden reappearance, although Zelazny shot her a bilious look as she slid into her seat in ancient history.

The students, though, were not so polite. She could handle the staring, although it made her skin crawl. But the whispered insults just loud enough for her to hear were harder to take. Most of the time she managed to ignore them. Until, in maths class, she heard someone stage-whisper, 'Do you think *she* killed Jo ... ?'

For a moment, Allie couldn't breathe. Then a flash of white-hot pain made her forget all her promises.

Holding her pen like a dagger she spun in her seat and levelled it at two girls who sat behind her. Amber and Ismay:

acolytes of Katie Gilmore. The 'twins of evil', she'd always called them back when she had a sense of humour. She didn't think anything was funny any more.

'If I were you' – her voice was low and surprisingly steady – 'I'd shut up.'

For a second they just giggled uncertainly. She could see that they weren't sure whether to ridicule her or be afraid.

Then Amber flipped her long blonde hair over one shoulder with practised nonchalance. 'She's terrifying,' she said. 'She has criminal eyes. I can't believe she's loose among us.'

This gave Ismay, ever the follower, the courage she needed to be hateful. 'She's some kind of monster.' Her lips curled up in a disdainful smile. 'Why don't you do us all a favour and run away again?'

Somehow the pettiness of their words defused the situation. Allie's anger receded, like a wave drawing back from the sand. When they weren't talking about Jo – when they were just insulting Allie – she could take it. Still, she ached to punch them both in their pert little noses and see what they had to say then.

But she'd promised Lucinda no trouble. No rule breaking at all. In return she'd get to hurt the right people.

Uncurling her fist from the pen she flipped it into writing position.

'Little tossers,' she said, loudly enough for everyone to hear. Then she turned her back on them and, cold with rage, tried to block out the sound of their insipid giggles.

Once class began, though, she had no time to worry about what anyone was saying about her. She was so far behind in her studies she wasn't certain what her teachers were talking about.

Chemistry was the worst. She took copious notes but, as the complex formulas and diagrams spilled meaninglessly across the pages of her notebook, panic rose in her throat like bile.

Am I too far behind to catch up?

Two days ago she wouldn't have cared. But she'd promised Lucinda she'd pass all her classes and with so much at stake she now cared very much.

The biggest problem was that the teacher was Jerry Cole and, even as she struggled to understand the lesson, she was also working studiously to avoid meeting his eyes.

He was back to his normal, good-humoured self, making bad jokes about atoms and molecular structure. He smiled easily and she could see he'd made an unsuccessful effort to tame his wiry curls. There was no sign at all of the angry man she'd faced the day before.

When the class ended, she raced to join the queue of students streaming from the room, losing herself in the crowd. She was already congratulating herself on making it away when he called her name.

'Allie – could you stay behind for a second?'

She froze, her heart sinking.

For a moment she considered just running out – pretending she hadn't heard. Then, with heavy slowness, she turned to face him. His wire-framed spectacles glittered in the light, hiding his eyes as he motioned for her to sit in a desk on the front row.

After a brief hesitation she perched stiffly, her arms crossed in front of the book bag in her lap.

He leaned back against his desk. Allie thought he looked uncomfortable; his feet moved restlessly.

'Allie, I wanted to clear the air about yesterday. It was a difficult day for both of us and I would just like to put it behind us.' Wary, Allie watched as he took off his glasses. His eyes looked tired. 'You know, the things that have been happening here – Jo's death, your injuries – they haven't only affected students. Teachers have feelings too. And we've all been under a lot of strain this term. But if I'm to teach you, then you need to be comfortable around me. You need to know I'm not judging you all the time. So I hope we can work together again the way we have in the past. I think you're a good student – and a good person – and I enjoy having you in my class.'

His words sounded genuine and she longed for things to be normal again. He was offering her something she really wanted.

'I'm ... sorry too,' she said shyly. 'For ... well, all the stuff I did.'

He visibly relaxed, as if he'd been as nervous about having this conversation as she was. It was disarming and she found herself feeling better about things.

'Good. I'm glad,' he said. 'Well, now that we've settled that ... I want to talk to you about something more mundane – chemistry.' He chuckled and Allie smiled politely as he polished his glasses on a cloth he took from his pocket. 'You're quite far behind with your work and I know how hard it is to catch up with this class. Once you're behind things can spiral out of control fairly quickly and before you know it' – he held up an empty hand – 'you're being held back.'

She kept her expression blank but tightened her grip on her bag.

Is he going to hold me back? Even hearing the possibility expressed aloud was humiliating. Hot blood rose to her cheeks.

'I don't want that to happen to you,' he continued, oblivious to her tension. 'But I think you'll need some extra help to get you up to speed. I've spoken to Rachel Patel, and she's offered to tutor you for the rest of term. As you know, she's one of our science stars so I think this is a great idea. Given your previous high scores, I think you can catch up with the class if you work hard – can I count on you to do that?'

A sudden burst of hope, warm as sunlight, filled her. He still had confidence in her. He thought she could do it. And best of all, she'd be working with Rachel – maybe she could figure out a way to mend their damaged friendship at the same time.

'Definitely,' she said with heartfelt enthusiasm.

'Good.' He stood up and she knew their talk was over. But as she headed towards the door, he called after her. When she turned back he was looking at her oddly.

'You're going to be just fine, you know,' he said.

Taken by surprise, Allie didn't have time to be anything but honest. 'I hope so.'

That conversation was the only light in an otherwise dim day, and Allie's feet dragged as she lugged her heavy book bag up the stairs towards the girls' dormitory wing after her last class.

When she saw a small familiar figure ahead of her, darting through the crowds of students, she swallowed hard.

'Zoe thinks of you as a big sister,' Isabelle had said. 'She needed you.'

'Hey, Zoe,' she called out. 'Wait up.'

The younger girl stopped in mid-stride. When she turned around, her expression was guarded.

Zoe was a prodigy – just thirteen, she was already studying well above Allie's level. The two of them had been close last term but after Jo's death Zoe acted as if nothing important had happened. She didn't seem to care. Allie never once saw her cry. She just got on with her life as if Jo had never existed.

Early on, Dr Cartwright had tried to explain to Allie how Asperger's worked but she hadn't wanted to hear it at the time. It had just been too hard to take.

Now, though, her own actions seemed mean to her.

When she caught up to her, Allie rushed into her apology. 'I just wanted to tell you again that I'm so sorry for the way I've treated you. It wasn't fair. I've been messed up but I shouldn't have . . . done that.'

Zoe's face screwed up, and Allie knew she was thinking it over – flipping through the words as if they were numbers. Adding them up. Coming up with a reply.

'I forgive you,' she said finally. 'But you can't do it again or I won't be your friend. And that's for ever.'

Something fluttered loose in Allie's heart. She couldn't lose Zoe. She needed her. She spoke with a fervour she hadn't realised she felt.

'I won't do it again, Zoe. I swear it. And I . . . I really hope things can go back the way they were. Please. Let's just . . . be normal again.'

Clearly satisfied by this, Zoe gave a nod that sent her pony-tail swinging. 'Good. I want that, too.'

Side by side, they walked down the narrow corridor lined on both sides with small white doors, each with a number painted on it in black.

Tilting her head to one side, Zoe spoke with her usual bluntness. 'Why did you run away? Because you were sad?'

Allie hesitated. 'Yeah . . .' she said eventually. 'I was sad.'

Zoe seemed to accept this. 'Where did you go?'

There was no easy answer to this question.

'To church, in the end.' Allie's voice was rueful. 'Although that wasn't the plan. Like . . . at all.'

'What was the plan?'

'To go to London and find out who hurt Jo.' Allie shrugged – it sounded so foolish now. 'Somehow.'

'Aren't you from London?' Zoe's gaze sharpened.

'Yeah . . . ?'

'Nathaniel would have found you immediately. He'd know right where you'd go. It was a terrible plan.'

Allie opened her mouth to reply then closed it again. Zoe had a point.

When they reached the younger girl's door, Zoe stopped. 'If you ever decide to run away again, come to me. I'll help you choose the best place to go. Statistically speaking.'

Allie was surprised by how much that touched her; for a second she didn't trust herself to speak. When she recovered, though, her reply was fervent.

'If I ever run away again you will be the first person I tell.'

*

When she opened the door to her room, the chemical-lemon smell of furniture polish greeted Allie before she'd even switched on the light. She inhaled deeply. Loath though she was to admit it to herself, she was glad her dirty clothes had been taken away and fresh towels stacked on the shelf by the door. Glad everything was orderly.

Outside, cold winter rain tapped against the bedroom window as if it was trying to get in. She dropped her book bag by the desk with a clunk and kicked off her shoes. The room was warm and snug.

Grabbing the thick stack of work assignments her teachers had given her to make up, she sat down on the floor to sort through it – she'd need a lot of space.

'Let's see,' she muttered, frowning as she looked at the first page. 'This is urgent.' She set it on the floor to her right. 'And this is ... sort of urgent.' She set another paper on top of the first. 'This is' – she held the next sheet – 'totally freaking urgent.'

The process continued in that manner for some time as the 'urgent' stack grew alarmingly. When she'd gone through everything in the file, she looked around in dismay; the floor was so covered in paper she could barely see the whitewashed wood beneath it.

'Bollocks,' she announced to no one. 'I'm totally screwed.'

In the end, she decided the biggest worry was an English essay for Isabelle's class – twelve hundred words on the Romantics in Italy due the next day. Allie hadn't read a single page of the assigned work.

She was flipping worriedly through her English textbook when someone knocked at her door.

'Come in,' she said without looking up.

'Hey, Al ... lie.' Rachel's voice trailed off as she walked in, her eyes widening at the scene in front of her. 'Yowza. That is, like, a whole tree on your floor.'

'Help.' Allie waved her assignment at her. 'What do you know about the Romantics in Italy?'

'That depends. In Tuscany?' Rachel walked the rest of the way in, closing the door behind her. 'Or in Rome?'

Allie gave her a desperate look. 'They went to more than one *place*?'

Without replying, Rachel held out her hand. Allie gave her the paper and she scanned it quickly. 'I did this one already so, let's see ... ' Looking through the books on Allie's shelves, Rachel pulled out a slim volume. 'This is what I used. Chapter eight has everything. Read that and you can write up a basic essay – quote some Shelley poems to take up space. That man liked the sound of his own voice. Check it out.'

Holding up the book in one hand, she intoned with great drama:

'Let a vast assembly be,
And with great solemnity
Declare with measured words that ye
Are, as God has made ye, free ... '

Allie held out her hand for the book. 'Rachel, God has made ye a life-saver.'

'That's what they tell me.' Rachel's smile was steady but Allie knew her well enough to see the hint of uncertainty behind it.

Still, she reassured herself, *at least the smile happened.*

A sudden silence fell. Allie flipped through the papers trying to think of something to say but Rachel filled the conversational gap. 'Did Jerry tell you I'm your chemistry teacher now?'

Allie tried to affect cool. 'Don't think this means I'm your bitch. I'm still a free woman.'

Rachel grinned, genuinely this time. 'Oh really? Who's your daddy?'

'Wait ... ' Allie swung cautiously back into the rhythm of their rapid-fire rapport, although it felt creaky after so long away. 'Are you saying my new daddy is a girl named Rachel? When I write a memoir I'm calling it "Allie Has Two Daddies and One of Them Is Rachel".'

'You will sell a million copies and I will be famous. I'll accept a percentage.' Rachel rubbed her hands gleefully. 'So, should we start suffering ... I mean working tonight? An hour of science torture will be good for you.'

The banter made Allie feel almost normal. Like she had her friend back.

'Do I have a choice?'

'No.' Rachel walked to the door. 'See you at dinner, minion. Where you can peel my grapes.'

EİGHT

'*Allie, help me! Oh God. Please help me . . . ' In the darkness, Jo's terrified voice sailed eerily on the breeze that rattled the tree branches above Allie's head.*

Each word cut Allie like a blade. Panicked and desperate, she ran left, then right, then left again. But the voice never seemed to get any closer and it was getting harder to breathe. Her chest felt as if it was wrapped in bands of iron, inexorably tightening.

Trying to summon the breath to speak, she panted harshly.

'I can't find you, Jo!' she called weakly. 'Where are you?'

'Allie!' For some reason the hope in Jo's voice broke her heart. 'Help me! Please!'

A sob tore Allie's throat as she ran. Trees that seemed to swoop down to snatch at her clothes with branches that ended in sharp points, like long, jagged nails. She ignored the pain. She had to find Jo. If she could just get to her in time, she'd live.

She was exhausted by the time she saw Jo in the distance, lying on her back in a grove of trees, blonde hair glowing around her head like a halo. Her cornflower blue eyes stared up at the sky, unseeing.

Dropping to her knees, Allie reached for her slim hand. 'I'm here, Jo. I'm here.'

Jo's breath rattled in her throat. As she turned to look at Allie her blue eyes clouded over and turned white.

'Too late, Allie,' she said bitterly. 'You're too late. I'm already dead. And it's your fault.'

Looking down, Allie realised she held the hand of a corpse – Jo's fingers were blue and cold, lifeless.

She opened her mouth to scream but no sound came out ...

Gasping for air, Allie sat bolt upright. Sweat streamed down her face as she searched the dark room with terrified eyes. She scrambled back in the bed like a cornered animal until she huddled against the headboard, trembling.

Strangled breaths burned her throat. Her heart thudded in her ears.

It was just that dream again. I'm in my room, she told herself. *I'm in my room and I'm safe and everything's OK. Everything's OK. Everything's OK. Everything's OK. Everything's OK ...*

But the walls closed in on her anyway.

Squeezing her eyes shut, she took in a long, slow, shaky breath, trying to force air into her compressed lungs. She wheezed as tiny wisps of air struggled to get through. Flashes of light sparked at the edge of her vision.

She used the tricks Carter had taught her for dealing with

panic attacks – breathing slowly through her nose and thinking of things that made her happy.

Kittens, she thought frantically. *Little fluffy ones! Sunny days! Chocolate ice cream! Beaches!*

Even as she was still trying to compile it, the list seemed so ridiculous she choked on a laugh, tears trickling down her cheeks.

As it had before, the trick worked. Gradually the walls began to return to their real locations and her racing heartbeat steadied.

But the experience left her shaken.

'It was just a dream,' she said aloud, clutching a pillow tight to her chest like a shield. 'Just a dream.'

The darkness felt oppressive and she flipped on the desk lamp, reaching for her alarm clock. It was half past four in the morning.

Taking a deep, steadying breath, she leaned back against the cold wall, shoving strands of her hair out of her face.

Today she started her garden detention – three days a week she was to work from six in the morning until eight in the walled garden. There was still another hour before she needed to get up but she didn't want to go back to sleep – she could feel the dream around her, coiled like a snake, waiting to strike should she doze.

Instead, she took a long hot shower then, back in her room, rooted through her dresser for her warmest clothes, choosing as many layers as she could stack – thermal underwear, exercise trousers and two pullovers under her heaviest jumper. When she was ready it was still too early, so she worked on her English essay until six.

The school was eerily silent at this hour; even the staff were nowhere to be seen as she made her way down the stairs. The creak of the back door as it opened echoed in the quiet like a scream.

Outside, it might as well have been midnight – not a glimmer of light showed on the horizon aside from the faint light of stars. The grass was covered in a thick frost that crunched beneath the rubber soles of her shoes as she headed across the back lawn.

God it was cold. It was so cold that breathing made her nose ache and her forehead seemed to tighten around her brain.

Shoving her gloved hands into her pockets, she tried to burrow deeper into her coat.

Gardening in February, she complained to herself. *Do people actually do this? On purpose?*

Denuded of leaves, the trees lining the footpath behind the school formed a gloomy, skeletal canopy above her. Lowering her eyes, she quickened her pace.

To her left she could just make out a ghostly white domed roof of the marble folly through the trees. Ahead of her, the footpath disappeared in the dark.

Uneasy, Allie broke into a gentle jog.

She didn't want to admit she was afraid. She told herself she needed to warm up her muscles so they'd ache less when she started working. But tension turned her stomach sour.

When she reached a long, tall wall made of heavy squares of aged grey stone she allowed herself to relax a little. The garden was inside it. Turning left, she followed it to a sturdy wooden gate. Normally it was kept locked but today the combination lock hung open and the gate stood slightly ajar.

At the sight of it, a tingle of unease ran down Allie's spine. Her mind flashed back to Jo, expertly spinning the little dials on the lock. The gate was never left unlocked.

Someone must have left it open for me, she reasoned. *It's not like I'm not expected. How else would I get in?*

Still, as she stepped through she moved with caution, lowering her centre of gravity, her muscles tense.

The walled garden was vast – in the summer it produced enough vegetables and fruit to feed the entire school, but at this time of year it looked bare and dead. And as far as she could tell it was deserted.

'Hello?' she called, standing on her toes to peer into the darkness. 'Mr Ellison?'

Her voice sank into the cold earth.

Someone should be here to meet her. It's not like going out to the garden in the middle of the night was her idea, after all.

This was starting to piss her off.

It must be well after six now. But here she was, alone in the dark, wandering aimlessly.

'This is so freaking stupid,' Allie muttered to herself as she pushed through a tangle of dry branches. 'I might as well have a sign on my back that says, "Please attack me, Nathaniel".' A thorn she couldn't see tugged at her sleeve and she yanked her arm free. '"I'm alone and vulnerable in the dark. Swoop in now and take me back to your hellhole of global domination." And why didn't I bring a bloody *torch*?'

At that moment, a sharp cracking sound rang in the air. She whirled towards the noise but could see nothing in the darkness.

Maybe I just heard myself step on something, she thought hopefully. *And it echoed.*

But a nerve fluttered in her cheek, betraying her tension.

'Hello?' Her voice sounded uncertain and she cleared her throat. 'Is anyone there?'

Nobody answered.

Allie stopped talking. Maybe it wasn't great to be advertising her location.

After a long moment of heavy silence she heard it again – the sharp crack of a branch snapping.

And she hadn't moved.

Allie's training kicked in – her heart pounding, she dropped down into a low crouch, muffling a grunt as her battered knee protested. Staying very still, she listened.

Snap.

There it is again.

Someone was definitely there – no animal could make that noise. But, whoever it was, they seemed to be at the far end of the garden, although it was hard to tell where precisely – the sound echoed off the encircling walls.

She stayed low, hidden by darkness and dry brush, thinking through her options. She felt strangely calm. Maybe it was the lingering effect of her panic attack earlier – her adrenaline failed to kick in.

She knew she should run back to the school to get help. That is what Isabelle would want her to do.

But what if it was Nathaniel? Or Gabe? What if they were here now? This could be her chance to end this. To pay them back for what they'd done.

75

She wasn't back to full strength. And she was alone. Fighting them now would be a bad idea. If she lost . . .

She didn't know what would happen if she lost.

But all she could think was: *If I won . . . it would all be over.*

In the end, the decision wasn't that difficult. Rising to her feet she looked for a makeshift weapon.

Whatever the odds – it didn't matter. If they were here she wasn't running away. She owed Jo that much. She owed her bravery.

Finding two sharp bamboo stakes, she yanked them free of the frozen earth and carried one in each hand as, with careful steps, she crossed to the edge of the garden. There she paused to listen then, moving with stealth and speed, she followed her instincts towards the fruit orchard at the back.

She couldn't feel the cold any more. Purpose made her warm and whole. She was entirely focused on what she was about to do.

She was almost there when she heard the sound again – much closer now. It came from the other side of the row of trees in front of her. Whoever it was, they were in there.

Her nerves tingled with anticipation – her stomach muscles tightened as she readied herself to spring.

That was when she heard the laugh.

The deep, familiar rumble was followed immediately by words she couldn't make out and then another chuckle.

She knew that laugh.

No longer trying to keep quiet, she shoved through the dense cluster of apple and pear trees, half hidden in the early morning dark.

'... and his face turned red, and his eyes bulged out of his face, and I swear to God ...'

Bursting through the trees she saw Carter with his back to her, breaking thin branches into smaller sizes and piling them up as he told his story. Nearby, Mr Ellison smiled as he sharpened a set of clippers. A battery-powered lantern sat between them on the ground.

Embarrassment made heat rise to Allie's cheeks. How could she have thought it was Nathaniel? She was paranoid.

But for God's sake, she thought, *why weren't they looking out for me instead of sitting back here nattering?*

Shame turned to anger in one red-hot instant.

'Hey!' She shouted louder than she'd intended. Carter whirled to face her, still holding a long branch in one hand. He looked gratifyingly startled. 'Why didn't anyone answer me when I called?'

She could hear the irritation in her own voice but before Carter could say anything Mr Ellison pointed his clippers at her, a frown lowering his brow.

'You're late, young lady. And I don't like how you say "hello".'

'*What?* But I ... I couldn't find you. Didn't you hear me calling?' Her mood shifted without effort from anger to defensiveness. 'I looked for you for ages. Nobody told me to come to the orchard, and' – they were both staring at her as she finished lamely – 'it's dark.'

At that, Mr Ellison began stacking his tools into a worn metal box. 'No need to go hiring a lawyer, Miss Sheridan. Just try to be on time from now on. And bring a torch. It doesn't get light until after six.'

Allie refused to look at Carter but she knew he was trying not to smile.

Embarrassed, and in a bid to change the subject, she pointed aggressively at Carter. 'What's he doing here?'

Carter opened his mouth to reply but Mr Ellison cut him off. 'Carter is going to be helping us out today for reasons that are . . . not entirely voluntary.'

His eyes twinkled as he said it, and this time Carter failed to stop his guilty grin.

Instantly, Allie's hackles rose. *So it's funny when Carter gets detention, but I get treated like an axe murderer?*

The injustice rekindled her rage.

'Awesome.' Her tone was sullen. 'So, are we just going to stand around chatting about how funny it is when Carter breaks The Rules, or is there something you want me to do?'

Mr Ellison's eyebrows shot upwards. 'I'd appreciate it if you kept a civil tone, Miss Sheridan.'

She couldn't remember him ever looking truly stern before. Tall and broad-shouldered, with warm brown eyes and skin the colour of burnished oak, the groundskeeper had always been kind to her.

Normally she would have apologised and defused the situation but right now she was cold and bruised, every single one of her muscles hurt, she'd had that awful nightmare and *nothing* was fair.

She glared at him in mute rebellion.

When Allie didn't respond, the groundskeeper spoke again, his tone signalling his disapproval. 'I believe you're right-handed, Allie?'

Some part of her wanted to end this standoff and just answer him straight but she was sulking in earnest now. So instead she gave a dismissive shrug and crossed her arms.

'Allie, come on . . .' Carter said softly.

She bit her lip hard to stop herself from telling him to just shut the hell up. Why wouldn't he mind his own business?

Evidently having decided she wasn't going to speak, Mr Ellison reached into the pocket of his dungarees and pulled out a pair of well-used secateurs, small enough to fit easily in her hand, and held them out to her. He made no move to step towards her. She was going to have to walk over and take them.

Allie's arms stayed folded stubbornly. She didn't want to give in. She wanted everyone to know how angry she was. How unfair everything was.

But he'd report her to Isabelle. And then Lucinda would find out, and she'd told her she had to cooperate completely, so . . .

She had no choice. With slow, resentful steps, she crossed the distance between them and reached for the clippers, trying to show him with her eyes how angry she was.

When she started to pull away, though, he held on to the clippers.

'I know you're better than this, Allie,' he said, not at all unkindly.

Her first instinct was to tell him he didn't know anything about her. Nobody did. But then, to her surprise, tears prickled the backs of her eyes. She didn't want to say mean things to Mr Ellison. She knew she wasn't in control of her actions right now. She was swinging wildly; hitting all the wrong people.

She had to stop.

Her rage dissipated, like a puff of breath in the cold air.

'I'm sorry,' she said, needing him to accept her apology. Needing him to forgive her.

His face softened. 'I understand more than you know, Allie.' The deep baritone rumble of his voice was comforting. 'I've lost people. Good people. So has Carter. People we loved just as much as you loved Jo. We know how much it hurts. But we got through it and now you have to get through it, too.'

Allie knew Carter's parents died when he was only a child. And they were good friends with Mr Ellison. That must have been devastating. They must have felt as bad as she did now.

She turned to look at Carter, but he'd dropped his gaze, as if Mr Ellison's words had brought back painful memories.

The tight strings that had seemed to bind her heart ever since that horrible night loosened, just a little.

She was not the only one to go through this. And she shouldn't punish them because of her own pain. All of them had lost someone.

She nodded fiercely. 'I'll sort things out, Mr Ellison. I promise.'

Perched high on a ladder, Allie trimmed twigs from the gnarled branches of the old apple tree as Mr Ellison had showed her, letting them fall through to the ground. From where she sat she could see the top of the school building – lights had just begun to come on in the dorm windows. Inside it would be warm and starting to smell of bacon and toast.

At the thought, her empty stomach rumbled.

She'd had to take off one glove to hold the clippers and she paused to blow warm life back into her frozen fingers. Below her she could see Carter dragging fallen branches into piles and raking leaves and twigs away from the base of the trees.

Across the orchard, Mr Ellison was busy sawing fallen branches into firewood, so they were essentially alone.

Amid the protection of the branches she watched Carter work, remembering what it was like to be close to him. She'd been his friend first – then his girlfriend. Now his ... nothing.

Since he'd got together with Jules they hardly spoke. She'd been stunned by how quickly he'd moved on, and he had just sort of avoided her. The air between them remained heavy with unspoken recrimination.

Climbing down, she dragged the ladder around the tree to a new spot.

Carter glanced up at her. 'Do you need some help?'

She shook her head. 'I've got it.'

With a shrug, he returned to his work.

When she'd set up the ladder on the other side of the tree, she turned back to him and spoke quickly before she could change her mind.

'Look. I'm sorry for ... like, earlier. That wasn't cool.'

His rake stilled and he looked up at her, surprise leaving his face unguarded for a second.

'That's OK,' he said. 'I don't blame you.'

'To be honest,' she looked down at her clippers, 'I got spooked in the garden. Thought I heard something. But it was just you guys. So ... I overreacted.'

'No one could blame you for being on edge, Allie,' he said. 'I am, too. We all are. You have nothing to apologise for.'

'Oh, I think I have a lot to apologise for.'

Carter didn't miss the wry tone in her tone and he looked at her searchingly. 'Why'd you do it, Allie?' he asked. 'Why'd you leg it?'

Leaning back against the ladder she glanced up at the lightening sky, remembering how she'd felt that day.

'I felt like ... like nothing happened,' she said. 'Like, Jo died and then everyone went back to business as usual except me. And I don't want business as usual. Ever again.'

He nodded to himself, biting his bottom lip. 'Thing is,' he said after a second, 'nobody went back to business as usual, Allie.'

She hadn't expected that.

'What do you mean?' she asked, her brow creasing.

'I mean, everything changed. I guess nobody told you because they knew you ... needed space or whatever.' He plucked a dead leaf from the tree, avoiding her gaze. 'But we've been having loads of meetings about it. All Night School training has changed, too. They are looking for the spy – everyone's completely paranoid about it. And Raj tracked Gabe and Nathaniel everywhere they've been.' He shook his head and his gaze glanced off hers. 'You know Raj is Batman, right?'

'So wait.' Allie needed him to get back to the point. 'Are you saying all this stuff has been happening but *nobody told me*?'

Carter's expression was hard to read. 'Isabelle said you weren't ready yet. You needed to grieve.'

Allie's jaw was so tight it was difficult to speak.

'I've grieved enough,' she said. 'Now I'm ready to make Nathaniel pay.'

NINE

Allie's classes went more smoothly that day – students paid less attention to her, and the lessons began to make a tiny amount of sense.

In her free moments she thought about what Carter had told her. Why hadn't Isabelle ever mentioned what they were doing? She tried to remember anything the headmistress had said about tracing Jo's attacker, finding the spy. But all she could recall was being told not to worry about it. That it was under control.

But as afternoon turned into evening, and evening into night, she grew increasingly jittery. She was about to find out for herself – her Night School training started that night.

When she joined Rachel and Zoe in the library after dinner, nerves gnawed at her stomach and it was hard to focus on Rachel's chemistry tutoring.

'You're not paying, like, a huge amount of attention,' Rachel complained when Allie stumbled over the same problem for the third time.

'Soz.' Allie dropped her pencil with a sigh. 'Maybe I just need to do something else for a while and come back to this. My brain is tired.'

Across the table, though, Zoe gave a significant look. Allie glanced at her watch – it was nearly nine. Time to get ready.

'Actually,' she said, pushing back her chair, 'I think I'm just knackered.' She began gathering her books. 'I guess I'll have an early night and start fresh tomorrow.'

Rachel gave a sympathetic nod. 'Probably a good idea. You do look worn out.'

'I have to go too.' Zoe jumped to her feet. 'I'm way ahead with my work, anyway.'

As they hurried out, guilt nibbled away at Allie's battered conscience. Lying to Rachel felt wrong. Their friendship was being re-forged link by link – deception made it seem more fragile.

Outside the library door, Zoe stopped. 'I'm going upstairs to drop my books first. Want to come?'

But Allie just wanted to get on with it and she shook her head. 'I'll meet you down there.'

After Zoe dashed up the stairs to the girls' dorm, Allie made her way down the grand hallway, her heart in her throat. She could do this. She could go back to Night School and not screw it up this time.

She was so lost in thought she didn't hear footsteps. Turning a corner, she ran headlong into someone coming the other way. Their shoulders collided with a jarring thud that sent a quick sharp pain down Allie's side.

'Ouch. Bugger ... I mean, sorry.' Allie reeled back clutching her arm. Only then did she see who she'd crashed into.

'Did I hurt you?' Sylvain's blue eyes surveyed her with concern.

'I'm fine,' she said, flushing, although she wasn't entirely certain that was true.

When he saw the way she held her arm, his brow furrowed. '*Merde*. I did hurt you.'

He reached for her shoulder as if he could fix her then thought better of it and dropped his hands. 'I'm sorry, Allie. I was in a hurry – I didn't see you.'

'It's not that bad,' she mumbled. Looking up, she met his vivid gaze. 'I don't think you broke me.'

'I can't believe I was so clumsy. I'm just late for ...' He gestured down the hall to where the door leading down to the basement yawned open.

'I'm going there too,' Allie said.

His eyes widened. 'You're back in it again? When did this happen?'

She shrugged, as if Night School was no big deal. 'It's part of my punishment.'

His eyes swept across her face – although he didn't mention it, she got the feeling he was surprised she was talking to him. She'd been diligently avoiding him since the night of the winter ball.

It wasn't that she didn't want to talk to him. She just hadn't known what to say. Their kiss that night had been so epic – so intense. Just thinking about it made her heart flutter.

But then Jo died. And the world changed overnight.

That night she learned Nathaniel would kill the people she cared about. That night she'd decided to try not to care about anyone ever again.

'It must be hard for you after everything that happened,' he said. 'Are you ready?'

'I don't know,' she admitted. 'But I have to do it. For her.'

He nodded as if he'd expected nothing else. 'I would do the same.'

Her eyes darted up to his. 'You would?'

'Of course,' he said. 'It's the only way. You have to get strong and you have to fight. And win.'

'Thanks,' she said, meaning it. 'That helps.'

When he smiled it softened his sharp features, making him look boyish – less sophisticated. Sometimes he seemed so grown-up it was easy to forget he was only sixteen.

Then he glanced at his watch and the smile faded.

'We will both be late, I'm afraid,' he said. 'I have to run upstairs first.'

'Of course,' Allie said, taking a step away.

'Allie . . .'

She looked up at him enquiringly but he seemed to change his mind.

'Nothing,' he said. 'See you down there.'

He sped away with the smooth gait of a panther.

Alone, Allie made her way downstairs. The once-familiar basement steps had never looked grimier or less inviting. And the walk down that dingy, narrow corridor had never seemed lonelier. She was relieved when she reached the girls' dressing room.

The big square space was mostly empty – only a handful of girls were getting ready, most already in their black Night School training gear.

In one corner, she saw Nicole, still in her school uniform. As she flipped her long dark hair up into a ponytail, their eyes met. Nicole didn't seem surprised to see her – or if she was, she hid it well.

'So, are you ready to return to the meat grinder?' Her French accent made 'meat' sound like 'met'.

'Is that what we're calling it now?' Allie forced a smile.

'It is an appropriate name, *n'est ce pas?*'

Nicole's bitter tone perfectly reflected the way Allie felt. A bit brave. A bit angry.

The two of them had only got to know each other at the end of last term but Allie had quickly started to like her. She was far too pretty – small and slim, with huge brown eyes – but she didn't seem to be afraid of anything.

'Good point.' Allie walked over to a hook with 'Sheridan' stencilled above it in neat square letters. Hanging from it were black leggings, two snug-fitting long-sleeved tops – one for inside, one for outside – and a zip-up jacket. Stacked on the wooden bench below were sturdy waterproof running shoes, a black knitted hat and thermal gloves.

She wondered if it had all been there the whole time she'd been out of Night School. Just waiting for her to come back.

Rather than unbuttoning her white blouse, Allie pulled it off over her head – turning it inside out in the process. As she reached for the pullover, she saw Nicole's eyes flicker across her scars, red against the white skin of her arms and torso. It was the first time anyone other than her doctors had seen what the accident did to her and, flushing, she hurried to pull the black top over her head.

Noticing this, Nicole shook her head. 'Don't be ashamed of your scars.' Startled, Allie glanced over at her. 'Be proud of them. They are a symbol of your survival. Of your strength.'

What bollocks, Allie thought, bristling. *I'm not strong. I'm a failure.*

But as they finished changing in silence Nicole's words stayed with her. After all, she was alive, wasn't she? She'd taken on two guys twice her size, and she'd won.

The scars were proof of that.

When she changed into her leggings, she didn't try to hide the ugly red mark on her left knee.

Nicole waited for Allie to finish; they walked together into the training room where several dozen Night School students stretched and chatted on the blue exercise matting. When those near the door noticed Allie, they fell silent.

Feeling exposed, she looked around for familiar faces. Jules and Carter stood on the far side of the room with Lucas. Carter had his back to her but Jules nudged him and he turned to see. Their eyes met. He gave her a polite nod and then turned back to his conversation.

Looking at the back of his head, she swallowed hard, angry with herself.

What had she expected? For him to run over and hug her? Welcome her back to Night School?

Still, after their conversation this morning she'd hoped for more than this and it hurt a little. The pain was quick and sharp – an emotional bee sting – and colour crept up her cheeks.

Turning to Nicole, she scrambled to think of something, *anything*, to say so everyone would know she didn't care one bit.

'So . . . how are you?' was all she could come up with.

I hate my own brain, she thought, anguished.

Nicole, though, missed nothing. 'Fabulous, darling,' she said with a delighted, musical laugh, as if Allie had said something clever and hilarious. 'Should we go over here?'

She tilted her head away from Jules and Carter.

'God yes.' Allie couldn't keep the relief from her voice.

As they sped across the room, someone called her name. Slowing, Allie turned to see Eloise walking towards them, a cheerful smile brightening her face.

Allie felt better instantly. The librarian was one of her favourite Night School instructors. Young and vivacious, she had always been someone Allie felt she could trust.

'Welcome back to Night School,' Eloise said, draping an arm across her shoulders. Then she lowered her voice. 'Are you ready for this?'

It was clearly the question of the night.

'I guess so,' Allie said. 'I mean . . . I hope so.'

'You'll be fine,' Eloise said with absolute confidence. 'I wanted to tell you about our plan.'

'Plan?'

'Because of the accident we need to ease you back into the physical work,' Eloise explained. 'We can't just drop you in with everyone else – you're not ready. So we've been working with your doctors on a strength-building programme for you. You'll have two training partners instead of just the one.' She grinned broadly. 'And I'll oversee your progress personally.'

Relief washed over Allie.Out of all the instructors, Eloise would have been her choice. Maybe this wouldn't be so bad after all.

Nicole leaned into their conversation. 'Who will her partners be?'

'You for one,' Eloise said, and Allie felt even more cheered.

'And the other?' Nicole asked.

Eloise looked at Allie. 'How would you feel about having your old partner back?'

Hardly believing it was possible, Allie said, 'Zoe? *Really?*'

The librarian's grin widened. 'Yep. The unholy alliance is back together, just as it should be.'

Allie smiled back at her. 'Thanks, Eloise.'

'Don't thank me too soon,' the librarian cautioned. 'You've got a lot of hard work ahead of you. This isn't going to be easy.'

But as Eloise walked away to talk to Jerry Cole, Allie felt better. She wasn't going to have to do this all alone.

'All right, gather up everyone.'

At the sound of Zelazny's booming voice she hurried to join the others encircling the history teacher. In the centre of the training room he stood ramrod-straight, his pate glistening through his thinning hair in the fluorescent light. His pale blue eyes scanned the group for anyone not paying full attention.

'We will start tonight as we did earlier this week with some basic krav maga techniques, so pair up with your partners, do some quick stretching and then we'll begin.'

As the students broke up into pairs, Allie looked around in confusion.

Krav maga?

Carter had told her things had changed down here since the attack. Now she was starting to see what he meant.

'There you are.' Dashing up to her, Zoe grabbed her hand and began pulling her to the back of the room. 'Did you hear we're going to be partners again? It's about time.' She glanced at Allie critically. 'I hope you don't slow us down too much. You're really out of shape.'

Allie winced. Next to her, Nicole fought a giggle.

'Zoe, sometimes you are a little ... too honest,' Nicole said.

'Too honest?' Zoe asked blankly.

Over her head, Nicole and Allie exchanged bemused looks.

'Never mind,' Allie said. 'Does anybody know what we're supposed to do now?'

Nicole pointed to the side of the room, where Eloise stood waving them over.

Crossing the room with Zoe on her left and Nicole on her right, Allie was conscious of other Night School students watching them and she raised her chin and lengthened her stride – hoping she looked confident. Fearless.

'Just ignore everyone else,' Eloise said when they arrived. 'We're having our own exercise party.'

So, as the other students practised dangerous-looking martial arts moves, throwing each other to the floor in complex ways and fighting over fake weapons, the three girls were an oasis of calm, warming up with a series of yoga stretches. Gentle as they were, every single one hurt Allie in some way –

as if they sought out each injury and poked it hard. But she kept that to herself, biting her lip when she wanted to cry out.

At some point, though, Eloise must have seen the pain in her face, because she whispered, too quietly for the other girls to hear: 'This will get better. One day you'll notice it hurts less. And then it will hardly hurt at all. I promise.'

Relieved somebody had seen through her, Allie nodded fiercely. She needed to believe those words. She had to get strong again.

Strong enough to fight.

When training ended, Allie was exhausted. She'd sweated more than she ever thought possible and her muscles felt so worn she wobbled when she walked.

She took a long shower to give herself time to recover. By the time she'd dressed, the other girls had gone and she was alone in the changing room.

The big room felt different when it was empty – sounds were hollow, and shadows seemed to move for no good reason. She threw on her clothes and hurried out – to find Sylvain leaning against the wall in the corridor.

At the sight of him, tall and lean, his blue eyes watching her cautiously, her heart sped up.

'Hey,' she said. 'What's up?'

'Nothing.' But he said it with such elaborate insouciance she knew he was faking it. 'I just thought I'd walk up with you.'

'Cool,' she said, faking it, too.

Their footsteps were nearly silent on the linoleum floor and they were halfway down the long corridor before Sylvain spoke.

'There was something I wanted to say earlier and I didn't have time.'

'OK ...'

'I wish ...' When he hesitated, she glanced up at him curiously – it wasn't like Sylvain to be unsure of himself. 'I wish you had come to me instead of ... when you ran away.'

Too tired to dodge the subject, Allie sighed. It was all anyone wanted to talk about anyway.

'I guess I should have. But I thought I had to do it on my own. I wanted to make something happen.' They'd reached the foot of the staircase and she turned to look up at him. 'Can you understand that? Does it sound crazy?'

'I can understand why you felt that way.' He was choosing his words carefully. 'But I think you should have thought it through. You could have come to me. I would have told you the truth.'

'Would you?' she asked with a touch of bitterness. 'Or would you have gone to Isabelle and told her what I was planning? To *protect* me.'

'Have I ever done anything like that?' He held her gaze and Allie realised that he hadn't. Not once.

'No,' she said slowly. 'I guess not.'

His eyes still held hers, as if he was waiting for her to understand something – to figure something out. Or as if he had more to say.

They were on the stairs now and as Allie reached for the banister her hand brushed his accidentally. She felt that touch like a shock, and jerked her hand away.

'Sorry,' she said, as heat rushed to her face.

'For what? For touching me? It's allowed, you know . . .'

His voice was gentle, teasing, but Allie wasn't ready for this. She hurried up the stairs.

'What is it, Allie?' They'd reached the ground floor now, and his voice echoed in the grand hallway. 'We've touched more than hands, you know.'

Instantly his words summoned images of that night. Snow falling. His lips warm against hers. Her fingers tangled in his hair.

She shook her head as if that could clear it all away.

'We can't,' she said. 'I can't.'

'Why not?' The vulnerability in his expression as he looked at her then made her heart flip. 'You know I like you. And I thought you liked me. But suddenly it's over and you won't even talk to me.' When she didn't speak he took a step closer. 'You can't lock yourself away for ever because of what happened, Allie. You have to keep living.'

'Gabe already tried to kill you once because of me, Sylvain,' she said. 'That's enough. No more. No one else dies because of me.'

He looked stunned. 'Is that what this is all about? You're trying to protect me from Gabe and Nathaniel?' He held up his hands, trying to make her look at him. 'Allie, I am not Jo.'

'I know that,' she snapped. 'But don't you get it? Someone in this building helped to kill Jo. And I've got to find out who that is and make sure they get what they deserve. And I don't want you to get hurt and mess everything up and . . . and . . . *distract me*.'

His eyes blazed. 'So you're going to do this on your own, and

I'm nothing more than a distraction?' He raked his fingers through his hair. 'You're still running away, Allie. You just don't realise it.'

With that, he stalked off, leaving her standing alone.

All the way up to the girls' dorm wing, Allie kept going over the conversation in her mind, trying to find a way to make it less horrible.

The worst part was that Sylvain was right in a way – she *was* trying to do this on her own. She was afraid to let him – or anyone else – help. When he was around things got confusing and it was hard to focus. They'd just end up kissing again and there could be no kissing until the spy was identified. It just couldn't happen.

Besides she hadn't let go of Carter yet – not completely. After they'd talked this morning, some fragment of her heart hoped it was all a horrible mistake and they could find a way to make things work again.

Although every time she saw him with Jules that became a little less possible.

As she walked down the long corridor, her rubber-soled shoes squeaking faintly on the whitewashed floor, she sighed.

What a mess.

In her room, she dropped her bag with a thud. The room felt stuffy and she walked to the window, leaning across her desk to reach the latch. It swung open like a shutter, letting in a blast of cold, fresh air.

Allie closed her eyes and breathed in deeply, trying to clear her head.

The moon was full – a bright spotlight in the sky illuminating the grounds with a wash of blue light. Still, even with its helpful glow, were it not for her Night School training she probably wouldn't have noticed the flicker of movement below her, it happened so quickly.

Frowning, she scanned the lawn two storeys below for a fox or a night bird.

Then she froze, fingers tight against the window frame. Because what she saw was a man, running into the trees.

TEN

She couldn't seem to catch her breath. Her chest was suddenly too small for her lungs.

Shoving things off the desk with a reckless sweep of her arm, she climbed up on top of it to try and get a better look through the window. But he'd disappeared completely.

For a second she stayed still, gripping the window frame. Then she tore across the room and out of the door.

Weariness forgotten, she pounded down two flights of stairs and along the wide, empty grand hallway to the front door, where she fumbled with the complicated old locking system, fingers numb with anxiety and excitement until, with an almighty clang, the lock finally gave and she was outside.

Leaving the front door open behind her she hurtled down the front steps. Her knee protested but she ignored its complaints and sped across the grass.

She wasn't afraid. She was going to catch that man. And she was going to make him suffer.

The moonlight lit up the grounds like a stage – silvering the grass and illuminating the trees. Allie made no effort to hide herself or to move quietly. This wasn't about stealth – it was about speed.

She'd made it across the lawn to the tree line, the spot where she'd last seen him, when her muscles – exhausted from the earlier training – began to give. She reeled drunkenly into the woods.

It was darker here – the moonlight couldn't penetrate through the canopy of pine branches. Slowing her steps, she suddenly realised she had no idea where to go – she didn't know which direction he'd taken after entering the forest.

Instinct led her to the chapel footpath where she sped up again, peering into the shadows. She stopped to listen, hoping to hear footsteps, breaking branches. But she could hear nothing except her own ragged breathing; her pounding heart.

I lost him.

Despairing, she bent over, resting her hands on her knees and taking shallow breaths. When she raised her head again, she noticed movement ahead – it was just a flitting shadow. But it didn't seem right.

'Stop!' She shouted the word at the top of her lungs, bursting into a run. The shadow moved – turning towards her – and as she grew nearer it became a man, dressed all in black.

Only then did Allie realise she didn't have a weapon. Desperate, she looked around for a long stick, a large rock – anything she could use. She grabbed a twig – too small and fragile to be of use – but now the man was coming towards her, fast.

'I said *stop*!' she bellowed ... but then her voice trailed off. The man had a familiar face.

'Allie?' he said. Then he stepped into a thin beam of moonlight that broke through the branches. It was one of Raj's guards – the one who had been with them in the SUV on the way back from the jail. 'What are you doing out here?'

'Were you just ... on the lawn?' She was breathing heavily. A stitch in her side had suddenly opened up like a knife wound and she dropped the twig to clutch her ribs.

'Yes – we're patrolling.' Puzzled, he moved towards her carefully as if she might bolt or bite him. He spoke with elaborate calm – holding out his hands. 'Do you remember me? I'm Peter. This is Karen.'

A guard with long blonde hair plaited into a single, shimmering braid stepped out from the trees to join him. Allie had seen her, too, working with Night School students.

'What's happened?' Peter asked. 'Why are you out here?'

'I thought I saw –' Allie said breathlessly – 'Gabe.'

Karen's eyebrows winged up. 'And you thought you'd just run out to catch him? On your own?'

'Well,' Allie said, feeling utterly exhausted and stupid, 'someone had to.'

The two guards took her down to a nondescript office in the basement near Training Room One, where Zelazny was less than pleased by what he described as her 'attempted vigilantism'.

'You could have been hurt,' he said with obvious exasperation. 'Someone else could have been hurt. Sometimes I think all our training is wasted on you, Sheridan. It doesn't matter what you're taught – you do the opposite whenever it suits you.' He gestured around the bare office where the guards stood in a half circle around them. 'This isn't your living room. We are not your servants.'

Heat flooded Allie's cheeks. 'I'm really sorry,' she mumbled, lowering her gaze. 'I didn't think.'

'No. You didn't.' He leaned forward until she met his eyes. 'There is a reason for everything we teach you, Allie. We're not doing this to amuse ourselves. You need to focus or you're not going to get through this.' Then he'd picked up a pen and waved a hand to indicate her dismissal. 'See Isabelle tomorrow after class for your punishment. Now, for heaven's sake: go to bed.'

The next day, Allie endured all her classes, knowing she'd have to explain her actions to Isabelle that afternoon. The headmistress would *not* be happy. She'd broken The Rules – did this violate her agreement with Lucinda?

Had she ruined everything?

When her last class of the day finally ended, she walked down the stairs with heavy feet. Her gaze was lowered when Katie Gilmore stepped into her path with such suddenness Allie nearly ran into her.

'Bloody hell, Katie . . . ' Allie grabbed the wide oak banister to keep herself upright. 'What is your malfunction?'

In the light of the crystal chandelier, Katie's fair skin was flawless; her clear green eyes sparked with malice. 'Well, goodness. I don't know. I was hoping a psycho liar who burgled the village church with some smelly pikey boy might be able to tell me. Do you know anyone who fits that description?'

Anger flared in Allie's chest, hot enough to singe, but she willed it away. She was in enough trouble already.

'Oh what*ever*, Katie.'

She moved to bypass Katie but the girl stepped smoothly in front of her, blue pleated skirt swinging.

'I don't know why they brought you back. It was the perfect opportunity to get rid of you. Raise the standards around here.'

'Katie, seriously. Seek. Professional. Help.' Allie kept her voice as steady and dismissive as she could but she could hear a slight tremor in her own words. It had been a long couple of days – she wasn't sure she could handle this right now.

'Allie's grades are very good, actually. Well above average.' At the sound of Zoe's piping voice, Allie and Katie both spun around in surprise to see her standing behind them. 'The standards are about the same whether she's here or not.'

Katie eyed her with malicious contempt. 'Oh look. It's Robot Girl. Shouldn't you be off memorising things? Or going through puberty?' She turned back to Allie. 'It's so appropriate the little weirdo likes you.'

Outraged, Allie opened her mouth to defend Zoe, but the smaller girl beat her to it, stepping closer to Katie until she was standing two steps above her, forcing her to look up at her.

'I'm already going through puberty,' Zoe said with typical pedantry. 'The same as you. You start at eleven and finish when you're seventeen. On average.'

Katie glared. 'I don't care, you creepy little android.'

Allie stepped between them. 'Leave her alone, Katie.'

A crowd began to gather, watching the skirmish with avid curiosity. This was getting out of hand.

Lowering her voice, Allie tried to speak in the same quiet, threatening way she'd seen Mr Patel do when he wanted to intimidate someone.

'I don't know what your problem is with me, and I don't really care. You know who I am; who my grandmother is. Leave me and my friends alone or I will ruin your life. I will make it my mission to *break you.*'

Katie stepped closer, until their faces were inches apart. 'I'm not afraid of you, Allie,' she hissed. 'And I'm not afraid of Lucinda Meldrum. No one is. You need to tell her—'

But mention of her grandmother's name was too much – Allie grabbed Zoe's arm and pulled her with her.

'Come on, Zoe,' she said, lowering a freezing glare at Katie. 'We're done here.'

When they reached the ground floor, the younger girl spoke, mostly to herself. 'Puberty is a notoriously difficult and emotional time. I studied up on it, so I'm ready.'

'That's great, Zoe,' Allie said absently. Her mind was on Katie's words. What had she meant when she said no one was afraid of Lucinda? Was that some sort of message?

Katie's parents were powerful members of the board. That was all Allie really knew about them.

Zoe, having finished her puberty point, was ready to get on with her day. 'Anyway, I have to go and study now.'

Her smooth, unworried face showed no signs of concern about the altercation on the stairs.

'Hey,' Allie said hesitantly. 'Thanks for standing up for me.'

Zoe swung her book bag over her shoulder. 'That's all right. Katie Gilmore is a bitch.'

When she'd gone, Allie turned towards Isabelle's door. After a brief hesitation, she knocked on it firmly. When there was no response, she jiggled the door handle – it was locked tight.

'Isabelle?' she asked the door tentatively. 'Are you in there?'

Silence.

'Balls,' Allie muttered.

For a few long minutes she waited outside, scuffing the toe of her black Oxford shoe on the polished wood floor. But Isabelle didn't return.

Allie wasn't sure what to do. Zelazny had been quite firm that Isabelle would expect her to be here. And the last thing she needed was more trouble.

Biting her lip, she looked around for a place to wait. Across the hall, a heavy ornamental table held a large vase filled with pale pink roses. If she sat on the floor next to it she was out of the way but could still see the headmistress's door.

Once she was settled, she pulled her history book out of her bag and began looking over her homework. A stream of students and staff ebbed and flowed in the hallway in front of her, but there was no sign of Isabelle.

More than half an hour passed before she heard the faint creak of Isabelle's office door. When she looked up, someone stood in front of it. Her back was to Allie, but it looked like the headmistress was having trouble with the lock.

At last.

'Isabelle!' Leaving her books on the floor, Allie ran across the hall. At the sound of her voice, the woman turned. But it wasn't Isabelle at all.

It was Eloise. And in her hand she held a small silver key.

Eloise's eyes widened as Allie skidded to a stop a few feet away, and for a moment the two just stared at each other in surprise.

What was Eloise doing in Isabelle's office? Was she in there all along? Did she just ignore me when I knocked? And why was she messing with the door just now?

Allie knew she needed to say something but her mind wouldn't seem to function.

'I ... uh ...' she stuttered, 'just ... I was ... looking for Isabelle.'

The librarian's eyes darted from Allie to the hallway beyond her as if she was concerned about being seen.

Up close, Allie noticed her cheeks were flushed and breathless. Her dark hair had begun escaping from the clips that held it, as if she'd been exercising or running.

Confusion and a dawning sense of suspicion made Allie's stomach tighten. She wrapped her arms around her torso.

Composing herself, Eloise lifted her chin in an imperious imitation of Isabelle's natural hauteur. 'She's away. Can I help you with something?'

Yeah, Allie thought darkly, *you could tell me what the hell you were just doing in Isabelle's office when she's not here.*

But she didn't say that.

'No ... no, I just need to talk to her,' she said instead, trying to sound casual. 'Do you, like, know when she'll be back?'

'She went to London for a meeting after her last class.' Eloise glanced at her watch. 'She won't be back until late tonight.' She studied Allie narrowly. 'Are you sure there's nothing I can help you with?'

'No thanks.' Allie took a quick step back, banging her head on the tilted underside of the staircase above them. 'Ouch.' Never taking her eyes off Eloise, she rubbed her head with one hand. 'I uh ... guess I'll just come back. You know. Tomorrow.'

Forcing herself to move with deliberate steadiness, she crossed the hall and gathered her books as if nothing was wrong.

The whole time she was conscious of Eloise watching her every move.

ELEVEN

That night Allie made her way down the basement corridor towards Training Room One with slow, heavy steps. She felt weighed down, as if something tugged at her, holding her back.

All she wanted was to tell someone everything, but when she tried explaining it in her head it sounded crazy.

Hey. So anyway, I thought I saw Gabe outside last night but I didn't, and Eloise is breaking into Isabelle's office when she's not there and by the way I'm totally sane. Don't you worry about a thing. Got a B on my history essay.

Nicole and Zoe were already in Training Room One when she arrived, warming up near the back. She hurried over to them but barely had a chance to say hello before Eloise walked up looking perfectly normal.

'How are you feeling today,' the instructor asked with solicitous concern. 'Any soreness in your knee?'

'A little.' Allie couldn't bring herself to meet Eloise's gaze.

'We'll take it easy today. But if it handled yesterday's work-out that's great news.' Eloise's smile appeared genuinely enthusiastic. 'You're making progress.'

As she went through her warm-up routine, Allie kept an eye on her but she seemed utterly normal – laughing at Nicole's jokes and keeping a close eye on Allie.

If she was the spy who thought she'd just been found out, she was hiding it very well.

This all left Allie conflicted. Maybe Eloise had a perfectly good explanation. It could probably all be explained if she could just talk to Isabelle – but the headmistress had still not returned.

After a brief warm-up, Zelazny stepped into the middle of the room. 'We will begin tonight with a four-mile competitive run.'

Zoe, who loved running, gave a small hop of excitement.

'About time,' she chirped to herself.

Allie, who was feeling particularly non-competitive, wasn't quite sure how this would work. On competitive runs the last student in was punished, usually with short-term detention or additional exercise. The punishment was mild but the humil-iation was intense.

As soon as Zelazny stopped talking, though, Eloise pulled the girls aside. 'I'm sorry, Zoe,' she said, smiling at the younger girl, 'but you're going to have to take it slow. Allie can't go fast and she certainly can't run four miles.'

'Rats,' Zoe muttered.

As the other students poured out of the room, Eloise gave them strict instructions that Allie could only do a walk-run combination and go no more than two miles.

107

'If you want to run further,' she told Zoe and Nicole, 'bring Allie back here first. Under no circumstances are you to leave her unprotected outside.'

Her use of the word 'unprotected' took Allie aback – it was the first time she'd realised Zoe and Nicole were essentially her bodyguards. But it made sense. She'd been given two partners instead of one, both of them known for their speed. In addition, Nicole – a senior member of Night School – was highly skilled in defence tactics and martial arts.

The other students were long gone by now, the training room was empty.

They were hurrying for the door when Eloise called out, 'And, Allie?' When Allie stopped to look back at her, the instructor's expression held a warning. 'Be careful.'

As she hurried to join Zoe and Nicole in the hallway Allie's mind teemed with doubt. No matter how she tried she simply couldn't square the way Eloise had acted earlier with the way she was now. It was as if she were two different people.

'She's nice, Eloise,' Nicole said. Allie shot her a surprised look – it was as if she could hear her internal monologue. 'She looks out for us in a way other teachers don't.'

'Mmm . . .'

'I think someone like Zelazny would throw you to the wolves, and Jerry would push you too hard, but Eloise is more compassionate,' Nicole continued as Zoe shot ahead of them.

'Do you trust her?' Only when she heard her own voice did Allie realise she'd asked the question aloud. She could have kicked herself.

Nicole cast her a curious look. 'Of course. Don't you?'

They followed Zoe up a staircase to a door leading out into the dark night.

Yes, Allie thought. *Say yes.*

'I don't know,' she said instead, 'any more. Who to trust, I mean. I used to . . . '

They walked up a short staircase to an open door; as the icy February air hit her, Allie let her voice trail off.

If she'd expected Nicole to be shocked at the suggestion Eloise might not be trustworthy she was disappointed. The French girl merely shrugged.

'You've been through so much, I'd be surprised if you trusted anyone now.'

Then she pointed to where Zoe waited in the distance, hopping up and down like an enraged elf.

'Should we run? It would make her happy.'

Her accent changed 'happy' to ''appy' and, in spite of everything, Allie found herself smiling.

'Yeah, if we don't run I think she'll explode.'

'That would be terrible,' Nicole said cheerfully. 'Because she's so young and Zelazny would make us clean up the mess.'

They took off at a slow jog. Zoe stayed ahead of them – zooming forward out of sight, waiting until they'd nearly caught up, then doing it all again. The other students were far ahead of them; they were all alone.

The night was clear and, for a while, the bright moon lit the path ahead. When they moved into the forest, though, it was harder to see where they were going. They hadn't gone far when Allie stumbled over a root, jarring her knee.

Swearing, she stumbled around for a minute clutching her knee.

'Have you wankered it?' Zoe asked, running back to her at top speed.

'Zoe!' Allie said, mildly scandalised. 'When did you become a professional swearer?'

'I've been practising,' Zoe explained. 'Lucas is teaching me.'

'How bad is it?' Nicole asked, drawing them back to the subject at hand.

Tentatively, Allie put her weight on her knee, wincing in anticipation of agony.

It held.

'Actually . . . I'm good,' she said. 'Let's keep going.'

With a hop Zoe zipped ahead again, but Nicole eyed Allie's leg critically.

'Let's walk for a few minutes,' she said. 'See how it does.'

Nicole's patience made Allie feel strangely humble. She felt as if she had to acknowledge it.

'Thanks for . . . you know,' she said, 'doing this, I guess. Going slow with me. You could be running off with the others.'

The cold had made Nicole's cheeks and nose red; with her pale skin and dark hair, she looked like Snow White in the cartoons. If Snow White was badass and dressed like a Ninja.

'Oh don't worry,' Nicole said. 'I like this much better than the usual thing. So you are saving me from something I despise.'

This was not the reply Allie had expected. 'Really? I thought you liked Night School.'

110

'Joining Night School was not my idea. My parents insisted.'
Seeing Allie's expression, she gave an eloquent shrug. 'It's
fine – I don't mean that I truly despise it, I suppose. Sometimes
it can be fun but –' she made a rueful gesture – 'there are other
things I'd rather be doing.'

Allie considered that for a while as they walked. 'You never
thought of saying no to your parents?'

Nicole's reply was instant. 'Never. It means too much to my
mother. You see, I'm the first girl in my family to be accepted.
My mother wasn't chosen for Night School when she was at
Cimmeria so . . . ' She shrugged. 'I think I am living her dream.'

Allie, who knew all about lost parental dreams, gave a bitter
chuckle. 'I think I'm living my mum's nightmare . . . Maybe
we're in the same boat for different reasons.'

For a while they walked in companionable silence – Allie's
knee felt better now but Nicole showed no inclination to run
again and that was fine with Allie. Eloise had said to take it
easy. The woods around them were quiet in that deep, winter's
night way – even the wind didn't blow through the branches.
The only sound was the crunch of their footsteps on the cold
ground.

She stole a surreptitious glance at Nicole, who seemed lost
in worried thoughts of her own.

Maybe she can be trusted. Maybe she would know what to do.

She worked to summon her courage then, clearing her throat
to break the silence, she said, 'Uh . . . Nicole . . . can I ask you
a question?'

The French girl turned to her enquiringly but at that precise
second Zoe shot down the path towards them again. This time,

though, something about her pace wasn't right – she was moving too fast. As if she was running from something.

Everything slowed. Allie reached for Nicole's arm to warn her but she'd already begun to run towards Zoe. Stumbling, Allie followed.

Too out of breath to speak clearly, the younger girl pointed into the darkness off the path.

'The chapel,' she gasped. 'Someone . . . in . . . there.'

The moment the words left her mouth, the cold earth seemed to take Allie's feet in an icy grip, tight as iron. She stood frozen, watching as if from far away, as Nicole moved closer to Zoe, asking her questions.

She recognised the look on Zoe's face – she'd seen it before. Zoe was afraid.

It was happening again.

'What exactly did you see?' Nicole's rational voice jolted Allie into action. She finally moved, joining the other two in a tight circle under the trees.

Zoe's face was taut, but she was trained for this.

'The door's open,' she said. 'The candles are lit.'

The hairs on the back of Allie's neck rose. There was no reason for anyone to be in that chapel. Every night it was closed before sunset. Students weren't allowed to visit it after that. Security guards would have been checking it every two hours.

So why is it standing open?

It made no sense. She could see the others knew that, too.

'Did you see anyone?' Allie asked, her voice taut.

Zoe shook her head.

'Are you sure, Zoe?' Nicole asked.

Exasperated, Zoe held out her hands. 'You have to see it for yourself. It's ... weird.'

Nicole bit her bottom lip. 'I don't like this. We should take Allie back.'

She and Zoe both turned to look at her as if she were a problem they had to solve. Heat rose to Allie's face. They couldn't do that. This could be their chance. What if it was Gabe or the spy? They could get him right now.

'I'll be fine,' she insisted. 'I can keep up.'

'You can't run,' Zoe pointed out.

'Yes I can.' Allie's voice was defensive. 'I just ran a few minutes ago.'

'Not fast,' Nicole said.

She was right. But Allie was not about to walk away from this. Although she had the uneasy realisation that if they wanted to they could make her go back.

'Come on, Nicole,' she pleaded. 'We have to do this.'

The French girl shook her head. 'It's too dangerous.'

'There are three of us and we're all trained for this,' Allie pointed out. 'What if Jo's killer is down there? We could take him. I know we could. But if we don't go now he'll get away while we're off running for help. We can't blow this chance, Nicole. He could kill someone else tonight. Please.' Her eyes pleaded for them to understand. 'Let's do this.'

Nicole and Zoe exchanged a long look. Zoe looked dubious but it was clear the decision would be made by Nicole, the most senior member of the group.

'OK,' she said finally, although worry creased her forehead.

'But we work together and we take no crazy chances. Agreed?'

She spoke to both of them but her eyes were on Allie.

Allie didn't blink. 'Agreed.'

Zoe led the way, Allie and Nicole followed, running side by side. When the path narrowed, Allie dropped behind but stayed hard on the French girl's heels. The run was tiring but she got the feeling they were holding themselves back for her.

Their quiet footsteps, thudding almost in unison, seemed deafening to Allie. The night had grown colder and their breath puffed out in small clouds, illuminated by the moon in the brief seconds before they disappeared.

The churchyard wall appeared first and they flattened themselves against it looking for any sign of movement. But the path that ran alongside it was empty. Soon they were on the move again.

They were close to the stream now. It was swollen from recent rains and the sound of its rushing water disguised any noise they made. They could move faster here – take more chances.

When they reached it, the old churchyard gate hung half open, as if it had been shoved recklessly.

Allie's breaths shortened.

Turning to catch her eye, Zoe pointed twice at the gate in a jerky motion. The girls gathered around it – Nicole on one side, Allie and Zoe on the other.

Inside, the old gravestones and tombs jostled with the bare trees for space; a low mist covered the ground. To one side, an ancient yew tree towered above the stone wall. Instinctively, Allie's gaze moved to its long, lower branches where she and Carter had often met when they were first becoming friends.

The gnarled branches were empty now.

Everything was just as Zoe described it. The little chapel's heavy, arched door gaped open. Inside, candlelight flickered and jumped, moving with a life of its own.

Zoe darted across the churchyard. Moving smooth and straight as an arrow, she stuck to the grass, where her steps were soundless. In seconds she'd disappeared in the shadows. After a moment, though, her hand appeared against the grey stone church wall, waving them in.

Catching Allie's eye, Nicole tilted her head, signalling her to go first.

Taking a deep breath as if she were about to dive into a pool, Allie ducked low and scuttled across the churchyard. The grass was slippery beneath the thick soles of her shoes. The world was muffled – all she could hear was her own breathing, which deafened her.

It seemed to take for ever to reach the church but it mustn't have, because as she slid into the shadows next to Zoe the younger girl merely nodded her approval before turning to the gate and making the same gesture again.

Nicole was at their side in seconds. She looked at Zoe enquiringly.

Zoe pointed at the door but Nicole shook her head.

The window then.

Moving as one unit, they stepped carefully down the wall to a stained-glass window. During the day, it filled the little one-room building with multicoloured light. But now the light was moving the other way.

Straightening, Zoe tried to see into the window but she wasn't tall enough. The window ledge was at least six inches above her head. She dropped down, shaking her head. Nicole tried next, but she was only a little taller than Zoe.

As she crouched down again, she made a gesture of frustration.

They both turned to Allie.

Standing on her toes, clinging with her fingertips to the cold stone of the window ledge, she looked inside. What she saw took her breath away.

All the candles inside were ablaze. Dozens of them. Maybe a hundred. The room was *filled* with light. Even the heavy, wrought iron candelabras that normally stood near the altar had been moved – they now stood in a semi-circle near the wall to the left of the window. Allie couldn't see what they were illuminating.

She dropped back down to face the others. Shaking her head she mouthed, 'I can't see anyone from here.'

For a moment they stood still, looking at Nicole, who appeared to be deciding what to do. Zoe pointed hard at the door. Nicole shook her head.

Narrowing her eyes, Zoe jutted her finger at the door again – more insistent this time. The look on her face said she wasn't about to back down. After a second, Nicole held up her hands in surrender.

They all took a step towards the door but almost immediately Nicole whirled on Allie, pushing her back. She held her hand up in a 'Stay here' gesture.

116

Allie couldn't believe it. Had she come this far only to be stopped at the end?

'Come on ...' she mouthed, pleading.

Nicole was unmoved. She pointed fiercely at the earth under Allie's feet.

Every muscle in Allie's body was tensed, poised for the fight ahead. Ready to catch Jo's killer if he was in there. Ready to *hurt him.*

But there was no way Nicole would let her in there first.

Fine then. They can go first. I will be right behind them.

She nodded her submission. Zoe, who would hate being told she couldn't go in, gave her a sympathetic look before shooting to the edge of the door where she waited for Nicole, who was soon next to her.

Nicole gestured at something Allie couldn't see, and then in an instant they were gone.

As soon as they were out of sight, Allie ran to the door and hid herself in the shadows beside it. If anyone tried to get out she would be on them before they knew what hit them.

She stood like a statue, staring at the doorway unblinking for so long her eyes filled with cold tears. She listened fiercely for anything – a scream, a cry. But the stream roaring in the distance and her heart thudding out a surprisingly steady rhythm were the only sounds.

Just when she thought she might go mad from not knowing, Zoe appeared in the doorway. The candlelight behind her was so bright for a moment it looked as if her hair was on fire.

Wordlessly, she motioned for Allie to follow her.

Inside, the air was hot and still, perfumed with the scent of smoke and melting wax. As the girls moved, the candle flames danced on the waves of air made by their bodies. In this light, the medieval paintings that covered the grey stone walls seemed to come alive.

They were meant to be seen this way, Allie realised.

On one wall, a gigantic red devil shoved suffering souls down into Hell, while others climbed a ladder to Heaven. But if they were meant to be saved, why did they look so afraid?

Elsewhere a dragon swooped upwards in pursuit of a dove just out of reach of its claws. The paint had always looked aged and dull before, but in the candlelight the dragon's rust-red scales shimmered with life.

But Zoe and Nicole weren't looking at those. They were staring at another painting: of a tree very much like the yew by the churchyard wall. The painted version was filled with colourful fruit and birds. Its tangled roots spelled out the words 'Tree of Life'. It was Allie's favourite painting in the heavily decorated church.

This was where the candelabra had been carefully arranged in an arc.

As Allie drew closer she could see that something was on the painting.

'What is it?' she whispered.

Nicole's eyes were still locked on the painting. Raising her hand, she pointed at the tree trunk.

Only then did Allie see the folded piece of paper impaled into the wall by a hunting knife.

Who would do that? she thought wildly. *Who would damage a painting that's nearly a thousand years old?*

The problem was, she knew exactly who would do that.

Moving slowly, as if in a dream, she stepped inside the encircling candles. She heard Zoe and Nicole whisper her name, cautioning her. Calling for her to stop.

But she didn't. She couldn't stop.

Because the paper held one word, written in confident, slanting handwriting: 'Allie.'

TWELVE

The heavily carved hilt of the dagger was cold in Allie's hand but she didn't flinch. She wrapped her fingers around it and yanked it from the old stone wall with force, catching the paper as it fluttered loose.

Silky to the touch, the heavy paper unfolded like fabric.

Dear Allie

I must apologise for choosing such a dramatic means of communication, but you see I needed to get your attention. I trust I have it now.

You have chosen the wrong side in this war, Allie. However, it may surprise you to know I don't blame you. I, more than anyone, know how convincingly Isabelle can pretend to love. How seductive Lucinda can be. How strong are *the ties of family that bind us. But they are lying to you, Allie.*

So far, you have disappointed me. For that there will have to be consequences. I'm sorry to say these consequences may be severe.

And yet the course upon which we find ourselves is not unchangeable. If you see the error of your ways and change your mind now, you will be welcomed into my organisation as Christopher has been. Everything will stop. You can take your rightful place in a seat of honour. You deserve that seat, Allie. You also deserve the truth. I alone am willing to give you that.

All you have to do is come to me. I am always watching. If you look for me, I will find you.

With me, you will finally be safe.
Nathaniel

'What does it say? Allie? Are you all right?' Nicole stepped inside the circle of burning candles.

As she turned to her, Allie realised her face was wet with tears of futile rage, although she had no memory of weeping.

Calmly, the French girl reached for the note. 'May I see it?'

Numb, Allie watched as she quickly scanned the words, her lips tightening. When she finished, she swore a stream of French curse words Allie suspected were stronger than anything she'd ever heard Sylvain say.

'This man is insane. Are you OK?' Without waiting for the answer, Nicole put a supportive arm around her. 'Zoe's gone to get help.'

'I just wanted to catch him.' Allie gripped the hilt of the dagger until her knuckles turned white. 'Why can't I ever catch him?'

Minutes later the churchyard was a hive of activity. Security guards, teachers and Night School students bustled between the graves setting up battery-powered lights, shouting orders, and running in and out of the chapel.

Standing in the shadows near the churchyard wall, the three girls were alone. No one had spoken to them after Raj had prised the knife and the note from Allie's fingers and hustled them out of the building.

'Don't move,' was all he'd said before disappearing into the darkness.

Allie wasn't sorry to see the note go. She'd read it enough times already to memorise the threatening message written in a neat, angular hand.

With simmering rage, she thought again about those last words. *Come to me . . .*

'As *if*, you utter tosser,' she muttered aloud. Standing nearby, Zoe looked over at her questioningly.

'Sorry. Not you,' Allie said. 'Nathaniel.' She glanced at her watch with barely contained irritation – it was after midnight. All around them guards and Night School students were doing things. She longed to do something. 'How long do you suppose they'll keep us here?'

'I don't know but I wish they'd let us help.' Zoe's nose was red from the cold and she hopped up and down impatiently. 'I don't know why they're keeping us here.'

'To talk to us.' Nicole's eyes stayed locked on the guards. 'They are securing the grounds and then they will want to ask us questions. It's standard.'

Raj's guards all seemed to be talking to themselves – Allie couldn't see microphones but she guessed it was some sort of communications equipment. That was a surprise – the school resisted almost all modern technology.

At that moment, someone switched on the lights and the churchyard was suffused with eerie blue-white light – after the heavy darkness that preceded it the effect was blinding.

Two figures approached them. Shielding her eyes with her hands, Allie squinted into the glare. In the fog and the light they looked like shadow-people until they were right in front of her.

It was Raj Patel and Zelazny.

'We need to get you girls someplace safe,' Zelazny announced without preamble. 'We want you inside the school building until the search is completed.'

Allie fixed him with a bitter stare. 'No place is safe.'

Before he could reply to that, three shadows detached themselves from the darkness and moved close enough for Allie to make out their features. Two were Patel's guards, Peter and Karen. The third was Carter.

'They're going to take you to the school and stay with you until the rest of us get back.' When he met Allie's gaze again, Patel's dark eyes were steely. 'I'm not taking any chances.'

*

They took off almost immediately and, within seconds, the churchyard with its bright lights and crowds of protective guards faded into the distance.

Allie's hackles rose. The woods were too dark. Too quiet.

But the guards moved quickly and, with Allie in the middle of a protective phalanx, they hustled down the footpath at a steady speed. Nobody spoke. They just ran in silent formation.

Allie felt drained. Each step seemed to require all the energy she had left. Then she had to do it again. Her knee throbbed and every other footfall sent a knife-jab of pain through her leg. But she endured it with grim acceptance – the pain helped her focus on what mattered. And honed her rage.

Nicole and Zoe ran at her side. Carter was right beside Nicole. Once, Allie glanced at him out of the corner of her eye but he was staring straight ahead, his expression alert and intense.

They broke out of the woods in half the normal time. As they ran across the lawn the school building towered over them like a fortress. Upstairs, the dorm windows were dark but light poured from the open front door, backlighting Isabelle who stood waiting for them at the top of the steps. Her golden-brown hair flowed down her back in shining waves. With an oversized white coat hanging from her shoulders, she looked like a goddess.

She rested a steadying hand on each of Allie's shoulders, her expression grave. 'Are you OK?'

Allie nodded. 'I'm good.'

'Thank God.' Isabelle turned to include the other girls in her gaze. 'Please go on to the common room and wait for me there.

I've had some tea and sandwiches put out for you – you must be frozen solid.' She turned to Carter. 'A word, please?'

As the two walked back down the stairs, talking confidentially, Allie wondered what they were saying.

'Come on, Allie. You should be inside.' Grabbing her hand, Zoe dragged her into the grand entrance hall where Nicole waited for them.

Usually dimmed at this hour, the chandeliers were all aglow. It gave the empty hallway an oddly festive feel, like a party to which no one had shown up.

The two guards were still with them – Karen walked well ahead; Peter had dropped behind. When they reached the common room they flanked the doorway – letting the girls in first then closing ranks outside the door.

After hours out in the cold, the deep leather sofas and Oriental rugs looked inviting. A fire crackled merrily in the large fireplace; nearby, a tea tray had been set out piled with sandwiches and biscuits.

Needing no more invitation, Nicole and Zoe dropped into chairs by the fire.

'This is much better,' Nicole said, stretching her legs out towards the flames.

But Allie stood just inside the door, staring around her blankly. It was all too civilised and ordinary – as if they'd just come back from a jolly afternoon of ice skating or shopping. She couldn't make sense of it. There were *guards* outside the *door*.

And yet she was starting to believe if Nathaniel wanted to, he could walk right past them.

She was so lost in thought she never heard Carter approach. 'You OK?'

At the sound of his low voice, Allie's breath came out in a sigh. When she turned towards him, his dark eyes surveyed her with concern.

The memory of how she'd felt in the training room when he hadn't come over to say hello came back to her, unbidden and bitter.

I guess it's OK to be my friend now, she thought dully. *Jules isn't here to see.*

'I'm OK,' she lied.

'Raj told me about the note . . . ' He shook his head, at a loss for words. 'Are you really fine?'

'No, I'm not.' Her voice was thick with emotion. 'I'm freaking out and I don't understand any of this. I hate myself for not catching Nathaniel and I hate Raj because he can't catch him and . . . I'm just scared. About what's going to happen next.' She covered her mouth with one hand as if to shut herself up. 'I'm sorry. I think it's all making me crazy.'

Carter shook his head. 'You're not crazy. The world is crazy. It's not our fault. We didn't make it this way; we just inherited it.'

As she looked into those familiar depthless eyes, her heart ached. She hadn't realised until this moment how much she'd missed his calm rationality. The way he got her. The way he could calm her down when she lost it.

It still worked. Her lips quirked into a shaky smile. 'I think the world's in trouble if we're the sane ones.'

'Doomed,' he agreed, grinning back to her.

Footsteps in the hallway interrupted her thoughts and the moment dissipated as suddenly as it began.

Zelazny, Raj and Isabelle walked into the room together. Their grim expressions made Allie's stomach tighten.

Motioning for the other students to stay where they were, Isabelle turned to face her. 'Allie,' she said. 'Please come with us.'

THIRTEEN

'There's nothing new in the note,' Zelazny said dismissively.

'I disagree.' Raj's voice was low but firm. 'You have to look beyond the superficiality of words on paper to what he's really saying. And I think his message has changed.'

They were all crowded into the headmistress' small office – Isabelle sitting at her desk with Raj and Allie in the chairs facing her. Zelazny stood with his back against the door, arms crossed.

With so many people in it, the room felt hot and stuffy. It smelled faintly of sweat.

'I'm not sure I see that – what's the new message?' Isabelle asked, frowning. With her dark blonde hair loose, she looked younger – more like a student than a headmistress. But her demeanour was authoritative. And angry.

'The note is addressed to Allie but it was meant for us. He's telling us he's about to make his move,' Raj said. 'He's not asking Allie to come to him. He's asking us to *send her* to him.'

The room fell silent.

Icy prickles of fear ran down Allie's spine. Now that Raj had said it, Nathaniel's underlying message seemed so obvious. He was giving Isabelle a way out. Inviting her to betray Allie and Lucinda.

Giving her one last chance.

Isabelle made an impatient sound. 'If so, then this was a waste of his time.'

The headmistress turned to Raj. 'We can discuss Nathaniel's wishes later. My immediate concern is how this happened. How was the chapel not secured and why didn't your guards discover the intrusion before my Night School students encountered it? This was a serious lapse.'

Her tone was ominous, and Raj shot her a sharp look.

'Actually, we don't believe there was an intrusion.'

'What does that mean?' Zelazny barked. 'Clearly someone was in the chapel.'

Raj kept his eyes focused on Isabelle – Allie saw her pale as she realised what he was about to say.

'There's no indication that anyone entered the grounds last night. The note may have come from outside the school – it could have even come through the post. But the scene at the chapel was arranged by one of us. It was an inside job.'

Isabelle slapped her hand on the desk hard. They all looked up at her in surprise. Allie could see she was fighting to control her temper. When she spoke, frustration was clear in her voice.

'Why haven't we been able to find this person, Raj? How have they eluded you? What are we missing?'

Raj just shook his head – if he knew the answer he'd have told her. What was there to say?

'August?' She turned to Zelazny but he tightened his lips and held up his hands.

Isabelle rubbed her eyes tiredly and turned back to Allie.

'Is there anything you haven't told us, Allie? Anything at all?'

Allie hesitated.

'Allie.' Isabelle looked at her with intense focus. 'Whatever it is, don't be afraid to tell us. You don't want to keep it to yourself and find out later it was important.'

Allie knew she was right but could she tell them? Could she do that to Eloise?

Then she remembered that note stabbed into the wall.

'It's just that ... I thought ... ' Allie felt like a traitor, but she made herself continue. 'I thought I saw something the other day. It's probably nothing. But you should know.'

A heavy silence fell as the three teachers stared at her. Raj was the first to speak. 'What did you think you saw?'

The glare of their attention unnerved her and she twisted the hem of her jumper around her finger tight enough to hurt.

'It was just ... Eloise.'

'I don't understand.' Isabelle had gone very still. 'What about Eloise?'

Isabelle and the librarian were friends; surely she'd given her a key. This was all a horrible mistake, Allie thought with a hot surge of panic. She had no evidence. She couldn't just go around accusing people of murder.

But she was in it too far now. She had to explain.

'I was looking for you after class.' She turned to the head-mistress. 'You were in London but I didn't know so I waited outside your office for ages. Then . . . Eloise was in there . . . I think . . . the whole time but she didn't answer the door. I just saw her come out. It's probably, like . . . nothing. But when she saw me, she acted weird – she was all sweaty and she looked kind of . . . scared. She had a key.' She looked at Isabelle hope-fully. 'Was she supposed to be there for a . . . thing?'

Isabelle and Raj exchanged a long look.

'There are a lot of possible explanations . . .' Isabelle cautioned.

'Of course. And she can tell us what those are.' Raj's voice was low and velvety, like a cat purring at the sight of a bird landing on the ground.

This was the opposite of everything Allie had hoped for. Goosebumps formed an icy trail down her spine.

Oh, God – what have I done?

For a long moment the headmistress held his gaze as if she were deciding. Then she nodded, just once.

Without another word, he sprang to his feet, crossing the room in a few long steps. Zelazny followed him out of the room.

When they'd gone, Isabelle stared at the closed door blankly. A heavy silence fell over the room.

Allie tried to think of something to say but the headmistress seemed to have forgotten she was there.

'Maybe I should . . .'

She half rose from her chair but Isabelle motioned for her to stay. Her face had turned pink, as if she held back tears.

Guilt made Allie's skin crawl – this was her fault for telling them what she'd seen.

Why did I have to see it? she thought angrily. *Couldn't somebody else have been the one outside her office that day?*

'I'm sure she'll have a good explanation,' Allie said.

Isabelle's golden brown eyes shone with repressed pain. 'I've known Eloise all her life. I simply do not believe she could be the mole.' Sounding shaky but determined, she repeated her words. 'I cannot believe it. There has to be something else, Allie. Something we've missed.' Grabbing a piece of paper she picked up her pen. When she looked up again her expression was resolute. 'So let's go over this again. From the beginning.'

It was nearly dawn by the time Allie climbed into bed. By then she was exhausted. But she couldn't sleep.

Her memory kept replaying the moment when Eloise had found out how much trouble she was in.

When she'd returned to the school building, Isabelle had gone to meet her, ordering Allie to stay in her office. But she left the door open. So Allie had heard Eloise's cheerful voice saying, 'I got your message. What's up?'

It was Raj who replied, but Allie couldn't make out his words. Whatever it was it had upset Eloise, whose panic was clear.

'What? *No*. That's ridiculous.' Then a moment later: 'Isabelle, *please*. Don't let them do this.'

Allie had reached the hallway in time to see them march the librarian away like a prisoner, Zelazny on one side, Raj on the other.

At the sight, her stomach flipped – she knew just what that felt like.

Giving up on sleep, she kicked off the covers and climbed on to the top of her desk to throw open the arched window. Closing her eyes she let the cold fresh air wash over her.

If only there was somebody to talk to about this. Last term, she'd be climbing out of the window right now and running across to the boys' side of the building to slip through Carter's window and tell him everything.

She looked longingly at the sturdy ledge beneath the window frame. Then she shook her head and looked away. Those days were over.

But who else was there to talk to? Rachel wasn't in Night School, so she couldn't really talk to her about it. Zoe was only thirteen and, although she was freakishly smart, she was just a kid.

The chill had begun to seep into her bones and she was closing the window when someone tapped lightly at her door.

Frowning, Allie glanced at the alarm clock beside her.

Half five in the morning. Who would be knocking at this hour?

When she opened the door, Nicole stood on the other side. In her dark blue pyjamas and thick, white dressing gown, she looked uncharacteristically imperfect – her long, dark hair was dishevelled and she wore no makeup; Allie could see a red map of tiny pimples scattered across one cheek.

So Nicole was human, too, behind her façade of perfection.

'I'm sorry,' the French girl said, blithely unaware of the intense scrutiny she was under at that moment. 'I couldn't sleep. I thought maybe you might be up, too.'

'Totally.' Allie stepped back to let her in. 'I'm glad it's not just me.'

'Well. It was a strange night.' Nicole's tone was wry. Without waiting to be asked, she sat on the end of the bed, pulled the blanket off the footboard and draped it across her legs.

'It's colder in here than in my room,' she observed.

Allie admired her confidence; she seemed to just take charge of the situation wherever she was, and to feel comfortable no matter what she was doing.

Climbing back into bed, Allie pulled the covers up against the chill that still pervaded the room after she'd closed the window.

'After you left, Zelazny and Jerry Cole came to talk to us.' Nicole spoke quietly. 'They asked so many questions, but they wouldn't tell us where you were. It was so stupid – like they're playing war games again, you know?'

Allie nodded. She hated when things went wrong and the teachers acted like Cimmeria Academy was MI5 or something.

'Did they ... did they mention Eloise?' Allie spoke hesitantly.

Nicole's huge dark eyes shot up to meet hers. 'They asked us about her a lot. Is she in trouble? I was very confused by that.' Her delicate brow furrowed.

For a second, Allie paused, unsure of how much to reveal. But Nicole was a senior Night School student so she'd find out soon enough.

'They think she's Nathaniel's spy.'

Although her voice was just above a whisper, her words seem to hang in the air, like the reverberations of a bell.

At first, Nicole was too shocked to respond. Then she gasped in dismay. 'Oh *no* – but that's ridiculous.' She muttered something in angry French. 'Why do they think this? I don't understand.'

Heat flooded Allie's face; she dropped her eyes. 'It's my fault,' she confessed. 'I ... saw something and I told them. Then they freaked.'

To her surprise, Nicole took this remarkably well. 'What did you see?'

Allie told her about Isabelle's office, Eloise and the key.

When she'd finished, Nicole frowned with thought. 'That is strange. I don't understand why ...' She glanced up at Allie. 'Isabelle said there was no reason for her to be there?'

Allie gave glum assent.

'Oh no.' Nicole slumped back against the wall. 'This is terrible. It can't be her. I don't want it to be Eloise.'

'That's what I thought but then ... I don't know. It looks bad,' Allie said.

'Wait.' Straightening, Nicole tapped a pale pink nail against her chin thoughtfully. 'Let's think this over.'

Burying her face in her hands, Allie groaned. 'Do we have to? Isabelle and I talked about it for hours. We found nothing to help Eloise.'

But Nicole was not dissuaded. 'I have had a thought. You say she was sweaty? And seemed nervous?'

Allie nodded.

Nicole absorbed this before asking, 'Was her hair ... what's the English term ... rumpled? Like bed hair?'

Allie was baffled – how could that help?

She gave a puzzled shrug. 'Yeah, I guess.'

'Did you see anyone else come out of the office? Any other teachers?'

Curious, Allie shook her head. 'No. But I left right after that.'

'Hmmm.' Staring off across the room, Nicole rested her chin on her hand. 'It could be.'

'Could be what?'

Nicole blinked at her. 'It could be that Eloise isn't a spy. It could be that she was in there with Jerry having sex.'

There is no way I heard that right.

'*What?*' Allie gaped at her. 'Are you saying Eloise and Jerry Cole are ...'

Nicole nodded. 'Shagging, as you English say. Yes.'

Allie couldn't seem to get her mouth to shut. The very idea of the librarian and the science teacher having sex was repulsive. Why would Eloise, so young and pretty, want a man so *old*? He had to be at least ... nearly forty.

Trying to imagine what the librarian saw in him, she had a sudden memory of Jo staring at him dreamily – she'd always had a crush on Jerry.

But still. Eloise wouldn't. She could have anyone.

'I think that's rubbish,' she announced. 'There's no way Eloise would want him.'

Nicole seemed surprised. 'Why not? I think he's quite handsome. He has a great body.'

'*Jerry?*' Allie stared at her in horror. 'He's an old man, Nicole. You can't think he has a good body. That's just ... gross.'

'Oh, you English girls are so naive.' Nicole sighed. 'Jerry is very good-looking, I assure you. And I know they are having an affair. That much is certain.'

'How do you even know that?' Allie tried to disguise her dismay but failed.

'I think the question is how do you *not* know? Haven't you seen the way they look at each other? They liked each other for ages and they got together last term. I kept seeing them going off into the woods together. Once I caught them kissing in the training room before the others arrived ... I thought everyone knew.' She shrugged carelessly. 'They are in love.'

Allie tried to force herself to process this information.

'OK, but even if they are together – which I am not OK with – how did they get in Isabelle's office? And why would they go in there to ... to shag? Why wouldn't they just do it in their rooms?'

'I don't know,' Nicole conceded. 'But teachers aren't allowed to date and sex is totally forbidden. So ... maybe they got the key somehow and, knowing Isabelle was away for the day, they went in there because it is private. I mean, I don't know, this is just an idea.' She looked up at Allie with a thoughtful expression, as if she were working out a complex homework problem. 'It is a small office but there is space in there enough for two people to make love, *non*?'

Allie wrinkled her nose. *This is grim, grim, grim.*

'It's possible, I guess. But if that's what she was doing, wouldn't she just tell them? Then Jerry would back her up and they would let her go.'

'If she tells them she and Jerry are having a relationship they will both get fired. So she could be protecting him. Or she could have told them and – but this is inhuman – he could deny it to protect himself.' Nicole's expression grew serious. 'Or it is possible Raj and Zelazny simply don't believe them.'

Allie held her gaze. 'What do you believe? Do you think Eloise is working for Nathaniel? Do you think she's the one?'

'Of course not.' Nicole's response was immediate and emphatic.

Until she'd asked the question, Allie hadn't realised how much, on some level, she'd hoped it really was Eloise. Even though it would be awful, at least they'd have answers. The hunt would be over. And that was something.

But in her heart, she didn't think it was Eloise either. It didn't feel right. It didn't fit.

Despair, black as a storm cloud, swept over her. She was so tired, and they'd tried so hard. All for nothing.

Nathaniel was still out there. The wrong person was being held against her will. The spy was still around, still threatening, still unknown. Nothing was better. Everything was just as bad as it had been before. If not worse.

She looked up at Nicole with empty eyes. 'Then who is?'

For a long moment Nicole held her gaze then, as if she'd had a sudden idea, she sat up straight. 'Let's work this out. Could I have a piece of paper, please?'

Climbing out of bed, Allie grabbed a notepad and pens from her desk and handed them to her. Nicole was, like Rachel, an advanced science student. It made sense she'd want to look at this as if it were a complex equation.

'Let's just stick to the actual attacks.' Nicole drew a few

squares on the paper. In one she wrote, 'Ruth'. In the next, 'Jo'. And in the last, 'Chapel'.

'Now.' She thumped the end of the pen against the paper. 'Where were we all when Ruth was killed?'

Painstakingly they pieced together the whereabouts of the Night School students and teachers the night of the summer ball, making a list of who was accounted for and who was missing. Then they did the same thing for the night of Jo's death. Who had they actually seen at the precise time the gate was opened and she was stabbed? And then they did it again with last night's incident. Nicole diagrammed out a list of names in small rectangular squares, drawing lines – straight and unerring – to those whose locations were not known.

Before long, Allie realised Nicole was looking for a pattern. Yes, someone from outside may have got in as well, but someone inside the school had to give them the key, open a lock, release the gate. Help them. And that's what they were looking for. A person consistently missing whenever anything happened.

When they'd finished, for a moment they both stared at the page in solemn silence.

With a fingertip, Allie traced the dark lines leading to a handful of boxes, each one holding a familiar name. Each line as slender as the strands of trust she'd built for these people.

But everything built can be destroyed.

'It's one of them, then,' she said.

Nicole nodded, her dark eyes serious. 'It's one of them.'

Allie stared at the incriminating paper in front of them then raised her gaze to meet Nicole's.

'What do we do now?'

FOURTEEN

I t was nearly nine by the time Nicole left Allie's room that
morning, and by then they had a plan. It was basic but it
was better than nothing.

The first step was to put together a team to help them.

They'd agreed that everyone chosen to be part of the plan
had to be approved by both of them but, in the end, it wasn't
hard to decide who to include.

Now they just had to convince them all to help.

Allie dressed quickly and hurried out. The hallways were
quiet; it was Saturday – most students would be playing games
or lazing around chatting. Some would be out in the cold kicking a football around. A low rumble of voices and laughter
tumbled through the open common-room door.

For a fleeting, melancholy moment, Allie missed normal
student life. It would be so good to be someone else for a
while.

She broke into a jog, speeding down the wide hallway to the library.

Walking through the library door was like entering a different school. A hospital hush hung over the room. Thick Persian rugs absorbed sound below while, above, high ceilings made small noises disappear. The effect was as if the room was wrapped in cotton wool.

The acrid scent of smoke from last summer's fire had long since dissipated; now the room smelled only of old leather books, nineteenth-century ink and wood polish.

All the bookcases looked identical but she knew that many of those at the front of the room were replicas, made precisely like the original shelves that towered into the dimness above her head. Even the new rolling ladders were identical to the originals.

In fact, every bit of physical damage Nathaniel had done to the building had been repaired; Allie knew she should find that comforting. But right now nothing made her feel any better.

When she noticed a slim, bespectacled man in Eloise's usual seat, her stomach tightened. It seemed so callous just to replace her as if she was already found guilty. As if she was disposable.

As she walked up to the desk, she recognised him as one of the lower-form English teachers, and she fought to quell her temper. It wasn't his fault. Probably.

Still, she had to challenge him. She wanted to see if he would lie to her face.

'Excuse me,' she said. 'Do you know where Eloise is?'

He set down the cards he'd been filing – the look on his face told her that, while she might not remember his name, he knew precisely who she was.

'I'm afraid she's in meetings,' he said with impeccable politeness. 'All weekend.'

The combination of his lies and good manners set her nerves on edge. He must know precisely where Eloise was and what she was going through but he didn't care at all.

What a wanker.

'Awesome,' she said coldly. 'I was afraid something bad might have happened to her.'

Without waiting for his reaction she spun on her heel and hurried to a dim section at the edge of the room. Rachel was right where she'd known she'd be. Glasses on the end of her nose, long hair twisted into a messy knot at the base of her neck and held in place with a pencil, one end of which pointed up like an antenna.

She'd been surprised by the ease with which Nicole accepted her request to include Rachel. Since she wasn't in Night School, she'd expected some objections.

'Including her will break most of The Rules,' Allie had pointed out, but Nicole only shrugged.

'We'll be breaking so many of The Rules I don't think it matters. If we get caught we'll all be expelled anyway.'

'Hey,' Allie said now, sliding into the seat across from Rachel.

'Oh good!' Rachel peered up at her. 'Are you here for your flogging ... I mean, science tutoring?'

When Allie didn't joke back, Rachel narrowed her eyes. 'What's up? Something's happened, I can tell. Your nose is doing that thing.'

Warily, Allie reached up to touch the end of her nose. It didn't feel like it was doing anything.

'What thing?' she asked, before deciding it didn't matter. 'Look, something's happened . . .'

'I knew it.' Rachel sounded smug. 'The nose never lies.'

Trying to get her to focus, Allie leaned forward. 'I need your help.' Nobody was sitting at any of the tables around them but, still, Allie half covered her mouth as she spoke. 'You're not going to like any of what I'm about to tell you.'

'Uh-oh.' Rachel took off her glasses.

'Eloise is in trouble and she needs our help.'

All traces of humour left Rachel's expression. 'What happened?'

Allie looked around at the other tables. 'Come with me.'

Leaving Rachel's books on the table, they headed to a dark corner of the library in the Ancient Greek section – no one was ever back there. Every step of the way Allie worried that Rachel would refuse what she was about to ask of her.

She hated Night School and all of Cimmeria's darker side. She'd tried to convince Allie not to join. But the library was her favourite place in the world and, to her, Eloise *was* the library. Allie knew emphasising the librarian's plight would help convince her to get involved, but she felt like a traitor for doing it.

This was everything Rachel loathed about the school and Allie was taking her right into the middle of it.

Quickly Allie told her what had happened last night – the knife in the wall. Nathaniel. Gabe. When she explained that somebody at the school was helping them, Rachel made a choking sound and half turned away.

'I was so afraid of that,' she said after a second. 'Something my dad said a while ago clued me in that it could be one of us. Who do they think it is?'

Allie held her gaze. 'Right now? They think it's Eloise.'

Curling her hands into fists, Rachel swore quietly. Allie couldn't remember her ever using a couple of those words before.

'The thing is, we're pretty sure it's not her,' she continued. 'But we need your help to prove it. Rach, I know how much you hate this stuff but ... will you help me?'

For a long moment, Rachel didn't speak. When she looked up, her almond-shaped eyes were dark with worry.

'What do you need me to do?'

The rest was easy.

Allie insisted Zoe be included because even though she was young she was also fast and smart. Best of all, she was innocuous – she could slip in and out of a room without anybody noticing. Nobody paid attention to a kid.

Nicole did her part – bringing Carter and Sylvain into the group.

When Jules' name came up in her discussion with Nicole, Allie shook her head. She just couldn't deal with the Carter–Jules love-nest right now.

And Nicole, to her surprise, refused Lucas without explanation.

'I don't want him in the team,' she'd said when pressed.

'Come on, Nicole,' Allie had said. 'He's Rachel's boyfriend. He's safe.'

But Nicole just shook her head and Allie had to drop it. No Lucas.

So that was the group: six people to find the spy Cimmeria's best instructors had failed to locate.

The first step was simple enough. They were to meet at midnight in the crypt beneath the girls' dorm.

After that things would get harder.

At three minutes to midnight, Allie tapped sharply on the wall separating her room from Rachel's. After a pause, one faint tap came back.

Time to go.

Her door swung open without a sound. Slipping out, she closed it with an expert flick of her wrist. The click as the latch caught was almost imperceptible.

The long, narrow corridor was empty and dark. Rachel's door was shut tight.

Clutching her torch in one hand, Allie bounced on her toes impatiently, careful not to make a sound. 'Come on, Rach ... ' she whispered under her breath.

For a few endless seconds nothing happened. Then Rachel's door opened with a creak.

She emerged slowly, her reluctance clear in every movement. Her eyes were downcast, her shoulders slumped.

Allie knew how much Rachel didn't want to do this but she willed her to do it anyway – she needed her.

Tilting her head to indicate Rachel should follow her, Allie headed down the hall without a word. The heating had been turned down and the building groaned and clicked around them as it settled into the cold winter night.

The door near the end of the corridor looked like an ordinary utility closet but swung open to reveal one of the old servants' staircases hidden within Cimmeria's walls. In Victorian times, this would have been how housemaids slipped around the building to perform their chores unseen. Now they were largely forgotten.

A cool draught blew through the open door, making the hairs on Allie's arms stand on end. After a glance over her shoulder to make sure Rachel was with her, she switched on her torch and headed down.

Four storeys lower, the narrow, winding, stone staircase deposited them in a large, low-ceilinged space. The limestone floors and walls acted like a refrigerator – it was freezing. It was also empty. And it shouldn't be.

Allie's hackles rose. Something was wrong.

She swung her torch around the room – the beam illuminating ghostly stone columns bearing the marks of ancient chisels, like scratches made by claws.

A shuffling noise arose behind them, as if the light had awakened something.

Allie whirled, pulling Rachel behind her and dropping into a low, defensive crouch, holding her torch like a truncheon.

'This is so awesome,' Zoe whispered, turning on her torch. 'Best idea ever.'

Allie sagged, the adrenaline flooding out of her. 'Bloody hell, Zoe. Why didn't you say something earlier? You scared me to death.'

'Hi, Allie. I'm here. Right where you told me to be.' Zoe's cheerful tone segued swiftly into alarm. 'Blimey, Rachel, you don't look so good. Maybe you should sit down.'

Looking back, Allie saw that Rachel's complexion had gone an odd pale green.

'Rachel!'

'Totally fine,' Rachel insisted, wobbling.

Taking her arm, Allie navigated her towards a dusty crate. 'Let's sit you down. You look like you're going to be sick.'

'Just . . . startled.' Rachel's voice was faint. 'Thought we were dead. Nothing major.'

'Put your head between your knees,' Zoe ordered.

'What's wrong with Rachel?' Sylvain emerged from a corridor as nothing more than a bright torch beam with a French accent.

'Zoe scared us.' Allie glared at the younger girl accusingly. 'Rachel had a heart attack.'

'Not a heart attack, exactly,' Rachel murmured, her voice muffled as her face was still pressed against her knees. 'But my life did flash before my eyes. I'm really sorry about Robert Peterson.'

They all stared at her.

'Who's Robert Peterson?' Allie and Zoe asked at the same time.

'I know him,' Nicole said, ducking through the same doorway Allie and Rachel had just used. 'He was in my physics class last year. A super student with very thick spectacles.'

'I kissed him once,' Rachel said. 'He slobbered.'

'Gross,' Zoe said, looking repulsed.

Nicole just shrugged. 'And yet you are alive.'

'Somehow,' Rachel conceded.

'Where's Carter?' Nicole asked looking around the vault-like space.

'I'm here.' They all turned as Carter's torch appeared through the corridor, gradually brightening as he neared them. Allie pointed her torch at him until they could see the shape of his body in the dark.

'Then we are all present.' Nicole's voice was solemn. 'Let's begin.'

FIFTEEN

They gathered in a circle on the dusty floor. The only light came from their torches. It occurred to Allie they looked as if they should be playing a party game – 'I Never' or 'Spin the Bottle'.

But this was a very different kind of game.

Looking around the circle of familiar faces watching her expectantly, she knew they wanted the same things she did. Answers. Resolution. Justice.

She couldn't give them that.

'You all know why we're here.' Her voice echoed off the cold stone walls. 'After what happened last night, I –' With a glance at Nicole she corrected herself. 'Nicole and I – we don't think Isabelle and the others are on the right track. We want to figure out who the spy really is. So we've mapped out where everyone was when all the stuff happened.' The others looked at her expectantly. 'We still don't know who the spy is. But we think we know who it *isn't*.'

She leaned back and the French girl scooted forward. Her dark hair had been pulled back into a sleek ponytail at the nape of her neck; when it caught the torchlight it gleamed like granite.

'We started from the basis that we do not think the spy is a student,' Nicole began. 'Only the most senior Night School students have the kind of access this person has. So . . . it would have to be one of us.' She swung her torch slowly around the circle, illuminating their faces one after another. 'And I don't think it is.'

'Why not?'

It was Rachel who spoke, and they all turned to stare at her.

'What do you mean why not?' Surprise made Allie's voice squeak.

Rachel shrugged. 'It could be one of us. We don't follow each other constantly.'

Alone among them, Nicole did not seem surprised by this. 'Yes. So, just in case, I researched each of us. Each time something happened, I could account for where we all were. When the knife was found in the chapel, not one of us could have done it. You' – she pointed at Rachel – 'were in the library.' Rachel nodded. 'Allie, Zoe and I were together. Carter and Sylvain were also there, along with Jules and Lucas and every single Night School student,' she said. 'And I have worked this out for the other incidents as well. At no time could the same senior student have done these three things. It is not one of us.'

'It's one of the teachers.' Carter's voice sounded hollow.

Even though she had worked this out with Nicole that morning, hearing it said made Allie's heart turn to ice in her chest. And she could see by the looks on the faces around her she wasn't alone. Sylvain had his head in his hands. Rachel looked drawn. Even Zoe appeared troubled, her bottom lip caught between her teeth, her brow creased.

'Yes,' Nicole said quietly. 'It has to be one of the Night School instructors. Someone very close to Isabelle. They have the freedom, the access and their time is more difficult to track.'

'Then why couldn't it be Eloise?' Zoe asked, frowning.

Allie thought of that sheet of paper on the bed this morning. Eloise's name with a line drawn through it. The strange mixture of disappointment and relief she'd felt.

'Eloise was with us right before the knife was found,' she explained. 'Whoever placed it in the chapel did it between the time when the other Night School students passed and when we came by later – otherwise someone would have seen it. Eloise didn't have time to get there and arrange it all before we arrived. So if no one intruded on to the campus last night – and Raj says they didn't – it couldn't be her.'

As they absorbed this, Nicole swung her torch in a little circle. 'Blaming her for it is ... how do you say? Theatre.'

The temperature seemed to drop further in the cold crypt.

'If that's true then one of the teachers accusing her is actually the one working for Nathaniel,' Sylvain said.

'It would make sense,' Rachel said. 'They'll stop looking if they all believe the spy is Eloise.'

Allie nodded. 'And while they're not looking, the real spy could be doing ...'

Nicole finished the thought for her. 'Anything.'

Zoe, her face scrunched up with thought, was trying to work it all out. 'If we're right about Eloise then that means the spy is either Zelazny, Isabelle, Jerry or Raj—'

'It's *not* my dad.'

Rachel's voice was sharp, and the others swung around to look at her.

'Rachel's right,' Allie said. 'No way is it Raj. He loves this place and Isabelle too much. And it can't be Isabelle for obvious reasons.'

'Could it be one of Raj's senior guards?' Sylvain asked. 'A few of them have full access.'

But Nicole had thought of this, too. 'Three guards are allowed access,' she said. 'Only two of them were working here the night Ruth was killed.'

The cellar fell silent. The list of possible spies was very short now.

'That leaves Zelazny, Jerry or one of Raj's senior guards.' Carter ticked the names off on his fingers with solemn deliberation. 'And Raj picks his guards very carefully.'

Sylvain looked like he'd been punched. 'I just don't believe it,' he said. 'It must be one of the guards. It's impossible Jerry or Zelazny would do this. Impossible.'

Allie and Nicole exchanged a glance. Nothing was impossible any more.

The next day was Sunday and Allie was outside Isabelle's office at nine o'clock, waiting.

The door was locked; the office appeared to be empty.

Leaning against the wall, Allie crossed her arms and settled in.

She has to come back some time.

Carter and Sylvain were looking for Zelazny and Jerry. Nicole and Rachel were trying to find out what they could from the other teachers. Zoe was snooping around Raj's senior guards.

Allie was assigned to find out everything she could from Isabelle.

One of them had to uncover something. Whoever the spy was he couldn't be perfect. He had to make a mistake some time. All they had to do was find it.

As the minutes crept by, though, she began to wish she had a different task.

She hopped from one foot to another. Sank down to the floor and stretched out her legs. She even counted the panels in the elaborately carved oak wall but her heart wasn't in it.

Next time she'd definitely bring a book.

When lunchtime arrived and Isabelle still hadn't appeared, Allie at first vowed to skip the meal in order to keep watch. But the alluring smells wafting down from the dining hall soon became too enticing to resist.

A short break won't matter, she told herself. *Wherever Isabelle is, she isn't here.*

When she walked in, Rachel and Nicole were already at the table, eating sandwiches and talking in whispers.

'Any news?' Allie asked, pulling up a chair.

They both shook their heads.

'Big fat zero,' Rachel said. 'You?'

'The same. Isabelle never showed. I was there all morning.' Gloomily, she surveyed the neat array of sandwiches on the platter in the middle of the table. 'I wish I knew where the hell she was.'

Still feeling chilled from last night's icy meeting, she half stood to peer into the tureen in the middle of the table.

'It's weird green soup today,' Rachel warned her. 'I wouldn't.'

The two watched doubtfully as Allie ladled soup of a startling hue into a white china bowl with the Cimmeria crest on the side.

'I just need something hot,' Allie said. 'Even if it's Soylent Green.'

'Soylent Green is people,' Zoe announced, sliding into the chair next to her.

'Oh great,' Rachel said. 'Now you've ruined the ending for me.'

'I thought everyone knew.' Zoe stared hard at Allie's soup. 'That looks disgusting. It might actually *be* people.'

'It tastes better than it looks,' Allie said, unbothered. She glanced up at Zoe. 'Did you have any luck?'

'With what?' Zoe asked blankly.

Allie tilted her head significantly. 'You know ... the thing? From last night?'

'Oh, the *spying*.' As they all shushed her, Zoe grabbed a sandwich off a tray. 'A little.'

She had their full attention now.

'What did you find out?' Allie asked.

'It's like we thought, they're holding Eloise.'

'Where?' the other three all asked once.

Zoe's reply came through a mouthful of cheese sandwich. 'I don't know – they didn't say. But the guards are cross. They have their limits. They're working double shifts. They've got families, you know. They didn't sign up for this. And they don't want to be involved in anything illegal.'

Her phrasing was odd – her accent changed subtly with each phrase – and it took Allie a second to realise she must be parroting precisely what she'd heard the guards say. Zoe's natural tendency for precision, it turned out, made her an ideal spy.

'We've got to find out where they're keeping her,' Allie said. 'That must be where Isabelle is, too. How can I talk to her if I can't find her?'

Frustration made her voice rise and she forced herself to lower it to a whisper again.

'I'll find her,' Zoe said confidently. 'One of the guards said ...'

Her eyes widened and Allie turned to see what she was looking at.

Carter and Sylvain were running across the dining hall. It was odd seeing them together – given how much they'd always hated each other. But now they looked like a team, moving in unison across the busy room.

A scene of confusion seemed to break out in their wake. The noise level rose and some students sitting near the door rose from their seats and rushed out of the room.

'Come quick.' Carter was breathless. 'Something's happening.'

Exchanging a puzzled look, the girls hurried after them for the door, where the sudden exodus was causing a bottleneck.

As soon as they extricated themselves the boys led them down the hallway to the front door, which stood open despite the cold February wind.

Seeing it, Allie's heart sank. Whatever was happening, it wasn't good.

In front of the school building a Bentley gleamed in the driveway. A powerfully built man in an odd uniform – half military, half bellboy – was marching towards it. In one hand he carried a designer suitcase. His other hand gripped the arm of a struggling girl.

'That's Caroline Laurelton. What's he doing to her?' Rachel frowned in dismay.

'What is it?' Zoe squirmed in front of them to try and see.

'Let me go!' The girl squirmed in the driver's grip, her short brown hair flying from the effort, her voice rising to a scream. But he was more than six feet tall and appeared to be made of muscle. She was small and slight. She didn't stand a chance.

'I don't . . . ' Allie turned to Sylvain, who stood next to her. His jaw was tight, and she could see the anger and disgust in his eyes. 'What's happening?'

'Her parents are taking her out of the school. They've sent their driver to take her home.' As he explained, Sylvain kept his eyes on the girl who, Allie could now see, was weeping. 'She doesn't want to go.'

His gaze shifted. Allie turned to see what he was looking at. One of Raj's guards stood to one side of the door, watching the scene. Meeting Sylvain's gaze, he shook his head.

They weren't to interfere.

Back in the drive, the man was shoving the tearful girl into the capacious car.

'This is wrong,' Allie said, mostly to herself.

'I know.' Sylvain's voice was bitter.

Straightening his cap, the driver picked up the girl's suitcase and tossed it on to the front passenger seat. Then, without acknowledging the crowd of students watching, he got into the driver's seat and drove away.

As the car disappeared into the forest, the students milled, their voices rising in a rumble of confused excitement.

Zoe reappeared at her side, with Rachel right behind her.

'Why didn't anyone stop him?' Zoe asked.

'Forgive me if I'm wrong but did that look like a kidnapping to anyone else?' Rachel asked. When no one replied, she looked around in bafflement. 'I don't understand what's happening. Where is my *dad*?'

Sylvain and Carter exchanged a look that spoke volumes. Carter tilted his head at the door behind them. 'Let's go inside.'

The dining room was mostly empty when they returned to their table. Shoving the plates out of the way they huddled, speaking in low voices.

'Here's the thing. Caroline Laurelton's parents are on the board,' Carter said. 'Not fans of Lucinda. Rumours are everywhere that they issued a statement to the other board members this morning saying Isabelle and Lucinda are dragging the school down and they wouldn't be part of it.' He hesitated for a second before giving the last bit of bad news. 'They said they were just the first to pull their kids out. They said everyone would go.'

Allie's stomach dropped.

'More theatre.' Nicole sounded bitter. 'That girl is a pawn in her parents' game. They don't care about her feelings. They're using her to send Nathaniel's message to Isabelle.'

'We think this is Nathaniel's next move.' Sylvain's face was intense. 'He's divided the board. Now they're dividing the school. It's started.'

SIXTEEN

'I don't get it.' Zoe said. 'If this is happening, the instructors must know. But they've all completely disappeared.'

'What do you mean, disappeared?' Allie asked.

'No one's seen Zelazny, Jerry, Eloise or Isabelle since last night,' Zoe explained. 'Everyone's talking about it. Jerry didn't show up for a weekend workshop. Zelazny was supposed to do an extra class today but he wasn't there. They're just –' she held up her hands – 'missing.'

'Well, where are they? Teachers don't just evaporate,' Allie said.

'They must be with Eloise,' Sylvain said. Next to him Carter nodded his agreement. 'They'll be questioning her with Raj – somewhere away from the school building because they don't want to be interrupted.'

Zoe perked up. 'Let's find them and tell them what's happening.'

'The thing that scares me is ... what if this is just what Nathaniel wanted?' Rachel mused. 'What if he set up Eloise just for this? The more chaos the better, as far as he's concerned.'

'He can't have done,' Allie said miserably. 'I'm the one who accused Eloise. He didn't make me do that.'

'I think Allie's right,' Nicole said. 'I think it's the other way around.'

'That makes sense,' Sylvain said. 'He found out Eloise was being blamed, so he's decided to strike now.'

'Yes, that is a smart move,' Nicole said. 'Hit us while all the teachers are distracted.'

Rachel's brow furrowed. 'Wait, how did you find out about what her parents said to the board?'

'Katie.' Sylvain spoke with clear distaste. 'She's telling everyone.'

The others groaned. Everyone knew Katie Gilmore's parents were very active members of the Cimmeria Board.

'But how did Katie find out?' Allie asked. 'She'd need a phone.'

Sylvain's brow creased. 'That's a good question. I'll go and speak to her – she was just outside so she can't have gone far. I'll see if she knows more as well.'

When he'd gone, the others were at a loss.

'We have to do *something*,' Zoe said, her sharp tone betraying her impatience. 'We've got to find the teachers and tell them what happened.'

'How?' Carter asked. 'Right now we don't even know where they are.'

Nicole looked at Zoe. 'Why don't we do a quick sweep outside? See what we can find?'

'I'll talk to the guards.' Rachel stood up. 'They might talk to me because of who my dad is.'

Relieved to have a purpose, they left in a rush. Now Carter and Allie were alone at the table.

'So ... what should we do?' she asked, twisting her napkin into a knot of white cloth.

'We need to find out what's really going on, and how much the teachers know.'

'How do we do that?' Allie asked.

His replying grin had a dangerous glint. 'I've got an idea.'

That afternoon, Allie was again outside Isabelle's office. This time, though, she wasn't alone. As she leaned back against the wall, crossing her arms in a pose of affected nonchalance, Carter stood across from her, his back against Isabelle's door, whistling tunelessly.

Every so often his eyes met hers and his eyebrow arched questioningly. Each time she shook her head.

Not yet.

She knew from experience he only needed a minute to do what he was about to do. But if he was spotted it would be disastrous; she had to be certain it was safe.

Finally, the hallway went quiet. Twisting her neck, Allie checked the stairs and the corridor behind them. Empty. She turned back to where Carter waited, poised.

'Now,' she said.

Moving with swift confidence he bent over the lock to Isabelle's office door and inserted a shiny metal pin.

As he worked, Allie stood beside him, blocking him from

view as she watched the empty corridor for any sign of activity.

'Still clear?' he murmured without looking up. Glancing down, she had to admire the way – even under pressure – his steady hands worked the pin in the lock.

'Uh-huh.'

The hallway was so quiet, the click the lock made when it gave seemed to echo.

'They really should replace this lock,' Carter said softly, as the door swung open. 'It's too easy.'

Slipping inside, they closed the door behind them.

The windowless room was very dark. The noises of the building were muted here; the quiet was unnerving. Allie could barely make out Carter's shape but she could hear the sound of his even breathing.

She moved swiftly, dropping her blazer from her shoulders, stuffing it into the crack underneath the door.

Feeling his way around the furniture, Carter flipped on the brass desk light and the room leapt into life.

In the yellow glow, he met her gaze and pointed at the desk. 'Let's start here.'

As usual the imposing, mahogany desk was covered in stacks of paper and they looked through them hurriedly for anything about Eloise or Nathaniel. Anything that could give them some idea what was happening right now.

With no idea when the headmistress might return – or even where she was – they had to be quick. Getting caught would be the end of everything for both of them.

For ten minutes they searched in silence. Most of the papers were English essays the headmistress had been reviewing or normal school paperwork, bills and accounts. Nothing useful at all.

As Allie opened a file that proved to contain only utility bills, Carter stopped her. 'Here.'

Looking up she saw he was reading something hand-written on a sheet of white paper.

'What is it?' He lowered the paper so she could see.

'It's the allegations against Eloise.'

The page held a numbered list of charges in square, precise handwriting, mostly related to the fact that she said she was alone on many of the dates and times Nathaniel's spy was suspected to be active.

'Look at that,' Allie whispered, pointing at the page. 'It ignores the fact that she couldn't have got in the chapel to light those candles before we got there.'

'It's Zelazny's handwriting.' Carter's tone was flat.

She looked up at him doubtfully. 'Do you think . . . ?'

He shrugged, his lips in a tight line. 'If he's accusing her . . . I have to wonder if he's got something to gain by doing it. The real spy knows it's not her.'

His words gave Allie that same sensation she'd had earlier of having ice at her core, and she shivered. 'It's just . . . hard to believe. Zelazny seems so loyal.'

In the glow of the desk lamp, Carter's eyes were fathomless. 'I don't trust anyone any more.'

Unsure of how to reply to that, Allie turned back to the papers on the desktop.

The history teacher was grumpy, yes, and a stickler for the

rules. But he'd always seemed like the most rock-solid of all the teachers. The one who never shifted. Utterly loyal to the school.

How could he possibly . . .

Her mind in a whirl, she was half looking at papers relating to the school's accounts when something about the numbers struck her. Picking up a page she held it closer to the light.

'Carter,' she whispered, 'this is weird.'

'What is it?'

'It's just . . . Are we broke?'

'Broke?' He frowned, reaching for the paper. 'What do you mean?'

'Look here . . . ' She pointed at the bottom line. 'It says the school has negative three hundred and seventy-four thousand pounds in its accounts. That's a lot of minuses.'

He scanned the paper quickly and shook his head. 'I don't understand,' he said. 'That's not possible.'

But Allie was looking at another paper now. 'Wait. Look at this one.'

She read aloud: ' . . . as nearly half the parents have failed to pay their fees this term, I'm depositing the necessary funds into Cimmeria's account to make up the difference. However, this indicates that Nathaniel is preparing to make a move during this term. Thus we must increase our efforts to stop him and his group before this can occur. Otherwise, the school could be destroyed. And the organisation lost to us.'

The letter was signed with Lucinda's sweeping signature.

'So they knew this was coming,' Allie said. 'That's why they're all hoping they've caught the spy.'

Carter met her gaze. 'They think it's their only chance to stop it.'

When he reached for the page to read it again, his fingers brushed against hers, causing an electric spark and Allie jumped back, letting go of the paper. The page floated to the floor.

'Sorry,' they both said simultaneously, bending over to pick it up at the exact same moment and hitting heads with a cracking sound.

Clutching her head, Allie didn't know whether to laugh or cry as she reeled away from him.

Carter held his own temple. 'Are you OK?'

Though her head was throbbing, Allie gave an embarrassed laugh. 'I'm fine, I think.'

But as she ran her fingers through her hair she felt a lump beginning to rise. It was sensitive to touch and she hissed from the pain. Seeing this, Carter's face darkened with concern.

'What is it? Let me see.'

'No, I'm fine, really ...' Allie demurred, but he shook his head sternly.

'Come on. Let Dr Carter have a look.' He held the lamp up close to her head and, with a touch as soft as silk, parted her hair.

Allie stayed very still – afraid if she moved he'd stop. And go back to ignoring her.

He whistled softly. 'That's a nice goose egg you've got there, Sheridan.'

She shot him an ironic look. 'Will I make it, doctor?'

His replying smile made his eyes crinkle.

It was just the way things used to be between them – so natural and easy. Allie wanted the moment to last and last. But as if he'd suddenly remembered who he was with, Carter cleared his throat and took a step back, returning the lamp to its place. When he spoke again his voice was cooler.

'We'd better hurry. Why don't you check the drawers?'

'Oh ... yeah.' She moved to the other side of the antique desk, keeping her face down so he couldn't see the colour in her cheeks.

This is so hard. Can't we just be friends again?

With a sigh, she tried the top drawer.

Locked.

The one below it was locked, too. And all the rest.

'No joy,' she said.

'I—' He began to reply then stopped.

They both heard the sound at the same moment. Frozen in position, Allie stared at the door in horror.

Somebody was trying to get in.

Without a word, Carter grabbed her hand, pulling her to his side. Then he turned out the desk light.

The room was plunged into darkness.

SEVENTEEN

Crouched low behind Isabelle's desk, Allie held her breath. In the darkness, she couldn't see Carter but she could sense him next to her.

Whoever was trying to get in was having a bad time of it.

The doorknob rattled again and they could hear the faint jingle of metal against metal.

'He has a key,' Carter whispered, so quietly his words barely disturbed the air. They stayed very still.

For a long moment the rattling sounds continued. Then, abruptly, they stopped.

'It doesn't fit,' a muffled voice said outside the door. 'She must have given us the wrong key.'

It was a man's voice. After that, they could hear other voices conferring.

If they have another key, Allie thought, *they'll use it now. Then they'll find us.*

The thought made her quiver – getting caught now would ruin everything.

But outside the conversation faded away. Holding her breath, Allie listened hard but could hear nothing.

A full minute ticked by as they huddled together in the dark.

'I think they're gone,' Carter whispered at last. 'We should get out of here before they come back with the right key.'

They stood, careful not to make a sound. Carter kept a hand on her elbow as they made their way through the dark room to the door. He didn't need to – Allie knew this room well. But his touch made her feel safer; she was sorry when he let go.

As they stood at the door, she looked at the shadow shape of him beside her – wishing there was something she could say that would make all the bad things that had happened between them go away. That would allow them to be friends like this again.

But there wasn't.

'Ready?' he said.

She lifted her chin. 'Yes.'

Then she opened the door and walked out into the light.

'We've found out they are keeping her somewhere else,' Nicole whispered.

'Could you be more specific?' Carter's tone was too sharp; a nearby student glanced up from his physics book.

'Carter,' Sylvain said quietly. 'Volume?'

Allie expected Carter to glower at him or say something

sarcastic. Instead he merely lowered his head in acknow-
ledgement.

Watching the two of them, she frowned. Something had
changed between them. They weren't enemies any more. They
didn't act like friends exactly, but there was clearly some sort
of understanding between them. They were like ... allies.

When Carter spoke again his voice was low. 'Sorry, Nicole.
Go ahead.'

They'd gathered in the far corner of the common room,
perched on a leather sofa and chairs and leaning in to hear
each other speak. The room was packed with bored students in
various stages of relaxation – some played board games, others
read books or gossiped.

The ambient noise was loud enough they'd thought they
could talk here without being noticed.

'Wait,' Sylvain said, before Nicole could proceed. 'Pretend
to talk about something fun. Like football.'

'Football isn't fun,' Rachel said pointedly and Nicole giggled.

Even though everything was still bad, even though nothing
had yet been resolved, the mere fact that they were at last *doing
something* lightened the heavy atmosphere. They weren't in the
dark any more. They were involved, investigating – and they
were finding out what was going on.

With a beleaguered sigh, Sylvain pulled a polished
mahogany box of chess pieces from underneath the occasional
table in front of them and began to set them up on the chessboard painted directly on to the table top. Black on the right,
white on the left.

Glancing up, he caught Allie's eye and motioned for her to

sit across from him on the floor. After a brief hesitation, she did as he requested.

'We can talk about anything,' he explained, 'as long as we look like everyone else. People see what they want to see.'

When he looked up from the board, the light caught his eyes and fractured like sunlight on water.

'I haven't played chess since ...' Allie's voice trailed off. She picked up a ceramic pawn; it was cold in her hand. The colour of snow. 'Well. I used to play with Jo.'

'I remember.' The compassion in his voice made her feel better and worse all at once. She was glad when he let the topic go. 'You be white.'

'Now,' he said to everyone else. 'Pretend to watch us while you talk. And try to keep your voices low.' He glanced back at Allie with an encouraging smile. 'Your move.'

Seeing that he was serious, Allie's hand hovered over the board for a moment. Then she chose a pawn and slid it forward one square. He countered instantly with one of his own.

'They're holding Eloise in one of the old staff cottages,' Rachel said, her voice low and steady. 'We saw Raj and Jerry and the whole Scooby gang heading into the school from somewhere, and then leave again. Zoe followed them.'

In the middle of a move Allie paused, a pawn forgotten in her hand. 'By herself? Was that safe?'

'Of course it was safe,' Carter snapped before Zoe could speak. 'The teachers aren't going to hurt her.'

His tone was unnecessarily sharp and Allie shot him a reproachful look before turning back to the game. The moment in Isabelle's office was obviously over.

She slid the pawn next to one of Sylvain's – close, but just out of reach.

'Whatever,' she whispered so quietly only Sylvain could hear. Across the chessboard he smiled at her conspiratorially and she found herself smiling, too.

'Tell them what you found,' Nicole whispered to Zoe, who sat next to her.

'They're in a cottage – not Mr Ellison's. Another one, near the pond in the woods. Kind of rundown, really overgrown.' She studied the chessboard critically. 'You're not using your bishop right, Allie.'

Perplexed, Allie looked at the piece with its mitred top and wondered what would be the right way to use it.

'I know that place,' Carter said. 'It used to be staff housing but then they quit using it for some reason a few years ago. I think it needed repairs or something and Isabelle never got around to it.'

'Did you see Eloise?' Rachel leaned closer. 'How is she?'

Zoe shook her head. 'I only heard her. They all went inside and then I could hear them talking. They said the key didn't work. They kept asking her for the right key.' She looked around the group. 'What does that mean?'

Sylvain moved his queen forward four squares.

'They had a key they thought would open Isabelle's office,' Carter said. 'They tried it while we were in there. Scared the hell out of us but they couldn't get in.'

'What's that about?' Rachel asked. 'Why would it matter if the key didn't work?'

An image of Eloise standing in front of Isabelle's door flashed in Allie's memory.

'Eloise had a key to Isabelle's office,' Allie said. 'She was holding it in her hand when I saw her that day – the day I thought she was the spy. I told them about it.'

'They must be trying to find that key,' Nicole said thoughtfully. 'They'd want to make sure it was secure so no one could use it.'

'But she gave them the wrong key?' Carter looked puzzled. 'Why would she do that?'

'Maybe she doesn't have the right one any more,' Rachel suggested.

'Then who does?' Sylvain asked.

No one had an answer to that.

Rachel broke the silence. 'What did you two find in the office?'

Allie let Carter describe what they'd learned. When he finished, the others looked stunned.

'So they knew this was going to happen all this time?' Rachel sounded shocked.

Sylvain's queen and a knight suddenly cornered Allie's king.

'Check,' he murmured, arching one eyebrow.

Allie glared at the board but couldn't find a way out. 'Balls.'

'What if our parents try to pull us out?' Zoe asked.

They all fell silent.

'That guy dragged Caroline to the car,' Rachel said. 'Are they going to do that to half the people in this room?'

'What can we do, though?' Allie asked.

Sylvain picked up a discarded chess piece. Holding the

white knight in his hand, he looked at it thoughtfully for a moment. Then he held it up.

'We can warn them.'

Sylvain's statement caused an instant outcry. How could they do that? If they did, wouldn't everyone know what they'd been up to? How should they say they found this information out in the first place? Besides, it wasn't like they could send everyone an anonymous email. If they spread the word, the instructors would find out what they were up to and put a stop to it.

It was Rachel who'd found the solution.

'Never underestimate the power of gossip,' she said simply.

They all looked at her with blank incomprehension.

'I do not understand?' Nicole looked around for an explanation.

It was Carter who figured it out first. 'Oh you are awfully clever, Rachel,' he said, as understanding spread slowly across his face. 'Tell the gossips and they'll tell the world.'

'Exactly,' Rachel said. 'We tell five of the biggest gossips in the school what Nathaniel's doing, and that their parents might be coming for them next.' She looked at them expectantly but they still didn't get it. She rolled her eyes. 'They'll tell everyone else ... Come *on*, you lot! It's better than Facebook. Everyone will know what's happening by sunset and it won't be traceable.'

As they absorbed this information, the others exchanged looks.

'And what happens then?' Nicole asked the question that was in all their minds.

'Then they can make a choice,' Sylvain said. 'What happens after that is up to them.'

'What could they do, though, really?' Carter asked. 'Run away?'

'They could run away,' Allie said. 'Or they could fight back.'

EİGHTEEN

The next morning, Allie was up and out in the frigid walled garden by six. It was the first real day of pretending everything was normal when nothing was. Her stomach was tight with nervousness and excitement – today they would put their plan into action.

She'd nearly forgotten about detention amid all the excitement, but as they all split up to their respective dorms the night before Carter had called after her, 'See you in the garden, bright and early . . . '

Allie had stopped in her tracks, staring at him in disbelief.

'Seriously? Do you think Isabelle *actually* expects us to stick to detention with all this going on?' She swung her arm around in an irritated gesture.

'Uh . . . yes?' He shot her a look that said he thought she was being dense on purpose. 'You have indefinite detention.

Indefinite. She will not be happy if we just decide not to show up because of the apocalypse we haven't been told about.'

'Fine.' Allie stomped up the stairs after the other girls. 'Because I have nothing better to do.'

'I'm busy too, you know,' he'd called after her but she hadn't looked back.

Clutching a torch, she slipped through the open garden gate. The weather had warmed slightly, and the frozen earth had thawed into a soupy mud. Her head filled with thoughts of spies and Nathaniel, she sloshed through it in search of Mr Ellison.

She found him setting up at the edge of the orchard, whistling tunelessly to himself as he worked.

'My best worker is the earliest one,' he said cheerfully. 'How are you today?'

'Fine.' She stood up straight, trying to look fine.

'That's good,' he said. He carried a massive armload of equipment out of an open shed. 'Makes an improvement. Feel good and others around you will feel good by association.'

Allie didn't notice she'd wrinkled her nose in disbelief until he waved a finger at her. 'It's true. Try it if you don't believe me. You'll see.'

'OK . . . ' Her tone was doubtful.

'You're going to be working in the berry section today.' He handed her a rake and clippers. 'Getting the bushes ready for spring. Follow me and I'll show you what to do.'

They headed back across the dark garden.

'Where's Carter?' Allie asked, jumping over a muddy hillock.

Mr Ellison's brow lowered. 'Late is all I know.'

176

'Oh.'

The gardener was demonstrating how to tell the leafless blueberry branches from the blackberries when the sound of fast heavy footsteps made them both turn.

Before Allie realised what Mr Ellison was doing, he'd moved in front of her wielding a heavy iron hoe in his right hand as lightly as she might hold a pen.

The gardener was very tall, about six foot five, and always had a lumbering gait, but suddenly he seemed capable of great swiftness and grace. Seeing this, Allie felt both awe and despair. Was nobody at Cimmeria what they seemed to be?

Within seconds, though, he'd relaxed and she heard him murmur under his breath, 'What is wrong with you, boy?'

Standing on her toes, she saw Carter pelting it across the mud, his torch flickering on and off weakly.

'Sorry,' he panted, skidding to a stop in front of them. 'I over-slept.'

'Late.' Mr Ellison uttered the word with the same contempt some might use for 'Traitor'.

As Allie watched in astonishment, Carter hung his head. 'I'm sorry, Bob,' he said. 'I can come back later to make up the time.'

'We'll see about that,' the older man muttered. But he seemed mollified by Carter's contrition, and soon he left them working on the berry bushes alone.

After Carter's mood swings the day before, Allie approached him with wariness. She didn't know what was going on in his head – but he couldn't just pick her up and put her down when he wanted to, like a toy. They were either friends or they weren't.

It wasn't easy work – the blackberry thorns were like tiny daggers and the way they worked through gloves and sleeves seemed almost malicious.

'Ouch, you bleeding, bloody, stupid ... *plant*!' Yanking off her glove, Allie examined the dot of blood on her fingertip. 'I am never looking at blackberries in the same way again. They are vicious little bastards.'

'You OK?' Carter, who was gathering pruned branches for burning, glanced over at her with a mixture of concern and amusement.

It was the first time he'd spoken to her directly and Allie looked up at him in surprise but recovered quickly, giving a nonchalant shrug. 'I'll live. I guess nobody was ever thorned to death.'

'As far as we know ... ' he said.

'Maybe it was covered up by the berry industry.'

They exchanged a smile; Allie relaxed a little.

As she pulled the glove back on, she thought about the way Mr Ellison had leapt in front of her a few minutes before. 'Is Mr Ellison Night School?'

Carter's expression darkened. 'Yes and no.' He looked around to make sure the gardener was nowhere near. 'He was once. He went to school here. Studied philosophy at Oxford. Went to work in the City for one of the big banks. Then something happened – something bad.'

Allie tried to imagine Mr Ellison, young and dapper, in a suit. It was almost impossible. She'd never seen him in anything but dark green overalls. Never seen him without dirt on his hands.

Allie stared at Carter, willing him to continue. 'Do you know what happened?'

'All he'll say is that he made a mistake that hurt a lot of people. Whatever it was, it was bad enough that he quit and never went back.' He threw a long branch into the compost pile. 'He'll never forgive himself.'

The story was sobering. The idea that you could make a mistake – just one mistake – and your whole life could be ruined was frightening.

Allie's thoughts drifted back to what was going on here right now. And she wondered if any mistakes of that magnitude were being made. She was fairly certain they were.

'I wonder . . .' she said.

'I think . . .' Carter said at the same time.

They both stopped and chuckled awkwardly.

'Sorry.' Carter waved a twig at her. 'You go first.'

'It was nothing,' Allie said. 'I just wonder if Eloise is OK out in that house by herself. I wonder if she's scared.'

'First of all she's not by herself,' Carter said. 'They'd never leave her alone. She probably wishes she was by herself. And second . . .' He looked at her speculatively as if trying to decide how much to say. 'Don't get too married to the idea of Eloise being innocent just because Nicole thinks she is.'

Allie stared at him, a rising sense of panic tightening the muscles of her throat. 'Wait. Don't tell me you think she's really the spy?'

'I don't know if she is or isn't. I just don't think Nicole's theory proves she's innocent. And I wouldn't assume she didn't do it.'

'Why not?' Allie's voice took on a defensive tone. 'She couldn't have done the chapel thing, right? I mean, not on her own.'

She hadn't realised until he'd taken it away from her how much her belief in Eloise's innocence mattered. She wanted that belief back.

His eyes were as bitter as dark chocolate. 'Nobody around here is really innocent, Allie. Surely you know that by now?'

'I should have known you'd be talking instead of working.'

Mr Ellison's voice cut off Allie's planned response. Looking up, she saw the gardener striding towards them, his green uniform already a bit muddy. Knowing what she now knew about him, she liked him even more somehow. There was something compelling about suffering – something uniting.

I'll talk to Carter later, she thought. *I'll make him see that he's wrong. It's not Eloise. It just isn't.*

Allie endured her classes with barely controlled impatience. None of the Night School instructors showed up to teach. A variety of teachers were shuffled in from other classes to take over and the whole exercise felt slapdash and annoying.

Word had also been passed out that Night School training was temporarily suspended – no explanation was given.

That afternoon, Allie and Rachel stood on the landing of the grand staircase, pretending to chat casually. Suddenly, Rachel straightened. 'Target sighted. Six o'clock. Battle stations.'

'Aye aye, Captain.' Allie followed her gaze. The vivid red of Katie's lush mane of hair made her easy to spot as she paraded up the stairs at the centre of a group of genetically perfect friends.

'What have you heard again?' Allie's voice was unnecessarily loud.

Rachel waited to answer until Katie had nearly reached them. 'Half the kids in the school will go. And nobody knows who. It'll be just like Caroline only times a hundred.'

'That's horrible.' Allie feigned shock. 'What can we do?'

Katie stopped walking so abruptly the girls with her had to backtrack to rejoin her, but she waved them away with an irritated flutter of her fingers.

'Go on. I'll catch you up.'

After a moment's hesitation they walked on. When they were out of earshot she turned to Rachel. 'What were you just saying, geek girl?'

Dropping the pretence, Rachel filled her in on what they knew. As she listened, Katie leaned against the wall, letting her head fall back until it thumped against the carved oak panelling.

'So this is what they're up to.' She looked pale. 'I should have guessed when Caroline left. How could I be so stupid?'

Allie frowned. 'They? Who?'

'My parents. Of course they have a plan. And of course it involves dragging me out of Cimmeria and ruining my life.' Turning to Allie she said, 'I tried to warn you something was coming. That Lucinda was losing it. But you wouldn't listen.'

'Wait,' Allie said. 'Your parents are on Nathaniel's side?'

Katie levelled an exasperated look at her. 'Of course. Don't be ridiculous. Haven't you been paying attention at all?'

Allie ignored the insult. She stepped closer to Katie, looking into her eyes. Challenging her. 'What about you? Are you on his side?'

Her directness seemed to catch Katie off guard; she shook her head so hard her red hair swished. 'No. Never.'

Her response was so passionate, so spontaneous. Allie had to believe her.

'What are you going to do if they send someone for you?' Rachel asked.

For a second, Katie didn't reply. When she did speak, her voice sounded strained. 'I don't know. But they will have to kill me to get me out of here. I'm not going like Caroline.'

'You'd really stand up to your parents like that?' Allie asked, surprised.

Katie's eyes glittered like chips of ice in the winter sun. 'I loathe my parents, Allie. I'm not going anywhere with them. And that slimy creep Nathaniel can kiss my perfect arse.'

Her cut-glass accent made even obscenities sound elegant and funny. It reminded Allie painfully of Jo, and she felt that sudden sense of loss that took her by surprise at the strangest moments, like falling into a hole you couldn't see.

Tilting her head, she studied Katie appraisingly. Maybe she'd misjudged her.

As if aware of Allie's reconsideration of her, Katie turned her haughty gaze back to Rachel.

'What can I do to help, geek girl? Say the word. It's yours.'

NİNETEEN

All the next day the gossips did their work with relentless efficiency. By dinner that night, there was no subject of conversation within Cimmeria Academy except the rumour that parents were pulling their children out of school.

Most of the students had known about Nathaniel already – rumours had been rife for ages about a divide among the school's administrators – but the idea that the division could go this far caused panic.

The elegant dining hall looked the same as it always did – candles glittered on the round tables, crystal sparkled at every place setting, heavy silver cutlery gleamed in the warm glow of the heavy chandeliers – but the mood was ugly.

Once again, none of the senior staff was present. It had been so long since they'd shown up for a formal meal Allie was beginning to wonder if they were starving themselves to death out in the woods. Part of her hoped so.

Across the dining hall two red-faced boys were having a shouting argument, one pounding on a table in rage. Nearby several girls seemed near tears.

Do they even know what's going on here? Do they realise they're losing control?

Although they'd all expected it to happen, no students had been pulled out of school by their parents that day. This fact only made the sense of dread worse. They were all waiting for something horrible to happen.

'What do you think he's doing?' Carter asked. 'If he's really planning to take half the school, why did he just pull one student out and then no more?'

'Perhaps it was a warning,' Nicole said.

'It's his way of telling Isabelle he's serious – and he's giving them a chance to give him what he wants,' Rachel said. 'Like blackmail.'

'He's wasting his time. They'll never do that.' Allie pushed the food around her plate with a desultory fork.

'Especially since they barely seem to have noticed Caroline is gone at all,' Zoe said.

Looking up at her, Allie noticed Jules watching them from a nearby table. She was sitting with Katie and a few other friends, as she had the night before. Her eyes looked hurt, and when she caught Allie's gaze she quickly looked away.

Allie wondered how Carter had explained what was going on. Why he wasn't sitting with her at meals any more. With all that had happened in the last few days, the two of them must barely be seeing each other at all.

'So there's no Night School training tonight ... ' Looking

across the table at Sylvain, Carter didn't appear to notice his girlfriend's expression. He was too focused on the project at hand.

Sylvain seemed to get what Carter was implying – he sat up straighter, his gaze fixed on Carter's.

'Yes,' he said. 'And the weather is clear.'

Some sort of agreement was being made between the two of them.

'What's going on?' Zoe asked.

A knowing smile tugged at Nicole's full lips. 'I think the boys are plotting.'

Sylvain and Carter grinned. Allie wasn't sure she liked this new alliance.

'OK. Here's the thing,' Carter said. 'We've been waiting for the teachers to come back so we can find out what's going on. Sylvain and I have been thinking it's time to go to them. And find out for ourselves.'

'What? We're going to go and find them?' Zoe's face brightened at the idea.

'We're going,' Sylvain said, 'to talk to Eloise.'

'Maybe this isn't such a great idea,' Allie said.

Perched on a bench in the Night School girls' dressing room, she loosened a knot in the laces on her trainers. 'It kind of feels like we're pushing our luck.'

'You *think*?' Rachel's sarcastic voice emerged from a borrowed, thermal top she was struggling to pull over her head. 'Just a little bit?'

'We will be fine.' Nicole pulled on thick, black leggings and reached for her socks. Allie had to admire her cool composure – nothing seemed to intimidate her. 'We will do nothing but look.'

The utilitarian room was painted plain white; the only decoration the shiny brass hooks that lined the walls, each one with a name painted above it in glossy black, and the black clothes beneath. Floor-to-ceiling mirrors lined one wall, making the room seem bigger than it was. It was a familiar place by now to Allie – but she knew Rachel, in all her years at Cimmeria, had never seen it before, because it was Night School only.

When the boys first told them about their idea, they'd all reacted with enthusiasm. If it gave them the chance to find out more about what was really going on, it was worth taking all the chances.

It was only now that they were in the middle of it that Allie's doubt gene kicked in.

They knew that by bringing Rachel into the section of the school reserved solely for the group's secret activities, and dressing her in someone else's Night School gear, they were breaking several of the school's inviolable Rules.

'How can you be so calm about this?' Allie asked Nicole. 'Aren't you worried about getting expelled?'

'I am sorry but if one of the teachers says to me, "You broke The Rules," I will say to them, "Well, where the hell is Eloise? Where the hell is Jo? Where is Ruth?"' Nicole's French accent grew thicker when she was angry. 'Where were you when the school fell apart? And I think that will be the end of that conversation.'

Allie had to admit she had a point. The whole situation was so intensely wrong, what did The Rules matter any more? Was anyone keeping score?

As they talked, Zoe stood in one corner of the dressing room, clad fully in her black Night School gear and kick-boxing the air, chirping with each move, like a small, angry crow.

Allie worried about bringing her, too. She was fast and smart but . . . so young. So small.

Before she could think it through, though, Rachel distracted her.

'This doesn't fit.' She stood in front of a mirror, eyeing herself dubiously; the pilfered top ended in the middle of her midriff, revealing a few inches of latte-coloured skin. 'I'm too tall.'

'Jules is tall like you,' Nicole said, pulling her long hair back into a ponytail. 'Try hers.'

Across the room, Rachel picked up the new black top, weighing it in her hands. Allie, who was wearing one just like it, knew it was light but very warm, made of the kind of material used for ski clothes.

'This is so weird,' Rachel said, pulling off the too-small top and trying on the larger size. 'I can't believe we're doing this.'

Zoe stopped kickboxing to look at her. 'We do this stuff all the time.'

Rachel studied her, a thin line appearing between her brown eyes. 'I know.'

All her life, Rachel had tried to learn nothing about Night School. She'd absorbed a great deal of information because her father was very involved in it but she'd always been resolute about having as little as possible to do with it.

Allie watched soberly as she pulled on the last of her Night School garb – transforming herself from a brainy student into a fighter. Jules was a couple of inches shorter than her, but her gear fit well enough. Like the others, she was now clad entirely in black, with thick leggings and warm running shoes. Her dark curly hair was tucked under a black knitted cap.

It gets us all in the end.

'I look like the Hamburglar,' Rachel grumbled.

'Can we get going?' Standing by the door, Zoe hopped on one foot impatiently until they all, at last, lined up behind her.

Then she flipped out the lights and opened the door.

It was midnight. Curfew began an hour ago.

The basement corridor was dark; they crept along it in absolute silence. Sticking close to Rachel, Allie lit the way with a special torch that emitted a pale blue light – enough to show obstacles in front of them but difficult to detect from a distance. The others didn't need a light – they'd been down this hallway so many times they could do it with their eyes closed.

Raj's guards weren't following their usual schedule so they couldn't be certain when the patrols would pass. But the guards were coming by less frequently than they used to so their chances of getting out unnoticed were good.

The decreasing patrols were worrying: the school leaders must truly believe they'd caught their spy if they were easing back on security.

Just what Nathaniel wanted.

Ahead, Zoe had stopped at the base of a set of stairs, holding up her hand. The others waited as the younger girl darted up to the top. A door swung open without a sound and a wave of cold damp air flowed over them. Steadying herself, Allie inhaled its cool freshness deeply.

She glanced surreptitiously at Rachel; like the others, she stood unmoving, staring at the opening through which Zoe had disappeared. Her nervousness was betrayed only by the fine sheen of sweat on her forehead and the way her hands clenched and unclenched at her sides.

Reaching out, Allie took Rachel's hand and squeezed it. Without looking at her, Rachel squeezed back.

Then Zoe appeared at the top of the stairs and motioned for them to follow.

Allie let go of Rachel's hand.

Ducking low and moving stealthily, the girls ran up the stairs and into the night. As they raced across the lawn, the only sound was the squelching of the cold mud under their shoes and the sound of their breathing.

With each step Allie waited for the shout – for someone to spot them and haul them in. Her muscles were tight with tension as they sped across the flat open ground. But the shout didn't come.

When they made it to the forest, she relaxed a little, falling into line behind Rachel but ahead of Nicole, who brought up the rear. They were safer here, virtually invisible in the dark.

With each step, Allie was reminded of how out of shape she was. How she was still healing. She was glad Rachel's presence gave her an excuse to take it slow. Rachel hated exercise –

Allie could hear how laboured her breathing was. But she kept going.

It took them around ten minutes to reach the edge of the stone wall surrounding the old chapel. Zoe slowed her pace and they followed suit. A few minutes later Allie saw the battered old gate ahead of them – it stood open.

Her heart tripped but she kept running, and reminded herself that this was the plan.

Right on time, two shadows slipped out of the dark churchyard – silent as wraiths. The girls increased their pace.

Allie watched as the Carter shadow sped ahead to join Zoe in the lead. The Sylvain shadow slipped back to the end of the line, joining Nicole.

Zoe and Carter led them past the chapel then turned on to a second path towards the stream. At Zoe's signal, they all crouched low and slowed, moving with absolute quiet.

On one side of the footpath a small stone cottage appeared out of the darkness. This was Mr Ellison's home, and the place where Carter had lived as a child. To Allie it had always looked like a house from a fairy tale, with gingerbread trim and a garden full of lush flowers.

The lights were all off but a faint curl of smoke still hung above the chimney; the gardener had gone to bed, but not long ago.

As they crept by, Allie noticed winter roses growing, pale and unexpected, along the stone wall. She touched one with her black glove as she passed – it seemed too beautiful to be real. Her touch shook raindrops loose from the bush and they pattered on to the ground below.

From out of nowhere, Sylvain grabbed her arm, pulling her away from the wall. Catching her eye he gave her a warning look. Even now, in these circumstances, his blue eyes made her heart stutter. She nodded apologetically and, after a second, he let go, dropping back out of sight.

The second path was narrower and rougher than the main footpath – it had been much less travelled upon. Fallen branches and stones made it treacherous. It slowed them down and made it difficult – if not impossible – to move with stealth.

When they reached a point where the path was blocked completely by a fallen tree, they stopped. Grabbing a branch, Zoe hopped up on to it and over to the other side, light and quick as a squirrel.

Carter followed with more effort. Then, one by one, they helped each other across. After helping Rachel over, Allie grabbed the branch to pull herself up but the movement caused a stabbing pain in her knee. She clutched her leg, willing it to stop.

From below, a warm hand grabbed her arm to steady her and she looked down into Carter's dark eyes.

'You OK?' he whispered.

She nodded and prepared to jump down. But before she could make the leap he grasped her waist and lifted her to the ground. It was exactly the kind of thing he used to do, back when they were friends, and Allie looked up at him in surprise.

Before she could think of the right thing to say though, Nicole jumped off the fallen tree, landing next to them.

'Go,' she hissed, pointing down the path.

Turning, Allie realised the others were already out of sight. The path ahead was empty.

Swearing under his breath, Carter took off into the dark.

Allie followed, but her knee was stiff and painful now and she couldn't keep up the same pace.

Remembering how agile she'd been before the accident – how fast she could run – she hated Nathaniel and Gabe even more. They'd ruined everything.

Rounding a bend, she saw Carter waiting for her ahead. He was holding up a hand in warning. She slowed her pace, trying to disguise her limp.

When she reached him, Nicole and Sylvain were right behind her. Carter pointed to the left. A tiny path disappeared under the trees. He motioned that he would go first and she should follow.

She nodded.

The new path was so small it was hard to see it in the pitch dark – she could just make out Carter ahead of her, moving carefully.

They came to a narrow stream – barely more than a trickle – and he jumped over it.

Saying a silent prayer that her knee could take it, she jumped after him. The soft earth cushioned her landing and her knee held.

Only then did she see the cottage in the distance. It sat on the far side of the pond where last summer they'd all gone skinny-dipping. She hadn't really noticed it then, probably because it was so overgrown it was nearly invisible. Bushes and trees surrounded it – ivy grew up its old stone walls.

She pointed at it and Carter nodded. This was the place.

Keeping a distance from the building, they made their way in a wide circle through the forest until they came to a cluster of bushes on one side. There Allie nearly ran into Rachel, who was huddled next to Zoe in the dark.

Carter hurried over to Zoe and spoke to her briefly, then returned to Allie's side.

Leaning closer, he whispered, 'We're waiting for the guards to leave.'

Allie nodded to show she'd understood, and stared at the little house as if she were trying to see through the walls.

Nicole and Sylvain had joined them now – Sylvain stood next to Zoe behind the cover of a thick pine tree, watching the house intently. Nicole crouched low, beside them.

The sound of a door creaking open echoed in the silent woods, and they all froze. Allie felt exposed – the others had found better hiding places. She'd thought they had more time.

Her heart pounding in her ears, she looked around for more cover but it was too late; if she moved now they might be seen.

There was nothing else to do – so she stood very still. And tried not to breathe.

TWENTY

The two guards made no effort to be quiet. As they emerged from the cottage, Allie could hear their voices clearly across the distance. One of them barked a laugh and it echoed in the quiet like a gunshot.

Next to her, Carter stood watching them with fierce concentration, as if he were willing them to leave. In their hiding place nearby, Nicole had a hand on Rachel's arm. Allie was relieved to see that Rachel's dark eyes were alert and interested – she didn't look afraid.

It seemed to take a lifetime for them to make their way down the footpath. When the guards disappeared into the trees, Allie inhaled deeply and felt the muscles in her shoulders relax.

Somewhere in the distance an owl hooted.

Emerging from her hiding place, Zoe sped silently to

Sylvain's side. After whispering something to him she took off into the forest.

When she'd gone, Allie caught Sylvain's eye and arched her brow questioningly.

'She's going to follow them,' he whispered. 'To make sure they don't double back.'

'You don't think they saw us?' she asked, alarmed.

He shook his head. 'We just need to be sure.'

Sylvain turned to ask Carter a question and Allie crouched down next to Rachel.

'You OK?' she said.

Her eyes sparkling in the moonlight, Rachel nodded. 'That was more exciting than I expected. I can see why you like this stuff. It's exhilarating.'

'Yeah,' Allie said grimly. 'It's ace.'

With a curious frown, Rachel opened her mouth to say something else, but at that moment Zoe appeared hurtling from the woods. They hurried to gather around her.

'They took the main footpath,' she whispered breathlessly. 'They're gone.'

'OK.' Sylvain looked at his watch. 'We should have half an hour before the next patrol.'

'Everyone ready?' Nicole whispered, her eyes sweeping the group.

They had planned it all down to the finest detail, so there was no need to go over it again – everyone knew what to do.

Nicole went first, running low and fast across the clearing until she reached the safety of the cottage, disappearing into the shadows around it.

The others waited, squinting into the darkness until they saw the pale blue light of her torch flash twice. After that they followed her one at a time. First Rachel, then Sylvain, then Allie.

For Allie, the run across the clearing seemed to take for ever – she felt so exposed. Gritting her teeth, she ignored the pain in her knee, forcing herself to run faster than she'd thought she could. Trying not to limp.

It only took seconds.

When she was safely beside the others, leaning against the cold stone of the house, she bent down with her head hanging between her shoulders and struggled to catch her breath. Glancing up, she saw Rachel watching with concern.

'You OK?' she mouthed. Allie nodded, aware of the irony of Rachel worrying about *her*.

When the others had made it across, Zoe led them around the building to the far side where she'd heard Eloise's voice before. A boarded-up window was just above their heads.

Nicole stood on her toes to whisper. 'Eloise?'

They all stopped to listen. There was no reply.

'She could be asleep,' Rachel whispered. 'It's late.'

They hadn't thought of this possibility. As they exchanged blank looks, Allie's heart sank. Had they risked so much for nothing?

Reaching up, Sylvain felt around the edges of the plywood covering the old window.

'Here,' he said, tugging gently at the lower right corner. The wood had been poorly nailed down and it could be pulled out a few inches – far enough for him to slip his hand underneath and tap the glass behind it.

Tap. Tap. Tap.

'Eloise?' he whispered. 'Are you awake?'

Tap. Tap. Tap.

Allie pressed her ear to the wall as if she could hear the librarian through the foot of stone that separated them. Silence.

Sylvain stopped tapping. 'Maybe she's not in there. Perhaps she—'

They all heard it at once, coming from the other side: *Tap. Tap. Tap.*

'It's her!' Zoe hissed. Reaching up, Sylvain tapped their reply.

'Is that you, Eloise?' he whispered.

'Yes.' Her reply was so faint it was hard to believe it was real. Through the walls it sounded ethereal; ghostly.

Her love of Eloise making her forget her concerns, Rachel stepped to Sylvain's side. 'Are you OK?'

A pause. Then, 'Yes.'

Carter leaned towards Sylvain. 'Ask her if she's guarded now.'

'Is someone in the house?' Sylvain asked. 'Guarding you?'

'Yes.'

Allie pictured Eloise standing by the window, whispering to them through the glass, lonely and imprisoned. Someone must be in the next room, keeping watch on her. As if she were a criminal.

Anger rose inside her like white heat.

She turned to Sylvain. 'Ask her if there's some way we can get her out.'

'Can we help you escape?' Sylvain asked. 'Is there ... a way out?'

This time the pause was very long. 'No.'

Allie wanted to weep with futile rage. There had to be *something* they could do.

Rachel turned to Sylvain. 'May I?' He inclined his head and stepped back, holding the plywood up so she could speak to the glass.

'Eloise, we know you didn't do it,' Rachel said. 'Or at least we think you didn't. I mean, you were with Jerry. Is there something we could do from this side to prove you're innocent?'

The silence that followed was so long, Allie wondered if Eloise had been found out – silenced somehow.

Then ... faintly, Eloise spoke again. 'The key.'

Rachel leaned closer to the window. 'What about the key, Eloise?'

'Isabelle's office ... the one I used ... find the key.'

Doubt squeezed Allie's chest like a vice. Why did she want them to find it? Did she expect them to take it so the teachers couldn't find it? To protect her? Was she guilty after all?

Wrapping her arms across her torso, she stared at the ground.

Rachel reached up to the window ledge. 'I don't understand, Eloise. What do you want us to do?'

When the librarian spoke again, Allie got the impression she was crying. Her voice sounded muffled. 'Zelazny gave it to

Jerry and then ... he took it back. I think he ... hid it. Find it. A small, silver key. Give it to Isabelle.'

At her words, Allie's head snapped up. Her eyes met Carter's. She could see the shock in his eyes.

Is Eloise saying Zelazny set her up?

Sylvain stepped closer to the window. 'Why would he do that, Eloise?'

She didn't reply.

Allie felt drained. They'd toyed with the idea of the spy being Zelazny but none of them had truly believed it. If he knew where the key was hidden ...

Anger made her shake.

How could he do that to her? How could he let her be held like this and not say anything?

The only reason for him to do that would be if he had something to hide.

She was so lost in her angry thoughts the faint creaking sound didn't register at first.

Then the front door thudded shut.

Allie's heart seemed to stop. She and the others stared at each other in horror. The moment seemed to stretch on for ever.

Without warning, Carter grabbed Allie's hand and began to run.

It all happened so quickly Allie didn't have time to react. By the time she thought about Rachel it was too late.

Sylvain will help her, she told herself. *He was standing right beside her. Surely he would have grabbed her, knowing she didn't have training.*

She kept trying to look back to see if the others were behind them, but Carter gripped her hand so tightly and moved so quickly through the rough terrain she could see nothing but darkness and blur.

They jumped over the stream and a twig snapped sharply under her foot; she winced and kept going – they didn't have time to be quiet now. They just had to be fast.

Air burned her lungs like fire and each step sent pain jolting through her knee. Carter's pace was relentless; they ignored the branches grabbing roughly at their arms and faces, and the stones that skittered under their feet. They crashed through the dried bracken and winter-dead brush. They must have run half a mile and Allie was just beginning to wonder if she could go much further when they reached a natural dip in the ground, shielded by a fallen tree. Leaping down into it, Carter pulled Allie in after him, down to the forest floor.

Then all was still.

For long minutes they lay without moving. Allie strained her ears to hear footsteps but the woods gave nothing away. A breeze blew through the branches high above them, crashing them together in a low roar.

When the wind finally quietened, the only sound was her heart hammering in her ears and her strained breaths.

They were completely alone.

Slowly her breathing returned to normal and she could pay more attention to where she was. She was aware of Carter's weight – he was almost on top of her, one arm thrown across her shoulders, his head resting in the cold, loamy soil next to hers.

She could feel his chest rise and fall against her with each breath; his body heat cut through the chill emanating from the damp earth.

Slowly, she turned her head to the right – careful not to make a sound – until she could see his face. He lay watching her steadily. She could sense a shuddering tension in his stillness – as if he was waiting for something.

She didn't know how long they lay there, unmoving – just staring at each other and listening for any sign that someone had followed them. At first she counted her breaths but then she lost track. Carter's proximity distracted her. She was hyper-conscious of his hand resting between her shoulderblades. And of the way he was looking at her.

Finally, his hand moved, sliding down to the small of her back.

Why did he do that?

Her breath hitched in her throat.

We are just hiding together, she reminded herself. *Nothing more. He's being kind.*

But his breathing had become more strained; his muscles tensed.

Allie didn't mean to kiss him. Later, she wouldn't even remember how it happened. Just suddenly, somehow, his lips were on hers and she was in his arms.

His lips felt so familiar it hurt her heart. She'd forgotten how good it felt to kiss him. The way he tasted. The feel of his body against hers.

His arms wrapped around her shoulders and she felt instantly warmer – instantly safer. She let herself sink into his embrace as his hands flattened against her spine. He drew her closer.

In his arms, Allie tried to forget everything that had happened – even where they were right now and why they were there. She needed this so much right now. She needed to be wanted. She needed to forget it all and just be the most important thing in someone's life for a few minutes.

But her brain wouldn't let that happen.

She kept remembering Jules' wounded expression when she wasn't invited to join them at dinner. How lost she'd seemed.

Think how much it would hurt her if she knew, a voice in her brain whispered. *How would you feel if you were her?*

The thought of how much pain they'd cause made her stomach churn.

They'd just begun to rebuild their friendship. This could ruin everything between them all over again. How would they act in the school hallway tomorrow? Would they just pretend nothing ever happened?

Dread chilled her. *We can't do this.*

Sensing her hesitation, Carter stopped kissing her. Leaning on one elbow next to her, he studied her sombrely. She could see her own confusion reflected in his dark eyes.

'I'm sorry,' he said. 'I just ... '

'I know.' She tried to think of something to say to make it all better but her mind was blank. Things used to be so easy between them. Now every single thing was complicated. 'It's not your fault. I'm sorry, too.'

'I guess I just ... missed you,' Carter said. 'And sometimes I ... '

His voice trailed off.

'I've missed you, too,' Allie said, her voice very small. 'I just wish ... this was easier.'

For a long second he held her gaze. Then he rolled over on to his back and stared up at the stars, one arm flung across his forehead as if to block some invisible glare. 'I know.'

Nobody teaches you how to do this. Nobody ever says to you, 'This is how you can break up and still be friends.' Or, 'Here's how to break up and not want to kiss your ex sometimes.'

It would be, basically, the most helpful advice in the world and it doesn't exist.

Sitting up, Allie pulled her knees close to her and wrapped her arms around them, staring off into the night.

Then, as if he'd made up his mind about something, Carter sat up and turned to face her. 'Look. There's something I have to say to you. And I wanted to say it a long time ago but I bottled it. I think I have to say it now.' His voice was taut with emotion and Allie looked over at him in surprise. 'It's just ... I am so sorry for the way I treated you when we were together. I know I blew it.'

Tears burned the backs of Allie's eyes but she didn't lower her gaze.

'At first I was jealous and acted like a dick. Then I was angry and that was even worse.' He ran his fingers through his tangled dark hair. 'I know I hurt you and I'm truly sorry.'

Something inside Allie's chest that had been holding tight for a very long time let go.

203

Whatever she'd expected to happen tonight, it wasn't this. With her lips still bruised from the force of their kiss, how could she tell him how much their breakup had hurt her? She didn't know how to describe the empty feeling of watching him together with Jules in those early days. Or the loneliness when he ignored her.

The problem was he'd just said everything she wanted to hear . . . four months ago. And now it was too late. She'd gone through the loss, through the pain, through the turmoil: and she'd survived.

She didn't want to go back.

But she couldn't say that right now. What she could do was try and fix whatever damage they'd just done to their own friendship, and to Jules. She could put this right.

'Thank you for saying that. It helps.' Her voice was surprisingly steady but in her lap she clenched her hands so tightly her nails carved crescent-shaped dents into her palms. 'But I shouldn't have kissed you tonight, Carter. It was wrong. You're with Jules now. She would be so hurt if she knew. She can't ever find out. I promise you I'll—'

Abruptly, he climbed to his feet and strode across the clearing where he stood with his back to her.

Allie's stomach dropped. Wondering if she'd gone too far, she scrambled to her feet. 'Carter, look . . . I'm sorry. I didn't mean to—'

'Don't do that,' he said, cutting her off. 'It's something you do, you know – apologising for things that aren't your fault.' She couldn't see his eyes in the darkness. 'You should never apologise for being right.'

Straightening his shoulders, he pointed north. 'We'd better get back. They'll be waiting for us.'

Without waiting for her response, he strode off into the darkness.

When they walked through the door of the Night School girls' dressing room twenty minutes later, the reaction was instant.

'Where have you *been*?' Jumping to her feet, Zoe ran across the room to hug her. The move was so unexpected Allie hesitated briefly before hugging her back.

Zoe never hugged anyone. Like, ever.

And yet the younger girl squeezed her tight. 'We've been waiting ages. We thought you'd been caught. Or ... something.'

Over her shoulder, Allie looked around the room, relieved to see Rachel sitting nearby. Everyone had made it back – she and Carter were the last to return.

'I'm sorry we scared you ...' she said, flustered. 'We ... uh ... hid for a long time to make sure ... it was, like ... safe.'

'You have a leaf in your hair.' Zoe observed as she released her.

Flushing, Allie hurried to pull the dried leaf loose from a tangle of dark hair and dropped it on the floor. Across the room Rachel gave her a searching look.

They'd all agreed in advance to meet back here if they became separated – it was one of few rooms in the school never checked by Patel's guards. Still, it was weird seeing the boys here.

'So, in the end, it was a success.' Sylvain's voice came from the corner and Allie turned to see him sitting on a low bench, his long legs stretched out in front of him. Meeting her gaze, he arched one sardonic eyebrow and she flushed, turning away. It was as if he knew, somehow, what had happened.

She and Carter had barely spoken on the walk back, making their way through the dark woods in near silence. Unfamiliar with this section of the grounds, Allie wasn't sure where they were but, even though they had to stay off the footpaths, Carter's unerring sense of direction led them straight to the school building.

'Depends on how you look at it,' Carter said now, leaning against the wall, his arms loosely crossed in front of him. Allie was sure he was avoiding her gaze – he seemed to look everywhere except at her. 'No one got caught but we haven't learned very much.'

'I don't want to say this but ... some of the things Eloise said sounded strange to me,' Nicole said. 'She didn't make sense.'

Her words yanked Allie out of her inner turmoil and forced her to focus on what really mattered – catching the spy. Jo. Because Nicole was right. Eloise had been oddly vague and unhelpful – even when her own fate hinged on their ability to help her. She hadn't sounded innocent.

'I thought that, too,' Rachel said, exchanging a despairing glance with the French girl.

A palpable sense of gloom settled over the room. Only Zoe still seemed to have hope.

'But we haven't tried yet,' she said. 'To find the key, I mean.'

'Allie, what do you think about this key?' Nicole looked up at her. 'Do you believe Eloise?'

Allie rubbed the back of her hand across her forehead – her

skin felt gritty. 'I don't know if I believe her or not. I know there is a key — I saw it. But as to where she got it or what she did with it . . . what she said sounded weird. Like she was protecting someone. Besides, if she's not the spy, and Zelazny's the one who gave her the key, and he hasn't told anyone that then . . . '

'Then that would mean Zelazny is the spy.' Sylvain finished the sentence for her.

He'd always been close to Zelazny, and Allie could see how much it hurt him to say that. It must be awful to think that his mentor could have fooled him the entire time. That he might actually be his enemy.

'I think,' Rachel said, 'we need to be very careful right now. Because, at the moment, we have good reasons to be suspicious of pretty much everyone.'

TWENTY-ONE

*T*he cold struck her first, then the wind. It must have picked up while she was walking. She didn't remember it picking up. But suddenly it was howling, crashing the branches together above her head until they roared like the sea, and nearly knocking her down with its sheer force.

Trying to get her bearings, Allie turned in a slow circle.

Where was she? She'd been running for so long she'd lost track of where she was going. Who she was looking for.

'Allie.' That was Sylvain's voice, his distinctive French accent making her name sound like a sigh, a caress.

But she couldn't see anyone in the dark. There was no moon – the trees were shadows against shadows. The night felt dark and ominous – it had a weight to it that seemed to press down on her, making it hard to breathe.

'Sylvain? Where are you?' She craned her neck but saw noth-ing – nothing but trees.

'Why did you do it?'

A sob shook her and she covered her mouth with her hand – he sounded so sad. Did he know she'd kissed Carter? How did he find out? They hadn't told anyone. They could never tell.

'Do what? I didn't do anything.' Her words were insistent but she could hear the lie in her own voice and she knew he must hear it, too.

'Why weren't you looking out for Jo?' Sylvain's voice sounded condemning. 'She trusted you. I trusted you.'

Tears were streaming down her face now. She needed to see him. If she could see his face she could convince him that nothing happened. Nothing at all.

'You can trust me,' she insisted. 'Jo can trust me. I won't let her down.'

His reply was cold.

'But Jo is already dead.'

It was Allie's own scream that ended the dream; her own strangled voice.

She must have been crying in her sleep; her pillow was wet from her tears. And she sobbed again now as memories of last night returned to her in a flood.

Why did I kiss Carter? Why did I do that? I've ruined everything. Why am I this person?

First she'd failed Jo, then she'd ruined her friendship with Carter *again*. She couldn't remember ever hating herself so much; she shook from it.

Without warning, her door sprang open and Rachel stood

there, her hair wild from sleep, her face pale with fear that quickly transmuted into concern.

'*Allie?* What happened? I heard you scream.' Seeing Allie's face, she ran across the room, kneeling beside her bed and pulling her into a rough hug. 'Are you OK? Was it another one of those dreams?'

Still sobbing, Allie nodded against her shoulder. 'I'm so sad, Rach. So sad. And I've done everything wrong and you can't undo it. Once you've done it you can't make it go away and I hate that.'

'Oh, sweetie,' Rachel's tone was soothing. 'You haven't done anything wrong, I promise. You haven't. There's nothing you need to undo.'

But that wasn't true at all.

'I didn't save Jo,' Allie whispered. 'And now I kissed Carter.'

For just a second, Rachel's hand stopped stroking her back then she resumed the calming motion.

'OK, first, you did everything you could to save Jo. *Nobody* could've saved her. Even God couldn't save her. What happened to her was not your fault.'

Allie didn't believe her at all but she wanted to.

'Now.' Rachel pulled tissues from a box on a nearby shelf and handed them to her. 'Why don't I get you some water and then you can tell me about kissing Carter.'

After she returned with a glass, they sat on the bed together, Allie clutching a handful of damp tissues in one hand and the water in the other, hiccupping as the tears slowed and then stopped. Brokenly, she told her what had happened that night in the forest.

'And how did he react?' Rachel asked, pulling a blanket over her knees.

'Like it was a mistake.' Allie held up her tissue hand as if to say *What else?*

'Do *you* think it was a mistake? I mean, do you still fancy him?'

'No . . . I don't know.' Allie sighed. 'I'm just confused. I mean, when you were with someone and you thought that you . . . loved him, I guess . . . how do you just say, "Oh, I don't love you any more." Just like that? I miss being with him, and being friends with him, and I wish we didn't have all this "formerly loving each other" thing hanging over our heads. But I can't make it go away and when I'm alone with him it all gets muddled up sometimes.'

'So . . . I think what you're saying is you want to be his friend again.'

Allie paused to consider this. 'I . . . guess so.'

'Because I've got this theory.' Rachel smiled and it seemed to warm the room. 'Do you want to hear my theory?'

Nodding, Allie snuggled closer to her. She was beginning to believe Rachel could actually make this better.

'I think that when we have a friend we love – like you and I love each other, right? Well, if that friend is the same gender, it's super simple. You and I are not gay, and we love each other so . . . boom. We're best friends.' Allie agreed cautiously as Rachel continued. 'But what if I was a bloke and you were my friend and we loved each other? It might get all confused. And if there was a lot going on and things were really emotional and dangerous, maybe your feelings of love for me could be misconstrued as romantic love. Then you might want to be my girlfriend and then it's all tangled up.' She leaned back to see Allie's face more clearly. 'I think what I'm saying is, it's easy to confuse friendship love for romance love when your friend is a guy. And that's why you're confused.'

Allie shredded a tissue into tiny pieces as she thought this through. If true, it could explain how torn she'd always been between Carter and Sylvain. Maybe she had friendship love for Carter and romantic love for Sylvain. But how could she tell?

'So you think I have friendship love for Carter?' she asked, with a hopeful look.

Rachel hesitated. 'I don't know,' she admitted. 'I can't know that. Only you can know that. But I know that you can love Carter and not be *in love* with him. And maybe, especially while he's with Jules, you need to consider that.'

At the mention of Jules, Allie winced. She didn't like the prefect, but cheating with her boyfriend was not anything she'd ever intended to do.

'What should I do now?' she asked with dull resignation. 'I have to make this right somehow. I didn't mean to be a cheater. And I can't lose Carter again. I just can't.'

'Well . . .' Rachel yawned and glanced at the clock on Allie's desk. It was nearly five in the morning. 'I think you need to talk this through with him and clear the air between you. And tell him that. Tell him you just want to be his friend, at least as long as he has a girlfriend. Then you have some time to figure out which kind of love you feel for him.'

'But how will I know?' Allie's voice was plaintive. 'How do you know which kind of love it is?'

'Oh yeah. That?' Rachel lay down next to her on the bed and pulled the duvet up over them both. 'That's the tricky part.'

School the next day was torturous. Classes seemed to drag on beyond any reasonable linear timespan. Allie, whose sleep had been shallow after her nightmare, even with Rachel beside her to keep her steady, struggled to stay awake as the dull replacement teachers droned through the day's text.

In English and history – the two classes they had together – Carter kept his distance, never once meeting her gaze.

Once, when she passed Jules in the hallway, guilt made her panic and she turned into the nearest classroom, colliding so violently with a teacher coming the other way that his papers went flying.

At lunchtime the group gathered to whisper through their plans. Although she sat between Rachel and Zoe, just being at the same table with both Carter and Sylvain made Allie's stomach flip, and she couldn't bring herself to eat. Instead she methodically vivisected a sandwich.

Jules sat at a nearby table with Lucas and some of her friends. Allie tried not to look at her, but her conscience drew her gaze inexorably in that direction and she kept catching glimpses of the blonde prefect talking and eating her soup.

Across the table, Carter talked intently with Nicole and Rachel. The shadows under his eyes were the only indication that he hadn't slept well last night either.

Two seats over, Sylvain was also listening to their conversation, his brow knitted with concentration. His long fingers toyed absently with his knife, flipping it end over end. Allie found it hard to take her eyes off it – his hands were gentle and skilful; the silver caught the afternoon light and flashed.

Abruptly, the knife stopped moving. Allie looked up to find him watching her. His expression was enigmatic – his eyes the cool blue of still water.

Her heart skipped a beat and she wrenched her gaze away.

Only then did she realise the others were looking at her expectantly.

'What?' Her tone was more defensive than she'd intended and she tried to lower it. 'I mean, did someone ... say something?'

'I said –' Rachel gave her an odd look – 'what do you think?'

'About what?'

'About the *plan*.' Nicole looked from Allie to Sylvain and back again, as if she suspected something had transpired between them. 'Do you think it's a good idea?'

'Sorry,' Allie said, flushing. 'I couldn't sleep last night. My head's not in the game. Please go over it again; I promise to focus.'

Carter gave an exasperated sigh. 'Right. I'll explain it again.' For the first time in nearly twelve hours he met her gaze directly. But his eyes weren't warm. 'Tonight we need to divide up the work. Nicole and I will search Eloise's room. Zoe and Rachel will search Zelazny's classroom.' He glanced from her to Sylvain, a small frown creasing his brow. 'You and Sylvain will search Zelazny's room – Sylvain knows where it is.'

Her throat tightening, Allie forced herself to nod calmly, but her heart was racing.

Some teachers lived in cottages on the grounds, but most lived in a separate wing of the main building. Allie had never been in it. Entering the teachers' wing was absolutely forbidden – only prefects were allowed, and even then they had to have a very good reason.

The others were all looking at her expectantly, waiting to hear what she thought of their plan, which fairly thoroughly broke any of The Rules they'd forgotten to break last night.

She squared her shoulders.

'Sounds great. I'm in.'

TWENTY-TWO

T hat night, in the shadows at the back of the library, Allie paced impatiently. Sylvain was ten minutes late. She was sure she was in the right place – he'd been quite specific, and the nine-foot-tall bookcases surrounding her held only old, leather-bound books written in French. Bored, she let her fingertips glide over the thick bindings with their gold-embossed names of writers like Laclos and Langelois.

Then, with a sigh, she glanced at her watch again.

'Come on, Sylvain,' she muttered.

A rolling ladder leaned against the tall bookcases so readers could reach the higher shelves and she climbed up a few steps to perch on a rung, letting one foot swing.

Even though worry was making her tense, the lack of sleep last night was taking a toll on her. Her eyes felt heavy. Resting her chin on her hand she let them drift shut. The darkness was welcome and soon she was dozing, her dreams filled with incoherent flashes of running and forests and a voice.

Wake up, Allie.

It was a familiar voice – one she liked. And for a second she kept her eyes shut, wishing it would say more. But it didn't.

Slowly, her eyes fluttered open.

Sylvain was on the ladder now, too, balancing on one foot so that his face was even with hers. She blinked sleepily into his eyes, sapphire blue in the dim light.

'Hey,' she murmured. Her thoughts were still fuzzy – the moment felt unreal; dream-like. She hadn't been this close to him since the winter ball. She could feel the warmth of his leg against hers, smell his distinctive cologne. 'I must have fallen asleep.'

'I'm sorry I'm late,' he said. For a second he stayed where he was, his face so close she could see flecks of violet in the blue of his eyes. Then he jumped down to the floor in a graceful, athletic move. 'I was delayed by one of the guards who wanted to ask me a million questions about whether I knew if someone had left the school building after curfew last night.'

'*What?*' Instantly wide awake, Allie leaned forward to see him better. 'Do they know it was us?'

Sylvain shook his head. 'They don't know who it was. But they know someone was there. We must be very careful now.'

The prospect of danger seemed to excite him – the colour was high in his cheeks and he bounced on the balls of his feet as if he had too much energy to simply stand still. A curl had escaped from his wavy hair and tumbled forward over his brow.

Seeing it reminded Allie of how she'd felt the first time she'd run her fingers through Sylvain's hair – the thrill of the forbidden. And the effect it had had on him. The way his arms had tightened around her waist; how he'd pressed his lips more firmly against hers.

It had all felt so different from kissing Carter.

So was that romantic love? She asked herself now, hopelessly. *Or the other kind?*

Climbing down from the ladder, she stretched her arms above her head trying to wake up her muscles. 'Cool. I'm ready when you are.'

Watching her, he gave a bittersweet smile. 'I wish that were true.' Then he pivoted and headed down the aisle of books. 'Come on. We should go.'

Dropping her arms, Allie rushed after him so hurriedly she stumbled over a stack of books someone had left at the end of the aisle.

'Here's your hat; what's your hurry . . . ' she muttered.

'What did you say?' Sylvain shot her an inquisitive look.

'Nothing.' Allie shrugged. 'I was just quoting a line from a film I like.'

'Do you like films?' He looked genuinely pleased at the idea. 'Which is your favourite?'

As always happened whenever someone asked her favourite book or film, Allie's mind went blank – it was as if she'd never seen a film in her life. Everyone was always trying to impress everyone else with their great taste. So it took her a second to realise she'd just quoted a line from one of her favourite movies.

'I like *It's a Wonderful Life*,' she said. 'I mean, I used to watch it with my family every Christmas before . . . I mean . . . It's pretty good, I guess.'

What she meant was, she used to watch the film back when she was happy. Before Christopher ran away and her world fell apart.

He looked at her seriously. 'I think it is an amazing film – one of my favourites. I love Jimmy Stewart.' His accent made the name sound adorable – 'Jeemee'. They'd made it to the door and he held it open for her as he warmed to the topic. 'I love films – when I'm at home I'm constantly watching movies – I particularly like old movies in black and white. They seem better than modern films, although I don't know why.' He cast a sideways glance at her. 'Have you seen *Jules et Jim*?'

Mutely, Allie shook her head. It sounded French and sophisticated. Of course her parents wouldn't have had that around.

'It is by François Truffaut, a great French filmmaker – I think perhaps the best ever,' Sylvain said as they stepped into the grand hallway. It was quiet at this hour and the polished oak panelling shone in the low light. 'You remind me, sometimes, of the actress in it. Your hair . . . other things . . .'

His words made warmth bloom in Allie's chest, uninvited. It was nice being compared to a French actress who was probably beautiful and mysterious as French actresses always were. The casual conversation served to distract her from worrying about the work ahead of them and she wondered if Sylvain had brought it up on purpose. It struck her that no one at Cimmeria ever talked about ordinary things any more. It was always Nathaniel, Jo, Isabelle, Lucinda, death. It felt almost odd to discuss something normal people talked about.

'I'll have to watch it,' she said. 'If you love it so much, it must be good.'

Jules et Jim, Allie said to herself, trying to memorise it. *Jules et Jim, Jules et Jim, Jules* . . .

'Maybe we will watch it together some day,' he said and gave her one of those Sylvain smiles that made her feel like no one else existed in the world except the two of them.

'Now, we should go this way.' Reaching for her hand, Sylvain pulled her with him to where the hall broadened to hold several classical marble statues. They ducked behind a wide plinth where they couldn't be seen by anyone passing through. The entrance to the staff residence wing was just a few feet away.

Crouched behind Sylvain, Allie studied him curiously. His breathing was even but his muscles were tense – she could see the tendons in his neck, raised in relief under the smoothness of his tawny skin. His tension was contagious, and she could feel her own breaths shorten. As if he'd noticed this, he glanced over his shoulder at her.

'Are you ready?'

Allie nodded. 'Yes.'

He stood, and she stood with him. 'Now.'

Moving silently, they ran across the empty hall to the door. Unlocking it with a key, he let Allie slip through first, running in after her and closing the door behind them.

On the other side, the corridor was dark. As Allie's eyes adjusted she could just make out heavy oak beams and carved wood. This must be the older part of the building. On either side, the hallway was lined with widely spaced doors, each with a number on it. These were the teachers' apartments.

They moved quickly down the hallway, walking in sync. Out of the corner of her eye, Allie noticed Sylvain was holding himself oddly. His biceps bulged as if he expected a fight; his hands were in fists at his sides. He was nervous.

The realisation sent adrenaline rushing into her veins. Sylvain was never nervous.

They were nearly at the end of the corridor when he held out his hand to stop her. Looking up and down the hall to make sure no one saw them, he stepped to the door marked with the numbers '181'.

He caught her eye. Each of them knew how much was at risk.

Allie kept her expression calm. She nodded her head.

Sylvain turned the handle.

TWENTY-THREE

The door wasn't locked. As it swung open, Allie could see only darkness ahead – hear only silence.

Holding up his hand to indicate that she should wait, Sylvain slipped inside.

Seconds later he returned and silently motioned for her to follow. Taking a steadying breath, she walked into Zelazny's room.

When the door closed the room was utterly dark. Allie stood still, afraid to move.

'Sylvain?' she whispered after a moment.

'I'm here.' His reply was muffled. She could hear the soft swish of his hands against the walls and realised he must be feeling for a light switch. Almost as soon as she thought it, the room was flooded with light. After the dimness, Allie had to shield her eyes.

'Blinding,' she said.

'Only for a second.'

Through the cracks between her fingers, she squinted into the glare. Sylvain stood near the door, watching her with a quizzical half-smile, as if she'd done something amusing. His earlier tension had disappeared.

They were in an orderly room with a leather sofa and a low chair with a padded seat and wooden arms. A television and DVD player stood in the corner near a fireplace. The walls were painted a matte, masculine shade of grey with a clean white trim. Turning a slow circle she took in the bookcases lining one wall and a door leading into another room, which must be the bedroom.

'It's so small.'

'It's not so bad.' Sylvain still stood with his back against the wall, looking around as if deciding where to start. 'Why don't you start with the bookshelves,' he said. 'I'll take the desk.'

Zelazny's bookshelves stood above low wooden cabinets and stretched all the way to the ceiling. Most of the books they held seemed to be about the military – *Battles of Britain*, *The Gathering Storm*, something that looked philosophical called *The Seven Pillars of Wisdom*.

Their dull navy and grey covers were rough beneath her fingertips. Their smell of ink and aged paper filled her nostrils.

With no clue how to really search, she felt around the edges and behind them for anything that might be tucked away. But they were just books. On a shelf.

She glanced over to where Sylvain rifled through the papers on the desk. 'Am I just looking for the key?'

'That is the main thing. But if you see anything odd or suspicious that would be good, too.'

Odd or suspicious? Like what? A gun with smoke rising from the barrel? A knife with blood on it? A pamphlet called How to Destroy Cimmeria Academy: A Rogue's Guide?

But now wasn't the time for sarcasm. She tilted books forward to look behind them, and dragged a chair over to climb on so she could see the higher shelves.

They'd been looking for quite a while in silence when Sylvain said, 'What happened with you and Carter last night?'

On top of the chair Allie wobbled, nearly dropping a book about the life of Winston Churchill. Catching it at the last second, she placed it carefully back on the shelf.

'Nothing,' she said, keeping her face expressionless. When he shot her a dubious look she held up her hands. 'It was just like we said: we hid out for a while in the woods until we were sure it was safe. Then we came back. Why do you ask?'

His eyed her speculatively.

'You were gone too long. Your hair was rumpled in that way –' he gestured vaguely with his hand. 'You seemed unhappy. You didn't look at him and he didn't look at you.' He picked up a stack of papers. 'Something happened.'

For a fleeting second, Allie imagined telling him the truth. *I kissed him. And he kissed me back. But it felt wrong and we were both sorry and now we're not talking and if Jules finds out I'll hate myself for ever. I think I only friendship-love him anyway. Whatever that is. And I'm not sure how I feel about you and I kind of wish you'd kiss me, too, so I could decide.*

Instead, she picked up another book and flipped through the pages.

'Don't be silly,' she said, although her voice sounded odd.

'Nothing happened. Carter just wanted to be sure it was safe before we headed back. You know how he is.'

'Yes,' Sylvain said dryly. 'I know how Carter is.'

Allie's head jerked up as she looked over at him, wobbling on her unsteady chair. 'What does that mean?'

Without looking up, Sylvain threw her own word back at her. 'Nothing.'

For a long few minutes the only sound in the room was the flipping of pages and the sliding sound the books made when she placed them back on the shelves. Sylvain asked no more questions but, for some reason, Allie wanted him to know she wasn't back together with Carter again.

But how do you even say that?

'Look,' she said finally. 'Carter and I are friends. Or at least, we're trying to be. That's it. He's with Jules. He ... cares about her.'

Across the room Sylvain set down a stack of papers. His gaze was piercing but he said nothing – he just let her talk.

'Being friends is just kind of ... hard after being ... other things,' she admitted. 'And last night we ... talked about it. It was fine.'

'If it was fine, why aren't you speaking to each other now?'
So he noticed that, too.

Allie flushed scarlet. 'Like I said. It's hard.'

Her words were flat and his eyes flashed to her searchingly but she wasn't about to say any more. She'd been as honest as she could be – she'd never betray Carter's trust in her.

It was time to change the subject.

'What's with you two anyway?' she said, pulling another

book off the shelf. 'You used to hate each other. Now you work together. You're almost *nice* to each other.'

Apparently unbothered by her question, Sylvain pulled a slim metal pin out of his pocket and began working the lock on a desk drawer. 'After what happened to you and Jo ... we talked. We decided it was time to stop fighting with each other, and to focus on Nathaniel. It has worked well.' The lock clicked open. 'We train together now.'

Allie nearly fell off the chair. 'You *don't*.'

'We do.' Seeing her disbelieving expression, he smiled. 'He is very good – very strong. I am more agile of course but ... he's not bad.'

'That ... is amazing.' She tried to imagine the conversation when they set aside six years of enmity. It was impossible.

Reaching the end of the bookcases, she climbed down from her chair, wiping her hands on the blue wool of her skirt. 'There's nothing here. Just really boring books.'

Sylvain was crouched low, trying another lock with his pick. He pointed at the door leading into the adjacent room. 'His bedroom's through there. Check the bedside tables.'

Allie made a face.

Zelazny's bedroom, she thought, revolted. *Gross.*

With slow reluctance she moved through the doorway and felt along the walls. The switch was cold under her fingers. Light flooded the small bedroom. It was painted the same shade as the sitting room – she had to admit it was a soothing colour.

On one wall was a double bed, covered in a dark blue blanket tucked in with perfect, square corners. Not a speck of dust could be seen anywhere.

'You could eat off this room,' she murmured to herself.

'What?' Sylvain called.

'Nothing.'

A table with two drawers, topped with a small brass lamp, sat to the right of the bed. Allie approached it as she might a viper. Steeling herself, she reached out for the top drawer, although every fibre of her being rebelled against the idea of opening it.

In her head she repeated a mantra over and over again: *Please don't let there be porn. Please don't let there be porn. Please don't ...*

It slid open silently to reveal a pair of wire-framed reading glasses, a pencil sharpened to a fine point, two books of crossword puzzles and one of sudoku.

Nothing useful but also, thank God, nothing creepy.

Just as she was about to close the drawer, two weird, pinkish plastic lumps caught her eye. She peered at them with unconcealed disgust before realising what they were.

Earplugs.

'Grim,' she whispered, slamming the drawer shut.

Having found nothing vile in the first drawer, it was easier to make herself open the second. A book entitled *Conflict and Resolution* sat on top, and she pulled it out to see underneath.

Beneath it was a notepad and pen, a CD, a small box of tissues and a jar of ointment.

Allie refused to look too closely at the ointment.

'There's nothing here,' she called out.

'Look under the bed,' he replied.

'Awesome,' she muttered.

Sighing heavily, she climbed down on to her hands and knees to peek underneath the pine bed frame. Clean as a whistle. There was nothing there but a suitcase and a cardboard box.

She pulled the suitcase out first to find it empty. Methodically, she checked all the pockets, finding nothing.

As she worked, she thought about what Sylvain had said. How easily he'd seen through her attempt at normality after what happened in the woods. And she thought with guilt about how she'd treated him since Jo's death – as if he were a problem she didn't have time to solve. In many ways, she'd treated him the way Carter had treated her.

The realisation made her stop in the middle of closing the suitcase. Turning, she stared over her shoulder at the open doorway behind her. Through it, she could hear the sound of Sylvain shuffling through the contents of the desk drawers. She could envision his quick, intelligent movements as he searched for signs that his mentor had helped a murderer.

The floor felt cold beneath her as she shoved the suitcase slowly back into its hiding spot.

Ever since Jo's death, she'd tried so hard not to feel anything. But now it was as if when Carter kissed her it opened a door she'd been pressing shut with all her strength. She was flooded with confusing feelings.

Sylvain was a complicated person, and they had a messed-up history, but he'd never once stopped caring about her. Never given up on her and found someone else. Never pressured her. She'd ignored him for weeks but still he'd waited for her. Been patient with her. He had been ... constant.

'Have you found anything?'

Sylvain's voice made Allie jump guiltily, as if he might know she was thinking about him.

'Nothing yet.'

The only other object under the bed was a cardboard box, and she pulled it now. The lid wasn't sealed, and it appeared well used, as if the box had been looked through many times.

It seemed to hold mostly keepsakes and records. There were some old bank statements – she studiously didn't read those – and a few bills and letters addressed to 'Mr August S. Zelazny'. (*What's the S for?*)

A book at the bottom caught her eye and she pulled it out. It was pale blue and white. The title read 'Your Baby Book'.

Frowning, she opened it to find a picture of a tiny red newborn, his face screwed up in protest. Above the picture was the cheery heading 'Your first photo shoot!'

The baby's name was filled in below it. Arnold August Zelazny. The birthdate was fifteen years ago.

Zelazny has a son? She read it again, puzzled. He'd never mentioned a child. And he was clearly not married now.

She turned the page. There was a photo of a younger, smiling Zelazny, hardly looking like himself. He had more hair, a dimple in his chin. He looked relaxed and . . . joyful. With him was a smiling brunette, her hair in slight disarray, as if she'd just been in bed. Between them they held the baby carefully, as if he were made of the most delicate glass.

Allie stared at the photo in dismay.

What happened? she wondered, her fingers lingering on the

edge of the page. The thick paper was slick beneath her fingers – designed to last for ever.

She had a horrible suspicion that something dreadful had occurred. Babies don't just *disappear* from your life.

She turned the pages to find more photos of the baby. Growing hair. Smiling with tiny teeth. Dates when he took his first steps, said his first words. Cards from his first birthday party.

Then it ended.

With deliberate thoroughness she looked through the rest of the box but there was nothing else there about the child. It was as if his whole life was contained in that book.

Arnold Zelazny: What happened to you?

Carefully, she put everything back, and returned the box to its hiding place.

Sylvain appeared in the door. 'There is nothing in the desk. Have you found anything?'

She shook her head. 'Nothing.'

He looked relieved and she didn't blame him. Maybe it wasn't Zelazny after all.

He motioned for her to follow him. 'We should go then. This is a waste of time.'

Standing, she turned to follow him. As she did, she noticed *Conflict and Resolution* still sitting on top of the bedside table – she'd forgotten to put it away.

'Just a second,' she called after Sylvain. Opening the bottom drawer, she grabbed the book hurriedly to put it away. But as she lifted it something slipped from the pages and fell, hitting the wooden floor with a metallic jangle.

Instantly alert, Sylvain returned to her side. 'What it is?'

Leaning down they both saw the small silver key gleaming against the dark floorboards.

'Oh no,' Allie whispered.

By the time they left Zelazny's rooms it was after curfew. They'd put everything back precisely as it had been except for the key, which was tucked in the pocket of Allie's skirt.

When everything was ready, Sylvain turned out the lights then stood with his ear pressed against the door, waiting for silence. After a moment, he pulled the door open a crack and peered out – the hallway was empty.

Silent as ghosts, they slipped into the long corridor.

They walked with purpose and speed but the door at the end of the corridor seemed a very long way away to Allie and she focused her gaze on it, willing it to come closer.

It seemed impossible to believe the spy was Zelazny. She still reeled from the idea. The key felt hot in her pocket, where she gripped it tightly in one hand. Zelazny helped to kill Jo? Zelazny, who was always trying to keep the school safe, keep Isabelle safe, who wanted everyone to follow all The Rules? Zelazny with his disappearing family and his neat-as-a-pin apartment ... he helped to kill people for Nathaniel?

It didn't seem possible. And yet ... there was the key.

Still, lots of people had keys. There was only one way to know if this was the right key and they were on their way to find out. First, though, they needed to get out of the staff wing without being seen. It wouldn't be at all unusual for a teacher to enter the residential wing at this hour. They could very easily be caught. And on this long, straight corridor there was nowhere to hide.

Forty steps, forty-one, forty-two . . .

They were close to the end when they heard the unmistakeable sound of a door opening behind them. But neither of them flinched.

Without looking right or left, they walked with confidence, in perfect sync.

Whoever opened the door didn't seem to notice them – no one called for them to stop.

Ten steps later they were at the door and through it. They'd made it out.

They slipped past the marble statues and down the broad, empty hallway. All the students were in the dorms now. Most of the lights had been turned off. In the dimness they moved like two shadows across the polished oak floors.

They didn't stop until they reached Isabelle's office.

Standing in front of the familiar carved door – looking like any two students at any school in front of any headmistress's door – they knocked and waited. When nobody answered, they exchanged a glance.

Allie pulled the small, innocuous-looking key from her pocket, and with a steady hand slid it into the lock. It turned smoothly. They both heard the lock click as it gave.

Turning his head away, Sylvain bit his lip. Allie could sense his bitter disappointment. He'd really believed in Zelazny.

Tentatively, she rested her hand on his shoulder, trying to tell him without words she knew how he felt. That she shared the awful, sinking sense of betrayal.

He lifted his head to meet her gaze and, for the first time in a long time, she felt again the power of the connection that existed between them. The feeling took her by surprise – like a sudden bright light in a dark room.

Reaching up, he rested his hand on top of hers.

I don't think this is friendship love, Allie thought, as her heart tripped at his touch.

The sound of soft footsteps shattered the moment. Sylvain's grip tightened and he held her gaze. She nodded very slightly to show she'd heard it too.

She took one silent step into the shadows under the stairs behind him. He didn't let go of her hand.

The footsteps approached them slowly. From the sound they made, Allie could make out two walkers – one had a heavier tread than the other. They didn't speak. Only when they reached the foot of the stairs did she see them – black-clad, stealthy, professional.

Guards.

In front of her, Sylvain was utterly still, watching their every move.

The guards walked by their hiding place without seeing them. At the foot of the grand staircase they turned and began to climb. Looking up, Allie listened to the creak of the steps as they walked to the first floor and turned down the landing towards the classroom wing.

When they were out of sight, she turned back to Sylvain. He was watching her, a smile curving the corners of his lips.

'You are getting very good at this,' he whispered, looking both proud and regretful.

'I know,' she said.

TWENTY-FOUR

The next morning at dawn, Allie stood in the garden, rain dripping into her eyes, whacking the mud hard with her shovel as she tried to make the furrow in front of her deeper and straighter.

One row over, Carter was doing the same thing only faster and better.

The rain had been falling for half an hour – an icy, relentless drip of misery. It was such a pointless waste of time – here they were doing detention when they could be inside the school finding the spy. And not freezing to death.

Muttering to herself, she pulled the edges of her wet woollen hat down, wishing she could pull it over her whole face.

She stopped for a second to watch Carter work. Having grown up on the school grounds – he was essentially raised by Mr Ellison – he was much more practised than her and yet he never got very far ahead of her. She had the feeling he was pacing himself to stay near her. And yet he hadn't said a single direct word to her all morning.

It was driving her crazy.

Last night with Sylvain had really made her think things through. Things were different with Sylvain from the way they'd been with Carter.

Sylvain seemed to have absolute belief in her ability to do things well. He made her feel confident. After the guards had left they'd sneaked back to their respective dorm wings in a hurry. There hadn't been a chance to talk. But that moment in the corridor – when their hands had touched . . . Thinking about it made her heart flutter in her chest. How could something as simple as the touch of a hand affect her like that? But then he always could. Sometimes, before Jo died, all Sylvain had to do was look at her and she fell to pieces.

Romantic love.

Carter's spade sliced through the mud with a clean thud, reminding her she should be working.

With a sigh, she whacked the mud ineffectually with her shovel. Raindrops clung to her eyelashes and she studied him through the watery prism. His cheeks were red from the cold and he was soaking wet. He never looked up at her.

She hit the mud again. Harder this time.

With Carter things were always so *complicated*. His emotions were like a labyrinth of trust and mistrust, faith and doubt. One misjudged step and you were lost for ever.

Today, for example. Here they were, alone in the garden. They had a lot to talk about. She knew Sylvain would have told him about the key last night. They'd agreed he would let Carter

235

know and Allie would inform the girls – she'd gone door to door in the dormitory wing to tell all three of them what they'd found.

Yet this morning Carter hadn't said a word about it. In fact, he hadn't said a word about anything.

They couldn't go on like this. Something had to be done.

'Are you going to ignore me all day?' she said finally. 'Or just when we're alone in the pissing-down rain and stupid-arse mud.'

He didn't look up from his work. 'Language.'

'Yeah, language.' She made an angry, half-hearted attempt to chop at the soil. 'It's that thing you use when you *talk to each other*.'

'Fine.' Straightening, Carter leaned against his shovel, studying her guardedly. 'Hi, Allie. How are you this morning?'

'Brilliant, Carter. I'm just brilliant.'

Rain ran down her face, seeping beneath her scarf to her shoulders. It was too much.

'I'm going to take a break and try not to die of pneumonia,' she said, looking at him. When he didn't respond, she tried again. 'Want to come with me? I'm just going in there.' She pointed her shovel at a small lean-to shed at the garden wall.

For a moment Carter didn't look up and she thought he might refuse. But then he straightened and hoisted his spade. 'I suppose I don't want to get pneumonia either.'

The shed had no heat but it did have doors to shut out the rain and a bench in one corner to keep them off the cold floor. After hanging her dripping hat and wet scarf from a rusty nail jutting out of the wall by the door, Allie shook out her damp hair sending a spray of cold water around her. Her hair was getting longer; it hung below her shoulder blades in long, dark strands.

'I kind of miss your red hair.'

Spinning around, she found Carter sitting on the bench watching her. When they'd first met she'd had dyed red hair. She'd let it go back to its natural colour months ago.

'You do?' She held up a strand, studying its darkness dispassionately. 'I always feel weird when I dye it now. Like, I look in the mirror and it's not me.' She dropped on to the opposite end of the bench with a sigh. 'Then again, maybe that's not such a bad thing.'

'Why?' he said. 'Don't you like you?'

'Sometimes,' she shrugged. 'Not so much right now.'

'Why not?' he said.

She gave him a look that said she was quite certain he knew the answer to that question already.

'Oh,' he said, dropping his gaze. 'That.'

'Yes. That.' She crossed her arms tightly. 'Can we talk about *that*?'

Carter made a noncommittal gesture.

'Look, I just ... ' Allie searched for the right words. 'I feel really weird about what happened. And ever since then we've both been avoiding each other, and being all cold around each other. It's like we were getting better at being friends and now we've taken this giant step backwards. And I ... ' She sighed, her shoulders slumping. 'I hate that.'

Carter shifted on the rickety bench and it swayed unsteadily.

'I know,' he said. 'But I just ... I guess I don't know how to handle this.' He was studying his hands intently. 'You have this

237

way of confusing me. I think I know what I want and then you come along and everything gets muddled up.'

Allie knew that feeling well. 'You do the same thing to me.'

Carter rubbed his eyes. 'The thing is – Jules and me – we've been friends since the first day she came to Cimmeria. Did I ever tell you that?' Allie shook her head. 'We were just kids. I was this angry, messed-up orphan. She walked in on her first day at Cimmeria with her expensive suitcases and her nanny, took one look at me and said, "My name's Jules. I'm your new best friend."' He chuckled at the memory. 'And she was right. We were always friends after that. She was so confident and determined. We studied together, grew up together, joined Night School together … I guess it was always sort of inevitable that we'd get together some time. But when it happened at the winter ball, it was an accident. We'd had too much to drink and it just … happened. The next day I thought it was a mistake. But then, as time went on, I thought maybe … ' He hesitated. 'Maybe this is right. She knows me so well and … we get along. It's different with her.'

She knew he didn't mean to hurt her but his words cut with the precision of a razor blade. The one thing she and Carter had never done well as a couple was to get along. The idea that he and Jules didn't argue – that they just understood each other – somehow felt like another indication of her own failure as a girlfriend.

'Then, the other night, you and I were running through the woods together, and … it was like it used to be. And I just looked at you and remembered how things were between us – the good things, anyway. And then … I don't know. I lost it. I messed up. I'm sorry, Allie, but I care about Jules. She's important to me. I can't ... ' Spots of colour had appeared high on his cheeks. 'If she ever found out what happened ... '

This was the opening Allie had been waiting for.

'She won't,' she assured him fervently. 'Not from me. And you mustn't ever tell her. I didn't mean to kiss you either. It was an accident. Like a ... a car crash or something. We were out there alone, it was dark and we're *used* to kissing. But now we have to pretend it never happened and learn how to be friends. We were good friends once. Really good friends. I want us to be that again.' Her voice was passionate. 'I can't lose you all over again, Carter. Please. Just ... be my friend.'

Clearly surprised by the depth of her emotion, he turned to face her. 'You never lost me, Allie. Not really.'

She knew that wasn't true.

'We lost each other. And if we ever get together I think it will happen again.' Her voice was resolute. 'Let's just be friends for ever, Carter.'

He met her gaze. 'I will always be your friend, Allie. For ever. I swear it.'

When her last class finally ended that afternoon, Allie hurried down the grand staircase, her heavy book bag thumping rhythmically against her hip with each step. She was nearly at the bottom when she heard someone call her name.

She turned to see Katie heading her way. Her hair hung in long copper curls that flamed in the afternoon light.

'I've been looking for your ... what should I call it? Gang.' Katie said the word with obvious distaste. 'I need to talk to you.'

Allie rolled her eyes. 'Gang. Friends. Whatever. What's up?'

'My parents got in touch with me.'

Allie frowned – Isabelle hadn't been around to take phone calls for students. 'Got in touch? How?'

Katie gave her a bored look. 'Seriously, Allie? They can do what they want. If they want to talk to me they talk to me. You know, it would help if you just didn't argue with me for, like, once.'

Allie held up her hands. 'So fine. You talked to them. Is everything ... OK?'

'No, everything is not bloody OK,' Katie snapped. 'Would I be standing here talking to you if everything was fine?' She adopted a wheedling tone. 'Oh, hi, Allie, I just need to tell you that *nothing interesting happened.*'

Allie fought to control her temper. 'Jesus, Katie. Don't have a *breakdown.* Just tell me what you need to tell me.'

'I can't believe you're the only people who can help me.' Katie sounded disgusted. Glancing around to make sure no one could overhear them, she lowered her voice. 'They told me they might like to *go away* this week, and that I might *come with* them. They said I should pack a bag just in case.'

'What ... ?' Allie began. But as the word left her mouth she realised what Katie meant. 'Oh.'

'Exactly.'

Allie looked at her in dismay. 'This *week*?'

Everything was about to happen – they were so close to identifying the real spy. They'd found the key, now they had to confront the instructors, form a plan, expose Zelazny, use him against Nathaniel in some way. And the Night School instructors were all still missing. The students were unprotected. Everything was half finished.

'Bollocks, bollocks, bollocks. Katie, we're not ready!' Desperation made Allie's voice rise. 'It's too soon.'

'Well, get ready.' Katie didn't appear sympathetic. 'We need a plan. Like, now. I do not want to be dragged out of here by one of my parents' thug bodyguards like poor, stupid Caroline.'

'We'll come up with something today,' Allie promised her. 'In the meantime, if they show up, hide. You have time to find places to go. The roof, the attic, the old cellar, the carrels in the library – the chapel has a priest hole; I can show you where it is.'

As she listed all the places she'd used to hide from teachers earlier in the term, Katie looked bleak. Clearly this wasn't the great escape plan she'd expected.

She ran her fingers through her vivid hair. 'This is such a nightmare.'

'Don't worry.' Allie tried to sound positive. 'We're working on a plan. We're meeting now to talk about it.'

'I hope . . . ' Katie bit her bottom lip. 'I hope you come up with something. Because this is bad.'

Her bluster had evaporated. She looked like a scared kid whose world was spinning out of control. Allie, who had never seen her looking anything but confident, didn't know what to do. She couldn't comfort Katie.

Besides, the others were waiting for her.

'I guess I better go . . . ' When she took a step away, though, Katie followed her.

'Hey, uh . . . wait.'

When Allie turned back to her she said, 'If you ever want me to come to one of your meetings, I could do that. And, you know ... help.'

Forgetting to keep her face blank, Allie gave her a look of pure astonishment. The redhead appeared anxious and almost ... lonely. As if she was the one left out of things.

Last winter Allie had asked her why she'd never joined Night School when she could have had anything she wanted, and she'd given her a flippant answer. But there must have been a reason why she'd so deliberately avoided the power group at the very heart of Cimmeria Academy.

But this wasn't the time to ask. So she nodded in a brisk, business-like way.

'I'll talk to them.'

'Her parents told her it's happening *now*?' Nicole's expressive eyes darkened.

'She didn't know the day for certain,' Allie said. 'But maybe this week.'

Carter's jaw tightened. 'If she's right we're screwed. We're not ready.'

They were gathered in the far corner of the great hall. Pale afternoon light trickled through the enormous windows behind them. The vast ballroom with its polished oak floors and huge fireplace held only a few tables and stacked chairs, waiting for the next elegant event; its emptiness made it feel even more cavernous.

Although they were alone, they talked quietly; if they spoke any louder their voices echoed in the hollow room.

'I've asked for word to be passed to my dad that I need to see him tonight,' Rachel said. 'He really can help us if we let him.'

'Is it time to tell him what we know?' Sylvain asked, turning away from Rachel to face the others.

When nobody responded, Rachel's face reddened.

'Come on. We can trust my dad.' Her voice rang with frustration. 'I don't know how many times I have to say it. He's on our side.'

'I agree with Rachel,' Nicole said. 'I believe Raj Patel is loyal.'

'I don't doubt his loyalty,' Sylvain said evenly. 'But I think anything we tell him will get to Isabelle. Because of that loyalty.'

'It's true,' Carter said. 'Are we ready for Isabelle to find out what we've been doing?'

'Not everything,' Zoe interjected. 'I mean, we don't want her to know we went out to the cottage to talk to Eloise, or that we broke into her office. That would not make her go, like, "Yay. My favourite students."'

'So we leave those parts out. Agreed?' Sylvain looked around the group – everyone nodded except Rachel. Sylvain held her gaze for a long moment. 'Rachel?'

Finally she nodded her reluctant approval.

'But we'll have to admit we broke into Zelazny's rooms,' Allie said. 'Otherwise we can't explain the key.'

'Agreed.' Carter said. He turned to Allie. 'Did Katie say anything else?'

'Nothing much,' she said hesitantly. 'Except that ... she kind of ... wants to ... join us.'

'What?' They chorused, and their voices echoed around the empty ballroom like a ricocheting bullet (*What? What? WHAT??*).

And so Allie found herself in the bizarre position of defending Katie Gilmore. Something she'd never thought she'd do in her life.

'She says she could help. She seems really scared. I think ...' She sighed, forcing herself to say the next words. 'I think she'd be useful. Even though she's an evil cow, obviously.'

'Oh God.' Rachel sounded horrified. 'Do we have to?'

'Her parents are hard-wired to this school, and she has very strong connections to the board and to the students whose parents are on Nathaniel's side,' Sylvain said thoughtfully. 'They think she's on their side, so they tell her things. Allie's right. She could be very useful.'

She gave him a grateful look and he held her gaze – the light from the window illuminated his eyes like cobalt glass. It was hard to look away.

The others were still arguing about Katie.

'She's vile,' Nicole said.

'She's insulting,' Rachel said.

'Crazy,' Zoe muttered.

'But we should invite her to join.' Carter looked around the group. 'Right?'

With clear reluctance they all nodded. There was no getting around it.

'Great,' Allie said, not thinking it was great. 'I'll tell her.'

'She shouldn't come to all the meetings,' Sylvain said. 'I believe we can trust her but we can't be certain yet. So we cannot have her there when we're talking to Isabelle, or ...' His gaze glanced off Allie's. 'Like yesterday.'

'Good point,' Carter said. 'She's very connected to things, but she's not Night School and she's not Rachel so we'll only invite her to certain meetings.'

'God help us,' Rachel said.

After dinner that night, they gathered again in a corner of the crowded common room to wait for Raj Patel.

Rachel, who had talked to the guards that afternoon, was adamant he would come but, as time ticked by, she grew antsy – looking up from her chemistry homework every time anyone walked through the door.

'Worst case scenario,' she said as ten o'clock passed with no sign of him, 'he just shows up in my room and I have to tell him everything myself.'

'If he does, just knock on the wall,' Allie suggested. 'Then I can come over and back you up. And also stop you from saying all the things.'

'He'll come soon.' Rachel looked around hopefully. But the spacious room with its leather sofas, bookcases stacked with board games and books, and tables topped with chessboards, was populated only by chattering students. Someone was playing *Clair de Lune* on the piano in the corner as others gathered around urging him to play something more lively.

Allie turned a page in her unread history book. The music – like everything else going on – was distracting. She was falling behind on her work. It was impossible to focus with so much happening. Lessons just seemed to be a tiresome interruption in her otherwise interesting day, and yet she'd promised Lucinda she'd make good grades.

From beneath lowered lashes, she glanced over to where Sylvain sat across from her in a deep leather chair, his chin resting on his hand. He looked lost in thought; she wondered what was consuming him – she had a feeling it was Zelazny.

Nearby, Carter was writing a geography essay – his neat handwriting slowly filling the page. Ever since their talk in the garden, he'd acted with extreme normality towards her, including her in conversations and even smiling sometimes. Things still felt formal with him but at least he wasn't ignoring her.

Something Katie said popped into her mind and she sat up straight, looking around the group brightly. 'Maybe we should have a name.'

The instant the words left her mouth she regretted it.

The others stared at her blankly.

'Excuse me?' Rachel said. Nicole stifled a musical giggle.

'Like, for our group.' Allie squirmed in their collective incredulous gaze. 'It's just . . . Katie . . . called us a gang.'

'I don't think we need a name.' Carter was trying not to laugh. 'Most of the good ones are taken anyway.'

The others tittered. Allie could feel heat rising up her neck. She wondered if there was some way to dissolve into the floor. She glanced desperately at Sylvain, but he didn't seem to be paying attention. There was no one to save her from this.

'Besides, if we're secret we don't need a name because we can't talk about us,' Zoe pointed out. 'Night School isn't really a name – it's, more like . . . a description. It's at school and it meets at night.'

'God. Just drop it. All right?' Allie tried not to look at anyone. 'Forget I said anything.'

'So,' Rachel said, deflecting the attention so Allie could recover, 'we should be keeping an eye out for my dad. He has this way of sneaking up on you.'

'He does! It is incredible.' Nicole sounded admiring. 'I don't know how he does it. He just' – she waved a graceful hand – 'appears. He is very talented in that way. Very graceful.'

'Yeah.' Clearly nonplussed by Nicole's enthusiasm for her father, Rachel glanced at her askance. 'Anyway. We need to be careful what we talk about. We don't want him to overhear anything.'

'Totally. It would be bad to be talking about penises when he walked up,' Zoe said.

'Zoe!' Allie and Nicole said at once.

The younger girl blinked at them. 'Well, it would, wouldn't it?'

'Yes,' Allie said primly. 'And you're too young to talk about penises to anyone.'

'Why?' Zoe seemed puzzled. 'How old do I need to be to talk about penises?'

'Sixteen,' Allie said. At the same moment, Nicole said, 'Fourteen,' and Rachel said, 'Fifteen.'

Exchanging a look the three of them burst into giggles.

'Older.' Allie felt breathless and hysterical. 'Just ... older than now.'

Zoe glared at them. 'I can talk about penises if I want to.'

'No one can stop you,' Rachel said. 'But it will be kind of

weird in your German lessons if you just sit there talking about penises.'

That set them off again. This time it took them a while to recover.

'I think you are all losing it.' Sylvain had noticed the hilarity at last and looked around in bafflement.

'Sorry,' Nicole said, wiping her eyes. 'It's the lack of sleep.'

'And threat of death,' Rachel added.

'It gets to you,' Allie said, trying to calm down. 'At least we're being careful what we're talking about so your dad doesn't hear anything.'

'Why?' Raj's voice seemed to come from nowhere. They spun round to find him standing behind Rachel. 'What do you not want me to hear?'

'Dad!' Rachel threw herself at her father. Caught off guard, he wrapped her in a reflexive hug as he tried to keep his balance. 'Where have you *been*? I've been looking for you everywhere.'

In the face of her relief, his expression softened. 'I'm sorry, honey. There's a lot going on.'

Allie's chest felt hollow; she looked away. There'd been a time when she'd been that close to her father. When he'd been glad to see her. She was surprised by how much it hurt to think about that now, when it had been weeks since she'd last spoken to him.

But Rachel's voice brought her back to what mattered right now.

'We know there's a lot going on. That's why we need to talk to you.' Extricating herself from her father's hug, Rachel moved back to stand among the others. 'Can we go somewhere?'

He looked around the group doubtfully. 'I don't have much time . . . ' he began.

'Please, Dad,' Rachel pleaded. 'It's important.'

Seeing the determination on their faces, he gave in.

'Very well,' he said with a resigned sigh. 'Come with me.'

He led them out of the common room to the empty classroom wing at a brisk pace. Flipping on the light in one of the science classrooms, Raj waited as they all filed in.

The faint tang of formaldehyde in the air was unpleasant – Allie breathed through her mouth.

The heat was turned down in the classroom wing out of hours – it was so chilly the hairs on her arm stood on end as she tried to avoid looking at the model of a human skeleton in the corner. She didn't like the way it grinned at them, as if being dead were just the best thing ever.

At the front of the room, Raj leaned against the teacher's desk, crossing his arms over his chest. The harsh fluorescent lighting cast his pallor in sharp relief. Allie couldn't remember ever seeing him look so tired. The circles under his eyes were deep and dark, and new lines had carved themselves on to his forehead at some point in the last few days.

'Now,' he said. 'What's this all about?'

For a second, no one spoke. Allie got the feeling they were all waiting for Rachel to do the talking because it was her dad but Rachel clearly didn't want to be the spokesman – catching Allie's eye, she motioned impatiently for her to talk.

'It's about . . . Eloise,' Allie said.

Before she'd even finished saying the librarian's name, Raj was shaking his head. 'You know I can't talk about—'

'We don't want you to talk about it.' Carter interrupted him. 'We want to tell you what *we* know. We think that ... maybe it could change your mind.'

Raj looked surprised at that but after a brief hesitation he motioned for him to continue.

Gradually, they filled him in on the basics of what had happened. When they reached the end, Carter turned to Rachel. 'Show him what we found in Zelazny's room.'

Rachel raised her hand; the key dangled from her fingertips, glittering like jewellery.

Raj's gaze was incredulous but Carter kept his voice even. 'It fits the lock on Isabelle's office door.'

'You went into Zelazny's private quarters?' Raj looked at them as if they'd lost their minds. 'Do you have any idea how much trouble you're in?'

'We had to do *something*,' Rachel said defensively. 'You all disappeared and everything went to hell.'

'Rachel—' His tone was sharp but she didn't let him finish the sentence; her face was pink with emotion.

'You don't know what's been happening, Dad. You've all been sitting out in the woods, telling each other how clever you were to figure it all out.' Her voice rose. 'Didn't you ever think that it was a little too easy? Did you consider who gains if you blame the wrong person?' She held the key out to him. 'Try it for yourself, Dad. It fits.'

For a long moment Rachel and her father stared at each other – his gaze warning her to back down. Her eyes undaunted.

It was Sylvain who broke the tense silence. 'Please just

consider what we're telling you, Raj. Remember, you trained us to ask these questions. And ask yourself what we've been asking ourselves: how could it really be Eloise?'

'It could be anyone,' Raj thundered, and the students went quiet. 'You do not know all the facts. What made you suspect Zelazny, anyway?'

Remembering Eloise's voice whispering through the walls, Allie dropped her eyes to her desktop.

'Just something someone said,' Carter said with deliberate casualness.

'Tell me this: did you break into any other teachers' rooms?' Raj asked.

They exchanged a glance.

'Eloise's room,' Rachel confessed.

Raj raked his fingers through his hair.

'I would like to know why you thought it was OK to do this.' His voice was deceptively calm but Allie knew he was furious.

This was going badly. He didn't look remotely convinced by what they'd told him. If anything he appeared to be more certain that he was right.

A sudden thought occurred to Allie and she leaned forward in her desk. 'You've known Eloise for a long time, haven't you, Mr Patel? Since she was a student here.'

His expression was stony. 'Yes.'

'Then how can you think she's the spy?' Allie couldn't keep the emotion out of her voice. 'I don't understand why you don't believe she was with Jerry. Why don't you trust her?'

'Because we have asked Jerry about that.' Raj spoke through

gritted teeth. 'And he wasn't with her that day. He can prove he was in his classroom, grading papers.'

The students looked at each other, shocked. Either Eloise was lying, or Jerry was. Neither of them seemed the type to deceive.

Raj rubbed his hands across his face; he hadn't shaved – his fingers rasped across his whiskers. 'You can't just trust people. Not when you're grown up. You have to constantly check up on them to make sure they haven't been corrupted by ... life. Circumstances.'

'Do you really believe it's her, Dad?' Rachel's voice was earnest, almost frightened. She'd never considered the possibility that Eloise might be guilty. 'Do you really believe she could have helped to kill Jo?'

Raj looked from one to another of them, scanning their faces with his piercing gaze. Then, shaking his head as if he couldn't believe he was saying it, he held out his hand.

'Give me that key. I'll talk to the others.'

When Rachel handed it to him he slipped it into his pocket.

'I promise I'll consider everything you've told me. But, please' – Raj surveyed them seriously – 'don't do any more investigating on your own. This is a serious situation. It's dangerous.'

At his words, a sudden burst of rage burned in Allie's throat. *It's dangerous? Could he be more patronising?*

It was too much.

'We *know* it's dangerous,' she snapped. 'We're not completely thick.'

Spinning around, Raj stared at her in disbelief. Suspecting she'd gone too far, Allie still couldn't stop herself from talking.

'Mr Patel, you have to come back. All of you. Do you even know what's happening here? It's bad. You're off in the woods playing your stupid war games.' She gestured around the room, her hand shaking with emotion. 'The real war? It's right here. Get back and help us fight it.'

'I'm going to ignore your tone,' Raj said evenly, 'because I know you're upset.'

But someone had to say this. 'I am not upset. The students already know what's going on. They know about Nathaniel. They know their parents are coming for them. And some of them aren't going to go. There's going to be trouble and you need to get back here. Now.'

'*What?*' Raj looked around the group as if seeking an explanation from each of them. 'How did that happen?'

Sylvain took over. 'We've been informed by one of the students whose parents are on Nathaniel's side that he is coming for them this week. The other students ... found out.'

'Oh they did, did they?' Raj turned away for a moment, his jaw tight. Allie didn't like the look on his face. 'You do not,' he said coldly, 'know everything that is going on. Do not for one second think that you do. You are sixteen years old.' His fist hit the desk beside him with such force a stack of papers jumped, landing in a disorganised shuffle. 'Did you really think we would tell you everything?'

'You should,' Allie said quietly. 'After all, we're the ones who'll die if you get it wrong again.'

Rachel gasped.

Raj flinched as if she'd struck him.

'Allie. *Stop.*' Carter sounded panicked.

'No.' Standing, Sylvain stepped to Allie's side. 'She's right. Raj, you need to come back.'

As the others began to talk over each other, Raj held up his hands for calm. He turned back to Allie. 'I understand why you're upset. And you've made your point. I get it – OK? I'll ... do what I can.' Including the others in his gaze, he said, 'Now. Tell me everything. Start at the beginning.'

When they left the science classroom some time later, no one wanted to hang around and talk. Murmuring excuses, they hurried off in their separate ways. Instead of feeling more hopeful after talking to Raj, everything felt worse somehow. The atmosphere seemed tainted with bitterness.

As the others left, Allie hung back, hoping to talk to Rachel alone. But Rachel walked out arm in arm with her father and didn't meet her eyes.

'I'm sorry ...' Allie whispered, when they were out of earshot. Her shoulders slumped.

She could hear her mother's condemning voice in her head. 'You always go too far, Alyson. You never know when to stop.'

Maybe her mother was right after all.

Burying her head in her hands she tried to erase her mother's voice from it, along with the guilt and the pain.

'It is hard to be the one who tells the truth.'

Allie whirled to find Sylvain leaning against the wall on the other side of the empty classroom. His face looked serious.

'Is that what I am?' Allie's throat tightened. 'Or am I just an arsehole? Because I feel like an arsehole.'

255

'Every leader must be willing to be an arsehole when it's necessary,' he said. 'You were the leader tonight.'

Allie wasn't convinced. 'You actually think I did the right thing?'

'If you'd behaved like an intimidated child Raj would never have taken us seriously.' He shrugged. 'You forced him to listen. By doing that you helped other people.'

Allie's chest ached with unshed tears. 'It's just that . . . I like Raj. And he'll never forgive me for saying that.'

Sylvain shook his head. 'Raj would have said precisely the same thing if he were you. He will respect you for saying it.'

His clear blue eyes held hers steadily. Even if she wasn't convinced he was right his approval made her feel better – more confident.

'How do you do that?' Allie said.

'Do what?'

'Make me feel braver.'

'You are always brave,' he said simply.

Heat seemed to flood through her.

If she was truly brave, then she could say what she needed to say to him.

She walked closer to where he stood, leaning against the desk across from him. The skeleton hung next to her and she touched the plastic bones of its hand without realising she was doing it.

He looked at her as if he was trying to figure out what she was thinking.

'There's something I wanted to say to you,' she said, uncomfortably aware that this was almost exactly what Carter had said to her in the woods the other night. 'I've wanted to say it for a while.'

'*D'accord*,' he said in French. '*Dîtes moi*. Tell me.'

It was devastating. He was always at his most charming when he spoke his own language.

She took a deep breath. 'Ever since Jo died, I've been avoiding you.' His eyes flicked up at hers sharply – almost in warning – but she kept going. She needed to say this. 'I avoided everyone but you most of all. I was a wreck, and I felt like I had to be alone. All the time. For ever. I even felt guilty for caring about kissing you when she wasn't alive any more.' She squeezed the plastic skeleton's hand as if for support. 'It seemed . . . selfish of me to want anything for myself when she would never have anything ever again. And I was angry, because I thought no one was looking for her killers. But I know how much it hurts to just be . . . dropped like that. And it must have hurt you that I was so cold and . . . distant.'

'You do not need to apologise.' His voice was gentle. 'You needed time. I knew that. I was never angry.'

'And you waited for me.' Her lower lip trembled and she paused to steady herself. 'You never gave up on me. Why? Why did you never give up on me?'

She looked up at him but he quickly dropped his gaze.

'There were times when I wanted to give up. I am not superhuman, Allie. Rejection hurts me as much as anyone. But I have always believed there was something between us that *mattered*. Something worth fighting for. And I believe you have felt that, too.' He lifted his bright blue eyes to hers and the vulnerability she saw there made her chest tighten around her

257

heart. 'But time after time you chose Carter over me. And the other night, when you and Carter came in from the woods and I knew something had happened . . . I thought, that's it. I'm not doing this any more. But then you came back to me again, looking at me like that.' He made a circle in the air with his fingers, like a frame around her face. 'And here we are.'

Allie fought for something to say. 'I'm not with Carter. He has a girlfriend.'

'I know that.' Sylvain shrugged. 'But I have seen how he looks at you. And how you look at him.'

She shook her head. 'No. He's been very clear that he is serious about Jules. And I know now we should never have got together in the first place. I feel friendship love for him. Only that.'

'Friendship love?' His eyebrows winged up.

Allie blushed. 'It's a thing . . . Rachel told me . . . Look. Never mind. What matters is we were meant to be friends, nothing more.'

Her tone was adamant.

'So.' He took a step closer, halving the space between them, and Allie involuntarily squeezed the hand of the skeleton, which she'd forgotten she was holding. 'Now you are free of your obligation to Carter and here you are. Because I am your . . . how do you say it in English? Your backup plan.'

She was so surprised by this she almost pulled the skeleton over; it rattled wildly as she pushed it back into place.

'No.' She took a half-step towards him. 'That's not fair . . .'

'Isn't it?' His gaze challenged her to be honest.

The problem was . . . he was kind of right.

For months now, Sylvain had fought to win her back. To earn her trust. But she was always waiting for Carter to decide what *he* wanted.

Heat flooded her face and she reached for his arm. 'Sylvain, I'm so sorry. I don't want you to be my backup plan. It's just hard to know what I want sometimes.'

'What do you mean, "sometimes"?' His voice was so low she couldn't be certain she'd really heard it. 'You've never known what you wanted.'

As he'd done the night before in the hallway, he put his hand on top of hers. The warmth of his skin radiated through her. She knew what it felt like to have his hands stroke her face, her hair. Pull her close.

'You have to make up your mind, Allie. I don't want you to choose me just because Carter is already taken. I want you to choose me because I'm the one you want.' His eyes were like blue flames; it hurt to look at them. 'All I ever wanted was to be the one you want. But I'm beginning to think I never will be. I can't wait for you for ever – no one could do that. Already I think I've waited too long. It hurts too much—'

Somewhere down the hallway a loud, unfamiliar voice shouted, 'Curfew!'

They stood close together for a second longer, Sylvain's eyes locked on hers. Then he took a step back and dropped her hand.

'It's late.' His voice sounded empty. 'We should go.'

TWENTY-SİX

Zelazny was at his desk when Allie walked into the history lesson the next day.

When she saw him, she froze in mid-step and the student walking in behind her ran into her.

'Sorry ...' Allie said, never taking her eyes off the teacher.

'Everyone take your seats *today* please,' he growled with characteristic grouchiness, as if he'd never been away. Never held Eloise prisoner.

Her heart hammered in her chest as she tried to figure out what was happening. Did this mean Raj had come through? Had he brought all the teachers back?

A few minutes later, Carter rushed into the classroom at speed and nearly tripped over his own feet when he noticed Zelazny.

When Sylvain walked in, she saw his eyes widen in surprise.

Catching Allie's gaze, he raised his eyebrows in a silent question. She shook her head very slightly to indicate she had no idea where the history teacher had come from.

The exchange calmed her down a little – at least they were still communicating.

She'd been up for hours last night thinking about what Sylvain had said and how badly she'd behaved towards him. The way he'd left her the perfect opportunity to say she chose him over Carter and she couldn't bring herself to say it. Why couldn't she just say it? He'd taken her by surprise but ... still. Why couldn't she just tell anyone how she felt?

Zelazny stood by his desk at parade rest, his pale eyes surveying the class shrewdly.

Pulling her notebook from her bag, Allie tried to act normal. What if Zelazny knew they'd been in his room? And *God* – what if he knew they'd accused him of being the spy?

The thought made her shudder. She waited, so nervous her hand trembled when she picked up her pen and drew shaky prison bars and a gigantic lock on the paper in front of her.

But then Zelazny just ... taught the class. They were studying the battle of Austerlitz and he picked up precisely where the replacement teacher had left off without a word of explanation or apology for his absence.

At first, Allie waited for the axe to fall, and for Zelazny to call her out. Accuse her of looking through his bedside table, the box under his bed. But as time went by, she realised that wasn't going to happen.

Slumping down low in her seat, she prepared to take sparse

notes and bide her time until she could talk with the others about this development.

But the lesson was surprisingly interesting. As Zelazny explained the battle between Napoleon and an overwhelming coalition of British, Russian and Austrian troops, she found herself absorbed.

'Napoleon was a master strategist,' Zelazny explained, drawing a quick map on the whiteboard. 'He knew he couldn't win by sheer force because he was outnumbered and outgunned. So he decided to create a trap.'

He wiped out part of his design on the right side and tapped it with his fingertip. 'He intentionally weakened his right flank to draw the coalition forces in. His hope was they'd throw everything they had at it, thus confusing their troops and weakening their own defences. Once they were in place, Napoleon's hidden forces would rush out and attack them.'

The history teacher drew a violent series of arrows swinging on to the board. When he turned back to face the class, he looked positively gleeful.

'They never saw him coming.'

As Zelazny described the battle in gory detail, Allie pictured Nathaniel's letter, stabbed to the wall of the chapel with a knife. What if that was something like Napoleon's ploy? Make them so paranoid they begin to suspect each other. Wait until they're confused and distracted. Then attack from the flank.

Zelazny was drawing more lines on the board. 'With the coalition forces weakened, Napoleon prepared his troops to deliver the *coup de grâce*. Famously this is what he told his generals then.' He wrote a sentence at the top of the board with such force the pen squeaked in protest. Then he stood back and looked out over the room.

The sentence read: 'One sharp blow and the war is over.'

As she stared at those ruthless words, a sudden chill made Allie shiver.

What if that's us?

After class, Allie met Carter and Sylvain in the corridor. It was lunchtime, and hordes of students rushed by them on their way to the dining hall.

'What in the actual hell is going on?' she asked.

Carter looked at Sylvain as if he would have the answer. 'Raj Patel?'

Sylvain shrugged. 'I guess so. He works fast.'

'If Zelazny's back do you think that means ...' Allie stopped as the realisation took shape.

'What?' Sylvain asked, a slight frown creasing his brow.

She shook her head. 'Nothing. Don't worry about it. There's just something I have to do.'

Turning on her heel she started walking away but Carter called after her: 'Aren't you coming to lunch?'

Without stopping, she threw her answer back over her shoulder. 'I'll meet you down there later.'

Running against the tide of students, she took the stairs at speed and jogged down the long hallway. She was moving too fast to stop when she reached the English classroom and skidded around the corner, fairly flying through the doorway until a voice stopped her in her tracks.

'Hello, Allie.'

Isabelle stood just inside the door, and she did not look happy.

'Where have you *been*?' Allie could hear the hurt in her own voice.

One part of her wanted to cry. Another – needier – part of her wanted to hug the headmistress. But she did neither. Instead she stood alone, arms at her sides.

'As I understand it,' Isabelle said, drawing out each word, 'you know perfectly well where I've been. And I would like to ask the questions right now, if you don't mind.'

'Actually I do mind.' Allie lifted her chin stubbornly. 'How could you just go away and leave us alone? How could you do that? We've had to deal with all this on our own. And now you show up again and you want *explanations*? What? Was this all some kind of test?'

If Isabelle was surprised by Allie's anger she didn't show it; her leonine gaze was steady, cold. 'You went into Mr Zelazny's private rooms—'

Allie wouldn't let her finish. 'And found what you were look-ing for, yes. You're welcome.' She rested her hands on her hips in a defiant posture. 'Anything else you want to thank us for? Warning the students their parents were on Nathaniel's side? Giving them a chance to make their own decisions? Thinking on our feet? Being innovative? Doing *your jobs*?'

'Enough.' Isabelle's powerful voice rang out in the empty room. 'You've made your point. Now sit down. I have a lunchtime work-shop scheduled and the students will arrive in a few minutes.'

Allie hesitated a second – she could, after all, just storm out in protest – but she really wanted to hear what Isabelle had to say.

With reluctant slowness, she lowered herself on to a nearby seat.

Placing her hands flat on Allie's desk, Isabelle lowered her gaze to hers. 'What you did – invading Mr Zelazny's private space – was in complete violation of The Rules. You had no right to take it upon yourself to do that. If he ever found out what you did I don't like to think what his reaction would be. If Lucinda found out you'd be lucky to still be at this school.'

Allie exhaled a long, relieved breath – Zelazny didn't know. They hadn't told him.

The rest – Isabelle's lecture – didn't really matter. She'd known all that when she walked through Zelazny's door.

'What was he doing with the key?' Allie asked, searching Isabelle's fine-boned face for clues. 'Have you asked him? Is he the one?'

The headmistress closed her eyes for a second as if summoning strength. 'Allie, you must let us handle this – this is what we *do*.'

Her voice fairly crackled with frustration but Allie refused to back down.

'You didn't even know he had the key—'

'We *did* know.' Isabelle's voice rose. 'And the key is now back in the book again. Please, for the love of God, leave it there.'

TWENTY-SEVEN

Disbelief made it impossible for Allie to speak for a moment. She couldn't seem to get her brain to function.

'You ... you ... *what?*' Allie stuttered in shock. 'I ... I don't ... '

'Understand? No, I don't suppose you do.' Isabelle smoothed the dark blonde hair which had begun escaping from her hairclip; as if her rage had been transmitted to her hair follicles. When she spoke again, her voice was more controlled. 'Allie, Raj and I are investigating all the people who could be Nathaniel's spy. All of them. And we have been for months now. We know everything in everyone's rooms down to the tiniest speck of dust. Down to the fingerprints on their books. And the earplugs in their bedside tables.'

As she tried to process this, Allie held up a hand – she needed Isabelle to stop talking while she thought it all through.

'Why did you leave the key there, though?' she asked after a second. 'Why haven't you just questioned him about it?'

'If he's Nathaniel's spy we can learn more by not making him aware we're watching him,' the headmistress replied. 'He could inadvertently lead us to Nathaniel, or reveal others who are working with him. Once we show our hand we'll get nothing from him.'

This made a dark kind of sense. But there were others involved, too. Other questions unanswered.

'If you think it's him, why hold Eloise?' Allie asked. 'Is she just, like ... what? A decoy?'

'Yes and no. At first we thought she might be the spy. Now we're fairly certain she's not but we're holding her so the real spy can believe we're not paying attention. We've reduced patrols of the grounds for the same reason, and suspended Night School.'

Sighing, Isabelle sat down in the desk next to her.

'Allie, there are more guards watching this school right now than there have ever been. The night you all went to the cottage, you were watched all the way there.'

All other sound receded. The noise of students chatting in the corridor outside the classroom could have been on another continent. Allie couldn't even hear her own heartbeat any more.

We were watched the whole time? Did they watch me and Carter?

Had someone watched them kiss? Stood by impassively as they revealed their deepest feelings about each other?

The thought of such an invasion of their privacy made her stomach churn.

When she looked up, she saw Isabelle was waiting for her to

say something. Trying to appear calm, Allie cleared her throat, but could only manage one word.

'How ... ?'

'The guards don't patrol any more,' Isabelle said simply. 'They hide and watch. They communicate using a new system Raj brought in. It's changed everything.'

Even as Allie absorbed this bit of information – nodding like a normal person – in her mind the same words were circulating on a vicious loop.

... watched all the way. You were watched all the way. You were watched ...

Isabelle was still talking but Allie only barely heard her. 'You must have seen them using microphones – they have tiny earpieces. It's the first technology we've allowed on campus in more than five years. It has changed the way we work.

'Very few people know this, Allie – the Night School instructors know about the tech but they don't know about the change in instruction for the guards. Only Raj and I and his guards know. And now you.'

'But ... I don't ... Why ... ?' Allie wanted to ask why Isabelle had her followed. Why no one had warned her this might happen. Why she'd been left so exposed when she'd *trusted* Isabelle to look out for her.

The headmistress thought she was asking something else. 'We haven't allowed technology – computers, phones, anything – since Nathaniel hacked our system five years ago. He gained access to all our files, student records, instructor information, Night School plans, guards' names and addresses, schedules – everything.'

'So why change now?' Allie asked dully. She wasn't sure she cared. But it seemed the obvious question.

'A recent Cimmeria graduate is a tech designer – young and innovative. He says this system is hack-proof. And after what happened with Jo and you … We knew things couldn't continue as they were. We had to find a better system. That's why the guards patrol less frequently. That's why you don't see them as much. They're trying a different tactic. And so far it's working.'

'Why didn't you tell me?' Allie searched Isabelle's face for clues that she'd done this out of malice, but all she found was weariness.

'No one knows. And I'd like to keep it that way. Until we know who the spy is, I need you to promise me you will tell no one about this. And I do mean *no one* – not Carter, not Rachel. No one.'

Allie felt blindsided. Isabelle was asking her to betray her friends. The people who'd got her through the last few months. Who'd stuck by her when she'd melted down after Jo's death. Who'd been dragged into hell because of her family.

'I can't do that,' Allie said. Isabelle's breath caught but Allie didn't give her a chance to speak. 'I'm sorry, Isabelle. I just can't. Those days are over. I'll decide who I trust from now on.'

'You could be making a very big mistake …' Isabelle said. But then the first student walked into the room, glancing at them curiously as he made his way to his desk.

Her eyes alight with disapproval, Isabelle straightened. But when she spoke her tone was as calm and professional as if they'd just been discussing Allie's marks.

'I need you to come to my office after classes today so we can discuss this further.'

'I can't.' Allie spoke without thinking. 'I've got a meeting with ...'

Her voice trailed off. She was supposed to meet the others to talk about their plans. She couldn't tell Isabelle that ... could she?

Isabelle's reply was sharp. '"Can't" is not a word I want to hear from you right now, Allie. I'll expect you there.'

As the headmistress strode away, her shoulders stiff, Allie sighed. The others would have to meet without her.

Still, when her classes ended that day, Allie didn't head straight to Isabelle's office. Instead, she intercepted Rachel in the hallway of the classroom wing.

'Help me,' Allie said. 'I have big problems and I need you to solve them.'

'Have you been doing calculus again?' Rachel asked sympathetically.

'It's worse than that.' Allie lowered her voice. 'It's Isabelle. And other things.'

'Boy things?' Rachel said hopefully.

When Allie nodded, Rachel's warm brown eyes lit up. 'At last! Interesting problems worth discussing.' She steered Allie down the corridor. 'Walk this way. The doctor is *in*.'

As they picked their way through hallways teeming with students, Allie spoke in quick quiet tones. She told her the basics about her meeting with Isabelle, leaving out the bit about the new security system and the spying it involved. That could wait.

'She didn't tell you anything else useful?' Rachel asked. 'Like where's Eloise? And who else do they suspect?'

Allie shook her head. 'Not much. We ran out of time. Anyway, she was more about the shouting and the threatening.'

'That's always nice.' Smoothly, Rachel dodged a junior student running straight at her. 'Everyone likes a bit of threatening.'

Watching the boy run laughing back to his friends, Allie envied his freedom to just be a kid. She couldn't remember the last time she'd felt that innocent and happy.

'Totally,' she said, her tone weary.

It had been a long day already, and she still had to go and talk to Isabelle again. Allie pressed her fingertips against her forehead.

'Are you sure she didn't say anything else bad?' Rachel watched her with concern. 'You look like someone punched you. Did she punch you?'

'No one hit me,' Allie said. 'Not, like ... physically, anyway. Look, I should go ...'

'Oh no, you don't. We haven't talked about boys yet.'

Ignoring Allie's protests, Rachel hustled her across the first-floor landing, out of the classroom wing and into the main building where classic statues stood in perpetual graceful postures. They slipped behind a statue of a young man with a ridiculously frilly jacket that jutted out over his behind, and sat down on a stone bench.

Tucked away in the quiet nook, they were hidden from view.

Rachel leaned back against the wall with a contented sigh. 'This is my happy place. Now. Tell me.'

Her voice halting at first but strengthening as she went along, Allie told her about her talk with Carter, deciding she felt only friendship-love for him, and then what happened with Sylvain.

'I blew it ... I blew it ... again.' Leaning forward, she pressed her hot forehead against the cold marble curve of the statue's heel. 'Oh, Rachel. Why do I feel like this? Why is it all so *confusing*?'

Rachel's voice was gentle. 'Allie, Carter was your first love. The first one is always the worst.'

'Oh, but why did he kiss me?' Allie said, miserably. 'It made everything so much worse.'

'It sounds like you're not the only one having trouble getting over it.'

Allie couldn't argue with that.

'What are you going to do about Sylvain?' Rachel said. 'What does your heart tell you to do?'

Allie sagged back on the bench. 'My heart is telling me to find out who helped Jo's killers and just stay away from all boys until then.'

Rachel looked thoughtful. 'You can't use Jo's death as an excuse not to make decisions about your own life – you know that, right?'

Allie blinked at her. 'I'm not ... am I?'

'Aren't you?' Rachel asked.

'Allie Sheridan!'

They both heard the voice at the same time. Someone on the landing was calling her. But no one could see them in their hiding place.

'Who is it?' Allie hissed.

'I don't know. I'll take a look.' Rachel climbed up to look over the statue's flying coat-tails. Standing on her toes, she craned her neck to see. Then she looked back at Allie wide-eyed. 'Jules. Mayday. Mayday. Dive. Dive.'

'Bollocks.' Allie ducked down low behind the legs of the statue. 'Why is she looking for me?'

'Well, she's a prefect, so she might need you for prefect ... ness,' Rachel reasoned. 'Or maybe she wants to beat you up for kissing her boyfriend.'

Allie swung at her but couldn't reach her.

'Steady,' Rachel said, and a fit of giggles threatened to over-take them both.

'Is she close?' Allie hissed, trying to stay calm.

Rachel pressed her fingers against her lips. Covering her mouth with both hands, Allie watched as Rachel peeked again around the statue's flared jacket. At that precise moment, Jules appeared in front of her, trying to see past her into the nook.

'Oh, Rachel.' Her tone was officious. 'Have you seen Allie?'

Allie knew how much Rachel longed to lie at this moment – she could see it in the set of her shoulders, sense it in the way she gathered herself as she prepared to speak. She also knew Rachel was a terrible liar.

'I'm right here.' She stood up, looking at the prefect over Rachel's shoulder. 'What's up?'

For a long second, Jules held her gaze. It was a challenging look; a warning. Maybe even a threat.

But all she said was: 'Isabelle wants you in her office.'

Allie nodded then turned to give Rachel a meaningful look. 'Take notes or something for me. When you see the others.'

'Will do. Good luck.' Behind Jules' back, Rachel saluted her sympathetically.

Staying a step or two behind, Allie followed Jules out on to the grand landing. Around them, the white statues caught the late afternoon light and glowed like angels preparing to fly.

With each step, Jules' Uggs made an annoying scuffing sound on the polished oak floors. Allie tried to work out which she hated more – the sheepskin boots or the fact that Jules got to wear her own shoes as a perk of being prefect.

'How's the gardening going?' Jules asked suddenly.

'Um ... what?' The question caught Allie by surprise. 'You mean detention?'

Never breaking her stride, Jules nodded.

'Fine, I guess,' Allie said. 'I mean, it's stupid and pointless; I'm learning a valuable lesson ... yadda yadda yadda ...'

They walked in silence for a long time after that, the only sound the shushing of Jules' shoes. Then: 'And Carter's still doing it too?'

Scuff, scuff, scuff ...

Her eyes lowered, Allie tried to figure out what Jules was getting at. Surely she knew her own boyfriend still had early morning detention?

'Yes, Carter too.'

Without warning, Jules rounded on her. 'Why?'

Her aggressive tone caught Allie off guard; she stepped back, stumbling over her own feet. 'Why ... what?'

274

'Why is he still gardening with you?'

Allie hoped her expression conveyed her belief that the prefect was losing her mind.

'Because he's got *detention*, Jules. Why else would anybody be out in the freezing cold at the crack of bleeding dawn three times a week?'

At that moment, to Allie's astonishment, all the fight left the prefect. Her eyes filling, she turned away.

'See, that's my question, too,' Jules said. 'Carter hasn't got detention. He hasn't had it once this term.'

Allie stared at her blankly. 'That's crazy, Jules. He must do. You've got your information wrong . . .'

'Oh please. I'm a prefect, remember?' Jules' tone was withering. 'I get the detention list every day. He's not on it. But he still goes out there with you . . .'

Allie's stomach twisted. 'I don't . . . understand . . .' she said faintly.

'Don't you?' Jules didn't look like she believed her. 'Well, let me make it clearer for you. My boyfriend pretends to have detention at the same time as you when he doesn't. He joins some imaginary *gang* and does God knows what every night. Again, with you.' Jules wiped her eyes with the back of her hands. 'He hardly talks to me any more but I see him talking to you all the time and he looks so . . . interested.' She took a shuddering breath, then held Allie's gaze with her wounded eyes. 'Tell me the truth. Are you two together again? Behind my back . . . is he with you?'

Allie found herself utterly lost for words.

Carter had been out in the cold and the rain with her, day

after day. Had he endured all that just so she wouldn't be alone?

For just a second she wondered. Then she reminded herself of the look on Carter's face when he talked about Jules and how much she meant to him.

This is what friends do for each other, she told herself. *This is what a true friend does.*

When she replied, she was surprised by how calm she sounded.

'No, Jules. Carter and I are not together behind your back. I know for a fact he cares for you very much and would never cheat on you. You're one of the people he cares most about in the world.'

Jules searched her eyes for any hint of deception but Allie didn't flinch.

'Then why is he doing these things?' Jules' lips trembled. A tear, crystalline as spring water, escaped from the dark blue pool of her eyes and tumbled down her cheek. 'I just don't understand him sometimes.'

Seeing imperious, unflappable Jules weeping was extraordinary. If she'd been anyone else Allie might have hugged her. But she was ... Jules.

'I know Carter is my ex-boyfriend but he's also my friend. Our break-up really sucked. And then other horrible things ... happened.' In fact, at that moment, Allie longed for nothing so much as to tell Jo about this conversation, and the knowledge that it could never happen was so overwhelming it shook her. She tightened her hands into fists to steady herself. 'I didn't know Carter didn't have detention. But I guess he's been worried about me because … I've been through so much. It was a really nice thing to do. And I didn't even …' She took a ragged breath. 'He's a good guy, Jules. He really is. Probably one of the best guys I've ever known. You're lucky to have him.'

Jules twisted her hands. 'I just … I wish he'd be honest with me. He keeps things from me. Secrets.'

Allie tried to think of something soothing to say but this was *Jules*. And Allie had been St Allie of Cimmeria long enough for one afternoon.

'I wish I knew,' she said, taking a step away. 'You should really … you know …' another step '– talk to him. Listen, Isabelle is waiting for me.' Making an apologetic face, she turned and walked away a little faster than was seemly.

As soon as she rounded the corner she broke into a run. With each step she felt lighter. Despite everything she'd just said her heart lifted at the thought that Carter had gone to such lengths to look out for her. To be her friend.

She skidded to a stop in front of Isabelle's office and rapped impatiently on the carved oak door. 'It's Allie.'

'Come in,' a voice called.

Her thoughts still tangled up in Carter and Jules, Allie didn't really pay attention to the sound of that voice. She turned the heavy brass handle. The door swung open.

Sitting comfortably in Isabelle's chair, Lucinda Meldrum looked at Allie with eyes the exact same shade of grey as her own.

'Hello, Allie,' her grandmother said. 'Tea?'

TWENTY-EİGHT

As Lucinda poured steaming tea into a bone china cup with the Cimmeria crest emblazoned on the side in dark blue, Allie sat across from her in a deep leather chair, watching her with hungry eyes, trying to memorise the details.

Lucinda's navy blazer contrasted neatly with her crisp, white blouse. Her white hair was done in a very short, stylish cut that made her look younger than she was. Diamond stud earrings glittered in the light.

It was only the second time they'd ever met. For most of Allie's life, she'd believed her grandmother was dead. She wanted to forget nothing.

'Sugar?' Lucinda asked brightly, her hand hovering over the fragile bowl.

Allie shook her head, reaching out for the cup. 'No, thank you,' she added with belated formality.

A smile played on Lucinda's lips as she handed her the cup on a matching saucer. 'You remind me of your mother at your age. She always forgot to say "thank you" until the last second. Always so eager to move things along.'

It was weird thinking of Lucinda – a former chancellor in the British government and renowned advisor to world leaders, famous to anyone who ever watched the news – as her mother's mother. It didn't seem possible they'd ever been family.

Allie's mother had run away from home after finishing at Cimmeria and had never looked back. She'd rejected her mother's wealth and power in favour of a simple life, and she'd hidden her family history from her children. Allie had only discovered it all once she was at Cimmeria.

Lifting the teacup to her lips, Allie inhaled its lemony bergamot perfume.

'Now.' Moving the teapot out of the way, Lucinda settled back in her chair. 'Let's have a chat.'

Up close, Allie could see the delicate pattern of lines around her eyes – they didn't look like laugh lines. You didn't become as powerful as Lucinda if you didn't have a spine of steel.

'We have a situation here, Allie,' Lucinda said. 'I don't have much time, but I think it's important you should understand exactly what's happening. Because you are in a great deal of danger. And I need you to be ready for whatever may happen next.'

'The parents,' Allie said, 'they're going to pull their kids out of Cimmeria, aren't they?'

Lucinda nodded. 'That's Nathaniel's plan. Then he'll call for a vote of no confidence, his supporters will identify themselves,

I'll be voted out, they'll take over the school and the entire organisation, I will be powerless, and he'll be free to continue his takeover, which I think will damage much more than just Cimmeria.'

As she described how she would be destroyed, Lucinda appeared unruffled. She could have been describing an ordinary business day for all the emotion she betrayed.

'Some of the kids don't want to go,' Allie said. She lifted her chin proudly. 'We're going to help them stay.'

Lucinda stirred her tea with a small silver spoon. 'It's a difficult situation. It would be very brave of them to try to stay but their parents will find a way to get them, I fear. They all have good lawyers and their children are underage. Nathaniel is very ... resourceful.'

'We can't just make them go.' Allie hadn't considered that Lucinda might not approve of their plan. 'They don't want to. Surely they have the right to decide which side they're on.'

'Not until they're eighteen they don't,' Lucinda said. 'Allie, I'm not saying they shouldn't attempt to stand up to their parents and stay here. Just ... speak to Isabelle about it. Make sure she knows everything you're planning. She can help you.'

'Can she?' Allie's tone was resentful. 'She's been away throughout all of this. We've had do everything ourselves.'

'She was never truly away. All you had to do was ask for her and she'd have been here,' Lucinda chided her gently. 'However, it certainly says a lot about you and the others that, instead, you made your own plans – found your own way. This is why you were chosen for Night School. I would expect nothing less.'

The glow of pride Allie felt from her words took her by surprise – she hadn't realised how much Lucinda's approval mattered.

'The problem is, Nathaniel has our backs to the wall with this,' Lucinda conceded. 'It's a masterful plan. There are few moves we can make to win.'

Allie clutched her teacup, considering what this meant. 'On the phone, a few weeks ago ... you said the organisation that runs Night School runs the government. Does that mean if Nathaniel takes over, he'll control the government?'

'I suppose I'd better start at the beginning.' Tapping her chin with one finger, Lucinda considered her. 'Have you heard of the Orion Project?'

Allie shook her head. She'd heard the term 'Orion' used somewhere at Cimmeria before, but she couldn't place it.

'That is the name of the organisation of which Night School and Cimmeria are one small part. It's a private group of very powerful people – members of parliament, judges, lawyers, financiers, CEOs, the owners of media corporations ... ' She waved her hand and her diamond ring caught the light, glittering like frozen fire. 'I could go on but that should give you a sense of who we are.

'There are similar organisations in other countries, but Orion is the oldest. I have been the head of Orion for the last fifteen years. It's a position I essentially inherited from my father. You see, it's always been a titular position ... ' Shooting Allie a sharp look, she paused. 'Do you know what "titular" means?'

Mutely, Allie shook her head.

'It means "in name only". So the chairman of this organisation mostly ran meetings, hosted dinners, and made sure things . . . happened. Until I came along.' She smiled demurely. 'I changed things.'

Fascinated and confused, Allie tried to keep up. She wished she was taking notes so she could remember it all later.

'How did you change it?' she asked.

'I instituted a voting system – so now the board votes on all our actions. And I lobbied to let children from different backgrounds into Cimmeria,' Lucinda explained. 'As you know, entrance to the organisation starts at school level. Night School is the main youth group, but there are similar groups at a few other top public schools. Until I came along, entrance was by heredity – if your family were members you were accepted. I changed that . . . as much as I could. Now some students – fewer than I'd like – are admitted based on ability and intellect. Fresh blood, they call it.'

Allie thought of Carter, the orphaned son of a kitchen worker and a mechanic. It made sense now, that he was in Night School.

'OK . . . ' she said. 'But what exactly does . . . Orion . . . do?'

Lucinda considered this for a moment before answering. 'It makes sure certain things are run properly.'

'What . . . things?'

'The government,' Lucinda said. 'The banks. Major corporations. The media. The courts.'

This didn't seem possible. 'Doesn't the government run the government?' Allie asked.

'Of course,' Lucinda said mildly. 'We just help them.'

'Help them how?'

'By making certain the right people are elected. People who are members of Orion. People who understand what we're doing.' Lucinda cocked her head to one side. 'Does that make sense?'

'No.' Allie didn't like the sound of this. 'Are you saying when people go and vote their votes aren't real?'

'Oh no. Their votes are very real,' Lucinda assured her. 'But the people they're voting for are part of Orion.'

A moment of stunned disbelief followed.

'All of them?' Allie's voice was small.

'Certainly not,' Lucinda said. 'Just ... enough of them.'

'And the judges?' Allie said faintly. 'Them too?'

'Absolutely,' Lucinda said. 'The court system is very important. Particularly the Supreme Court. Actually, we do run that one completely. It's ... necessary.'

A long pause followed as Allie digested this. The normal sounds of everyday life around her suddenly seemed out of place – the kettle in the corner ticking as it cooled; laughter floating in through the walls. As if a secret organisation were not running everything around them.

'So Orion controls ... everything.'

'It doesn't completely control,' Lucinda said. 'But effectively. Yes. I suppose that's fair.'

'Why?'

'It's a long story.' Lucinda poured more tea into her cup. 'You see, Orion is a very old organisation. It dates back more than two centuries to a time when the crown had lost most of its power and Parliament's strength was growing but still unsteady. After the revolutions in France and America, the noble families feared a revolution would happen here. The king was too weak to control his government, much less his country. So a group of the country's most powerful land owners and parliamentarians joined together to ensure the government was run well. They called themselves the Orion Society.'

'Orion ...' Allie said with a thoughtful frown. 'Like the stars?'

'Orion the hunter,' Lucinda said. 'In Greek mythology, he was a god. The founders chose to name their group after him because he could walk on water. Hubris if you ask me, but –' she held up her hands – 'it's only a name.'

'So ... what did they do?' Allie prodded her.

'They took over the reins of power. They helped each other. Made sure they became prime minister, chancellor, regent – whatever was needed to make sure power was held smoothly, transferred without interruption. Controlled.'

'And nobody knew they existed?' Allie's tone was dubious. 'How is that possible?'

'We are very good,' Lucinda said, 'at keeping secrets.'

'How did you end up in charge of everything?' Allie said. 'And your dad? How did he?'

'It's very simple: we inherited it. The leadership passes from one family to the next in order. Each family acts as chair for three years and then passes it on. Or, at least, that's how it worked until I came along. My great-great-great-great grandfather was one of the founders. The Earl of Lanarkshire.' Her piercing gaze held Allie's. 'That's who we are, you know.

Technically, I am Lady Lanarkshire. So is your mother. And so are you.'

Allie gaped at her. 'I'm a ... Lady?'

For the first time that afternoon, Lucinda truly smiled. She had even, white teeth, and her eyes crinkled warmly. 'Yes, you are.'

'But you're a baroness,' Allie said accusingly. 'I heard your guards call you that the night of the winter ball.'

'I choose to use that title, rather than Lady,' Lucinda said. 'You see, I earned that one.'

Bloody hell, I'm a Lady. Lady Allie Lanarkshire Sheridan Something ... Allie thought dizzily. *That is so messed up. Wait until Rachel finds out.*

'You said the leadership used to just go from one to another of the families in Orion,' Allie said. 'It doesn't any more?'

Lucinda's smile disappeared. 'No. I changed that. I thought the leader should be voted in. Some of our members are idiots and I couldn't bear the idea of them making decisions about the future of the country simply because of who their parents were. It was an archaic system. One of my first acts as leader was to change the original charter. We all agreed. Now the chair is elected. I've been re-elected three times.' She made a wry face. 'I'd be rather surprised to be elected again under the circumstances.'

A sudden realisation struck Allie with almost physical force. 'That's what Nathaniel's so angry about, isn't it? You changed the rules. My brother Christopher said something about you throwing away our inheritance. That's what he meant, isn't it?'

'Precisely so,' Lucinda said. 'He would automatically have

285

taken over after me, as your mother would have refused, and he is her eldest child. Had I not changed the rules, all of this would have been his.'

'But he can't care that much,' Allie said. 'I mean, I don't care. And I don't get to do it either. Why would Christopher care so much?'

'Christopher probably wouldn't have cared at all, Allie, were it not for Nathaniel.' Lucinda leaned forward, her face very serious now. 'You see – despite everything you've personally experienced, Nathaniel is very charismatic. Very charming. Very convincing. And a fragile young man like Christopher, searching for a path to follow in life, is easily seduced. Nathaniel showed him how your mother deceived him about his own history. Convinced him he couldn't trust his own family. Promised him a life of power and privilege. It is the traditional method – he broke him down. And then he built him up again. In his own image.'

As she spoke, Allie's blood seemed to chill in her veins. Could her grandmother be right? It would explain so much. Christopher's strange behaviour when she'd seen him last December. The way he'd seemed like a strange, angrier version of himself.

Remembering that day, the two of them standing on opposite sides of the running water, she felt colder. She tried to focus on asking more questions.

'Why does Nathaniel hate you and Isabelle so much?' Allie asked. 'What happened? Is he just crazy?'

'I've known Nathaniel since he was very young,' Lucinda said. 'I knew his father. We were . . . very close. Sadly, he died when Nathaniel was still a teenager. In those days, he was a frightened, lonely young man, who'd lost his mother when he was a child, and then his father died, too. All he had was his half-sister . . . '

'Isabelle.' Allie finished the thought for her.

'Exactly.'

Allie picked up her cup. 'So Isabelle and Nathaniel – they have the same father?'

Lucinda nodded.

'And you knew their father well . . . ' Allie said. 'How did you know him? Did you work with him?'

'Not exactly.' Lucinda's smile was wry. 'I married him.'

Allie, who had just taken a mouthful of tea, choked on it. Sputtering, she set the cup and saucer down and leaned forward trying to get her breath.

'You *married* him?' Allie croaked. 'Are you Nathaniel's mother?'

Looking supremely unruffled, Lucinda handed her a tissue. 'Oh no. Their father, my ex-husband, had several wives – not all at the same time, of course. He never could settle down. I was his first wife. After we divorced, he married Nathaniel's mother, who sadly died in a riding accident while still in her twenties. He then married Isabelle's mother.'

Allie blinked. 'Blimey, he must have been good looking to have so many women chasing him. Who was this guy?'

'"This guy", as you describe him, was Alistair St. John. He was a Scottish government leader and the owner of ILC, the biggest technology company in Britain,' Lucinda said. She took a prim sip of tea. 'He was very charming.'

'Wait,' Allie said. 'Is he ... was this St. John guy my grand-father?'

Lucinda rested her hand on Allie's arm. 'Oh no, darling.'

'Then who ...' Allie held up her hands in frustration at the confusing maze of old people's love lives.

'Your grandfather was a lovely man – a good man – named Thomas Meldrum,' Lucinda said simply. 'He was my second husband. He was much older than me; he died before you were born.'

She said no more about it, but her face settled, suddenly, into well-used lines of sorrow.

In the awkward pause that followed, Allie scrambled for something to say to change the subject. 'So, was Mr –' she tried to remember the first husband's name '– St. John important in Orion or Night School, or whatever?'

'Of course,' Lucinda said, as if the alternative were unthink-able.

'What happened after he died? Like, to Nathaniel and Isabelle.'

'Alistair and I were always close,' Lucinda continued. 'He made me godmother to both his children. Isabelle's mother was still alive – is still alive now, in fact – so she lived with her. But for Nathaniel, there was no one but me.'

'What was he ... like?' Allie asked curiously.

'Difficult,' Lucinda said. 'I was often away on business. Nathaniel and Isabelle were both attending Cimmeria at that time, it was his last year. Then when the will was read ...' She shook her head.

This sounded familiar to Allie. She thought Isabelle had

mentioned something about an inheritance long ago. 'What happened? What did the will say?'

Lucinda set the teacup down carefully on the delicate, white saucer. 'Alistair had left everything to Isabelle. The youngest child. The *daughter*. Not to his eldest son. It was a shocking decision and Nathaniel took it to mean his father never really loved him. Of course his father had provided for him, a large portion of all the income from the companies and investments goes to Nathaniel to this day, but that was meaningless to him. What mattered was his father didn't trust him with the family fortune. He trusted Isabelle.'

Allie let her breath out in a low rush. 'Why did he do that? I mean, leave it all to Isabelle?'

'Alastair was a businessman to his very core.' Lucinda's gaze was shrewd. 'He had devoted his life to his work. I know he saw weaknesses in Nathaniel's character – in his mind – that concerned him deeply. I'm quite certain it was purely a business decision.'

'Is that why Nathaniel hates her now?' Allie asked. 'Why he's doing all of this? Because of their dad's will?'

'I believe so,' Lucinda said. 'Or at least, that's at the root of it. I haven't helped, of course. With my decisions as head of Orion I insured he can never inherit that either, so he hates us all.'

For a long moment Allie sat still. The longer Lucinda talked, the more pieces of her life fell into place. It was like a complicated jigsaw puzzle in which you suddenly recognised the sky.

But there were still many empty spaces.

'You said on the phone that the police are on his side, that he meets with government ministers. I still don't understand, I guess, how he can do that,' Allie said.

'Ah, now. This is an indication of how clever – how thorough – Nathaniel is,' Lucinda said. 'After attending Oxford he came to work for me. He seemed to have calmed down – to have accepted his situation. I had hope for him again. He started as a clerk, but he was terribly good at his job. Very trustworthy.' She gave a bitter laugh. 'He progressed quickly. Eventually I made him my deputy. He was in charge of day-to-day operations of my offices and of my work with Orion. He represented me when I was away on business, which was often. This meant he got to know the Orion board personally, and they socialised with him. To my eternal sorrow he spent that time gathering information he could use against me. Finding out who was dissatisfied, who wanted more, learning what people didn't like about my leadership, what changes they would like to see. Planting seeds of unhappiness among them. After a few years, he had all the information he needed to begin to undermine me. To try to destroy me.'

She leaned her chin lightly on to her hand, troubled grey eyes looking out across the room. 'One day, about six years ago, I came back from a business trip in Russia and he was gone. He'd ransacked my office safe for critical documents, and disappeared.' Her eyes met Allie's again. 'That was the beginning.'

Something in her tone made goosebumps rise on Allie's arms. 'The beginning?'

Lucinda gestured at the room around them. 'The beginning of his battle for Orion, for Cimmeria, for you ... for everything.'

'He planned it that long ago?' Allie was incredulous. 'But I would have been ... what? Just ten years old.'

'I think he started planning the moment the lawyers read out his father's will,' Lucinda said. 'This is his revenge against a long-dead man.'

The temperature in the room seemed to drop; Allie rubbed her arms as she thought it all through. The story Lucinda told was so sad – so hopeless. 'After he disappeared – you never found him? You can find anyone.'

'Oh, I found him,' Lucinda said. 'Or rather Raj Patel found him. Within a month or two, I had a good idea of where Nathaniel was living, but ... what could I do? I had no hold over him. No crime to charge him with. Everything he'd taken I'd have given to him if he asked for it. And he was like a son to me. I just ... wanted to talk to him. To tell him how much I cared about him. That I forgave him. But he refused.' She rubbed her eyes, tiredly. 'When I heard about his plotting – forming allegiances with members of the board against me – I thought it was a pathetic sign of his desperation. And then ...' Her face saddened. 'Then Christopher went missing.'

Allie's mouth went dry. 'So he'd just been ...'

'Waiting,' Lucinda said. 'Watching and waiting for Christopher to be old enough. He knew it would break my heart – my "fake" son, as he saw it, taking my real grandson away from me. Further poisoning my relationship with your mother. He knew it would cause untold damage. That's why he did it. In its own way it was a brilliant move. And now ...' Her gaze met Allie's. 'Well, you're the missing piece in his puzzle. The last remaining member of my family. The final piece on his chessboard. He wants you on his side, too. Then –' she held up her expressive hands – 'checkmate.'

Reaching across the desk, she held out a hand to Allie, who hesitantly placed her own hand in it. Lucinda's grip was strong. 'There was no way for him to know that instead of driving us apart, he would bring us closer together. That I would do everything I could to protect you from him. And that we would fight back.'

Warm with pride, Allie squeezed her grandmother's hand. But when she spoke, her words were cautious.

'You said we're in trouble – that we're trapped. Do you really think we can win?'

'We have no choice, Allie.' The look in Lucinda's eyes startled her. All the warmth was gone; her gaze was utterly ruthless. 'Because he's coming for you.'

TWENTY-NINE

When Allie finally stumbled out of Isabelle's office, her head reeled from the information. In the end, they'd talked for more than an hour, mostly about Nathaniel and Christopher, but sometimes Lucinda revealed fascinating snippets about her life and work.

They'd been talking about a meeting Lucinda had once had with the prime minister of Japan when Isabelle tapped on the door.

'I just wanted to remind you that you've a meeting in five minutes with Raj,' she told Lucinda apologetically.

Taking her cue, Allie had stood. 'I should go.'

Lucinda walked around the desk to stand in front of her. With a gentle touch, she tucked strands of Allie's wavy hair behind her ears. It was such an unconsciously maternal gesture it made Allie's heart ache.

'It has been,' Lucinda said, 'such a pleasure to speak with you. I hope we can do it again soon.'

Uncertain of when she'd see her again, and not wanting her to leave, Allie spontaneously reached up to hug her.

'Thank you, Grandmother.' It was the first time she'd said the word to Lucinda; it felt strange but *good*. 'I'm so glad I know you now.'

Lucinda's arms had tightened around her shoulders – her perfume smelled of exotic flowers.

'And I you, Allie.'

She didn't know how she would begin to explain all she'd learned to the others. But they needed to know some of it, at least. They had to understand how serious things were.

First, though, she had to find them.

She knew the others had planned to meet in one of the library's study carrels, so she tried there first. But when she tapped on the door, with its carvings of acorns and leaves, a senior student she vaguely recognised threw it open with an impatient look.

'What do you want?' he snapped, peering at her through expensive glasses. His hair stood on end, as if he'd been raking his fingers through it repeatedly. The desk behind him was so thick with papers, some had slid on to the floor in an unruly heap.

'Sorry . . .' Allie jumped back so quickly she nearly tripped. 'I was looking for someone else.'

Muttering to himself about 'junior idiots', he closed the door without another civil word.

After that, she'd tried the common room, the great hall; even the dark and echoing top floor of the classroom wing.

There was no sign of them.

Finally – her mind teeming with new information and thoughts, with Orion and Lucinda, Jules and Carter – Allie settled down in a heavy leather chair in the crowded common room to wait. Everyone always looked there first. They would find her.

Filled with boisterous students playing games, chatting and studying, the big room was typically noisy. Next to her, a group of six younger students played a raucous game of poker, which seemed to involve rampant accusations of cheating and assertions of doubt about each other's parentage. But the sound washed over Allie virtually unnoticed.

Curling up in the deep leather chair, she waited. But it was ages before Zoe shot through the door, like a sparrow swooping from the eaves.

Her quick gaze alighted on Allie, who leaped to her feet. Zoe looked relieved.

'No one knew where you were. Sylvain and Rachel are losing it. Come on.' She shot down the wide hall with easy speed and Allie hurried after her, fumbling to shove her unread book into her bag.

When she looked up, Zoe was leading her across the building's grand entrance hall to the front door. For the first time she noticed the younger girl's jacket and hat.

'You're outside?' she said, surprise making her voice rise.

'Yeah.' Zoe wrestled with the complex ancient iron lock. 'It's so freaking cold, Sylvain said no one would think to look there.'

The lock gave with a clang. Zoe needed both hands to open the heavy door. The winter air hit them like a fist.

'See what I mean?' Zoe said, hopping up and down. 'Cold.'

'Exhilarating,' Allie said dryly. She wondered how long she'd last out there without a coat but she didn't want to take the time to run all the way upstairs for hers.

'Like an ice cube in your face,' Zoe agreed, heading down the front steps and across the muddy lawn.

It was a clear evening; silvery-white stars spread like frost across the black sky as they turned right on to a footpath.

Pulling the sleeves of her jumper down over her icy fingers, Allie ran faster as they entered the forest.

Ahead of them, the top of the summer house rose through the trees like a ghost, its sharply peaked roof seemed to float above the pines until they rounded a bend and could see the rest of the building.

Allie knew it was made of a fanciful mosaic of coloured tiles, set against white stone, but in the dark the colour faded to grey. They could hear voices talking excitedly as they approached, taking the stone steps two at a time.

'Allie's here,' Zoe announced, her breath emerging as a puff of white. 'She was doing her prep.'

'I wasn't prepping,' Allie objected. 'I was . . . thinking. And I did look for you.'

'We knew no one would think to look here.' Nicole's French-accented voice came from the shadow. Allie could see only her slim leg, clad in dark tights, dangling from the stone banister upon which she'd draped herself.

'I thought *someone* might have kidnapped you.' Rachel gave her a significant look before noticing her attire and becoming distracted. 'Where's your coat?'

'Zoe forgot to mention the outside part,' Allie said. 'But I feel fine. The run warmed me up.'

In reality, the perspiration had already begun to chill against her skin, but she didn't want anyone to make her go back.

'You're good until the hypothermia sets in,' Rachel said.

'Can we get serious here?' Carter sounded exasperated. 'I think we've got ten minutes before we have to get back for dinner. Allie, what did you learn from Isabelle?'

'Actually, I wasn't with Isabelle,' she said. 'I was with Lucinda Meldrum.'

At this bombshell, they all fell silent.

'Blimey.' Zoe sounded impressed. 'I didn't even know she was here.'

'Did she say anything we need to know?' Nicole's leg moved as she shifted her position.

'Loads but ...' Allie thought about all her grandmother had revealed about her family, her history, Nathaniel, Orion ... She didn't know where to start and they only had a few minutes. 'I couldn't even get started in the time we have. I'll have to tell you later. Did you meet with Katie? Why are you all out here?'

She was shivering so hard now her voice shook a little; the pillar behind her was like a block of ice and she stepped away from it.

'The meeting was ... disturbing.' As he spoke, Sylvain unbuttoned his jacket and pulled it off. Catching her gaze, he held it out for her.

The gesture reminded her so much of the night of the winter ball that, for a split second, she couldn't move. She remembered the way he'd taken off his tuxedo jacket that night, and what had happened next.

Goosebumps traced a pattern on her arms.

Then she reached out her hand.

The jacket wasn't long but it had weight. The warmth of Sylvain's body and the scent of his cologne lingered in the jacket's soft fabric. It slipped around her frozen shoulders like a hug.

'Katie thinks about ninety students will go with Nathaniel. We've been talking about how to handle it.' Rachel's voice dragged Allie back to reality.

'*Ninety*? That's half the school!'

'Yeah, it's way more than we expected,' Zoe said.

'I've already spoken to my dad,' Rachel said. 'Even they weren't expecting that many to go. They're having meetings about it now.'

'But some will stay ... right?' Allie said.

It was Carter who replied. 'Out of the ninety, she thinks ten are willing to stand up to their parents. I mean, most of these kids aren't Night School and they have no idea what's really going on here.'

Allie's heart thudded as their words sank in. Ten students. It was nothing. Half the school would be gone. Nathaniel would get his shock and awe moment.

'Based on what her parents have told her, she believes it will happen this week,' Sylvain said. 'Perhaps as soon as tomorrow.'

Too soon.

'No no no ... ' Allie pressed her fingertips against her temples. 'We're not ready. What are we going to do?'

'We told her our plan for those who want to stay – places to hide. Ways to avoid being found.' Carter's voice emerged from the dark. 'Katie's passing them on to those she trusts. Rachel and Raj talked about it and he knows everything we know. Did you discuss it with Lucinda?'

'She said ... ' Pulling the too-large jacket more tightly around her, Allie tried to remember exactly what her grandmother had said. 'She said she's working behind the scenes with the board – lobbying those who are unsure who to support. If she can get most of them to side with her, she has a chance. If more than half the board side with Nathaniel ... ' Her voice trailed off. Lucinda hadn't gone into what would happen if most of the board sided against her but the danger of that had been clear. 'The thing is she needs time to convince them.'

She looked around the open stone structure. The others formed a rough circle around her, their breath rising in clouds. Everyone looked tired and defeated. There were so few of them. How could they stop this?

'Time is the one thing she hasn't got.' With a sigh, Carter leaned back against the stone pillar behind him, staring up to where the ceiling of the summer house disappeared into a high peak, lost now, in the darkness. 'What happens if Nathaniel moves quickly? What happens if he comes tomorrow?'

The sleeves of Sylvain's jacket hung down below Allie's hands. When she held up her empty hands, they slid back just far enough to reveal her fingers.

'She also told me if students refuse to leave, Nathaniel could send the police.' She laughed with bitter irony. 'Isn't it funny? The police will come if students don't want to go, but we can't call them if there's a murder. It's just like . . . the world's gone crazy.'

'Clever tyrants are never punished.' Sylvain's voice was so low only Allie heard him. She glanced over at him. As he leaned back against the stone balustrade he seemed tense and tired.

'So what happens now?' Rachel asked.

'Now, we work on our plan.' Carter sounded grim. 'And get ready.'

Just before seven, they headed back to the main building for dinner. Nobody was hungry but attendance was required.

Sylvain swung into step beside Allie as they left the summer house.

'How were things with your grandmother, really? Were you glad to see her again?' His eyes searched hers.

'I was,' she said. 'I like her, you know?'

He nodded. 'She's intimidating,' he said. 'But she is also charismatic.'

It was weird to think that Sylvain understood her grandmother better than she did. But his parents were French billionaires. Sylvain had known people like Lucinda all his life.

'Still,' she said, 'it was worrying, too.'

'Why was it worrying?'

She pulled his coat tighter around her. 'Because I think she's scared.'

Behind them she could hear Zoe and Carter talking quietly and she remembered her conversation with Jules. She had to tell Carter before they went inside – he needed to know.

'I've got to talk to Carter for a second,' she told Sylvain, noticing as she did so that in the light of the stars his eyes were the precise colour of his dark blue sweater. 'I'll see you inside?'

He inclined his head with cool politeness, his face betraying no emotion.

Allie slowed her pace until she was walking beside Zoe and Carter. She turned to the younger girl. 'I need to talk to Carter alone for a second. Is that OK?'

Unbothered, Zoe shrugged and ran to catch up with Rachel. Allie heard her say 'Did you finish your chemistry assignment?' as if today were a perfectly ordinary school day.

When everyone was out of earshot, she turned to Carter, slowing her pace. 'Have you seen Jules since this afternoon?'

He gave her an odd look. 'No. Why?'

'I ran into her after class . . .' Allie started then she corrected herself. 'Actually, she came to find me. She was really upset.'

Carter stopped and turned to face her. She saw that the cold had made his cheeks red.

'About what?'

Allie's stomach tightened as she tried to decide how to tell him.

'She knows . . . she said . . . ' She exhaled a cloud of warm air. 'She knows you don't have detention. She wanted to know why you were working in the garden with . . . me.'

His jaw tight, Carter looked out into the darkness ahead of them. His cheeks were redder now.

'I didn't know what to tell her.' Allie shoved her hands in the pockets of her skirt and looked down at her shoes. 'She thought you were cheating on her with me.'

He didn't look at her. 'What did you say?'

'I told her we weren't, of course. That you're my friend and you look out for me and that she needs to accept that.'

He exhaled. 'Thank you.'

'And, look.' She tried to catch his gaze but he was looking past her. 'I just wanted to say ... thanks. I mean ... it was hard work and ... I didn't know you ... I mean, I thought you had to ...'

She hated her own stumbling words. He'd got out of bed, three days a week, at five thirty in the morning to spend two hours in the freezing cold doing hard work, just so she wouldn't be alone. Why couldn't she think of the right thing to say?

Finally he met her eyes.

'It's OK. You don't have to thank me.' Unexpectedly, he flashed a rakish grin. 'I just didn't have anything better to do.'

As Allie gaped at him, trying to think of a response, he turned and loped towards the school.

In the dining hall, most of the other students had already gathered by the time Allie arrived. She paused in the doorway to take in the scene. Carter stopped with her and followed her gaze.

White linens covered tables topped with glittering candles, crystal glasses and white china plates, all bearing the Cimmeria crest. Above their heads in the cavernous room, the chandeliers glowed. A warm fire crackled in the gigantic fireplace. The room smelled of roasted meat and wood smoke.

This was Cimmeria at its very best. It seemed too beautiful – too perfect – to be destroyed.

What will it be like if Nathaniel wins? Allie wondered as her eyes swept the room. *Who will be here tomorrow?*

'I'm going to sit with Jules tonight.' Carter said.

'Oh.' Thrown, Allie fumbled for a reply. They'd all been sitting together every day since the group had formed but of course after everything that happened he'd need to sit with Jules. 'I mean, great. That's a good idea ... '

She watched as he walked to the table where Jules sat with Katie and other friends. She saw Jules' face light up when she spotted him and realised he was coming to her. Watched her leap up to wrap him in a hug. Saw his lips brush hers as he bent to whisper something in her ear ...

'Take your seats, please!' Zelazny's roar startled Allie so much she jumped.

She walked to where the others sat at their usual table. Sylvain's cashmere coat was lined in expensive silk; it slipped easily from her shoulders. When she held it out to him he accepted it with a guarded look, as if he was afraid of what she might say.

But all she said was, 'Thanks for the loan. I hope you didn't get chilblains ... or whatever you get from the cold.'

'You're welcome,' he said. 'I don't know what chilblains are but I don't think I have them.'

'What *are* chilblains, anyway?' Nicole asked, looking around the table. 'People only seemed to get them in Dickens.'

'I don't know.' Allie dropped into a seat next to Zoe. 'And I don't want to.'

Zoe, who had opened her mouth to explain chilblains, snapped it shut. 'I know what they are,' she said. 'But if you don't want to know I won't tell you.'

'Where's Rachel?' Allie said, suddenly noticing her absence.

'Sitting with Lucas.' Nicole gestured to a nearby table. Lucas had his arm across Rachel's shoulders and their heads were close together.

'And Carter is with Jules tonight.' Looking thoughtful, Sylvain glanced over to where the two seemed to be sharing a private joke then back at Allie again. She avoided his eyes.

'It must be date night.' As she spoke, Nicole's doll-like eyes studied Sylvain and Allie, missing nothing.

'At least there's still us.' Oblivious to the unspoken drama happening around her, Zoe was so peppy and *normal* Allie wanted to squash her under something heavy.

She thought about telling them the things she'd learned from Lucinda, what Orion really was, and why Nathaniel was doing this. But it seemed weird to tell only a few of them and leave out Rachel and Carter.

Besides, nobody seemed very interested in that stuff right now. The idea that the school could be emptied tomorrow – that Nathaniel's plan could work – had drained the energy from them all. Everything felt futile. It was as if, instead of readying for battle, they'd begun preparing themselves for defeat.

Holding up her water glass, Allie watched the liquid swirl. Remembering her history lesson that morning, she thought about Napoleon's plan – the way he defeated a larger army through cunning and deception.

But who is Napoleon? she wondered. *Is it us? Or Nathaniel?*

B ut Nathaniel did not make his move the next day. Or the day after that.

Or the next day.

As time passed, the school fell into an uneasy sort of normality. Students went to class, studied, played games … and waited.

When a week had passed without any sign of Nathaniel, Allie began to allow herself to hope that maybe they were safe after all. Perhaps Lucinda had got to the board in time. Maybe they'd stood up to him and he'd been forced to back down.

When she asked Isabelle about it, though, the headmistress just shook her head. 'He's letting us get comfortable. Hoping we drop our guard.'

After the Night School instructors returned to the school, the group met less often. Raj and Isabelle had ordered them to stop looking for the spy and, under the circumstances, they had little choice – the teachers watched them like hawks. Now there was nothing for them to do but wait. Jules and Lucas began joining them for meals again and conversations about lessons replaced Nathaniel and spies.

It was a kind of false normality and Allie hated it. It felt like they were all pretending something awful wasn't about to happen. But what else could they do?

She found she missed the adrenaline rush of meeting in secret out of hours, of sneaking into locked rooms and searching for evidence. She missed the feeling of actually doing something. They were back on the outside of things again. On some level, maybe they always had been but, at least for a while, it had felt like they'd had some control.

Without the daily gatherings, she found it easy to keep her distance from Sylvain. And she wanted to do that. She needed time to think about things.

Every so often, though, she'd look up and find him watching her from across a room, a lost look in his bluer than blue eyes. And her heart would twist inside her.

Each time it happened she remembered what he'd said: 'I won't wait for ever . . . It hurts too much . . .'

Sometimes, when he made no effort to pursue her, or he didn't laugh at one of her jokes, she'd worry he'd decided not to wait any more and panic would unfurl in her chest unexpectedly, making her heart stutter.

He just . . . had to wait. Just until this thing with Nathaniel was finished. After that . . .

For his part, Carter never returned to the walled garden.

Allie had suspected he wouldn't after their talk, but she still felt bereft that first sunrise when he didn't appear.

Still, though, at least they were getting along better. He treated her like a normal friend – not a good friend – but a friend, nonetheless.

Baby steps, she told herself.

The weirdest development was she was starting to *like* gardening. She remembered something Jo had told her once about falling in love with the gardens after she'd been given weeks of detention. At the time Allie hadn't understood but now she could see what Jo meant. There was something therapeutic about the smell of damp earth; about dropping seeds into it and covering them up. It was calming.

It helped that the cold was less biting now. March had arrived in the midst of all this and green shoots appeared everywhere, all at once, as if someone somewhere had pressed a button marked 'Grow'. The neat, straight furrows she and Carter had made that morning in the rain were already lined with tiny green plants that would someday be carrots, cabbages and potatoes. Looking at them, she felt a sense of accomplishment – she'd helped to create that.

Mr Ellison had become less fierce once he and Allie were alone again, as if he felt sorry for her. Most days, he brought out a thermos of hot sweet tea and packets of biscuits, and they'd take a break, sitting on a bench, munching the biscuits and watching the birds work. They talked about a lot of things then – about his childhood in London, and how he came to Cimmeria to escape the city. He never told her the story Carter had told, about making a mistake and losing everything, and

Allie didn't ask. But she found herself telling him things she wouldn't have wanted to tell anyone else. How she and her mum couldn't talk any more. How she missed her dad. There was something about him – a kind of thoughtfulness and wisdom – that made her feel she could really talk to him. He'd made mistakes in his life, too. And so he, perhaps alone among the adults she knew, was unlikely to judge her.

Lately, Allie had been having long talks with Isabelle, too. After Lucinda's visit she'd plied her with questions about Orion and Nathaniel and Gabe.

It was Isabelle who told her about the other secret groups like Orion elsewhere in the world. That the one in Europe was called Demeter. The one in America, Prometheus. That Orion was the oldest but no longer the biggest or most powerful.

The headmistress also told her more about Nathaniel's plan. As they sat in her office one Friday after the day's classes ended, Allie asked her about Nathaniel.

'What does he really want?' she said. 'I mean, I know he only wants me to get back at Lucinda. And I know he hates you because of the inheritance. But why is he really doing this?'

As if she'd felt a sudden chill, Isabelle pulled her navy cardigan off the back of her chair and draped it over her shoulders. Under it she wore a white polo-neck top and slim, grey trousers. There was no way you would look at her and think she was organising a fight – preparing for an attack. She just looked like a teacher.

'For the last few years, Nathaniel has travelled the world seeking support for his plan to overthrow Lucinda and take full control of Orion,' Isabelle explained. 'Some of the reason is personal, as you know, but some of it is pure hunger for power and wealth. To be richer than his father ever was. Better. On his own, he hasn't got enough support within the organisation to do it so he's looking for international backers. He visited Demeter in Zurich in January and I'm told they sent him packing.' Her gaze hardened. 'But I fear he received a warmer reception from Prometheus.'

'America?' Allie blinked. 'Why would they listen to him? He's crazy.'

'They're not really listening to him,' Isabelle said. 'They want to use him. You see, there are people in Prometheus who have been arguing for precisely what Nathaniel is offering for many years. They see in him a potential ally. With Britain on their side that would tip the balance. They could have what they've always wanted – more control, more power. Unimaginable wealth. The return of the oligarchs. An end, I fear, to the modern experiment with democracy.

'If they can rid themselves of the shackles of laws designed to protect people . . . just *think* of the money they could make. They would be kings.'

Allie looked at her doubtfully. 'But that's bonkers. Surely there's no way it would happen. People wouldn't accept it.'

Isabelle's expression held an odd mix of cynicism and melancholy. 'People wouldn't even notice,' she said.

'Of course they'd notice – everything would change.'

'Yes, things would change. But not obviously,' Isabelle said. 'And most people aren't paying attention. They've got jobs and children, mortgage payments and problems . . . they don't have time to notice little changes in the law that don't seem to affect them anyway. Look at what Orion's accomplished already – it has infiltrated every major branch of British leadership from the government to the media to the courts. It has never overtly tampered with an election as far as I know, but it could if it wanted to. And if it did, no one would ever find out.' She leaned back in her chair. 'Because Orion controls the organisation that monitors elections.'

Allie stared at her open-mouthed.

'Are you saying Nathaniel could actually do what he wants to do? He could –' she didn't even know the word for what he wanted to do – 'take over?'

'I'm afraid he could,' Isabelle said. 'That's why this matters so much. That's why people have died. Because what's at stake is everything.'

With so little action, Allie had no choice but to catch up on her school work. Every afternoon she and Rachel could be found in the library studying at Rachel's favourite tucked-away table, sitting in soft leather chairs in the glow of the green-shaded desk lamp. Just like the old days.

One Wednesday, nearly two weeks after the instructors first returned, Rachel was tutoring Allie in chemistry. It was late afternoon and Allie was thinking very strongly about going to the kitchen in search of a snack.

'I think you missed part of that molecule.' Rachel pointed at the diagram in Allie's notebook. 'There should be another bit. Like this.' Sliding her textbook over, she showed Allie how the design should look. 'Otherwise you'll end up with, I don't know, a badger molecule.'

Drawing the new section, Allie didn't look up as she replied. 'A badger molecule?'

'You know how badgers kind of look like someone dropped some of their molecules and then accidentally added parts of something else's molecules? That's what I mean.'

As Allie's molecule began to make more sense, though, a disturbed murmur swept the room. Glancing around, Allie could see no obvious problem, but some students had left their tables and now gathered in clusters, whispering. A few of them ran from the room.

'What's going on?' she said, mostly to herself.

'Someone probably broke up with someone.' Rachel kept working. 'I can't believe I didn't know before now.'

'You still don't actually know,' Allie pointed out.

'Good point,' Rachel said, half standing. 'So if I go and ask . . .'

Then she saw something that made her stop talking.

Her footsteps silent on the Persian rugs, Katie was running across the room towards them, her vivid ponytail streaming behind her. She must have run a long way – she was breathless; her milky skin even more pale than usual.

When Katie reached them, she gripped the table so hard her knuckles turned white.

'It's started.'

THIRTY-ONE

'**G**o.'

When Katie didn't move, Allie shoved her hard.
'Now!'

She almost shouted the word and the girl turned and ran
without looking back at her.

Adrenaline poured into Allie's veins, setting her pulse racing
as she turned to Rachel. 'Are you ready?'

Looking scared, Rachel took off her glasses and tucked them
into her skirt pocket.

'What about our things . . . ?' She gestured at the table in
front of them, piled with books and papers and pens, all the
normal accoutrements of student life.

'Leave them.' Allie's tone was gentle. She needed Rachel not
to panic. 'They'll be here when we come back.'

If we come back, she thought.

Rachel nodded as if this all made perfect sense.

The library was almost empty now.

'Come on, Rach.' Allie took a step towards the door. 'We've got to bail.'

Still not moving, Rachel looked around the room. 'Lucas.'

Allie took her arm. 'He knows where to go. You told him. He'll be there now. You have to trust him. OK?'

Taking an unsteady breath, Rachel nodded and straightened her spine. 'Let's go.'

Then they ran out of the room into the suddenly empty grand hallway and up the grand staircase, to where groups of confused students had clustered.

Through the windows on the landing they got a glimpse of the row of gleaming limousines, Rolls Royces and Bentleys outside, stretching as far as they could see.

Rachel blanched. 'There are so many.'

'There should be ninety.' Allie's tone was tense as her gaze swept down the row of dark cars. 'Come on.'

Quickening their pace they ran down the hallway. A winding stone staircase led them down to the ancient cellar. As they hurtled into the coolness of the dim, stone room they found most of the others had already arrived. Zoe, Nicole and Sylvain were clustered in a tight knot, talking in urgent whispers.

'There you are.' Nicole looked relieved.

'Where's Carter?' Allie asked.

Silence fell. Allie had the sickening sense that something was wrong.

It was Sylvain who broke the news.

'He's searching for Jules.' Sylvain held her gaze steadily. 'Her parents were among the first to arrive.'

The floor seemed to sway under Allie's feet; she stared at him in horrified disbelief. 'Jules . . . ? No, that can't be right.'

But even as she said it she knew it was true – he'd never get that wrong.

Raking her fingers through her hair, she tried to think this through. Carter had never once mentioned which side Jules' parents were on. He'd never said a word about it. Allie had just assumed they supported Isabelle – the alternative was unthinkable.

Poor Carter.

With that, the awful reality of it all set in. Anyone's parents could be out there. Panic made it hard for her to think.

'Did Jules get away?' Allie asked, trying to steady herself. 'Did everyone get away? Do we know?'

'We came down here right away so we don't know what's happening upstairs,' Zoe said.

Next to her, Nicole looked worried. 'Their arrival happened so quickly.'

The students who didn't want to go should now be scattered in hiding places all over the campus. Isabelle, who was fully involved in the plan and had arranged its finer details, was probably telling some parents right now that she had no idea where their children were.

'Someone should go up to keep an eye on things,' Allie said. 'Rachel and I are safe, we could both go.'

Rachel gave a tense nod, her dark hair bouncing against her shoulders.

'You shouldn't go alone,' Sylvain said. 'I'm safe. I can go as well.'

Looking down at her nails, Nicole hesitated just a little too long.

'I will stay down here,' she said at last. When they all turned to stare at her she gave a delicate shrug that pretended non-chalance she clearly didn't feel. Her dark eyes betrayed her nervousness. 'Just in case. I think my parents are ... undecided.'

Zoe tugged on Allie's sleeve insistently. 'I want to come with you.'

Apprehension made it hard for Allie to breathe. It was too much – Zoe was so small. She was only thirteen.

If anything happened to her ...

'Come on, Zoe.' Allie's tone was gentle; convincing. 'It's not fair to leave Nicole alone down here.' When Zoe lifted her chin stubbornly, she tried a different tack. 'Look, it won't be for long. I'll come back in a few minutes and we can switch. OK? We need to stick together.'

For a moment it looked as if Zoe might refuse, but then she relented, her shoulders drooping.

'Sure,' she said, jutting out her lower lip. 'I'll stay here and *hide*.'

'All right.' Sylvain turned to Rachel and Allie. 'We must divide. I'll take the boys' dorm. Rachel, you take the girls' dorm. Allie, you're the main building – the library and common room – and try to find Isabelle. We'll meet back here in twenty minutes precisely.' He looked from one to another of them, his expression deadly serious. 'Don't be late. Don't make us come and look for you.'   .

There were several ways into the cellar. Sylvain headed down a narrow corridor to a staircase leading to the main building. Allie and Rachel turned back to the staircase they'd come down earlier – it led straight to the girls' dorm.

As they headed up the stairs, Nicole called after them. 'Be careful.'

Her French-accented words echoed off the stone walls around them as they climbed.

Rachel and Allie ran all the way to the top of the dark, dusty staircase – the only sound their harsh breaths, the pounding of their feet on the uneven steps.

They emerged into the girls' dormitory to find it a scene of utter upheaval. In the corridor girls were hugging each other and crying as male bodyguards and drivers in a variety of uniforms hurried them along with the barely controlled violence of riot police.

'Get your things,' one man in a black uniform barked at a twelve-year-old girl who cowered away from him, clinging to a friend's hand, 'or we're leaving without them. It makes no difference to me.'

Tears streaming down her cheeks, the girl – about the same size and build as Zoe – let go of her friend and walked fearfully down the hall in front of him.

Left behind, her friend sobbed brokenly. Meeting Allie's shocked gaze she held up her hands. 'I don't understand ... what's happening?'

'Bloody hell,' Allie whispered to Rachel.

The girl's long blonde hair was tied back with a blue bow – she was skinny, with a light dusting of freckles on the bridge of her nose. She looked somehow familiar, but Allie couldn't place where it was she'd seen her before.

Crouching down until her gaze was on the girl's level, she took her by the shoulders, her hands gentle but firm. 'Listen to me. Do you see that door right there?' She pointed at the door to her own bedroom. The weeping girl nodded. 'Go in there and do not come out until the cars are all gone. Not even if someone calls your name. Not even if it's someone you know.' Clearly terrified, the girl nodded. She'd stopped crying, and she stared at Allie as if she were a rescuer, descending from a helicopter to pluck her from a flooded house.

Her eyes were the same cornflower blue as Jo's.

Allie's throat had gone so tight she could hardly speak. Jo didn't have a little sister – it must just be a coincidence. But the similarity was so striking ...

'What's your name?' she whispered.

'Emma.'

'Your *last* name.' But Allie's tone was too insistent and the girl began to cry again.

'Hammond,' she said, sobbing.

Rachel had crouched down next to her too, now. She took the girl's hand. 'Emma Hammond, how old are you?'

'T-twelve,' the girl replied.

Rachel nodded seriously as if twelve was a very good age to be. 'Will you be OK for a little while by yourself? While we go and try to help some other girls?'

The girl nodded, although it was clear she wasn't at all sure.

Allie had control of herself now. She wasn't related to Jo. Her eyes were just blue.

People have blue eyes.

'There are biscuits in the top right drawer of my desk,' Allie said. 'I expect you to eat them all. Now go.'

They watched as the girl ran into the bedroom. Their eyes met for a second as the door began to close and Allie again saw a resemblance to Jo that made her shudder.

Swallowing hard, she nodded at the little girl. The door latched with a sturdy click.

'I wish those doors had locks,' Rachel muttered.

'Me too.' Allie squeezed her hand.

Rachel caught her gaze. 'You did the right thing,' she said, answering the question Allie was afraid to ask.

'But she's too young,' Allie said. 'Too young for us to include her in our plan. Nobody under sixteen could stay without their parents' permission, remember?' She kicked the wall next to her with such force a feather-sized piece of plaster floated down to rest on the floor next to her foot. 'Why don't we have a *better plan*? Why are we so stupid?'

Rachel's jaw was tight. 'We did the best we could.'

But at that moment it felt like they'd failed.

Looking at the bizarre scene around them, Allie said, 'Are you OK to be up here alone? This is worse than I expected.'

Some part of her expected Rachel to tell her not to go – she didn't really want to be alone right now herself. But, to Allie's surprise, Rachel just squared her shoulders.

'I'll be fine. But, Allie?' The look on her face gave Allie an idea of what was coming next. 'I'm not going to leave the young ones. I'm going to hide them, too.'

Allie couldn't ever remember being more proud of her.

'It was a crap plan, anyway,' she said, a smile quirking up her lips.

Rachel held up her fist. 'Stay safe.'

As Allie raised her own fist a sudden thought made her hesitate. *This is the first time I've ever seen Rachel really behave as if she was in Night School.*

Before Rachel could notice the pause, though, Allie recovered and bumped her fist with her own. 'Always.'

Downstairs, the scene was even worse than the girls' dorm. As students wept and struggled, and uniformed men shouted, Zelazny stood red-faced near the door bellowing, 'Please return to your normal activities! Do not linger in the hallway. If you are collecting students, do so in an orderly fashion. School must not be disrupted!'

No one was listening.

'There's no need to be so grabby!' A tall, bookish-looking boy said, wrenching his arm free from a uniformed muscleman's grip. 'I'm cooperating. You can tell them I cooperated.'

Allie recognised the stressed-out boy from the study carrel – the one who'd snapped at her the other day. But now he looked young and frightened – his glasses had been knocked crooked on his face as he tried to walk with elaborate dignity, just out of the man's reach.

'Hey!' Running to his side, Allie touched his shoulder and he spun round to look at her. Behind his dark-framed glasses, his eyes looked afraid. 'Are you OK?'

'Oh, I'm just fine,' he said with false bravery. 'I'm going home, though. Pete here won't have it any other way, eh, Pete?'

The dark sarcasm in his voice was not missed by the man, who shot him a threatening look.

'Think you're funny? I am allowed to subdue you, boy. You do not want me to subdue you.' With that, Pete shoved the boy so hard he took an involuntary sprawling step towards the door.

'See?' he said despairingly as he caught himself. 'Everything's just fine.'

As they walked out the door, the driver turned to look at Allie with appraising eyes – something in his gaze made her blood chill in her veins. He knew who she was.

Suddenly afraid, she ran across the entrance hall to where Zelazny had given up shouting and now muttered at a clipboard in his hand. He seemed to be ticking names off as students walked out, dragging their suitcases behind them.

'Mr Zelazny—' Allie began, but he cut her off without looking up.

'Not now.'

But she was not going to be put off. Not today.

'Mr *Zelazny*.' This time she said his name with such authority the teacher looked up, his mouth open in surprise.

When she had his full attention, Allie spoke clearly, enunciating each syllable: 'Where is Isabelle?'

For a moment he looked at her as if he'd never seen her before. As she studied him with a frown, she noticed the clipboard quivering very slightly.

Blustering, raging, fearless Zelazny was frightened. But if he was the spy . . . wasn't this what he wanted?

'Isabelle?' she said again.

He rubbed a weary hand across his face.

'Great hall.' His voice was hoarse from shouting, his eyes bloodshot from lack of sleep.

Without waiting for more information, Allie fought her way back through the noisy, frightened crowd, across the polished oak floor, past the tapestries where ladies in long, medieval gowns looked upon the chaos but passed no judgement, under the sparkling crystal chandeliers.

The door to the great hall stood open. Clad in a dark skirt and crisp, grey blouse, a silk scarf draped around her neck, Isabelle stood on the low platform she used for induction days, surrounded by a crowd of worried teachers and a handful of students.

She appeared as calm and unruffled as Zelazny had looked panicked. But Allie knew her well enough by now to know it was an act. She could see her tension in the way she held her hands, in the high set of her shoulder and the tiny lines around her eyes.

'There is nothing more we can do right now,' she was saying as Allie walked in. 'We must wait for them all to go before we know how many we have left.'

The teachers grumbled, clearly not satisfied.

'It's not just students leaving,' one of the science instructors said. 'Sarah Jones is gone.'

Someone gasped and a whisper swept the room. Allie had to think for a moment before realising they must be talking about the biology teacher. Rachel had mentioned her before.

'Are you certain?' Isabelle's face betrayed no emotion.

'Her room was cleared out when I stopped in on my way

here.' The woman looked shaken. 'We were friends. I didn't know she was one of Nathaniel's supporters.'

Isabelle didn't pause to comfort her. 'Does anyone know of other teachers who are missing?'

'I haven't seen Darren Campbell,' a voice called from the back, and the crowd murmured restively.

'What about Ken Brade?' a maths teacher asked.

But someone quickly said, 'I saw him out front helping August Zelazny.'

A sigh swept the group like a breeze as the teacher's loyalty was confirmed.

'I need specifics,' Isabelle said. 'Will two of you volunteer to verify all the teachers who are missing?'

Allie waited as the volunteers were chosen and Isabelle stepped down from her platform. The headmistress was instantly swamped in a sea of anxious instructors but she moved through them with steady determination.

'I don't know,' she kept saying. 'We'll discuss this at the seven o'clock meeting. I'll have all the facts then.'

As she emerged from the crowd her steely gaze met Allie's. Her eyebrows winged up, and she motioned her closer. 'With me.'

As they moved out into the hallway, Isabelle took her arm, pulling her swiftly through the crowds. Two of Raj's guards materialised as if she'd conjured them, flanking them protectively.

'Did Jules get away?' Allie asked urgently. 'Did Katie?'

Isabelle turned to face her. 'I need you go to the agreed place until this is over,' she said. 'I can't protect you right now. There's too much happening at once.'

322

'I can't just hide while this is happening.' Even as she said the words, Allie realised how much like Zoe she sounded. 'I have to help.'

'You cannot help. No one can help us now.' Just for a moment Isabelle's guard slipped and Allie saw anguish in her eyes. Her voice sharpened. 'Just go back to the agreed place. Raj has guards all around it. I need you there. If you see the others on the way send them back, too but do *not* go looking for them. Not anyone.'

Allie opened her mouth to protest, but Isabelle grabbed her arm. The strength of her grip caught Allie off guard; Isabelle's nails dug in like blades.

'Allie, listen to me. Do you think for one moment all those *drivers*,' she spat the word out, 'are who they say they are? They have all the right paperwork but ... *look at them*. Those are highly trained security personnel. Those are Nathaniel's guards and they are all over my school.' For a brief angry second, she shook Allie so hard her body quivered. 'I need you all in a safe place. Now. Any of you could be taken and I wouldn't know until it was too late. I cannot protect any of you right now. The plan is off until this is over. Go now.'

Her ferocity had the intended effect. As soon as she was released, Allie ran. But it wasn't herself she was thinking about and, despite Isabelle's words, it wasn't the cellar she headed for. Instead, she vaulted the stairs two at a time, one word ringing in her panicked mind like an alarm bell.

Rachel.

THİRTY-TWO

I left her completely alone. If anything happens to her ...

As she hurtled up to the top floor, Allie's breath came in short gasps. At first she thought it was from the exertion of moving so fast but then, to her horror, her vision began to darken. Her throat had narrowed until she felt as if she were choking.

No please. Not now.

She fought to stave off the panic attack – breathing in through her nose and letting the air whoosh out through her mouth as she'd learned to do. Even as the walls closed in on her, she forced herself to keep moving.

I will not give in to this, she thought. *I will get to Rachel and then I will have a nice, quiet nervous breakdown in the cellar with my closest friends.*

At the thought she tried to laugh but it came out as a sob. Still the action served to loosen the constriction on her lungs and she took a welcome gulp of air as she crested the top of the stairs to find . . . nothing.

The long, narrow corridor lined with plain white doors was empty. The crowds from earlier had dissipated. There were no crying girls, no angry men in terrifying uniforms. There was nobody at all.

'Rachel?' In the emptiness the word echoed back at her mockingly.

She looked around in bewilderment. All the doors were closed. Would she have to go through each one?

'Rachel?' She tried again louder.

Halfway down the hallway, one white door swung opened with a quiet click.

A rush of relief made Allie dizzy. It was her own bedroom door.

Of course! Rachel must have gone in there to hide with Emma.

She hurtled down the hallway to the open door.

'Rach!' she called as she skidded through the doorway. 'I was freaking—'

But it wasn't Rachel waiting for her. It was Emma. And she was covered in blood.

Whirling, her heart hammering inside her chest, Allie searched the room for an attacker but, other than the blood-covered girl, it was empty.

She crouched down in front of her, resting her hands gently on shoulders as delicate as a bird's wings, and looked for wounds. The girl appeared to be frozen with fear.

'Emma!' She turned the girl round and back again but could find no cuts. 'Who hurt you?'

'A man came.' Emma's big, frightened eyes stared up at her. 'He was looking for you.'

Allie swallowed hard. 'What did he say?' Her voice sounded as if it came from far away. 'Emma, where did the blood come from?'

Tears streaming down her face, the girl held up a folded piece of plain white paper, stained with bloody fingerprints.

'He said to give this to you.' As Allie took the page from her hands gingerly, a tear rolled down Emma's cheek, tracing a path in the gore.

With her heart pounding out no recognisable rhythm and her head beginning to swim, Allie knew she couldn't stop to read the note. Clutching it in her hand she turned back to Emma.

'Can you run?'

The girl nodded.

Standing, Allie grabbed her hand – it felt so small and fragile.

'As fast as you can, Emma.' She was surprised by the steadiness of her voice.

They ran down the hall to where a door hid the old servants' staircase. As the door swung open revealing the winding stone staircase, Emma recoiled.

'It's dark.'

But Allie wasn't about to stop now. 'Don't be afraid of the dark, Emma. Be afraid of that man.'

Then she pulled her on to the stairs.

Emma's broken sobs and the scuffing of their footsteps were the only noises that accompanied them down for what felt like eternity. Around and around the staircase twisted and turned until Allie was certain they must be halfway to Hell.

But she held back the rising tide of panic until she saw Zoe waiting for her near the foot of the stairs.

'She's here!' Zoe called over her shoulder. Then she looked back at Allie and her eyes widened. 'Who's that with you? What happened?'

Carter and Sylvain appeared behind her as Allie stumbled into the room, still clinging to Emma's hand. She could see their shock as they saw the blood-covered girl.

'Rachel.' Allie gasped, trying to breathe. But she couldn't get any more words out. There seemed to be no oxygen down here.

Moving quickly, Carter grabbed Emma and examined her for wounds.

Realising she was about to fall, Allie put one hand on a stone column. It felt cold as ice under her fingertips.

'Is she here?' she wheezed. The walls moved rapidly towards her, as if they were about to attack her. 'Rachel ... is she here?'

'Rachel?' Sylvain's voice seemed to come from far away. 'She was with you. Allie ... ?'

He caught her as she fell, his arms warm and strong around her.

'Sylvain ...' She struggled for air.

'I've got you,' he said, lifting her from the earth.

'We must find Raj Patel.' Nicole sounded frightened. It was the first time Allie could ever remember her sounding scared.

Sylvain said something to her in French before switching back to English. 'It's not safe yet.'

They were all sitting together in a tight circle on the gritty stone floor. It seemed like they were talking in circles, too.

They needed to do something but there was nothing to be done.

Allie's head felt as if it had been stuffed with feathers that were occasionally kicking her in the face.

After she'd nearly passed out, they'd forced water on her and made her sit still, her head resting on her knees. Her breathing was steady now. In fact, her lungs were working so perfectly it was kind of enraging.

They told her what they knew – the students they'd seen going and those who'd made it to the safe places.

She still clutched Nathaniel's blood-splattered letter in her hand like a weapon. Although the light in the cellar was dim she could make out the words he'd written. It was obvious he'd been rushed – his handwriting was usually so precise and neat; this was a hurried scrawl.

Dear Allie

I looked for you but could not find you. Unfortunately, no one was willing to tell me where you were. Your friend Rachel was singularly uncooperative. I was forced to punish her for her rudeness. I'm keeping her with me.

Allie, I've grown impatient with our little game. So here is what you will do. You will come to me tonight and offer yourself in exchange for Rachel. Come alone. Do not *bring Raj Patel or Isabelle or any of the other instructors or guards.*

When you have done this, Rachel will be released, alive and well. If you fail in any regard, if you break any of the rules I've set out here, she will die precisely as Jo died.

And you will know, for all your life, you could have saved her.

I will be at the castle ruins at midnight. Do not be late.

Nathaniel

The thought of Rachel alone with that monster made Allie's stomach twist; doubling over she dug her fists into her abdomen, pressing back against the pain.

We underestimated Nathaniel again, she thought, despairing. *Oh, Rachel, I'm so sorry ...*

Reaching across her body to free one of her fists, Carter squeezed her hand. 'She's still alive, Allie,' he said, his tone gentle.

She shook her head so fiercely her hair stung her cheeks as it swung. She couldn't afford to hope now; hope was nothing but delayed heartbreak. He should know that anyway – Jules was gone. He hadn't got to her in time.

'You don't know that, Carter. He lies. He killed Jo ...'

'I know.' His tone was measured. 'But we have no reason to believe he killed Rachel.'

'The blood.' Allie pointed at Emma who now sat with Nicole, who'd cleaned her face with bottled water and draped her own jumper around her. Staring at them all mutely, the girl appeared to be in shock. 'Where did it come from?'

'It's Rachel's,' Nicole said. 'But the wound Emma describes sounds superficial.'

'That much blood was from a superficial wound?' Allie's voice was sceptical.

Sylvain crouched down in front of her; his blue eyes dark in the shadows. 'He cut Rachel's arm with a knife. And smeared the blood on Emma. He said it would –' He stopped, his jaw tense, and Allie saw that he was fighting to control his temper. 'He said it would get your attention.'

'I hate him,' Zoe muttered to herself, stabbing at the ground with a piece of wood she'd picked up somewhere.

Still holding on to Emma, Nicole leaned forward to catch Allie's gaze. 'Emma says he made a bandage for Rachel's wounds and the cuts were not deep. Allie, he wouldn't be so careful if he intended to kill her.'

'The thing I can't figure out is how Nathaniel got into the building in the first place,' Carter said. 'How did no one see him? Is our security that weak?'

Allie rubbed her face tiredly. 'The drivers. Isabelle said the drivers were all Nathaniel's guards. That's how they got in. They walked in together, in a crowd. It caused such chaos they couldn't keep track.'

'And one of them was Nathaniel.' Sylvain said bitterly. 'It's so brazen – it's just his style.'

'They didn't get a chance to count them in and out, then.' Carter's jaw tightened. 'Some of them could still be in the building.'

'That's why Isabelle said we had to stay down here,' Allie said.

'I don't care. We have to get out of here.' Jumping up, Zoe threw the stick across the cellar. It bounced off something in the shadows and hit the floor with a thud. 'We have to tell Raj about Rachel. He'll know what to do.'

Pressing her fingertips against her forehead, Allie tried to make herself think. 'Should we tell him, though?'

The others stared.

'Of course we have to tell him, Allie,' Nicole said. 'She's his daughter.'

Do not bring Raj Patel or Isabelle or any of the instructors or guards . . .

Thinking of Nathaniel's words, Allie felt cold inside, as if ice water ran through her veins instead of blood. But she had to stay focused. For Rachel.

'He'll want to run out there to fight Nathaniel,' she said. 'And if he does that, Rachel will die.'

Sylvain and Carter exchanged a look.

'What do you think?' Sylvain asked.

'I don't know . . . ' Carter sounded worried.

'He's tactical.' Sylvain reminded him. 'Always tactics.'

'Yeah, but this is his *daughter*,' Carter said.

Allie looked back and forth between them as they worked it out. They knew Raj better than she did. Better than any of the students. They'd been working with him nearly every day for months.

'Even then' – Sylvain's voice was firm – 'he believes in strategy. He'll be able to handle it.'

331

After a second, Carter nodded and turned to Allie.

'Sylvain's right. We should trust Raj. He's too smart to just rush out without thinking it through, even if it's Rachel. He'll help us plan.'

Allie held Sylvain's gaze. 'You're certain?'

He didn't hesitate. 'I'm positive.'

She trusted him. 'Then let's get Raj.'

First, though, someone had to get out of the cellar.

'Isabelle says the cellar is safe because Raj's guards are all around it – they know we're down here,' Allie explained. 'If they're around us there must be some way to find them.'

Zoe looked around the circle. 'Let me do it.'

Everyone objected at once, their voices making an echoed cacophony, but Zoe held up her hands. Her determination made her face look more grown up.

'Look, I'm small and fast. I won't go into the main buildings. I'll search the stairwells and corridors – all the places they could be guarding. I'll find them.'

'No!' They all said it together.

Her face reddening, Zoe glared at them. 'I could do this *better than you.* Do not forbid me just because I'm young and a girl.'

A heavy silence followed.

Carter gave in first. 'I think we should let her.'

Allie's chest tightened. 'Carter, no . . .'

'She's faster than any of us.' Nicole took his side.

'Sylvain . . .' Allie appealed to him, but, although his expression was sympathetic, he shook his head.

'I agree with the others.'

After a quick discussion about where she should go, Zoe leaped to her feet to head towards the stairs but, as she did so, Sylvain caught her arm. Pulling her closer, he whispered something to her.

Her small face serious, she nodded. Then as Allie watched, helpless to stop her, she ran into the shadows.

After she left, the atmosphere developed a kind of claustrophobic emptiness. Time seemed to stretch – the hands of Allie's watch slowed.

To keep herself calm, Allie walked the borders of the ancient cellar. It was never used for any purpose any more, and held only a few old trunks and some long-forgotten stacks of bricks. Dim light came from a few old wall sconces, so yellowed and dirty the few bulbs that did work emitted only a weak, flickering glow.

She glanced around to see what the others were doing. Nicole was talking to Emma in a low voice. Carter stood at the foot of the stairs like a sentinel, his hands in his pockets, his expression unreadable. Sylvain stood with his back against the wall, lost in thought.

By now it must be getting dark outside. She thought of Rachel, alone with Nathaniel and Gabe. Helpless. Terrified.

A sob welled in her throat and she forced it back – she needed to stay focused.

She shoved her hands into the pockets of her skirt, and her fingers encountered the sheet of blood-spattered paper Nathaniel had left for her.

Pulling it out she unfolded it carefully and read it again, frowning at each word.

Suddenly she straightened. As if she'd made a sound, Sylvain turned and cast an enquiring look at her.

She held out the note. 'I think I know what we have to do.'

THIRTY-THREE

They were all sitting in a cluster, sketching out Allie's idea in the dust on the floor when the sudden clatter of heavy boots on the stairs jarred them into instant action. Leaping to their feet they ran together to the foot of the stairs.

Carter looked pale but determined; his jaw set. Beside him, Nicole seemed less tense. She held a thick board in one hand like a police truncheon and Allie got the feeling she'd relish the chance to use it. Allie and Sylvain stood on opposite sides of the cellar entrance; Allie held a brick in her hand.

The men who burst out of the stairwell wore the black uniforms of Raj's guards but nobody cared. They all knew clothes meant nothing any more.

'Does anyone know them?' Carter called out, his voice urgent.

The others' response was immediate. 'No.'

It was all the invitation Nicole needed. She swung the board with all her strength, hitting the first man in the gut. He grunted in surprise and pain. Allie lunged forward with a brick in her hand.

'Stand easy!' Raj's disembodied voice caught her in mid-stride – the brick tumbled from her fingers. She spun round in confusion as he stepped out of the narrow corridor, Zoe bounding at his side. 'They're the good guys.'

His clothes were muddy and new lines had appeared on his face, but he did not look defeated.

As Nicole offered an apologetic hand to the wounded man, Allie walked slowly over to Rachel's father. How could she tell him what happened? What words were there in the world to explain how she felt?

But he didn't wait for her to speak. He pulled her into a hug. 'I know what happened.' His voice was rough. 'We'll get her back.'

'I'm so sorry, Mr Patel.' Tears burned the backs of Allie's eyes as she stood stiffly in his arms. 'It's my fault.'

'No, it isn't.' He held her at arm's length so she could see the determination in his face. 'This is Nathaniel's fault. And when we find him I'm going to make sure he knows exactly how I feel about that.' As he spoke, his eyes changed. Suddenly he looked predatory; dangerous.

As quickly as the look appeared, though, it faded, and he glanced around the room, in complete control. 'Everyone OK?'

They all nodded.

'Can I see the note, Allie?' Raj held out his hand.

For a second she hesitated. A few weeks ago, she wouldn't

have let anyone see this note. She would have run out there to try and get Rachel all on her own. And Rachel probably would have died.

But she'd learned. She'd watched the others sacrifice themselves for her, for Jo. She'd seen them take chances that could have cost them everything they cared about.

She trusted them. She believed in them.

So she turned to where they stood watching her. Catching her eye, Sylvain nodded once.

Only then did she pull the crumpled, blood-stained page from her pocket and hold it out to Raj.

'We need to talk to you,' she said. The others gathered around her, supporting her. 'We have an idea.'

'Isabelle will never agree to it.' Raj's words were emphatic.

'We know.' Nicole shot him a significant look. 'So we have to decide how to handle it.'

Raj had sent his guards back into the corridors and stairwells. Emma had been taken to the infirmary to be checked out. Only he and the group remained in the chilly cellar.

He rubbed his eyes. 'Let's go over this again.'

'Nathaniel says I must come without you, Isabelle, or any of the guards or instructors,' Allie explained patiently. 'But he doesn't mention students. I will go to the castle. The others will follow through the woods in case I get into trouble. You and your guards will already be there, hidden. Nathaniel will think I've followed his rules so Rachel will be –' she almost couldn't bring herself to say the word, she so wanted it to be true – 'safe.' She took a steadying breath. 'I'll go to him alone – the others will stay near me. You wait until Rachel is free then you come in – he won't be expecting you.'

'My guards are all over the grounds right now.' Raj spoke thoughtfully as he studied the sketch they'd made on the dirty floor: a partial circle with space on one side left open, arrows swooping towards it. It was Napoleon's plan from the Battle of Austerlitz but Allie had thought it best not to mention that part. 'I could tell them to get into place one at a time. No group movement. They'd be virtually impossible to detect.' He glanced around the group, and Allie could tell by his expression he'd already made up his mind. 'It's a good plan.'

She kept her face blank but her heart leapt with excitement. They could make this work.

'What about Isabelle?' Zoe sounded doubtful. 'She won't let us do it.'

Standing, Raj wiped the arrows from the floor with the sole of his boot. In an instant the evidence was gone. 'She won't know.'

They gaped at him surprise.

'How—' Allie started but Raj held up his hand. He looked tense, his jaw squared as if anticipating a blow.

'I'm in charge of the operation. Isabelle and I have already decided to leave the Night School instructors out of any plan because we don't know which of them to trust. I have nearly one hundred guards on their way now, and they all report directly to me.'

The others murmured.

'A hundred?' Carter looked stunned. 'Where . . . ?'

'Lucinda.' Raj held Allie's gaze. 'She sent her own personal security team. I've called my guards in. By midnight they'll be here and ready.'

Allie sent a silent prayer of thanks to her grandmother.

A hundred guards. We can do this.

'What will you tell Isabelle?' Sylvain's practical question brought her back to earth.

'She asked me to keep you all under guard for your own protection in one of the classrooms.' He shrugged. 'I'll tell her that's where you are.'

'But she'll . . . ' Allie faltered. 'She'll never forgive you.'

Raj's expression told her he knew that already.

'Let me worry about that,' he said. 'You worry about staying safe.' With a glance at his watch, he motioned for them all to stand. 'I need you all in gear and ready to go. Stay in the training room until I come and get you. My men will take you there now.' His gaze glanced off Allie's. 'I've got to go and meet Isabelle now.'

After Raj left, the guards led them silently through a series of dark underground corridors. Allie, who thought she knew the school well, had never seen some of them. The school's cellars were a labyrinth – at times they climbed up one level only to descend again moments later.

She was thoroughly lost by the time a door opened on to the hallway outside the familiar Night School training rooms.

After changing quickly into their dark Night School gear, they gathered in Training Room One. The square chamber felt hollow and empty without the other Night School members.

Zoe was the only one who seemed unaffected by the

situation. She limbered up on the thick elastic matting as if this were any other training exercise.

The others exchanged anxious murmurs and tried to stay calm. Allie's nervousness made her muscles stiff. It was hard to warm up.

She wasn't alone. Across the room she saw Sylvain exhale through pursed lips as if trying to force himself to relax. But his shoulder muscles bulged from the tension.

After a while, there was nothing to do but wait. Allie leaned back against a wall, her arms wrapped tightly around her legs, and rested her chin on her knees. She tried not to think about how Rachel might be feeling right now. What she might be thinking.

Why was Nathaniel making her wait until midnight? It seemed so long. She wanted Rachel out of there.

When Carter sat down next to her, she welcomed the distraction.

'You ready for this?' he asked.

She looked at him soberly. 'I just want to get it over with.'

'Me too.'

Allie watched his face as he looked out across the room. She thought about how he must feel after everything that had happened today.

'Carter, I'm so sorry about Jules.' Her voice was tentative. She wasn't certain how welcome her sympathy would be. 'I didn't know about ... about her parents.'

His face darkened. 'I missed her by minutes. She was supposed to go to one of the hiding rooms but she didn't make it. By the time I got outside the car was gone. It happened so fast.'

Allie looked at him sadly. 'I didn't know her parents were . . .'

He shook his head. 'I didn't want to advertise it. Besides, you two . . .'

Hated each other.

'Yeah,' she said, ashamed. 'I'm sorry about that, too. All that fighting . . . it seems so unimportant now.' She turned to face him. 'Do you think she'll get away? Come back? She's trained.'

He shook his head, a muscle flickering in his jaw. 'I don't know. Could we just . . . talk about something else?'

But what else was there to talk about?

When Raj walked through the door some time later they were all sitting in tense silence, waiting. He looked around the room, his eyes missing nothing.

'Let's go,' he said.

'All you do is put it in your ear, like headphones.' Raj put a small silver device on Allie's fingertip, and she placed it cautiously in her ear.

It felt cold against the sensitive flesh and she shivered. 'Won't it just fall out?'

'Adjust it until it feels snug but don't force it,' he said.

She moved it until it seemed to fit. 'I think it's in there.'

'This is your microphone.' He showed her a tiny piece of what looked like black plastic no larger than the head of a pin. 'Here. Lean forward.'

She did as he asked, and he stuck it to the fabric of her jacket, just below her jaw. She craned her neck to look for it – it was invisible.

He placed an earpiece in his own ear. 'Say something.'

His voice rang from the device inside her ear and she flinched. 'Wow. That is way too loud.'

'It's because I'm standing so close to you. The transmission is not strong – as soon as you leave the building my voice will seem faint to you but you should never lose contact at any point.'

Biting her lip, Allie nodded. They were standing at the end of the corridor, by the stairs leading out on to the grounds. She'd been through that door a hundred times in the last few months with the other Night School students. She knew the path she was about to take like the back of her hand. She knew where she was headed and what she was going to do. She was ready.

She'd never been more frightened.

As if he could see it on her face, Raj took her by the shoulders. The others were gathered behind them so he lowered his voice until only she could hear. 'You're sure you want to do this?'

Allie thought of Rachel, sitting at her library table bending over her chemistry books, glasses sliding down her nose. Throwing back her head to laugh at one of Allie's bad jokes. Calmly explaining complex molecules. Running into her room when she had a nightmare.

Terrified, with blood running down her arm and Gabe holding the knife.

Lifting her chin she met Raj's gaze with fierce eyes. She might be scared but she wasn't about to back down. This was her chance to get the bastards who killed Jo. Beautiful, happy, crazy Jo. And who now wanted to kill Rachel.

They were all just pawns in Nathaniel's game.

Allie was sick of being a pawn.

'I'm ready.'

Her words were simple but her tone was eloquent – Raj didn't ask her again.

'OK.' Stepping back, he looked at them all, pride in his eyes. 'You know the plan. I know you can do this. Go out there. And bring her back.'

THIRTY-FOUR

Allie walked along the dark path with quick purposeful steps, her eyes fixed on the path ahead. Her senses were so alert it felt as if her hair stood on end. She tingled with nervous anticipation.

Keep it together, Allie, she told herself. *You can do this.*

She thought of the way she'd felt when, just before she'd gone, Sylvain had pulled her into a rough hug. He'd whispered something to her in French and she hadn't known what it meant and yet thought she understood, all at once.

She could do this.

The night was quiet. The only sounds were the thudding of her feet on the soft soil, the rapid pounding of her heart; her breath. The others should be in the woods around her by now, following her steps through the trees. But she didn't hear a thing.

There was no moon – clouds obscured every star. The air felt heavy with impending rain. It was so dark she could barely see the path at her feet but she hesitated to use the torch that dangled from her hand. If she relied on the torch, its beam would be all she could see. Her eyes would adjust, but the darkness was so complete it was taking time.

Ahead, the path began to ascend, twisting and turning steeply, becoming rockier.

'I'm at the hill.' She whispered the words, lowering her head towards the tiny device affixed to her jacket.

'Clear.' Raj's voice was steady and calm in her ear.

For a while she was too busy focusing on it to be frightened. Stones skittered out from under her foot. Once or twice she stumbled, but she always caught herself before she fell.

She was nearly at the top when she heard a sound in the woods. It was faint but clear – a snapping branch, then ... silence.

Allie's mouth went dry and she peered into the darkness around her. But the night revealed nothing. She turned back to the footpath and took one step forward.

'Hello, Allie.'

She froze. Nathaniel's chillingly familiar voice seemed to come from her earpiece, but that wasn't possible.

Her hands shaking, she fumbled with her torch. Suddenly her fingers were so numb everything felt like nothing at all. Finally, she managed to press the button and a bright beam sprang out. She held the torch above her head, pointing it straight ahead.

The path was empty.

Her breath came out in a choked sob.

Where is he?

Panicked, she swung in a circle, the torch beam swinging drunkenly.

Nothing.

'I need you to walk to the top of the hill, and into the castle.' In her ear Nathaniel's voice was calm.

That only made Allie more frightened.

He hacked the comms system.

'Once you're there, I'll tell you where to go. Do as I say and Rachel will be fine.'

He can hear everything we say.

Allie's heart hammered against the walls of her chest so loudly it was hard to hear his voice.

'It was naughty of you to try to subvert my demands by using these earpieces,' Nathaniel chided her. 'I know my letter did not strictly forbid this. Still, I'm instituting a new rule. Alert Raj that I am talking to you and Rachel dies like Jo. I hope you understand how serious I am.'

For a second Allie was immobilised by fear. He'd said she shouldn't alert Raj – did that mean she could hear Nathaniel but Raj could not? Should she say something back? If she did, Raj would hear.

She thought longingly about running back down the hill and warning Raj. He needed to know.

But then she thought of Rachel – alone and held prisoner by that monster. She couldn't go back. She had to try.

'Allie, check in.' At that moment, Raj's steady voice came through her earpiece. He didn't sound at all rattled. He had no idea what Nathaniel had done.

'Allie?' Raj called again. This time he sounded concerned – she had to reply.

'Clear,' she whispered, her voice tight.

There was nothing to be done. She couldn't warn Raj without risking Rachel's life. She had to go on, but she was so frightened her feet seemed frozen to the earth, her hands glued to her sides.

Come on, Allie, she urged herself. *Rachel would do this for you.*

Gritting her teeth she took one step. Then another. In that fashion she stumbled up the hill, clutching her torch in a death grip. Its beam unsteadily illuminated the emptiness ahead, making shadows of tree branches that reached out for her like long fingers.

The crest of the hill lay just ahead. Beyond it, she could make out the jagged rocks of the castle tower.

Lowering her head she walked on, her footsteps uneven but determined.

When she reached the remains of the castle's once formidable stone wall, her heart pounded so quickly she felt dizzy.

The old wall had crumbled over time but still stood more than six feet tall in places. She picked her way through the fallen rocks to a spot where the wall was at its lowest. Here, battered stones had been piled into makeshift stairs, and she climbed to the top.

The winds had picked up and her hair blew around her face as she stood on top of the wall looking out over the old stone tower, gloomy and ruined. Tonight, with storm clouds swirling overhead, it looked every bit as haunted as its reputation held it to be.

Next to it, a scorched circle marked the spot where the

students had held a bonfire in the autumn term. It felt like a hundred years ago.

She could see no sign of Nathaniel but she knew he was there, somewhere. Waiting for her.

Steeling herself, she climbed down and headed across the uneven ground.

'I'm at the castle,' she said into her microphone.

'Clear,' Raj said. 'You have ten minutes.'

Ten minutes until he came with his guards to get her. Ten minutes to free Rachel. Ten minutes to survive.

A light mist began to fall; tiny raindrops clung to her eyelashes.

Raj's plan required her to stand in the middle of the castle yard and call Nathaniel out. 'Whatever you do,' he'd said, 'do not go into the castle tower. Understood?'

But now when she reached the centre of what had once been the castle keep, Nathaniel's voice, so low and preternaturally calm it sent goosebumps cascading down her spine, spoke in her ear.

'Walk into the castle tower.'

Horrified, Allie replied aloud: 'No.'

'Allie?' Raj's voice in her ear.

She bit her lip. 'Clear,' she said.

Clenching her hands into fists at her sides, Allie tried to stay focused. She needed to *think*.

Nathaniel had said if she refused any of his commands, Rachel would die. But would he really do that? Once Rachel was gone he'd have no hold over Allie. There'd be no reason for her to speak to him.

A sudden adrenaline-burst of confidence in her own logic made her feel dangerously brave. She could do this.

Taking a deep breath, she stood amid the ruins, her arms flung out at her sides.

'Nathaniel! You said you'd find me if I came looking for you. Well? *Here I am*. Show yourself.'

Her voice seemed to disappear into the glowering clouds. Turning in a slow circle, she looked for any sign of him. Her eyes darting into the shadowed corners and rocky ledges of the hilltop castle.

Rain had begun to fall harder now. Her hair clung to her scalp and snaked over her shoulders in dripping strands.

Raj had told her not to attempt to provoke Nathaniel, but she was angry now, and she couldn't stop herself. 'Come on, Nathaniel. You didn't lie to me, did you? You wouldn't do a thing like that, would you?'

'Don't push me, little girl.'

The calm voice emanated from the base of the tower and Allie's earpiece at the same moment. She whirled in time to see Nathaniel step out of the darkness.

Frantically she looked around for any sign of Rachel. But he was alone.

As she had the first time she saw him in the heat of last summer, Allie marvelled at his sheer ordinariness. His neat dark hair and average build would not have been out of place among Cimmeria's teachers. His face was pleasantly but not spectacularly designed – his nose slightly too big, his eyes a little too small to be perfect, but he did not look like a monster.

His expensive suit looked out of place here, though. He was dressed like a banker. His cufflinks caught the light from her torch and sparkled coldly.

'You disappoint me,' he said. 'I thought you cared enough about your friend to do as you were told.'

'I care enough about my friend not to believe a single word you say,' Allie replied, her shoulders squared although her hands trembled. 'Where is she, Nathaniel? Where is Rachel? Show her to me or I will walk away right now.'

To show she meant it, she took two steps away from him. He held up his hand.

'Christopher's right about you – you're always in such a rush,' he said with a chilly smile. 'You never take the time to think things through.'

His casual mention of Christopher made Allie draw in her breath sharply but she wouldn't let him see how much it hurt to think about the brother who'd abandoned her.

He needed to think she didn't care.

'Don't talk about Christopher or I might have some sort of a crying fit.' Her voice dripped sarcasm. 'Now I want my friend back. Where is she?'

'You're spectacularly stubborn. Has anyone ever told you that?'

Allie fixed him with a challenging stare. 'Yes. Where is she?'

Sighing dramatically, Nathaniel raised his right hand. 'Gabriel. Show her the girl. She won't talk sense until she's seen her.'

Gabe.

Allie's heart seemed to shrink to the size of an ice cube.

Jo's killer stepped out from the shadows, dragging Rachel

like prey. One of his thick arms crossed her chest, holding her immobile. The other held a knife pointed at her throat.

Pale and terrified, Rachel trembled in his grip. One eye was swollen shut. Blood had dried under her nose. Her arms were wrapped in bloody bandages.

They'd beaten her.

Despite all her efforts to stay calm, anger coursed through Allie's blood like flames.

'Gabe!' she screamed, her voice breaking into a sob. 'You psycho bastard, you *let her go*.'

But he only grinned and brought the knife closer to Rachel's fragile neck, pressing the tip into her skin.

Something about his smile caught Allie's attention and she focused her torch beam on his face. Gabe had always been Cimmeria's golden boy – handsome and athletic, with perfect features. In those days, he only had to smile for a girl to fall for him.

His thick, dark blond hair had been shaved close to the scalp. An angry, red scar crossed his face from the outer corner of his left eye to his upper lip.

Realising he must have received that scar in the kidnapping attempt last year, Allie felt a rush of bitter pleasure.

Then Nathaniel flipped his hand back in a dismissive gesture and Gabe stepped back into the shadows. Rachel gave a terrified, animal cry.

'Rachel!' Allie shouted desperately.

But she was gone.

'Oh God.' Allie trembled with such violence the torch beam shook.

She had to stay calm or she wasn't going to be any help to anyone, so she took a deep breath and, although it turned her stomach, she walked closer to Nathaniel, stopping about fifteen feet away from him.

'I did what you wanted.' She was surprised by how calm her voice was. 'I came to you. Now let her go.'

His smile was easy, as if they were having a pleasant chat about the weather. 'I will let her go when I know for certain I can trust you, Allie. And I will know that when I hear your response to my offer.'

Allie held her gaze steady. 'What offer?'

'As I said in my note, I want you to come with me, willingly, as Christopher did. I want you as part of my team. I will bring you back to Cimmeria once I take over running the school – you will complete your education here, I promise. Christopher wants his sister back and I want to see your family reunited. With me you will have all that you deserve based on your impressive bloodline – your life will have purpose. You will be an important part of Orion and I will make certain you get the training you need to prepare you for the role you will some day have in the organisation. You will have wealth and power you can only dream of now.' He held out his hands, palms facing upward. 'So that is my offer, Allie. Give me your answer and Rachel can walk out of here alive.'

The rain fell hard now, pattering off the ancient stones around them with a million tiny thuds. She dropped her head, watching the water run from her hair to the dirt at her feet. There was bound to be a trick. He'd never let Rachel go. She needed to be ready.

Finally, she straightened, looking at Nathaniel through the falling water. 'Fine,' she said. 'Yes, I'll go with you.'

Clearly delighted, he held out his arms as if he expected a hug. She stared at him, her expression incredulous.

Grinning, he dropped his arms. 'For the first time you've surprised me, Allie. I was certain you'd say no.'

'But –' she held up her hand – 'I'm not going anywhere until Rachel is safe. I will go with you, only if she walks out of here right now. This second.'

'Now, Allie . . .' he began, his tone placating.

She shook her head so hard drops of water flew around her in a circle. '*Don't*, Nathaniel. You have your rules, and I have mine. I came alone. I did as you said. Let Rachel go now and you can have me. Otherwise the deal is off.'

He shot her a sour look.

'I should have expected something like this.' He glanced at his watch. 'Still, I think we can make this work. In the interest of our new relationship and to prove my sincerity.' Turning, he called back into the darkness. 'Gabe. Release her.'

A voice from the shadows said something Allie couldn't make out. Whatever it was it infuriated Nathaniel, who spun with the speed of a cobra strike. 'I did not ask for your opinion. Release her.'

For a long moment nothing happened – Allie could see only darkness. Hear only the rain and her own ragged breathing.

Then something moved in the shadows.

A second later, Rachel stumbled out into the light of Allie's torch. As she passed Nathaniel she ducked fearfully as if anticipating a blow. She looked so weak, Allie feared she'd fall.

'Rachel!'

Allie ran to her side and slid an arm under her shoulders, pulling her away from Nathaniel. Ripping the tiny microphone from her jacket, she whispered rapid-fire instructions, hoping Rachel was strong enough to absorb the information.

'The others are in the woods. Your dad is coming. Run to the trees and hide until this is over. Don't get caught.' But Rachel seemed to be in shock; she stared at Allie blankly.

'Rachel, do you understand?' Fear burned Allie's stomach like acid. If Rachel couldn't get out on her own, the whole plan failed. 'Can you do it?'

'I won't . . . leave you with them.' Rachel's voice was weak.

I will not cry, Allie told herself. *I will not.*

'I'll be fine,' she said, loud enough for Nathaniel to hear.

'This is so touching.' Nathaniel sounded bored. 'But I really don't have time.'

'Please, Rach,' Allie whispered, squeezing her shoulder. 'Trust me. There's a plan.'

She held her breath as Rachel studied her for a long moment. Then she nodded and let go of Allie reluctantly. 'I'll go.'

With a sigh of relief, Allie released her, watching with worried eyes as she began to walk away – she was unsteady but upright. She'd make it.

Turning, she walked back to where Nathaniel watched her with clinical interest, as if she were an experiment in a lab that had done something unexpected.

Stopping just out of reach, she stood with her hands on her

hips. 'What now, Nathaniel? Does Gabe stick a knife to *my* throat now? Is that your big, clever plan?'

Above the sound of rainfall, a deep rumble caught Allie's attention and she frowned, looking up at the turbulent sky. Was that thunder?

'No.' Nathaniel gave a delighted grin. 'That is not my plan at all.'

The noise, which, now that Allie thought about it, had been there for some time, grew louder.

The wind picked up, whipping her wet hair into her face so hard it stung.

A bright light appeared above them, illuminating the castle ruins and highlighting the rain so it looked like tiny diamonds falling around them.

Blinded, Allie shielded her eyes as she looked up for the source.

The noise had changed into a repetitive thudding. It was louder now, and familiar. The air whipped around her like a mini-tornado. She knew what it was before she could see it.

A helicopter.

'No knife,' Nathaniel shouted at her above the steady *thump thump thump* of the rotors. 'I have a more sophisticated method.'

Raj was shouting something through Allie's earpiece but the noise of the helicopter was deafening. She cupped her hand over her ear, trying to make out what he was saying as the helicopter began to lower itself on to the castle grounds.

At that moment, a hand grabbed her arm roughly, twisting it behind her back sending a stabbing pain through her. She looked up to see Gabe's scarred face. He was smiling at her.

She screamed.

Holding her in a bruising grip, Gabe dragged her roughly towards the helicopter, which now hovered ten feet above them. Struggling with all her might, Allie tried to swing at him with the torch but she couldn't hold on to it, and it flew from her hand.

Then, through the wind and the rain, and the thudding of the rotors, Allie heard Nathaniel shout, 'What the hell . . . ?'

Twisting in Gabe's grip, she saw the others hurtling across the stones, Zoe in the lead – always the fastest. The others were right behind her. Sylvain and Carter divided. Sylvain headed for Nathaniel.

Without breaking his stride, Sylvain drew back his fist and punched him in the face. The force of his forward motion added power to his the blow. Nathaniel dropped instantly.

Allie's heart leaped with excitement, but Gabe's grip tightened around her throat and he dragged her more quickly towards the helicopter.

Suddenly, though, Carter stood in front of them, blocking their path.

'Let her go, Gabe.' His voice was steely, his gaze didn't waver from Gabe's.

They'd been friends once, before Gabe had betrayed them all. And Allie could see the loathing in Carter's eyes.

'Oh, Carter,' Gabe sighed pityingly. 'Still in love with the girl who doesn't love you back? How pathetic. Wasn't Jules—'

At that moment, something hit him on the back of his neck and his grip loosened enough for Allie to squirm free.

Whirling, she saw Nicole standing behind him with the same board she'd used earlier in the cellar. The French girl's eyes met Allie's.

'I'm starting to like this thing,' she said of the weapon.

Then, just as suddenly, she fell with a scream of pain.

Stunned, Allie looked down to see Gabe holding a heavy stone he'd used to hit Nicole in the knee. As she writhed in pain, he knelt above her and lifted the rock over her head.

Carter shot past Allie, throwing himself at Gabe, knocking him off balance. The rock fell to one side and Gabe and Carter rolled into the mud. Allie was scrambling for the stone when she heard a cry from behind her. Turning, she saw Nathaniel pick Zoe up off the ground. Sylvain crouched in front of him looking for any opportunity to pounce.

'Is this what you want, Allie?' Nathaniel cried, tightening his grip on Zoe's slim throat. Her face had begun to turn purple. 'Do you want her to die so you can live?'

The corners of Allie's vision darkened.

Propelling herself at him with all her might she screamed, 'You let her go.'

Before she could reach him, though, Nathaniel hurled Zoe at Sylvain, knocking them both down. By then, though, Allie was moving too quickly to stop. She ran directly into his arms.

Nathaniel wasn't as strong as Gabe, but he was skilled. He had Allie by the throat in seconds. A knife appeared from nowhere and pressed against her cheek, she could feel the sharpness of the blade.

'It's you,' he said into her ear. 'Or them. Choose.'

The helicopter was now just a few feet above the ground. The wind from its spinning blades hit them with the force of a hundred fists.

Allie's gaze skittered around the castle yard. She saw Carter and Gabe still fighting. Nicole lay on the ground clutching her leg. Sylvain and Zoe were on their feet, circling Nathaniel, looking for an opening – a chance.

They could all live if she just went with him. There wasn't really a choice.

'Take me.' She let her body go limp – she stopped fighting him. She pressed her face into the knife, hoping for the bite of the blade. Hoping for all of this to be over. 'Let them go. Just take me.'

When Nathaniel smiled she saw his teeth were covered in blood. Sylvain's punch had been accurate.

'Good girl.' Still holding her, he stepped towards the helicopter. Numbly, she stumbled with him.

Her heart seemed frozen in her chest. Everything felt unreal. Was she really going to go with the man who killed Jo? Really going to give in? Was there no other way?

In the distance, Gabe hit Carter with a sickening crunch. Allie watched in horror as Carter toppled like a felled tree. For a moment, Gabe stood over him, looking down at him, and she stiffened, fearing he'd try to finish him off. But then Gabe turned and limped towards the helicopter. Behind him, Carter lay still in the mud.

The thump of the rotors seemed to come from a hundred miles away as she stared at Carter's body.

He isn't moving. Why isn't he moving?

She had to know Carter was alive. Suddenly, she lifted her feet, letting her body weight drop like a stone. Caught off guard in mid-stride Nathaniel grunted in surprise. The rain made her skin slippery and he lost his grip. As he fought to hold her the knife sliced through the flesh of her shoulder.

She hit the ground and rolled. Gasping, she rose on to her knees, clutching her bleeding arm. It felt as if someone had set her arm on fire. Hot blood poured over her fingers and she stared down in puzzled dismay, too stunned to flee.

But Sylvain and Zoe were between her and Nathaniel now. Zoe held a heavy stone in one hand. Sylvain didn't need one.

The wind from the helicopter rotors buffeted them – she saw Zoe's jacket inflate around her like a balloon, and felt herself being thrown around by the deadly, spinning blades. Fighting the force of it, she threw up a hand to protect her eyes from beads of rain being thrown with such force they struck like stones.

Then, looking past her, Nathaniel cursed.

Following his gaze, Allie saw a mass of black-clad guards climbing over the castle walls. Dozens of them. Moving in silence, with deadly grace, they poured over the stone like black oil.

Raj was here.

Nathaniel turned back to her, his gaze narrow.

'You made the wrong choice, Allie,' he shouted above the cacophony. 'You will pay for this. Tell Lucinda she's already lost.'

Around them, black-clad guards swarmed the castle yard.

His shoulders high, Nathaniel climbed into the helicopter. Through the rain, she saw him motion to the pilot and it began to climb, swinging dangerously in the wind.

Allie leaned back to watch it go, willing it to crash. But it rose into the storm and disappeared, the rhythmic thud of the rotors gradually fading.

THİRTY-FİVE

'Ouch!' Allie jerked her wounded arm out of Sylvain's grip, wrapping her hand round it protectively.

'Allie, I must roll up your sleeve to see the wound,' he insisted gently. 'I know it hurts but we have to stop the bleeding.'

'I know,' she said. 'It's just ... ow.'

Around them, guards swarmed like insects, searching the castle grounds for anything Nathaniel might have left behind.

'Hang on a second,' Carter said. He turned to one of the guards. 'Excuse me, mate. Have you got a knife I can borrow?'

The guard stopped and took in the scene. Blood still dripped from Allie's arm, mixing with mud on the ground. Pulling a dangerous-looking blade from a holster on his hip, he flipped it over expertly, handing it to Carter hilt first.

'Thanks.' Carter held the knife out to Sylvain.

'Come on, Allie.' Sylvain held out his hand. 'One more try.'

Biting her lip hard, she held out her arm to him. Very carefully, he lifted the cuff of her sleeve and slit it with the knife. The blade was sharp. The fabric gave easily, all the way to the shoulder. Handing the knife back to Carter, Sylvain peeled the sodden fabric back. The cold air felt good against the wound.

Sylvain's breath hissed between his teeth as he saw the cut. His grip tightened on her wrist.

All Allie could see was blood. Wincing, she tried not to look at it.

'It's a long cut but I don't think it needs a tourniquet.' Sylvain glanced at Carter for confirmation.

Peering at the wound, Carter nodded. 'The bleeding is slowing. Bind it and let's get her back for stitches.'

As the others watched, Sylvain pulled off his own jacket and cut off one of the arms with the knife. He wrapped that around the wound snugly then used a strip of her shredded sleeve to tie it in place.

The makeshift bandage was secure. Allie's arm instantly felt better.

'Hold it like this.' Sylvain demonstrated, holding his arm across his chest. Obediently, Allie emulated him and he smiled, squeezing her good hand. 'Now, we need to get you back.'

'We have to find Rachel first,' Allie insisted. 'I'm not going without her.'

Frowning, Nicole peered into the distance. 'Zoe went after her ages ago. She should be back by now.'

'Let's find Raj,' Carter said. 'He'll know.'

'I think I saw him over by the wall.' Sylvain pointed.

They headed that way. Carter had one arm around Nicole, whose damaged leg barely bore her weight.

Allie didn't like the bruise on his jaw – it was purple and swelling. 'That looks bad, Carter.'

'It just needs some ice.' He rubbed the back of his neck. 'It's my neck that really hurts. I didn't like the way it crunched when Gabe hit me.'

Sylvain looked at Allie. 'It's you I'm worried about – you've lost a lot of blood.'

'I feel OK,' she said. She looked over at him. 'You and Zoe were great back there. I haven't had a chance to thank you.'

His lips tightened. 'I'm sorry Nathaniel got away.'

'Me too,' Allie said quietly.

When they reached the wall, one of the guards directed them over it towards the woods, where he said they'd find Raj.

Carter helped Nicole over first. Sylvain climbed up next and helped Allie across, lifting her gently as if she weighed no more than a child.

'There's Zoe.' Ahead of them, Carter pointed towards the woods to where a small figure had emerged, leading a taller one by the hand.

Allie's heart seemed to stop in her chest. 'Rachel,' she breathed.

She took off towards them, ignoring the jarring pain in her arm.

'Rachel!' She shouted it now, running to her. She heard Rachel call her name, saw her stumbling towards her and then they were both sobbing, hugging each other.

Stepping back, Rachel studied Allie with fear in her eyes. 'What happened? You're bleeding everywhere.'

'I'm fine,' Allie said with false bravado. 'I just need a few stitches. I should watch where I'm going.'

Rachel looked at the others who had reached them now. 'Is she really fine? How bad is it?'

Sylvain stepped to Allie's side. 'She's OK. We're taking her to the infirmary now. What about you?' He gestured at her bloodied nose and bruised cheekbone.

'It's superficial,' Rachel said. 'I'll live.'

But she looked weak and exhausted.

'Did you see your dad?' Allie asked her. 'He was worried about you.'

New tears filled Rachel's eyes. 'He found me as soon as I got to the woods.'

'Good.' Allie nodded, trying not to cry again.

Everyone was OK.

'We need to get going,' Zoe said impatiently. 'Raj said we had to go straight back to the school.'

'Yeah, let's keep moving,' Carter agreed. 'I don't know how long Nicole's leg's going to make it.'

'I'm fine,' Nicole insisted, but Allie could see the pain etched in her face.

The rain had stopped but the footpath was slippery mud and they moved with caution.

The adrenaline that had kept Allie going up until now was wearing off, and as they made their way down the hill she began to *feel* again. The cut on her arm throbbed. Her entire body felt stiff and bruised – as if she'd been in another car crash. But she knew the others were hurting, too, so she set her jaw and kept going.

When she tripped over a rock, though, the movement sent pain shooting through her shoulder and she was unable to suppress a whimper.

'Here.' Sylvain slipped his arm round her waist, supporting her weight. 'Lean on me.'

'I'm OK,' she lied and he almost smiled.

'I know you are,' he said.

It seemed to take hours to reach the school, although Allie knew it couldn't have been more than twenty minutes.

When they limped across the terraced back gardens and through the door, they found the building flooded with light and almost too warm after so long out in the rain. Allie hadn't realised she was shivering until she reached the heat.

But the wide hallway was strangely empty.

Exchanging puzzled looks, they walked past the marble statues and oil paintings, their footsteps echoing in the quiet. When they reached the foot of the grand staircase, they stopped, looking around them in bewilderment.

'Where is everyone?' Zoe whispered.

Carter shook his head. 'The great hall?'

But when they pushed open the door the big ballroom was dark and empty.

'Maybe we should try Isabelle's office.' Allie's voice was calm, but her heart had begun to race. Something was wrong. It was too quiet.

They made their way back to the staircase. Underneath it,

the door to Isabelle's office was ajar, but the light was turned off. The office was empty.

'I don't get it,' Zoe said. 'They have to be somewhere.'

'Maybe they're all outside,' Nicole suggested.

'Not Isabelle and the teachers, though . . . ' Carter said. 'Not all of them.'

Stepping away from Sylvain, Allie turned a slow circle, listening to the silence. The building didn't feel the way it should. There were no creaking sounds of footsteps above them. No distant laughter from the dorms.

It felt . . . hollow. Empty.

In the silence, they all noticed the soft sound of shushing footsteps above them; someone was coming down the stairs.

Sylvain, Carter and Zoe – the only ones not too beaten to fight – stepped forward with caution.

The footsteps continued at a slow, steady pace until they reached the landing above them – then the sound stopped.

'Oh my God,' Katie said, horrified. 'What happened to you?'

Her red hair was pulled back in a loose ponytail and she wore her white Cimmeria pyjamas and slippers. In her hand she carried an empty hot-water bottle. She looked so clean – so *normal* – that for a long moment they all just stared at her.

Tired and trembling from the cold and the loss of blood, Allie ran a shaking hand through her wet hair, as if to smooth it, before she realised what she was doing.

'Where is everyone?' Zoe hopped up a few steps towards the redhead.

'Everyone . . . who?' Katie asked, giving her an odd look.

'She means the teachers,' Carter asked.

'The teachers are meeting in the classroom wing,' Katie said. 'Or at least they were an hour ago.'

But Allie still had a bad feeling. Something about the quiet.

'What about the students?' Her voice sounded hoarse and tired. 'Where are the students?'

Katie walked closer to them, her slippers shushing on each step.

'The students who remain are in the dorms.' She held up the bottle. 'I'm getting this for Emma. She can't sleep.'

'You say those who remain.' Nicole looked pale and drawn in the white light of the crystal chandelier. 'How many students are left?'

Katie's gaze took in Allie's torn sleeve and bloody arm, Carter's swollen chin, Rachel's bruised face.

'There are about forty of us,' she said gravely. 'I'm sorry.'

Allie's chest tightened. This morning there'd been nearly two hundred students at the school. Now there were *forty*?

She wanted to cry but she was too exhausted. They'd fought and struggled and nearly died tonight. They'd defeated Nathaniel and saved Rachel and yet they *still lost?*

How?

Despair was like a weight in the air, dragging them all down.

Katie seemed to try and fail to think of something to make them feel better. Then, she held up the bottle in her hand. 'Look, I've got to get this filled. Emma can't be alone.'

Numb, they stepped back to let her pass, and she shuffled down the hallway. She'd only gone a few steps, though, when she stopped and turned back. 'You did the best you could. We all know that.'

When she'd gone, they stared at each other helplessly. Allie couldn't think of one word to say — nothing would make this better. The students were gone. They hadn't found the spy. And Nathaniel was still out there.

Her arm throbbed a reminder of how hard they'd fought, and she gripped it with her good hand to hold it steady.

In her mind she saw Nathaniel's face, the victory in his eyes. *'Tell Lucinda she's already lost.'*

Was he right? Was it all over? It seemed impossible to imagine. But this felt like failure.

'What happens now?' Zoe asked, her voice echoing.

Allie looked at her muddy face. She'd fallen and scraped the skin on her forehead at some point but her brown eyes were bright.

It was Carter who replied, gruff but unflinching. 'We fight. And we win.'

Sylvain made a soft sound and stepped away. Allie knew without a word what he was thinking. Because she was thinking the same thing.

How?

EPİLOGUE

'This way, Miss Sheridan, Miss Patel.' The man in the uniform handed their passports back with elaborate formality and gestured for them to follow him.

Exchanging a glance, the two girls walked behind him down the stairs. The morning light was unforgiving – Allie could see how Rachel had attempted to cover her black eye with makeup and failed. The powder only made the marks on her skin more obvious.

Allie's wounded left arm was held tight against her chest in a sling. She'd had to cut the sleeve off her blouse to accommodate the thick bandages. She could only imagine how they must look to a stranger but their escort hadn't raised an eyebrow when he saw them.

At the foot of the stairs, he opened a door and they stepped out on to the tarmac. The air was cool and damp. Allie's nose wrinkled at the acrid smell of jet fuel.

Ahead of them, Lucinda's private jet gleamed silver on the runway. At any other time she would have been thrilled at the chance to ride in it. But this wasn't any other time.

They were running away.

Lucinda had explained it simply on the phone. 'Until we establish who the spy is, the school isn't safe for you.'

'But where am I going?' Allie had asked.

'I'm not telling you or anybody else that information,' Lucinda said. 'You will find out when the plane lands. This has all become too dangerous, Allie.'

Allie, who now had fifteen new stitches in her body to remember Nathaniel by, knew this already. But she wasn't going without a fight.

'I'm not leaving the others,' she'd said stubbornly. 'What about them? It's dangerous for them, too.'

'It's not them Nathaniel wants,' Lucinda said. 'It's you. And if I can get you out of the picture I think it will make them safer, at least for a while.'

'But why can't they all just come with me?' Allie had asked, not giving up.

Lucinda's reply had been simple. 'Because it's easy to hide two people. It's harder to hide six.'

She said she was sending Rachel with her so she wouldn't be lonely and also to act as a tutor. Raj would coordinate their security.

Ahead of them, the plane's door swung open; its stairs unfolded like an insect's legs, stretching down to the runway.

In silence the two girls followed the uniformed man to the plane.

Inside, it was all luxury. The cabin's twelve armchairs were upholstered in buttery leather dyed a tasteful shade of taupe. The furniture wouldn't have been out of place in an upscale hotel or a fine office. The jet had a clean scent of leather and furniture polish – nothing like the commercial jets Allie remembered from family holidays.

Allie and Rachel sat where they were told, facing each other across a polished walnut table. A flight attendant brought them glasses of iced orange juice and Allie watched the beads of condensation gather on the glass and fall like rain.

Her arm ached and she touched it gingerly. The doctor had given her painkillers but she hadn't taken any yet. She knew they'd make her sleepy and she wanted to know everything that was happening – she needed to stay alert.

Most of all, she wanted to know where they were going.

The engines roared into life.

Across the table, Rachel looked tired and scared. Allie reached out her good hand; Rachel took it and squeezed it lightly.

'You OK?' Allie asked.

Rachel nodded. 'Fine ... just ...' She made a vague gesture that said, *'All this.'*

Allie knew what she meant. It had all happened so fast. There hadn't been time to process it. There wasn't even a chance to say goodbye properly. Zoe would be so upset when she found out they were gone. Nicole was still in the infirmary. And Carter and Sylvain ... they'd all risked their lives to save her last night. And now she was leaving them behind.

Leaping on to the plane just before the doors closed, Raj strode to their table. 'Are you both ready?'

They gave dutiful nods.

He rested a hand on Rachel's shoulder before heading up to the cockpit to sit with the pilots and, a few minutes later, the wheels began to turn. The plane sped down the runway with a kind of eagerness – as if it couldn't wait to be in the air.

But all Allie wanted to do was stay.

In physics they'd studied the way aeroplanes take off. There's something called the point of no return, when the plane's speed is so high, and the amount of runway ahead so limited, there's no physical way to stop safely. The plane must either take flight or crash.

That's what this journey felt like – like they had to go. They had no other choice.

The jet was so powerful, so fleet, when the wheels left the tarmac Allie barely felt it but she gripped the edge of the table as the world dropped away. The green English countryside spread out beneath them, with its ancient hedgerows and castles, small villages and busy motorways, all fading slowly behind a curtain of grey clouds, and then disappearing entirely.

Allie saw it through a haze of unshed tears.

There was no going back now.

ACKNOWLEDGEMENTS

If you are reading this book you are one of my favourite people in the world and I would like to thank you so much for coming with me on this journey so far. Your emails, letters and tweets fill my days with joy. I am forever in your debt. Thank you.

I want to thank the amazing Madeleine Milburn, who is both my friend and the best agent a girl could ever have. Were it not for her, there is no way this book would be in your hands right now. She makes things happen. Maddy, you are my *hero*.

Huge thanks also go to my international team of amazing editors and translators. First, to the team at Atom/Little, Brown in the UK – especially the fabulous and ludicrously talented Samantha Smith. Sam – I will follow you to the ends of the earth. Thank you for everything. Also to my French team at Collection R/Robert Laffont – led by the brilliant Glenn Tavennec, who is just as suave and calm under pressure as you'd hope – and my incredible German group at Oetinger, led by the unflappable and wonderful Doris Jahnsen. And to all my international publishers – thank you so much for your hard work! We are doing this together.

The first readers of this book are a group of my friends who do the difficult but so important thing of being honest with me. Laura Barbey, Kate Bell, Catriona Verner-Jeffries, and Hélène Rudyck, you are my muses. I couldn't do it without you. Thank you all so much. Please read all my books for ever. In return, I will give you all the cupcakes.

To all the booksellers and librarians who have personally put my books into people's hands – if I weren't already married I'd want to marry you all. If it weren't for people like you I'd never have read so there's no way I could ever have written. You make people's lives better. Thank you.

And, finally, to my patient, thoughtful husband, Jack, who reads my bad early drafts, helps me work out sticky plots, picks me up when I fall down, and convinces me not to give up when the going gets rough – thank you *so much*. I love you.

C.J. Daugherty was 22 when she saw her first dead body. Although she left the world of crime reporting to edit travel books instead, she never lost her fascination with what it is that drives some people to do awful things. And about the kinds of people who try to stop them. *Night School* is the product of that fascination.

C.J. lives in the south of England with her husband and a small menagerie of pets – you can learn more about her at www.cjdaugherty.com.